The E

To Elspeth

The Epistle

A Story of the Early Church

David Martyn

David Martyn

Blue Forge Press

Port Orchard ✿ Washington

Blue Forge Press is the print division of the volunteer-run, federal 501(c)3 nonprofit company, Blue Forge Group, founded in 1989 and dedicated to bringing light to the shadows and voice to the silence. We strive to empower storytellers across all walks of life with our four divisions: Blue Forge Press, Blue Forge Films, Blue Forge Gaming, and Blue Forge Records. Find out more at www.BlueForgeGroup.com

Blue Forge Press
7419 Ebbert Drive Southeast
Port Orchard, Washington 98367
blueforgepress@gmail.com
360-550-2071 ph.txt

Dedication

To Jennifer DiMarco, an amazing woman
who convinced me that my story of Isaac, Rebekah, and
Deborah, *The Oak of Weeping* should be but one book in
a series, 'The Hall of Faith.'

Preface

I have heard Christians reminisce for the days of the early church. They are drawn by the excitement of the times, the miracles, the widespread outpouring of the Holy Spirit, the teaching of the Apostles and love and fellowship of the early believers. The New Testament and the writings of others who lived during this tumultuous time certainly support this understanding. But such a romantic view of the first century overlooks the tension, division and persecution which accompanied the founding of our faith.

It is an undeniable truth that good and evil exist together in our world. We know that our faith does not take us out of the fallen world but empowers us to rise above and live victorious lives despite our trials and tribulations. The first Christians faced more challenges and dangers than most of us are willing to undertake. The first Gospel was not written for nearly twenty years, Paul's letters followed over the next seventeen years. John did not begin to write until fifty years after the crucifixion of Christ. Yet the church was immediately under attack from within and without. A spiritual battle was underway. Heresies needed to be addressed. Old prejudices and scores to settle led to division and separation. All the time, persecution continued.

It is no accident that the greatest outpouring of the Spirit today is at the edges of the church where new tribes, new people are hearing the call of the Holy Spirit and that call is being contested. It is these frontier believers who most closely understand the trials of the early church. Thankfully they have the Word of God, the fellowship of saints and the prayers of all God's people.

For those of us who find no challenge to our faith, or worse, see our practice of the faith as an opportunity to correct others not living up to our standards, perhaps it is time to look back to those who paid the price before us.

The Epistle

A Story of the Early Church

David Martyn

Chapter One

The great stones beneath him began to groan. Their painful lament, like giant teeth grinding in despair growing stronger as the afternoon darkness deepened. A wind a came up circling and twisting, looking for a direction to follow, whistling the tune to the stones. The groaning blocks of limestone began to shake, rhythmically at first, swaying side to side, each sway greater than the last. Ezra was thrown violently down onto the dancing hard rock floor as he heard crashing stone upon stone and metal upon rock and the eerie screams of others reminding him that he was not alone until at last the great stone blocks gave out one long shudder before coming to rest.

Ezra looked at the massive doors of the Temple before him, thrown wide open like outstretched wings of an angel in mourning, their lower outer corners resting on the now still stone floor. Their lower pintles were bent grasping with tiny fingers holding secure the mass of the great doors freshly adorned in King Herod's gold. The upper pintles had sheared and lost their grip. Ezra's sight was drawn inside, and he saw the golden menorah candle stand lying in the middle of the floor. The showbread was scattered about in the ashes and embers of the golden altar of incense lying forlorn on its side.

As Ezra lay prone before the Holy court looking through to the Holy of Holies, a new sound, a tearing, drew his eyes to the enormous blue curtain at the far end of the Temple. 'Do my eyes deceive me,' he thought, as two ghostly hands appeared at the top center of the curtain grasping and renting. His ears confirmed what his eyes were seeing. The curtain was being ripped, torn apart from top to bottom. The massive curtain beam was broken and there before his eyes, for all to see was an empty room with only a foundation from Solomon's Temple where once lay the glorious gold covered Ark of the Covenant with its carved, gilded Cherubim wingtip to wingtip protecting the ark from above. Ezra stared at the destruction before him, and he wept. He heard only the gentle bleating of a lamb who escaped sacrifice.

The young priest slowly stood up and turned around. Behind him, other priests, worshipers, many pilgrims, and sacrificial animals were also finding their feet. Some dazed and frightened and some hurrying to avoid rivers of embers and ash still crawling along the stone floor where the altar fire spilled from above. The High Altar was still intact, but the ramp from the court of the priests lay in ruin with stone and earth fill covering the milky white limestone floor. Priests caught in the act of sacrificing at the altar stood and stared, their way down destroyed.

Then the rain came. It quenched the fire and gathered the ash. Rivulets became rivers and the mud, ash, and coals swept across the court of the priests through gates into the court of the women and the court of the Gentiles. The rain continued, and the whole Temple mount bled, spilling over the walls and down into the lower city and the Kidron valley. Ezra walked slowly out the of the court of the priests into the court of the Gentiles. He walked all the way to the north end of the court and looked out, past the Fortress of Antonia towards the Damascus road. And there, at a place called Golgotha, through flashes of lightning, he could see three men hanging on Roman crosses of crucifixion.

Memories returned, of the man Jesus, one of the three now hanging in agony and humiliation. Only days ago, Ezra listened as Jesus taught in the Temple. Ezra was sitting with the scribes, listening. The words of Jesus were full of strength and authority, though the man himself was non-assuming and ordinary. His voice was soft and his tone gentle, but there was something else, something behind the voice and the words spoken, a verity, truth, yet a mystery. As appealing a teacher Jesus was, in the end, Ezra could not quite understand his message. Ezra recalled being spellbound by this simple Galilean with an incredible mind and how the spell was broken when Caiaphas, the Temple High Priest, challenged Jesus, saying, "By what authority do you teach?" Jesus responded with a question of his own, "The Baptism of John, was it of heaven or men?" Caiaphas turned to the scribes beside him for an answer. They argued among them, "If we say, 'of heaven,' Jesus will say, 'then why did you not listen to him.' And if we say 'of man,' the people will be angry because they believe John to be a prophet." Caiaphas' face flushed with anger, and he turned to Jesus and said, "We do not know." Jesus calmly replied, "Then neither shall I say by what authority I teach."

Ezra remembered the reports he heard of Jesus' trial before the council last night. It was all that his fellow priests could talk about that day. He heard of the witness who reminded the council that Jesus had said, "Destroy this Temple, and in three days, I will raise it up." There were many witnesses against Jesus, but their stories did not agree. Finally, Caiaphas took matters into his own hands, and in violation of the Law, he badgered Jesus with the question of his guilt, "Are you the Messiah, the Son of God, the Blessed One."

Jesus had been silent before his accusers. He had not uttered a single word during his trial. But now he turned and looked straight into Caiaphas's angry eyes and firmly said, "I AM. And you will see the Son of Man seated at the right hand of the Power and coming with the clouds of heaven."

All those there said that the council was silent. The Sanhedrin was stunned by Jesus' words. Then Caiaphas violently tore his robe and shouted, "What need of further witnesses? You have heard the blasphemy. What is your decision?"

All the witnesses confirmed that the council agreed Jesus was worthy of death. Caiaphas spent the night dragging Jesus first to Pilate, then to Herod and finally back to Pilate. Caiaphas arranged for a crowd to shout and insist Jesus be crucified by the Roman Procurator. Reluctantly Pilate agreed and handed Jesus over to his guards to be beaten and taken out of the city and crucified. Friends told Ezra that Caiaphas and his father-in-law Annas were so determined to see Jesus dead that they followed him as he carried his cross out of the fortress, through the streets and to the crucifixion site, Golgotha.

Staring at the man on the center cross, Ezra wondered, 'Why does Caiaphas fear Jesus? Where does such hatred come from? I suppose he is out there in the storm waiting for him to die. What will he make of what has happened here? Did I really see the hand of God tearing at the curtain? Was it my imagination? My fascination with the story of Daniel? Seen or unseen, I believe God is speaking to us. Why does God shake the foundations of His own Temple?'

As Ezra walked back from the court of the Gentiles to the court of the priests, he noted how quickly the priests at the altar were working to relight the fire as men shoveled and piled stone and debris to rebuild a crude ramp. Ezra knew that the Law of Moses forbade stairs or a ladder to be used to climb up to the High Altar. Others were shoveling the coals up for disposal under the Law outside the city wall. As he watched, more men appeared with tent cloth to cover the doorway to the court of the Holies. They worked quickly and deliberately knowing they must finish before the sunset when the Sabbath began.

Ezra remembered his own new responsibilities and walked back to the court of wine and oil, where the olive oil and sacrificial wine for the drink offering were stored and prepared. Entering the storeroom in the corner of the priest's court, he was relieved to see that the large jars of oil, barrels, and skins of wine were undamaged. The priest in charge of the drink offering snapped,

"Where have you been? Fortunate for you, there is no damage. Go clean yourself and remember you serve the wine offering this Sabbath!"

Then staring at Ezra, he said softly, "Ezra ben Haggai, your first duty is as a priest! Become a scribe like your father on your own time!"

Ezra bowed slightly and said, "Yes, forgive me I was startled by the quake and the storm. You say rightly, my first duty is as a priest."

Ezra tried to concentrate on his duties as a priest of the wine offering that Sabbath. As a new priest consecrated little more than a month ago, he was yet to grow comfortable in the ritual. He was still overwhelmed by his responsibility to intercede on behalf of all Jews in worshiping the God of Abraham, Isaac, and Jacob. Approaching the high altar of the One True God, the great refrain would repeat in his mind, "Hear O Israel, the Lord our God the Lord is One." Ezra believed the sacrifices made in the Temple honored God and atoned for the sins of the people. He held the Law of Moses as sacred and perfect. He determined years ago to serve in the Temple faithfully and wholeheartedly. He decided to study the Law, to know the will of God, for himself and for the nation of Israel he served.

Ezra's idealism was not shared by all the Levites he met at the Temple. The Levites were a large tribe in the nation of Israel. Since the days of the Exodus, they were set aside to serve first in the Tabernacle and then the Temple. Of the Levites, only the sons of Aaron could serve as priests. The Temple was both their calling by birth and their portion. They were fed by the meat, bread, wine, and oil offered to God. All produce was tithed, even the spices to season their food. All the bounty of the earth came from the Lord, and all were presented before the altar. The life of a Levite was very good, and the privileged life of the priest was secure from birth until death. Some saw this privilege as an entitlement, some saw it as a job, some saw it as an opportunity for power and influence. But many saw the same honor that captured the heart of Ezra.

Ezra greeted the first day of the week enthusiastically, not because it was the festival of the first fruits, with the joyous procession of singing priests and Levite musicians leading pilgrims into the Temple to offer their sacrifices upon the High Altar. Instead, he selfishly awaited the teachers of the Law to return to the Temple courts. Ezra walked past the Levites handling heavy ropes from the roof of the Temple, lifting the high doors from the hinges before replacing the pintles. It did not occur to him that it would take a host of Levite artisans weeks to replace the heavy felt curtain that separates the court of the Holy from the Holy of Holies. He made no notice of other Levites carefully putting the unhewn rocks back in their place on the ramp, wagons of sand and gravel waiting to fill the voids. He gave no thought to the command of God to use only unhewn stone for the altar as a remembrance that nothing that is sacrificed comes from man. It is God who gives to man all that he has.

Ezra's mind was elsewhere. Ezra sought out Gamaliel under his favored portico. Perhaps the master teacher, or Rabban, Gamaliel would have comments on the storm and damage to the Temple, or as a member of the Sanhedrin, he would comment on the rumored trial of Jesus.

As Ezra approached the Rabban, seated in the middle of a growing group of men, a man in a rich and flowing robe walked up to Gamaliel and whispered something in his ear. Gamaliel stood and said a few words to his chief disciple, a young man in the dress of a Pharisee, before walking off with the wealthy stranger. Ezra did not hear the disciple but could see the lesson would not take place. Curious, he walked up to the disciple and asked, "Will we not hear from Rabban Gamaliel today?"

The disciple brusquely replied, "The Rabban has been called away. Tomorrow. Return tomorrow."

Ezra, stood perplexed, "Forgive me, I am new, but this seems most unusual, I have never known the Rabban to walk off without teaching, without explanation."

The disciple looked at Ezra, "Yes, I remember you. You sit at the back. Never have a question. With such poor interest, why do you question me?"

Ezra replied, "I listen, and I learn. I learn from the questions of the others. Their questions are much better than any I have. I am new here as a priest and new to the court of the teacher. So, tell me, where has Rabban Gamaliel gone?"

"What is your name, priest?"

"I am Ezra ben Haggai. My father trained as a scribe, and I would follow him."

"I am Saul, a disciple of Gamaliel. If you insist, the master has been called to the Sanhedrin. Something to do with the Galilean, Jesus."

Ezra's eyes widened, "The one they condemned? The one crucified on the day of preparation? Does it regard the damage to the Temple in the great storm? Has God judged us for this man's death?"

Saul shook his head, "The Sanhedrin meets to discuss rumors of the crucified man Jesus. The damage to the Temple is not God's judgment for the man Jesus' death.

If any man deserved death, it is the blasphemer Jesus. God's judgment, indeed! Now, I must get about my business."

"Wait!" Ezra exclaimed, "Blasphemer? Jesus was a blasphemer? How do you know this? The trial, were you there? Was the master there? Certainly, as he is a member of the Sanhedrin, he would know. Please, tell me. The Temple curtain—I saw it, I saw it tear. I saw the hands… It wasn't the storm. When the sky was at its blackest when Jesus was on the crucifixion cross."

Saul stared at Ezra and said. "I'm going. The teacher will be here tomorrow."

Chapter Two

The wine court was one place in the Temple where Ezra could relax. The unadorned storeroom shielded him from the awe and majesty in the court of the priests, dominated by the High Altar and the entrance to the court of the Holies. The large room could have been a wine merchant's warehouse. It smelled of wine, wood, goatskins and olive oil. The priest in charge noted how the young priest was quickly making this room his sanctuary from the sanctuary.

"Not at the foot of the teacher today?" He said as he prepared for the next wine offering.

"Rabban Gamaliel was called to the Sanhedrin."

"So, do you come here as a priest to serve or just to

hide until you can sit with the scribes once more?"

"It is the one sacrificial rite I know. I am not hiding. Baruch, you know I perform my duties. Was my service not acceptable on the Sabbath?"

Baruch replied without looking up, "You should be about learning all of the Temple rites. You could visit the keepers of the bulls, or if they are too big for you, start with the doves and pigeons."

Ezra smiled, "I have just started in service with you, and you wish to send me off already?"

The older priest looked closely at Ezra. "I thought I heard a smile in your voice and there I see you can smile. We serve God, and He is holy, but we are men. We must do this every day. We have lives and cares, and even at times, we are permitted to laugh. When you are before the altar, give reverence, but among your fellow priests and Levites, be a friend and a companion. Did not your father teach you this?"

Ezra laughed lightly, "My father had many friends here. He often spoke warmly of them. I dare not tell them, but some I feel I know well for all the stories I heard. But he spoke most warmly of his fellow scribes, men he debated and whose opinions he respected. My father wanted both to serve God and know God."

Baruch sighed, I knew your father, Haggai. That is why I asked to be your trainer since your father is no longer alive to teach you here. He was a good man and a faultless priest. A stickler for the Law. Not afraid to challenge even the High Priest. He never trusted Annas and had little use for the Sadducees. He often claimed their philosophy, denying the resurrection of the dead, led only to selfishness and indulgence, seeking to enjoy the here and now. Few Sadducees worried that their opportunity to serve others was limited or spurred them on to give more of themselves to others."

"It seems to me the Sadducees dominate the council leadership and the decisions of the Sanhedrin," Ezra noted.

"They dominate the positions of authority in the Temple, that is why your father never rose to a high position. Remember his lesson. Remember also, the Roman Procurator must approve the High Priest. The Sadducee's lifestyle is less offensive to the Romans. Even so, the Sadducees know when to work with the Pharisees."

"My father told me, 'Serve faithfully and stay away from politics.'"

"Good advice."

Baruch paused, then said, "I have a new lesson for you, young Ezra. Tomorrow I will take you to the court of the Nazarites. You shall learn of your brothers and sisters not born Levites who vow to live sacrificially for our God. I have always found them a strong reminder that service to the Temple is service to our God and should never be taken lightly."

Ezra replied, "Though I have known Nazarites, and respect their vow, I always considered the Pharisees as having a zeal for God."

"Yes, I understand what you are saying. It is how many Pharisees wish to be viewed."

"You say, 'wish to be viewed?'"

Baruch nodded, "The Nazarite sees his own sin and a need to make further sacrifices in his life. He is less about judging others and more about serving God and God's people. It is my observation that too often our Pharisee friends want to appear more righteous than the rest of

21

us. It is the Pharisee who is more likely to tell you how to live your life and the Nazarite who is too busy struggling to live his own life, does not feel worthy to judge others. Now, this is not always the case. Remember, the Nazarite vow was given by Moses and is recognized by the Law. It is God's law and his office. The Pharisees arose from the days of the Maccabees and a desire to show a life lived according to the law. But anything made by man, even with the best of intention, can be corrupted by man's pride."

"You speak of humility?"

The old priest put his hand on Ezra's shoulder, "What man should not humble himself before our God?"

Ezra replied, "It is true, even for the scribes and the teachers of the Law."

The old priest nodded, "And for priests and High Priests!"

"Baruch," Ezra asked, "You were a friend of my father?"

Baruch nodded.

"I thought all of my father's friends were fellow scribes."

Baruch smiled, "Your father was my most challenging debater of the law! He could breathe life into an interpretation like no other scribe. He looked to the heart of God before the mind of men."

"Then, you are or were a scribe?"

"The closer the Law brought me to the heart of God, the more I was drawn to serve Him."

Surprised, Ezra said, "You're that Baruch! I did not know—yes, my father spoke of you often. He always said..."

Baruch cut him off, "There is no need to apologize,

and please do not try to flatter me with your memories of praise. My friendship with Haggai is secure on its own."

The next day Baruch introduced Ezra to the priest of the Nazarite Court, asking to observe the rites. The Nazarite court was in the southeast corner of the spacious Women's court. A priest was always present at the court where Nazarites came when they had fulfilled their vows under the law of Moses. He watched as each Nazarite would bring to the Temple a one-year-old male lamb, without blemish, for a burnt offering, and one-year-old ewe-lamb without blemish as a sin offering and a ram as a peace offering. Also, the Nazarite brought a basket of unleavened bread, flour mixed with oil and their grain and drink offerings. The male lamb and the ewe were taken to the high altar and presented to the priests as the burnt and sin offerings. The Nazarite then went to the court of the Nazarites and gave the ram and bread as a peace offering. The ram was slaughtered, and its meat was cooked in the pot at the Nazarite court.

Ezra watched the priest use a large three-pronged fork to take the shoulder after it had been boiled, place it in a clay pot and give it to the Nazarite. He then took a loaf of bread from the basket and placed them in the hands of the Nazarite, made a wave offering of the grain and presented the drink offering. When the offerings were complete, the Nazarite's consecrated head was shaved, and the hair was thrown into the fire under the cooking pot. Only then was the Nazarite released from the vow made to the Lord.

As they stood in the morning sun among the worshippers, Baruch asked Ezra, "What does the Law require of the Nazarite?"

His eyes still on the priest performing the rites in the court, Ezra replied, "The Law requires abstinence from wine, grapes, raisins and any product of the vine, or alcoholic drink. The Nazarite must not cut or even comb his hair during the vow and take care not to become ritually impure by contact with a corpse or cemetery, even the body of a close relative. Any such contact would violate his vows, and he must begin again. The law requires the Nazarite not to ignore his duty to a corpse he may discover, but even doing so the vow is broken and he must begin again."

Ezra turned to Baruch, "All this I know as a Levite and as the son of a priest. What I do not understand is the motivation or the heart of the Nazarite."

Ezra stood on the fringe of the court of the Nazarite transfixed as he watched and listened as the ritual was repeated. "I see nothing in common of the Nazarites other than their hair and their single-minded reverence. They are men and women, old and young, their dress, speech, and sophistication are as varied as the pilgrims who come to the Temple from Jews dispersed throughout the world."

He sighed and then said, "I am surprised that nearly all of those released from their vow immediately make an oath of a new vow to the priest who just released them."

Just then the sight of a young woman with tears in her eyes as she stepped away from the priest after renewing her vows for another year so captured Ezra that without thinking he stopped the woman and said, "Mistress, I am a new priest and seek to learn. Tell me, why do you make the vow of the Nazarite?"

The woman stared at Ezra and said, "I am neither wife nor mistress to anyone. Why do you ask such a question?"

Ezra embarrassed, continued, "I mean no offense, mistress..."

"My name is Mariam, not mistress. You, a priest serving in the Temple, and you ask such a question?"

Ezra replied defensively, "From my youngest days, my father has prepared me to perform the duties and rituals of Temple worship. I was taught the sacrifices for sin, both known and unknown. I was schooled in the Law. I know the need for atonement for every man and woman and for our people Israel. I know the Law regarding the Nazarite given by Moses. I ask you why you take the vows when atonement is available to all in Temple sacrifice?"

Mariam looked at Ezra wondering why this strange young priest was asking a worshipper when every priest she had ever known had only told her authoritatively what was required to do. "Why do you not take your questions to the teachers of the law or the high priest?"

Ezra earnestly replied, "I know of no teacher of the law or high priest that has taken the Nazarite vow."

"Was not the prophet Samuel, a Levite, consecrated a Nazarite for life?"

"Yes, the Nazarite vow is available to all. I spoke of my own acquaintance. At the day of my birth, it was known that I would be consecrated a priest in service to the Temple. You are under no obligation, and yet you seek a similar consecration."

"Priest..."

"My name is Ezra."

"Ezra, you answer your own question. Your consecration was determined at birth. Are you truly surprised that among all of God's people some outside of males of the tribe of Levi may have the heart to serve God? You say all that is required is met in the law in the Temple worship. Yet you also say the Nazarite vow is lawful. Why, then did God give the Nazarite law to our father, Moses? Was it not but to open a consecrated life of service to all His people? I am no teacher of the Law, but I know God will consecrate any whose heart it is to serve Him. Even priests."

"Truly, our God raises his servants from among all of our people. I speak of his prophets and chosen leaders, but tell me, Mariam, what is it that drew you to the Nazarite vow?"

Baruch had been listening to the conversation now stepped forward and said, "Mistress Mariam, you are not compelled to answer to this priest what is between you and our God. I pray His blessings to be upon you as you seek to serve Him and observe all that your vow requires."

Mariam looked into Baruch's face and then turned to Ezra, "No, it is an honest question from an honest priest, I will say more. I am Levite, but as a woman, my consecration was not decided at my birth. My father saw our family was well fed from the Temple and clothed in the finest dress. I will not say his name. He owns flocks and vineyards and is skilled among merchants. He is a Sadducee and performs his duties according to his schedule, but his heart is not at the Temple it is at his villa and his barns. He arranged for my marriage to a Levite, a Sadducee like himself. The marriage never took place. I will only say that it was the prophet John, the one called the Baptist that opened my eyes. I never met anyone like him. He was fully dedicated to God, only God. John was a Nazarite. After he baptized me, I made my vow. John showed me who I was before God."

Mariam's face turned stern, "I have answered all that I will. I must leave."

Chapter Three

Gamaliel was teaching under the shade of his favored portico. The disciple called Saul was seated on a chair behind him, his dark eyes watching Ezra as he found a shaded place to sit. "Rabban Gamaliel," someone asked, "This man Jesus, the one crucified on the day of preparation, all of Jerusalem speaks of him. Some say he has risen from the tomb like Lazarus who he raised up. You were called away to the Sanhedrin, what is the truth?"

Gamaliel sighed, "I thought this was to be a discussion on the Law."

Ezra was surprised to hear his own voice ask, "Was Jesus condemned under Jewish law or Roman law?"

Gamaliel nodded, "Yes. Let us discuss Jesus and the

law. You asked was Jesus condemned under Jewish or Roman law. Whose was the crucifixion cross on which he was executed?"

Ezra new this was a simple evasion, "Of course the Romans were the executioner, but wasn't he tried before our Jewish Sanhedrin first? Was it not Temple guards who arrested him? Was it not a Jewish trial that sent him to the Roman Procurator for execution?"

The disciple Saul stared coldly at Ezra and waited for his master to respond. "It is well known that only Roman courts can order a death sentence, but even Rome operates under laws. If Jesus was executed by Roman authority, it was because he was found guilty of a crime deserving death under Roman authority."

Ezra stood up and moved closer to the teacher, "Teacher, the question remains. It was Temple guards who made the arrest and brought Jesus to the council. Having no authority to execute Jesus, he was sent to the Procurator. The rumors agree that the witnesses against Jesus were all members of our council. Jesus was not arrested by Romans, and no Roman testified against him. That the Procurator saw some advantage in granting the desired execution does not change the underlying question. So, how can it be other than Jewish law that condemned Jesus to death? Answer us, then, was the execution of Jesus lawful?"

Gamaliel folded his hands and tapped the ends of thumbs together before answering, "Jesus knew the law. It was clear from his teaching. I have known no other teacher of the law like him. He only taught in the Temple when he came to Jerusalem for Passover. He chose to teach in the villages, to peasants, fishermen, tradesmen, and sinners—even women! He did not teach scribes and priests, Pharisees, and learned men. He chose not to debate his radical view of the law but to plant it in hearts and instill it in our nation's people without the authority of the priests and scribes. He taught as a prophet, yes, much like the Baptist, but here too, he was different. He did not call men to repentance and a return to the Law given by Moses. He challenged the Law as it has been passed through generations. He saw the Law differently than any man before him."

Saul listened intently as Gamaliel spoke. But again, it was Ezra who questioned, "Rabban, you are a great teacher in our Temple and a member of the council. That is why I ask you, as one who can separate fact from rumor. I have heard it said Jesus repeatedly taught, 'Do not think that I have come to abolish the Law or the prophets but to fulfill them....'"

Gamaliel finished the sentence, "Yes, and he said, 'I say unto you, until heaven and earth pass away, not one iota or one stroke will disappear from the Law until everything is accomplished.' You are going to ask if Jesus held to the Law, and that is debatable. Was it the Law of Moses he sought to teach or was his interpretation so radical and different as to be a new law of his own making? Yes, the council debated, we all debated, the scribes the Sanhedrin the priests, what to make of this man. But Jesus did not come to answer our questions. And when we sought him out, we felt only his ridicule and that of the people with him. Even so, I recommended we do nothing. If his teaching was false, nothing would come of him or his teaching. If his teaching was from God, well, all our strivings would not just be of naught but perhaps an affront to the Holy One of Israel. But our hand was forced at the trial."

31

Ezra was now standing right in front of Gamaliel. "Rabban, you were there. We have all heard rumors, but you can tell us plainly, was Jesus found deserving of death under the Law?"

Gamaliel nodded yes, "The Chief Priest, to his shame, did not conduct a lawful trial. To be sure, I do not say that justice was not served, but the trial was not lawful."

A voice asked, "Rabban, can justice be served where the trial is unlawful? We are trained..."

Gamaliel interrupted, "We will debate another time if justice can be served when the course of the Law that is intended to ensure justice is denied. Now, as to the question whether Jesus was deserving of death under the law, I can say it was not contradicting witnesses or perhaps even witnesses paid to say what they did not know to be true that condemned Jesus. It was not Caiaphas putting words in Jesus' mouth. No, it was his very own words. When Caiaphas asked Jesus, 'Are you the Messiah, the son of the Blessed One?' Jesus answered directly. He was most emphatic. He said, 'You have said it yourself. But I tell you, from now on, you will see the Son of Man seated at the right hand of Power coming on the clouds of heaven.' At this, Caiaphas tore his robes and shouted, 'You have heard the blasphemy! What is your decision?'"

The disciple Saul spoke, "Rabban, the council had no choice. Blasphemy is deserving of death under the law. They were forced into the humiliation of seeking the Roman authority for his execution. Stoning. Would that he could have been stoned under the Law of Moses."

Gamaliel closed his eyes and said, "Brother Saul, there was another choice. The other choice was to fall prostrate and worship him. But you are right in saying the council chose the humiliation of seeking a Roman crucifixion. But the humiliation became more disgusting when Temple priests arranged for a crowd to shout for crucifixion before the Procurator in his palace."

Ezra softly asked, "Thank you, Rabban, for sharing this painful event. Tell me, was there not one who spoke for Jesus? I have heard he had defenders in the Sanhedrin."

Gamaliel said, "You speak of Nicodemus and Joseph. They were there. I saw them walk off in silence."

A voice asked, "The rumors of the tomb?"

Gamaliel immediately answered, "Only rumors. The tomb of Jesus, the tomb meant for Joseph, is indeed empty now. The guards testified that they fell asleep and when they awoke the tomb was empty. We do not know who took the body or where. No one in authority believes other than the obvious, Jesus is dead."

"Rabban Gamaliel," Ezra asked with hesitation in his voice, "The storm when Jesus was on the cross. The damage, the torn curtain to the Holy of Holies—you spoke of the second option—if it is so, what can be done, I mean under the Law, how should we live?"

Gamaliel smiled, "Just as you said, 'Under the Law.' With Jesus, you have two choices. If you believe his word, you agree he speaks under the Law. If you do not believe Jesus, you still believe the Law. Here there is no choice; live according to the Law! God gave us His Law. It is here we can be made righteous. You are a priest. Serve God in his Temple and observe the Law in all that you do."

The tempting smell of the burning fat of the sacrificial bulls and rams on the high altar, the savory aroma of boiling meat in the great cooking pots of the offerings and the inviting aroma of the baking showbread was ever present in the Temple. The orderly chaos of priests, Levites, pilgrims, scribes, Nazarites, lepers, teachers, money traders and merchants selling doves, pigeons, lambs, and goats provided a constancy and a sense of stability not found outside the Temple. Ezra's life was adjusting to the rhythm of the Temple, and with the encouragement of Baruch, he poured himself into mastering his duties. He had served at every station and every ritual not reserved for the high priest. He was confident and poised even in the court of the lepers, where he carefully inspected those healed of rash and skin disease for any small sign of imperfection and the whitened diseased bodies of lepers for any evidence of healthy skin, proclaiming ritually clean the leper with no unblemished skin remaining. Baruch, a faultless priest, and trained scribe answered every question his young charge asked.

"Why is the complete leper declared clean?" He asked.

"The Law is more than rules and rituals; it is a life lesson to us from the LORD. The law of the leper is the same for buildings, clothing, and people. It is a living lesson in sin. Sin is a blemish that must be removed and the infected cleansed. Consider the pain of a man who first sees the white scab of leprosy. He sees both a disease that will grow worse and require the humiliation of calling out to others 'Unclean! Unclean!' announcing to all people to beware of him. He faces separation and loneliness away from friends and family. He is the right company for only fellow lepers. Imagine watching yourself, and others grow whiter, perhaps losing fingers and toes. He holds onto the remaining clean flesh as a badge holding him somehow better than the next, until one day there is no clean flesh, he is only blemished. There remains no pride. He is fully sin. When a leper is all sin, the Law tells him to show himself to the priest, and we must declare him clean. Only then can he offer a sacrifice, thanking the LORD for finding him clean. What becomes of such a leper? Most often, he dies. But he dies clean in the sight of God."

Ezra thought and said, "That is why offerings and sacrifices to the LORD are made after confession and after the fulfillment of a vow. The LORD desires confession and repentance. He asks we bring our offerings to him with clean hands and a clean heart. He allows us to begin life again. Is this not what awaits us in the resurrection?"

Baruch smiled, "Your eyes begin to see! Now, I must remind you that your duty time is nearly complete. You must go back into the world. Consider what you have learned. Consider how a righteous priest can serve when he is outside the Temple."

"I can return to the Temple at any time to sit under the teachers to train with the scribes. It is written, 'Thy Word is a lamp unto my feet and a light unto my path.'"

"Yes, but strive to pursue wisdom, not mere knowledge. Learn to read the Law through the prophets and psalms. What do the Temple musicians sing, but the psalms! It is also written, 'Your sacrifices I do not desire. A broken and contrite heart I will not despise.'"

"Baruch, your interpretation of the Law, is far more radical than the words I hear from Rabban Gamaliel and the scribes. They judged Jesus as a teacher of the Law with radical interpretations. Could the high priest, and the Sanhedrin be wrong in their teachings? Do they not understand God's law given to Moses? Have you heard

Jesus teach? Is he where your radical teaching comes from?"

Baruch replied, "Gamaliel was correct when he said, 'If Jesus' teaching is of God, it will not be stopped.'"

Baruch paused and continued, "My young friend will you continue in your father's work copying the Sefer Torah?"

"It is my desire. I regard it as service to the LORD, though I have yet to establish the reputation of my father before me. My work copying the sacred scrolls demands my full attention and lifts me from the troubles of the day. It is just my mother Naomi and me in a small house here in Jerusalem. She insisted we move here so she would never be alone even during my Temple duties."

"I remember the devotion of your father Haggai to Naomi and to you, Ezra. But you cannot hide away even in the Torah, though it brings great comfort. We spoke of the debates your father, and I had. I continue in them with good men, men like your father. But we do not meet in the Temple. Come and listen. Hear what good men, priests, council members of the Sanhedrin who have a heart for the LORD and serving his people have to say. Would you come?"

Ezra's eyes widened, "It would be a great honor! Yes! I will come."

Baruch smiled, "Good! I will send for you. And please give my blessings to your mother."

Chapter Four

Naomi wanted to hear everything her son had to tell about his first Temple duty. She made sure he was comfortable and afforded the honor as head of the house. Of course, Ezra was uncomfortable with such deference from his mother, but she insisted, and soon he was well into his stories. When he recounted the particular interest Baruch had shown him, Naomi interrupted, "Baruch, a scribe, a friend of your father? Yes, he spoke of him often. Baruch is a relative of another priest, an older man than your father, Zechariah was his name. He was remembered for returning from the Altar of Incense struck dumb. He insisted the angel Gabriel spoke to him and his speech only returned to him when his son was born. I recall his wife, Elizabeth was her name, was very old when she bore her son, John. Many say this John was the one known as 'the Baptist.' Yes, your father debated Baruch. He is one who looks for the Messiah."

"Baruch still holds my father in high esteem and has indeed shown me goodwill in instructing me in my duties. He is different than the other priests and scribes. His priesthood is not one of ritual, though he is faultless in his duties, no, he looks to see the LORD's heart for his people Israel and the heart of all who come to sacrifice. He has invited me to hear debates with friends. Influential men. Priests and scribes, members of the Sanhedrin. He says they do not debate in the Temple but in the intimacy of the home."

Naomi replied, "My son, his views may be too radical for the Temple. In these times."

"Mother, he agrees with father's advice to avoid the politics of the day. I have listened to the scribes and teachers. They are careful not to offend the high priest and the Sadducees who hold all the high positions. Only Rabban Gamaliel complains of their actions, but he teaches only the intricacies of obeying the law. He takes no positions in the issues of the day. And he has a chief disciple, a foreigner, by his accent, a Pharisee named Saul. This man Saul is one zealous for the stoning of any he believes transgress the Law. No, mother, I desire to listen, to hear, and judge for myself. But tomorrow I begin another Torah scroll, perhaps we will find a buyer before it is finished."

Naomi hugged her son, "You are a good man, just like your father. A faultless priest and a loving son. The LORD has blessed me! Now come to the table. I have prepared your favorite!"

The narrow streets of Jerusalem were alive with people. Shoppers, merchants, pilgrims, and priests all noisily went about their business. Ezra found his way to the house of Baruch on a very narrow quiet street. Baruch received Ezra warmly and introduced him to his other guests, "Joseph, Nicodemus, Mathias, this is the young priest of whom I spoke. His name is Ezra, the son of my late friend Haggai, a faultless priest and scribe. From their names, you can know they are descended from Shelemiah, high priest in the days of Nehemiah and the building of the second Temple when our people Israel returned from Babylon."

"Welcome, Ezra. My name is Joseph, from Arimathea in Judea," he said as he greeted Ezra with a hug a kiss.

"I join my brothers in welcoming you. I am Nicodemus," he said as he too greeted Ezra with a hug and a kiss.

Wordlessly, Mathias stepped forward a gave the young man the warm hug and kiss of friendship.

Baruch hugged young Ezra and said, "We debate the man Jesus. The second option you heard from Rabban Gamaliel, can he indeed be the Messiah, the Blessed One of God? Nicodemus has visited Jesus and spoken to him privately. Joseph, too, has followed the teacher and listened. Joseph was just telling us about the tomb. It was Joseph who sought permission from the Procurator to bury the body of Jesus in his own tomb. With the help of Nicodemus, they carried the body to the tomb but were unable to complete the preparations before the Sabbath. Joseph, please continue you telling of the events."

"As you say, I went to Pilate for the authority to take the body of Jesus, while Nicodemus went for the burial spices. Pilate was surprised that Jesus was already dead, but the centurion confirmed the news and the Procurator consented. The storm made it difficult to carry his body. Only his mother Mary, her sister, the wife of Clopas, another Mary, the one they call Magdalene, and his disciple John were still there when we took his body. They followed after us to see where we took him. When the Sabbath approached, the women insisted they be permitted to clean and prepare the body on the first day of the week."

Ezra asked, "The rumors, the empty tomb."

Nicodemus replied, "Be assured it is true. When the women returned at first light on the first day of the week, they found the tomb was empty. They claimed they saw an angel and asked where they had taken his body. It was Jesus they saw! Alive! The women returned to the disciples, who in disbelief ran to the tomb and found it empty, with only the linen that covered his body, just as the women had said. Peter, too, saw Jesus alive on that day."

Mathias added, "Cleopas and another disciple saw Jesus that day. They were walking to Emaus and talking about all the events of Jesus' crucifixion and the reports from the women. They say a stranger came alongside and asked them what they were discussing. Well, they told him about everything that happened regarding Jesus. Then the stranger explained to them why everything that happened to Jesus was required to fulfill the Scriptures. When they arrived in Emaus and stopped at an inn to eat, the stranger broke the bread. Cleopas insists it was Jesus. Both of them recognized him, and immediately, he was gone!"

Nicodemus now continued, "There is more. That

evening he appeared to his disciples, hiding in their room behind closed doors. Of the twelve, only Thomas was not there. When told later, Thomas did not believe his brothers. But Jesus appeared again when Thomas returned, and said, 'Thomas put your hands in my wounds.' Thomas exclaimed, 'My Lord and my God.'"

Ezra was stunned, he looked to Baruch and then studied Nicodemus, "Master Nicodemus, you say you met with Jesus. You are a teacher of the Law and a member of the council. Did this Jesus live according to the Law?"

Nicodemus nodded knowingly, "Jesus was indeed a teacher of the Law. Both a teacher and a faultless follower. No man taught the Law with such authority. In Him is the truth. His truth brings freedom to see God. Our tradition has blinded us to the truth in the Law. Our tradition is bound up in things of the flesh, we do not see the things of the Spirit. When I went to Jesus, he told me I must be born again. I must be born in spirit to know the things of the Spirit of God that He freely gives to all His children. He is the true Father to Jesus, and we are as brothers, knowing His love. This is the Law that Jesus taught."

Ezra asked, "You believe this Jesus is the Messiah? Perhaps this I can understand. But all of you believe he is the Son of God? He is of God Himself? No, I don't understand your teaching. The Law declares, 'Hear O Israel, the LORD our God the LORD is One!' No. I must take my leave. I am a priest. I am a scribe; I return to the Law."

Ezra got up and left. Baruch followed after him and said, "Study the Scriptures; they speak of Him!"

Two days later, Ezra walked with his mother to the

Temple for their portion of bread and meat, intending to return through the market for fresh vegetables. A breeze began to stir in the fresh morning air, but then it started to swirl and grow stronger, and stronger yet. Memories of that day in the Temple filled Ezra's mind. He listened to the pilgrims in the market, shouting, "Who are theses Galileans that speak in my tongue?" Pilgrims dressed in the manner of Greeks and Egyptians, Cretans and Arabians, all were amazed by what they heard. Some Jews of Jerusalem were saying, "They must be drunk!"

A leader among the Galileans spoke, "Men of Judea and all who dwell in Jerusalem, let this be known to you, and listen to what I say. For these people are not drunk as it is only nine in the morning! But this is what the prophet Joel spoke: 'And in the last days, it shall be, God declares, that I will pour out my Spirit on all flesh....'"

The words grew fainter as Ezra felt himself rise from the ground, the Galilean's voice still speaking, and he saw himself in spirit move up above Jerusalem, circling with the whirlwind into a darkening sky. He was transported over the Temple, over the fortress of Antonia to Golgotha, where three men hung on crude Roman crosses. Ezra heard through the wind the voice of one, somehow, he knew it was Jesus. He clearly heard the voice cry in agony, 'Into thy hands, I commend my Spirit.' The wind itself howled and groaned in agony as it carried Ezra back to the Temple, back to the shuddering stones. Once again, Ezra was prone on the floor, staring at the curtain before the Holy of Holies, the wind spoke, "The LORD has forsaken me, and my Lord has forgotten me!" Again, the hands appeared, and another voice spoke, "Can a woman forget her nursing child? Can she feel no love for the son of her womb? Even these may forget, but I will not forget you. Behold, I have inscribed you on the palms of My hands; your walls are ever before Me."

Ezra's eyes were fixed on the curtain as the hands effortlessly tore it in two. As the curtain split, he heard another, the voice of Jesus on the cross, 'It is finished!' Again, Ezra closed his eyes and wept.

The wind became still. Ezra opened his eyes, and the Galilean was speaking, "…and your sons and your daughters shall prophesy, and your young men shall see visions, and your old men shall dream dreams; even on my male servants and my female servants in those days I will pour out my Spirit, and they shall prophesy. I will show wonders in heaven and signs on the earth below, blood and fire and vapor of smoke; the sun shall turn red and the moon to blood before the day of the Lord comes, the great and magnificent day. And it shall come to pass that everyone who calls on the name of the Lord shall be saved.'"

Ezra looked to Naomi beside him, holding tight to his hand listening, transfixed by the words of Jesus' disciple. She glanced for a moment at her son and smiled. Then she turned back to the Galilean, "Men of Israel, hear these words: Jesus of Nazareth, a man attested to you by God with mighty works and wonders and signs that God did through Him in your midst, as you yourselves know— this Jesus delivered up according to the definite plan and foreknowledge of God, you crucified and killed by the hands of lawless men. God raised him up, losing the pangs of death because it was not possible for Him to be held by it. For David said of Him, 'I saw the Lord always before me, for he is at my right hand that I may not be shaken; therefore, my heart was glad, and my tongue rejoiced; my flesh also will dwell in hope. For you will not abandon my soul to Hades, nor let your Holy One see corruption. You made known to me the paths of life; you will make me full of gladness with your presence.'"

As the Galilean went on to preach from the Psalms, the visions came back. The words of Baruch echoed in his ears, "Search the Scriptures; they tell of him!" Ezra looked at Naomi, and with teary eyes, he said, "It is so. Jesus is the Messiah, the Blessed One of God. I will follow Him. He calls for me to come and be Baptized. Will you come with me, mother? Do you believe as I do?"

Naomi squeezed Ezra's hand. "I will go with you. I believe."

As Ezra and Naomi walked forward, they saw Nicodemus, Joseph, Mathias, and Baruch among the followers of Jesus. Standing ahead of him was a young woman, as she turned for a moment, he recognized her face, Mariam the Nazarite.

The leader, who they learned was called Peter, a disciple of Jesus, led those seeking baptism to the Pool of Siloam. Ezra found himself leading the people in singing a psalm of ascent even as they descended to the clear pool fed by the Gihon spring:

> "Out of the depths, I cry to you, O LORD!
> O LORD hear my voice!
> Let your ears be attentive
> to the voice of my pleas for mercy!
> If you, O LORD, should mark iniquities,
> O LORD who could stand?
> But with you, there is forgiveness,
> that you may be feared.
> I wait for the LORD, my soul waits,
> and in His word. I have hope;

My soul waits for the LORD
more than the watchman for the morning.
O Israel, hope in the LORD!
For with the LORD, there is steadfast love,
And with Him is plentiful redemption.
And He will redeem Israel from all his iniquities.

Naomi clutched Ezra's arm, her face beaming as she sang along with her son. At the pool, Ezra counted eleven lines of people moving forward. One by one, they would step into the pool, the water up over their knees. When told, they would kneel, the cooling water was now chest deep. A disciple of Jesus would take a bowl of water from the pool and pour it over the head and body of the new believer while saying, "I baptize you in the name of the Father, and of the Son and of the Holy Spirit for the cleansing of your sins. Buried with Christ, receive his Spirit, and rise up in new life."

Those who were baptized were asked to make way for those behind. Mariam turned to see Naomi waiting behind her and Ezra singing in anticipation. When Naomi was baptized, Mariam took her hand and said, "I will wait with you, mother, while your son is baptized," and both women carefully stepped out of the pool. After Ezra was baptized, he joined his mother and hugged her tightly. Mariam said, "You are the priest with all the questions."

Ezra nodded, "Mariam, is it not? The Nazarite baptized by John? You seek to serve the LORD. This is my mother, Naomi. Thank you for attending to her."

Naomi said, "Yes, thank you, Mariam, I feel like a new a woman! Who would know that I am a widow, late in my years! Such excitement! And hope! You must join us. You are alone? I Insist you come to our house and rejoice with us!"

Mariam hesitated, "I must be about..."

Ezra interrupted, "You have told me you are not of Jerusalem, you have no husband or family here, please, accept my mother's hospitality. Truly this is a day of rejoicing."

Mariam nodded, and the three began making their way back into the streets of Jerusalem. Ezra again began singing, Naomi walking on his arm. Mariam quietly walked alongside, smiling and weeping.

In Ezra's comfortable home, Mariam sat nervously while Naomi prepared a meal. "You must tell me how you met my son at the Temple."

Ezra reminded Naomi. "Remember her vow, no wine, no grapes, raisins, wine vinegar..."

Naomi quietly cut him off, "Yes, son, I know."

Mariam continued loudly for Naomi to hear, "I had gone to the court of the Nazarites, as I had completed the year of my vow. Your son, Ezra, asked after me. He was curious as to why I sought consecration as a Nazarite."

Naomi, determined to maintain the conversation, replied, "You say you are a Nazarite? I do not recall meeting any other woman who has made the Nazarite Vow. And baptized by John? You followed him in the wilderness?"

"Yes, I heard of a prophet sent from God preaching in the wilderness. I went to see for myself. His words convicted me of the sin in my life, and I heeded his call to repentance and was baptized."

Naomi stepped away from what she was doing and stood before Mariam, "My dear child, you are young and tender, your eyes speak to me of a gentleness. Surely your mother and father worry for your well-being. I cannot imagine you bringing anything but pride and love to your house, how did it come about—forgive me, Mariam, I did not mean to pry. But it is sweet to me to share with a young woman. I have no daughter of my own, or sisters. As fine a young man as my Ezra is, there is are times a woman wishes to speak only with another woman."

Ezra could see the confusion in Mariam's face. He laughed lightly and said, "Perhaps I should wait in my scriptorium."

Mariam blushed, "No, Ezra, you can stay. Tell me about your work. I have heard the rules are stringent in copying the Torah and the Prophets."

Ezra nodded, "Indeed, the work is very detailed. Every stroke must look like the original, the script cannot be changed. There are two columns of forty lines on each page, each stroke and every iota counted. The linen pages are sewn together and rolled as a scroll onto two acacia rods. The quills, paper, and ink are kosher, set aside for this work. Any letter or mark that is not identical to the master copy must be scraped off entirely and rewritten. If the name of our LORD is not perfect, the entire page must be cut out, buried, and the page rewritten. Indeed, it can seem tedious and requires one's full attention, yet the work brings fulfillment and wonder. When the Sefer Torah is open in my hands, I feel the wonder of holding the LORD's very word to our people."

Ezra blushed, "Forgive me. I know my work seems boring to many."

Mariam shook her head, "No, I can see that you have a passion for the Law and the Prophets, just as you have a passion for serving in the Temple. No, Ezra, do not apologize. I desire to know the joy of serving our LORD myself."

Naomi called from the kitchen, "Come, all is prepared. Let us eat."

Ezra blessed the food, then Naomi said, "Tomorrow we are to return to hear Peter teach. The Messiah has come! Our lives—all of Israel, will be changed! I never thought my eyes would see this day. And our new friend Mariam will share it with us!"

When they finished the meal, Mariam stood up and said, "Your hospitality has been most kind, now I must leave."

Naomi asked, "My dear, you have no family in Jerusalem, where do you go?"

Mariam mumbled, "I must go, there are places..."

"Places?" Naomi asked. "What places? You have no home. Stay here with us. You are our guest."

"No, I will not be a burden to anyone."

"You are no burden. Stay. How is it a young woman, a Nazarite lives in Jerusalem with no family, no relatives? You must tell me, for surely guilt would fall on my head if something were to happen to you. How do you make your way?"

Mariam replied, "I take care of myself. I hire out my services where I can. I clean, I carry water from the pool or well, whatever might be done. I am often given meals, sometimes money, though I will keep no money and give it to those who beg by the Temple gate."

Naomi looked at Mariam's calloused hands, blackened feet and sun-browned face. She considered the soiled heavy woolen cloak, her only possession, and saw the toll that field work and servitude had taken on her young body.

Naomi looked into Mariam's warm brown eyes and declared, "Today, you have become our sister. You will stay with us. You will eat with us and serve with us."

Turning to Ezra, Naomi said, "Ezra, make your bed in your scriptorium, our sister Mariam will have your room!"

Mariam protested, "I could not take Ezra's room!"

Naomi was giving the orders, "Ezra, go find something to do. Visit your friend Baruch. I will not permit Mariam to go to bed until she has bathed and has clean clothes. Go! Don't stand there!"

Without a word, Ezra was obediently out the door. The events of the day played over and over in his mind. When he found himself facing Baruch, he fumbled for words, "Forgive me, I was asked to leave my house, and I didn't know where else to go."

Baruch looked puzzled and said, "Come in, brother. Your mother has expelled you from your own house? Is because you were baptized?"

"No, nothing like that. Yes, I was baptized, and so was Naomi. It is indeed a wonderful thing! You were right all along, and so too, were Joseph and Nicodemus. No, Mariam—remember the Nazarite woman I questioned at the Temple? Mariam. She was there and was baptized. She is staying with us. She has no home; Naomi insisted. She is bathing and is to have my room."

"Ezra, you are welcome to stay here until Naomi allows you to return home. Naomi has once again become a mother! I remember my mother and my wife were just the same. A priest's authority ends at the door to his house!"

Ezra blushed, "It is as you say. But I must tell you about my vision. When the disciples of Jesus were speaking this morning, I was caught up in a whirlwind. It carried me over the city to Golgotha. The wind spoke. I saw Jesus on the cross. I heard him crying out to the Father. I was transported back to the Temple and relived the events at the Temple on the day of his death. I saw again great hands appear and the curtain to the Holy of Holies torn from top to bottom and I heard in the wind Jesus cry, 'The LORD has forsaken me, and my Lord has forgotten me!" Another voice spoke, "Can a woman forget her nursing child? Can she feel no love for the son of her womb? Even these may forget, but I will not forget you. Behold, I have inscribed you on the palms of My hands; your walls are ever before Me.' After this, I found myself standing beside Naomi, holding her hand."

Baruch nodded, "The Holy Spirit came in power upon the disciples of Jesus. I was in a room with the twelve. There were one hundred twenty in all. The Holy Spirit descended upon us like tongues of fire. We all began to speak. Tongues. Tongues we did not know. Peter led us outside and began to preach. That is the preaching you heard."

Baruch paused and closed his eyes in meditation before continuing, "Three thousand were baptized today! God has breathed upon his people! His kingdom has come in power and authority. Tomorrow you shall join me and other priests, believers as we teach in the Temple. Joseph and Nicodemus have been called to the council. They will not be intimidated! Caiaphas will not stop us!"

Chapter Five

Jerusalem was reborn. A new excitement moved through the homes, shops, streets, and markets all the way up into the courts of the Temple. Followers of the Galilean, Jesus seemed to be ever-present, ever loud and ever joyful. There was no place in the city large enough to accommodate Peter and the Apostles as they daily taught, prayed with, and fellowshipped with the growing group of followers. The spacious courts of the Temple became the meeting place for this new Jewish movement called, "The Way."

The followers would meet at the Temple to be taught the sayings and stories of Jesus. They would then move off in small groups to homes and rooms in the city where they would pray for one another and share in "The Lord's

Supper," a communal meal, commanded by Jesus to his disciples on the night before he was betrayed. The faithful joyfully complied with this and the other command of Jesus to his disciples when he said, "Go and make disciples of all nations, baptizing them in the name of the Father and of the Son and of the Holy Spirit, teaching them to obey everything I have commanded you. And surely, I am with you always to the end of the age."

The followers shared with friends, relatives, neighbors, customers, visitors, and pilgrims to the Temple. Every day, many spoke of visions and dreams. Some described being taken away by the Spirit God. It was common for pilgrims to hear the words preached by Peter and the other apostles leading the movement, in their own language, one unknown to the simple fishermen from Galilee. Many reported miraculous answers to prayer. Peter, their leader, spoke boldly with authority. Many people, even those opposed to his teaching, witnessed miracles.

Once, when entering the Temple, Peter met a lame beggar who asked for a coin. Full of the Holy Spirit, Peter loudly exclaimed, "I have no silver or gold, but what I do have I give to you. In the name of Jesus, the Nazarene, get up and walk!"

Peter took the man by his hands to help him up. Immediately the lame man's feet and ankles were made strong. The lame man leaped up and began to walk. The healed man walked with Peter into the Temple, jumping, skipping, and praising God as he went. Following this public healing and filled with the Holy Spirit, Peter preached that it was Jesus who has the power over life and death. Jesus had conquered death once and for all.

That day five thousand men answered Peter's call to follow Jesus.

The Temple authorities did not rejoice with the lame man. They did not praise God for this miraculous healing. They met to conspire just as they had before against Jesus. Caiaphas did not summon the Sanhedrin or the council, only his closest allies, former high priests, Annas, John, and Alexander were present when he ordered Peter and John arrested. After leaving them in jail overnight, Caiaphas called the council as he did not have authority to punish them. He sought to question Peter and John as they did Jesus but this time away from the public eye.

Caiaphas coldly asked, "By what power or what name have you done this?"

Then Peter, filled with the Holy Spirit said, "Rulers and elders of the people, if we are on trial today for a good deed done to a crippled man, by what means this man has been healed, let it be known to all of you and to all the people of Israel that by the name of Jesus Christ of Nazareth, whom you crucified, whom God raised from the dead—by Him this man is standing before you well. This Jesus is the stone that was rejected by you, the builders, which has become the cornerstone. And there is salvation in no other name under heaven given among men by which you must be saved."

The chief priests and the council were amazed by the boldness of Peter and John. They were common, uneducated men who followed Jesus. The man who was healed, standing beside Peter and John, would say nothing against them. The council sent them out while they debated what to do. Calling them back, the high priest demanded them not to speak or preach in the name of Jesus.

Peter and John replied, "Whether it is right in the sight of God to listen to you rather than to God, you must judge, for we cannot but speak of what we have seen and heard."

Not knowing what else to do the council released Peter and John. But Caiaphas determined this was not over.

Ezra's life was never busier. Every morning he went with Naomi and Mariam to the teaching. Together, they would take the meal, "The Lord's Supper." Ezra would join Baruch and other priests at a place in the Temple to search the Scriptures for evidence of Jesus' claims. They were amazed that familiar passages spoke of Jesus, but they never before recognized what was now so clear. Ezra then returned home and spent hours copying the Torah and the Law, chuckling to himself when the passage he copied spoke of his Messiah.

The short hours Ezra spent with Naomi and Mariam were intimate and warm. Ezra could see that the two women were bonding and quite content in their relationship to permit Ezra the time to debate and copy Scripture. He was pleased to see warm eyes and warm smiles on their faces. He found himself watching Mariam, no longer the hardened, austere field girl, but a bright, thoughtful, and beautiful young woman. *'What a special young woman she is,'* Ezra thought as he watched her. Any thought of Mariam leaving was gone. In truth, he realized that Mariam's departure would be most painful. She had become dear to both Naomi and him.

During the teaching one morning, a foreign-born Jew, a Levite from Cyprus, named Joseph, also called Barnabas or 'Son of Encouragement,' brought with him a pouch of money and laid it at Peter's feet. "I sold a tract of land and want to give the money for the good of all the brothers and sisters of 'The Way.'"

Many others followed his example, and they desired to have all things in common. They believed that Jesus would return soon and in power and that his followers should spend all their time making disciples. Surely, they argued, if we pool everything we own, we have enough to allow us to devote all of our time to His work and can forego time spent earning a wage.

As contributions were made, some who had given all and some who had nothing to offer sought support from the money provided. Nicodemus heard that the large inn, where Jesus and his disciples shared the Passover supper on the night that he was betrayed, could be purchased. The inn close to the Temple, was used as a rooming house for pilgrims coming to Jerusalem for the festivals. The apostles used some of the pooled money to buy the inn as a common house for widows and their children. The large kitchen made meals, and the widows ate at the inn. They set aside the upper room for Peter, the apostles, and leaders as a meeting room for counsel and prayer. They welcomed the skills of believers, and God added daily to their number. Soon James, the brother of Jesus, joined them, a man with an unquenchable thirst for prayer. Every day he would listen to the apostles as they discussed their calling to make disciples of all men. James would pray the whole day for God's leading and blessing on their work.

The needs of the widows and the concerns of those seeking to help soon found their way to the upper room. Now rather than preaching, the apostles spent most of their time administering between the givers and those seeking help. In frustration, the apostles decided to appoint deacons to do this work so they could return to fulfilling their calling to make disciples of all nations.

Naomi brought the question home to Ezra, "Son, all that we own is under your authority. Can you not give all that we have as well? Mariam and I will be cared for, and you can continue to serve in the Temple and receive all that is due to you as a Levite?"

Ezra sighed, "Mother, I have considered what you are asking for many days. I am pleased your desire is to give everything. I would believe you have discussed this with Mariam as well, and she feels the same. Truly, it is my heart's desire to give, and this giving is to the LORD. I have searched the Scriptures and considered the Savior's teachings. They tell me first, above all, the LORD desires gifts from the heart. 'The sacrifices of God are a broken spirit; a broken and contrite heart, O God, you will not despise.' But I also remember Jesus confronting the Pharisees on the practice of declaring their parents 'Corban.' If Jesus condemned the Pharisees for declaring what they owed for caring for their parents as given to God and releasing them from their obligations, as both hypocrisy and sin, how then could I do the same? Did not our Savior give his mother Mary into the protection of John while he suffered upon the cross? No mother, I will not give up a house for you for as long as you live. I shall not allow my duty to care for you to become someone else's burden. I will seek other ways to give."

Naomi offered, "There is the master Sefer Torah. It is ancient; it must be of value?"

Ezra nodded, "It is a valuable Torah. But it is but one copy. From it, I can make many more copies. No, I do not believe God would have me give it up. And I must sell the copy I make because I do not have enough money to pay for paper, quills, ink for the next. When I sell the Sefer Torah I now copy, I will keep just enough for one more, and we can give the difference to the work."

Ezra took Naomi's hands, "Mother, I will give to God. He is calling for me to give something. I earnestly seek to know what it is that he calls me to give. Mother pray. Pray that I do not disappoint the One who has called me to his work."

Naomi smiled, "Then I will join Mariam in her work with the widows. The deacons Stephen and Philip always welcome new helpers. I will help until my strength gives way, and then I will continue to serve, to devote my time in prayer."

"By all means, speak to Stephen, he is a man with a heart for God and all God's people. The Sefer Torah is nearly complete, pray someone will buy from a young scribe!"

The next day Ezra returned to the Temple to keep his appointment with Baruch, priests, and Levites who were followers of The Way. As he climbed the steps, he met Saul, the disciple of Gamaliel coming down. Saul said to him, "You are the priest who questioned Rabban Gamaliel concerning Jesus and the Law."

Ezra nodded, "Yes, I sat under the Rabban Gamaliel."

Saul replied, "We have not seen you in some time. Do you still study the Law?"

"I search the Scriptures daily. I am a scribe; I copy the Safer Torah. The Law of the LORD is ever before me."

Saul stopped and turned to Ezra. "You would do well to avoid the followers of the dead Galilean Jesus. They fall into blasphemy and pollute our Temple. Their days are numbered."

Saul looked squarely into Ezra's eyes and said, "If you love the Law of the LORD, you will return to the truth. You will stand against this false Messiah whose words have tickled the ears, but in the end, bring only death and destruction. Better it falls upon a few than upon our nation, Israel." Saul walked off towards the Council court.

Ezra continued to the Court of the Gentiles and to the side known as Solomon's portico, that had become the meeting place of the followers of Jesus. Baruch was there patiently going through the suffering servant passage of Isaiah with new believers. At an opportune time, Ezra asked, I have a request of Joseph. I hoped he could find a buyer for the Torah and prophets that is nearly finished. He has wealthy friends and connections."

Baruch replied, "Joseph and Nicodemus have been called to the council. But I will be sure he gets your message. Your first Safer Torah not supervised by your father, a blessing indeed! Yes, Joseph can help. I know he will help you, brother. Now, perhaps you would teach us this morning what the Law says regarding sin and atonement."

An honorable man in Israel would never run. A man in authority and privilege takes his time. People wait for him. Therefore, the sight of Nicodemus, out of breath from hurrying up the stairs and out onto Solomon's porch, startled Ezra, and all the followers of Jesus gathered for the teaching. Gasping for breath, Nicodemus shouted to Baruch, "Where are Peter and John? I must tell them. It's Stephen. They mean to stone him!"

Alarmed, Baruch asked, "Who means to stone him? Where is Stephen now?"

Still gasping, Nicodemus replied, "He was teaching in the Synagogue of the Freedmen, and they became angry. A mob dragged him before the council and accused him. Many accusations—they did not agree—but they insisted he is a blasphemer and demanded he is stoned. Caiaphas agreed. There was no defense, the council did not vote. There was shouting, and condemnation and Caiaphas declared it agreed that he was deserving to die."

"Only the Romans can put a man to death lawfully."

"There was nothing lawful about it. This was no trial. I saw an angry mob and a hateful high priest grasped the opportunity. They dragged him off to stone him in the valley of Kidron outside the walls of the city."

Baruch cried out, "Come, there is no time to spare. Perhaps we can stop them!"

As they made their way to the gate, they could hear the loud jeers of the angry mob. They rushed forward, and they saw men hurling stones at the bent and bleeding Stephen. As they arrived, they saw Stephen on his knees and heard him cry out, "Lord Jesus receive my spirit." Then lifting his head, his eyes bloodied and blind, Stephen said, "Lord, do not hold this sin against them." He fell forward and died.

Ezra found himself standing beside Gamaliel's disciple, Saul, holding the robes of those stoning Stephen. Their eyes met, and Saul said, "This is only the beginning. I will not stop until every blasphemer receives the same as this, man."

As the mob slowly wandered off, Baruch and Nicodemus led a small group of followers to take the body of Stephen to be prepared for burial. Nicodemus spoke slowly, "He defended himself before them. He was calm. He was filled with the Spirit, I am certain of it. He preached to Caiaphas and to the Council. He told how the history of Israel leads to Jesus. He opened the Scriptures to his accusers. In truth, he asked them, 'Which of the prophets did your fathers not persecute?' He challenged them all, 'They killed all those who had previously announced the coming of the Righteous One whose betrayers and murderers you have become. You received the Law as ordained by angels, and yet you did not keep it.'"

Ezra wiped away his tears, "No man spoke more truthfully from the Scriptures. Why did God let this happen?"

Nicodemus continued, "His accusations cut them deeply. They flew into a rage, and then—and then the Spirit came upon Stephen. I could see it. He was transfixed. His eyes gazed upward to what was unseen by anyone else. He said, 'Behold, I see the heavens opened up and the Son of Man standing at the right hand of God.'"

The men fell silent. They gathered up the body and left.

Naomi and Mariam did not see the pain in Ezra's face when he returned home. They were anxious to share their news with him. "We met Mary today, Mary, the mother of Jesus! She was serving the widows. She would not leave until everyone was served. Her son, James, a brother of Jesus, came to her and asked that she let the others serve, but she would not be dissuaded. She answered him, saying, 'This is my religion to visit widows and orphans in their affliction and keep myself unstained from the world.' All the apostles and leaders defer to her, yet she is humble and unassuming. She smiles upon all whom she serves."

"Mary lives among the widows?"

"She lives in the house of Salome, mother of John. John cares as for her Jesus desired. John's brother James, lives with them as does James, the brother of Jesus."

Ezra managed a smile, "Who is more faithful than Mary? She has suffered more than all others, yet she serves with grace and love. Should not the Apostles give her pre-eminence? She is the first of our Savior's disciples, and she is steadfast in the faith. Who can doubt that she is blessed by God? And yet, she suffered. I can only imagine how she suffered, never abandoning Jesus as he hung and died on the cross. Can we learn from her? We must learn from her. If Mary, blessed of God has suffered, can we expect any less? We must be prepared to give more than what we own. We must prepare to give our lives for the Blessed One our Savior."

Ezra sighed and continued softly, "I too have news. Hard news. Stephen is dead. He was stoned outside the city wall. But his death was different. Before he died, he saw the heavens opened and the Son of Man seated by the Father. He showed no fear, only compassion on those who murdered him. As Mary teaches us how to live, Stephen teaches us how to die."

Ezra began to weep. The emotions of the day overwhelmed him. Naomi and Mariam were struck dumb by the news, and they cried.

Ezra began to speak, "There was a man I knew from sitting under Rabban Gamaliel. His disciple, a man named Saul. He knew. Before it happened, he knew, and he warned me. He was there when they stoned Stephen, holding the robes of the men stoning our brother. He recognized me and said, 'This is just the beginning.' I fear a time of trial is upon us. Now is the time we must learn to live by faith."

Naomi thought about Ezra's words and answered, "Somehow, I trust Jesus more. I love him more. I am drawn closer to Jesus. Closer to Mary. Closer to the brothers and sisters."

Mariam said, "I have nothing else to give. I will give my life. I want to be closer, still."

After a time of silence, Mariam asked quietly, "Ezra, when you take the Lord's Supper, do you come closer to Him?"

Ezra thought before he answered, "The Lord's Supper draws us close, indeed. But it is more than a memory. We join with Him and with the Father and the Holy Spirit. We join with every brother and sister in the Lord. It is nourishment for the soul. Stephen will continue to join with us in the supper, as do the patriarchs and prophets and everyone before us who hoped in His coming."

Mariam nodded, "Then as a priest answer me this. Do I disobey the Lord's command to remember him if I refuse the wine at the Lord's Supper? For I have vowed before God not to drink wine. If I taste the wine at the supper, do I break my vow and covenant I made with God?"

Ezra hesitated, and began to reason out loud, "Jesus said, 'If you love me, obey my commands.' Indeed, it is his command to partake of the Supper. But the Law requires a Nazarite to continue his vow until it is fulfilled. Even if you bury a loved one, the vow must begin again until all is fulfilled. The wine at the Lord's Supper would restart you vow each time you partake. Then again, our Lord taught us that the Law was made for us."

Ezra fell silent, finally saying, "I don't know. I will ask the other priests and scribes. Truly, Jesus compels us to look at the Law differently than we practiced it in the past. I cannot counsel you on this question yet. You can assuredly take the bread until your vow is complete. For now, Mariam, take the bread with a clean heart, and he will in no way withhold his grace and mercy."

Mariam nodded as Ezra spoke, and she said. "Forgive me, Ezra, I am not a priest trained in the Law. But I know I love Jesus above the Law. What is the Law, but a rule of righteous living? We believe Jesus is the Son of God, the Father, author of the Law. Is not the creator above what He makes? I hear it said that when Jesus was asked, 'What is the greatest commandment,' He answered, 'The greatest commandment is to love the LORD your God with all of your heart and all of your mind and all of your soul. And the second is like it: love your neighbor as yourself. For in these two are all of the Law and the Prophets.' You look to the Scriptures to see what it says of Jesus. Perhaps you priests should look at the words of Jesus to understand the Law."

Ezra closed his eyes, "God charged our father Abraham just as you quote Jesus. This has been the command of God before Moses. It has never changed. There is truth in your words, Mariam, and instruction in my faith. This truth comes from God's unchanging command before Aaron, the first priest of the Law. Aaron's consecration was of God. I cannot believe the same for Caiaphas. We will search out this matter. We will search out if Jesus brings a new Law."

Chapter Six

Ezra was rechecking each page and recounting each stroke of his newly completed Torah when a visitor came to their door. Naomi called for Ezra, who met a tall black man wearing a magnificent white linen robe trimmed with gold. He wore a magnificent hat covered in the whitest of linen and long bright feathers. A large shining sapphire was mounted in the center. Ezra had seen Ethiopians before, but never one so richly attired.

"I seek the scribe, Ezra. A friend, Joseph, sends me. I must depart tomorrow and return to my duties at the court of my queen Candace. I urgently seek a Sefer Torah and Prophets. I am told you may have one. I will pay you well."

Ezra, surprised, said, "God is good! I have just completed a Torah with all the Scriptures, the Prophets, Psalms and Chronicles. Yes. You say Joseph sent you? Joseph of Arimathea? Well, please come in. I will bring it to you."

Ezra returned with the Sefer Torah, he respectfully removed the embroidered mantle and unrolled it to show a complete page. The Ethiopian looked closely and read a few words.

"You read Hebrew, my friend?"

"Yes, it has been handed down to our priests and scholars since the days of the great Queen of Sheba. We have preserved the wisdom of your Solomon. Show me, friend, where I can find the Prophet, Isaiah."

Ezra unrolled and rolled until Isaiah was in the center of the two acacia rods. "I have put the Prophet Isaiah in the center for you to find immediately."

The Ethiopian opened the scroll and read the first few verses of Isaiah. Smiling broadly, he said, "I shall study the Scriptures!"

Lowering the scroll and looking into Ezra's face he said, "All Jerusalem is in turmoil, 'Study the Scriptures, they speak of him.' It is all I hear!"

Returning the Sefer Torah to its mantle, the Ethiopian said, "I am told a scribe may work a year to copy the Torah. I will give you one year's wages of our high priest in gold, 100 Roman Aurei."

"That is most generous, my friend," Ezra said as he handed him the scroll.

"This is the greater treasure! I will share it with my Queen Candace."

After Ezra purchased the highest quality linen paper,

quills, ink, and mantle for his next Sefer Scroll, he put all of the remaining money into a pouch and carried it to the teaching. As Peter began a psalm of thanksgiving, Ezra went forward and laid the pouch at his feet. As he walked back, Peter called out to him, "Brother, do you wish to give us a word?"

"I have no word to give and desire no recognition. The gift is for our widows and orphans."

Peter asked, "What is your name, brother?"

"I am Ezra. Ezra ben Haggai. I cannot give everything I have. My mother is a widow under my roof. I am a priest and receive from the Temple. But I will not be like the Pharisee who calls his mother 'Corban,' so I provide for her. I am a scribe and have sold my first Sefer Torah at a high price. I have made a vow to the LORD to keep only enough to purchase the linen paper, quills and ink for another and the remainder I give to Jesus, to care for the widows and orphans. God be praised he sent a wealthy Ethiopian to purchase just as I completed the Torah. Forgive me if my gift is not enough."

"Tell me, Ezra, does it pain you to make this gift?"

"I gladly give, and desire to give all that I have, but I will not rob from others who depend on me, or make others assume my debts and burdens."

Peter said, "Your gift is pleasing to the Lord!"

When Ezra returned to his place, Joseph, called Barnabas, came alongside him and said, please, come with me. There is someone who seeks your help."

Barnabas led Ezra to the far end of Solomon's porch where a young Galilean was in conversation with Baruch. As they walked up, Baruch said, "This is the man. You can ask him yourself."

The Galilean bowed stiffly and said, "My name is

James, ben Joseph. Jesus is my brother. I seek to know more. I have questions. I did not understand but now, but now I know he is more. Mother always knew, but my brothers and I—well, your vision, I have heard of your vision and the Temple. What you saw. What you heard. I would listen. Please, tell me."

James nodded along as Ezra recounted the events on the day of Jesus' crucifixion. Ezra shared every detail. He told how on the day of the Holy Spirit, when Peter and Jesus' disciples preached, how the Spirit took him back to the crucifixion. He described hearing the voice in the wind, the voice of Jesus and the voice in the Temple as the curtain was torn. Ezra mentioned how he joined the others who were baptized in the Spirit and in the water of the pool of Siloam -how he is now a follower of Jesus.

All the time James was nodding as he listened, his eyes closed in concentration. When Ezra finished, James said, "I too was taken in the Spirit, and I know what you say is true. Peter and the Apostles preach, and many follow. It is their calling to make disciples, and I will serve as our Lord leads. I pray to God that His will be done. I pray that our people Israel repent and believe."

Ezra smiled, "It is a good thing that you do, brother James."

James continued, "And I seek to understand God's will for us and all men. I have heard the Baptist say of Jesus, 'The lamb of God who takes away the sins of the world.' I am a witness that He knew no sin. He was always righteous and obedient to the Law. The storm, the earthquake, the torn curtain to the Holy of Holies. It means something. Jesus died as an atonement for our sin, just as John prophesied. The torn curtain. It matters."

Ezra looked to Baruch and then to James. "I am glad

that you have come. I am glad that you say to me of the curtain, 'It means something.' It is as you say. Jesus died for our sins. The righteous for the sinner. It pleased God to accept Him as a sacrifice for us. A sacrifice that never need be repeated to atone for the sin of all men."

Ezra pointed through the gate to court of the Holies, "Look at the great altar. Sacrifice never ending, never enough! Now it is enough! I will help! Baruch and priests like us will help. We must examine the Law and know the will of the LORD our God. We are with you, brother James!"

James hugged Ezra and Baruch, "Brothers, teachers. Study the Law. I am a simple man from Nazareth. But I know there is much to learn—to understand. I will pray."

Baruch smiled, "Yes brother James, pray for us."

James was smiling, his head nodding affirming his words, "It is what I can do. I will pray that God sends a Spirit of knowledge and of discernment. I will pray that he will guide his priests called by his name. And I will pray that his strong arm protects you and shield you from all those who in ignorance or led by the evil one, seek to destroy you or any who have called on the name of Jesus for salvation and forgiveness. Yes. I can pray. This is now my calling."

Barnabas also hugged Ezra and said, "Be strong! Our God has called you. His Spirit is within you. You are his chosen priest. Be assured if He called you He will give you strength and knowledge. He will never fail you. Be of good cheer. You are a son of God. Who can stand against you?"

The men returned to the teaching as it was ending for the day. Ezra stopped and said, "I see Temple guards leaving as our brothers and sisters depart. They follow at a distance."

Naomi and Mariam were nearing the bottom steps exiting the Temple when a guard two steps behind pointed to them. Two Temple guards stepped forward and sternly announced, "You two. Come with us!"

"Why? Where do you take us?" Naomi protested loudly.

"No questions. You will come with us. If you resist or object once more, you will be carried forcibly."

"Is this the respect you show to the widow of a priest and her friend, a Levite from the country?" She replied.

"Speak once more, either of you and your mouths will be gagged and your arms tied. Is this how you wish to be seen by your neighbors?"

Mariam shouted, "It is written in the Prophets, 'Seek justice, reprove the ruthless. Defend the orphan, honor the widow!' And Moses commands, 'The Levite because he has no portion or inheritance among you, and the alien, the orphan and the widow who are in your town, shall come and eat and be satisfied. So that the LORD your God may bless you...' "

A guard's hand covered her mouth as his arm wrapped around her head. His other arm grabbed Mariam from behind, as jammed his knee in her back and he bound her hands behind her. Turning to Naomi, he asked, "Do you desire the same?"

The guards led them to the prison outside the Temple near the court of the Council. They were led to a large bleak room filled with women. Naomi and Mariam were immediately embraced by the others who said, "Be of good cheer sisters. We stand fast in the service of our Savior, who brings joy even in sorrow. Rejoice with us for we have been chosen among all who believe for the honor of bearing witness. For what prophet did they not kill? And are we more deserving than our Lord who said, 'Do not fear the one who can kill the body but cannot kill the soul. Rather fear him who can destroy both body and soul in hell.'"

Mariam began to sing.

More arrests came at night. They were made quietly in the homes of the followers of Jesus. No one was told where they were taken or what charges had been made against them. The few arrests that were made in public were led by the Pharisee, Saul, and his contingent of six Temple guards. Saul wanted his arrests made known—to send a message. Most were beaten. If he could stir the on-lookers to demand the accused to be stoned, he encouraged the mob to take them. He ordered his Temple guards to maintain good order—to clear a path for the mob and ensure the executions outside the wall. Man or woman, young or old, it made no difference to Saul. Every blasphemer was deserving of death. Ever the lawyer, Saul's only care was to assure the stonings could be laid against a mob.

The high priest soon realized Saul's method was having an effect. People were afraid to be associated with these Jesus followers. The teaching in the Temple stopped. Having no authority to execute prisoners, and limited room to house them, they ordered the imprisoned to be beaten and released. They gave a free hand to the zealous Pharisee to accomplish their purpose.

Ezra wept with joy when Naomi and Marian returned rejoicing from the council prison. He hugged them tightly, caressing their heads as he thanked God for their salvation.

Word was passed between believers to meet quietly in homes, in the small groups who gathered for the Lord's Supper. The Apostles and deacons would visit groups under their care to encourage, teach, and share information. Prayer dominated these meetings, but signs of the Spirit continued, and the followers remained steadfast in their faith.

Saul found it difficult to identify his blasphemers. Followers were no longer conspicuous in the Temple, and the public lost its taste for the heavy-handed pharisee's bullying of harmless, peaceable people. Frustrated in Jerusalem, Saul went to Caiaphas and asked for a letter authorizing his arrest of any blasphemers preaching Jesus to the Jews in Damascus. Shortly after this, Ezra's time of Temple service came, and he returned to his duties.

Chapter Seven

Everything at the temple appeared normal. The priests, the musicians and Levites, the pilgrims, and worshippers, the merchants, sacrificial animals, even the lepers were in their usual places following the rituals of the Hebrews since the days of Aaron. But things were not the same. How could they be? Sizeable numbers of all the people had been baptized in the Holy Spirit. They knew things were not the same. The followers of Jesus in the temple were not the same. They had been born again, and everything in their lives made new. They came to the temple and worshipped in the manner of their forefathers for they knew no other way. They were redeemed. Set free. Free from sin and all that came with it. Yet the temple stood and drew them. It was the house of the LORD God of Israel. Where else should they worship? They knew God does not change. His word is forever. His covenant is without end. So, they came and offered sacrifices, the believers with their persecutors, shoulder to shoulder singing ancient hymns of praise.

Things were not the same among the many priests who now followed Jesus. Slowly, they came to know one another, to identify brother from the unpersuaded or persecutor. Sides were drawn, but the work of the temple continued as it always had. The believers found every opportunity to share and debate, to pray and encourage. Baruch's wine and olive oil court became a safe place for believing priests to congregate for fellowship and prayer. It was here that Ezra brought the concerns of his heart.

"Brother priests, how often I have heard the debates whether Jesus is the Messiah and the Blessed One of Israel. We have searched the Scriptures, and we know they speak of him. It is right that we find every place our Savior is foreshadowed, but there is a more critical debate we have not begun. A sister came to me, a good woman who loves the Lord. She is a Nazarite and takes only the bread at the Lord's Supper. She asks a hard question. Should she follow the command of our Lord and drink the wine at the Supper, or does she honor the vow she made to God as a Nazarite?"

Ezra paused and looked at his brother priests, and he could see the same uncertainty he felt when asked. He continued, "Brothers, we must seek answers to such questions. We all believe Jesus was faithful to the Law of Moses. His brother James testifies that it was always so. Jesus taught that not one stroke or iota of the law would be taken away until all things are accomplished."

Ezra watched as his brothers nodded, "We must study the Law as Jesus taught it. We must examine all that we have learned in the power of the Holy Spirit that has come upon us. What does our Master mean when he says, 'all things are accomplished,' or again when he says, 'I have come to fulfill the Law?' The Law is linked to the Covenant God made with Moses. Can the Covenant be fulfilled? I can never forget the damage to the great altar and the tearing of the curtain to the Holy of Holies at the very moment our Savior died. Surely, it is a sign. Is it a sign of the grief tearing at the heart of our Father God at the suffering of his only son? Has God been torn apart as the torn animals he walked between when he gave us the covenant? We have received the Holy Spirit. Is the sign that God no longer remains behind the curtain in the Holy of Holies and now freely lives with his people made clean by the atoning death of his son on the cross? Then why do we sacrifice? Is it necessary or a tradition now fulfilled by Jesus? Brothers, these are hard questions. I do not say I know the answers. I say we must search them out."

Baruch walked over and stood beside Ezra, "Brothers there is truth in Ezra's words. These are indeed hard questions. We know Jesus is the Christ, the anointed, and the long-awaited Messiah. We must learn his teaching on the Law and the Prophets just as we determined who he is, and we must understand what he teaches. Are the Law and the covenant fulfilled? Does Jesus bring us a new Law and new covenant? How then shall we live? What shall we teach our people?"

One said, "Young Ezra, the Law we know. 'The Law of the Lord is perfect.' You ask us to throw away everything we know of God and the Law? By speculation? I say we continue as we always have but, in the knowledge that the Holy One has come and he will come again to establish his kingdom!"

Ezra started to answer, but Baruch interrupted, "Neither Ezra nor I say we cease our duties as priests. I speak for myself when I say; I have never had more assurance of my service to God as a priest than I have since I have come to faith in Jesus! No. We do not say stop ministering, for surely, we must. We are priests. But so also must we consider the teaching of our Lord carefully. Is any here opposed to searching out Jesus' teaching on the Law and the Prophets? I have often pondered on the Master's parable of the wineskins. Jesus taught that the new wine must be put into new wineskins. He taught that the new wine would cause the old wineskin to burst. Brothers, we must prepare new wineskins for our Savior's lessons."

When Ezra left the meeting with his fellow priests, he passed through the court near Solomon's porch and came upon James, the brother of Jesus, on his knees praying alongside James, the apostle who was lying prone before the temple in prayers. Ezra marveled at the time the men spent in prayer. They never stopped! Only when Peter lightly tapped on James the son of Zebedee's shoulder did James show any awareness to the noise and bustle of the people about him.

Sitting up and accepting Peter's help to his feet, he quietly asked, "Peter, do you not recall the times our Lord took you, John and me with him to pray? Do we have any better memories of him? I know you to be a man of action, and my brother John, a man of compassion, can you not let me be a man of prayer?

James, the brother of Jesus, understands. He joins me as we lay the work before the Father in heaven."

"James, I know you to be a man of prayer, and it is a good thing that you disciple James, the brother of Jesus, but there is important news. News for all of us. The others insisted you know as well."

"What news brother, that you take me from my prayers?"

"Our God is truly at work. It is confirmed our persecutor, Saul of Tarsus, has arrived in Damascus praising God and glorifying the name of Jesus. He insists he met Jesus on the road and blinded by the brightness of his glory. He sought out a brother, Ananias, who had a vision that Saul would come to him blind. Ananias prayed for Saul, and he was healed. The reports say Saul has been preaching the salvation of Jesus everywhere in Damascus, and Jews who do not believe, for they knew he carried a letter to arrest our brother followers, these Jews sought to kill him. Saul has escaped to Caesarea, where the brothers sent him home to Tarsus."

James nodded, "Should we be surprised that our Lord answers prayer? No sin is too great to be forgiven and no heart too hard for the Spirit to penetrate. I will pray that Saul's gifts are shown to him. Now, brother, is there anything else? I should like to resume my prayers."

When James returned to his knees, praying softly, Ezra stepped over to Peter and said, "Brother, I am Ezra, a priest. There are many among us and the Levites who follow Jesus. I am a friend to Baruch, Nicodemus, and Joseph of Arimathea, whom you know. I have met Saul, the man of whom you spoke. A zealous man indeed. A Pharisee and a disciple of the Rabban Gamaliel. This man is an expert in the Law. Pray that his mind is renewed, and he studies the Law through the teaching of Jesus, for we priests have been asked questions we cannot answer."

"I know of you, brother. I remember your gift. Your friends hold you in high regard. You have a mother, Naomi, and a sister, I believe, Mariam. Mary, the mother of Jesus, tells our brothers, the sons of Zebedee, of their tireless service among the widows. God's blessing be upon your house and upon your mind that the Spirit brings an understanding of Jesus' teaching of the Law. I will remember what you ask and pray for Saul."

Ezra was able to spend the night at home and happily shared the kind words from Mary to Naomi and Mariam. Both women were embarrassed yet pleased. "The three Marys all serve so faithfully and with great joy. Such energy! It is a wonder any of us can keep up with them!" Naomi replied.

"The squabbling always stops when they are present," Mariam added.

"Squabbling?"

Mariam looked at Naomi, who answered, "It is most unfortunate, but very often those attending the widows show favoritism for the widows of Jerusalem. The Greek-speaking widows from our people having returned from foreign cities are asked to wait."

"How can that be?" Ezra asked.

Mariam answered, "I don't believe they mean to ignore the Greek-speaking Jewish widows, probably they want to help their friends and neighbors first. But I must say, the offense is taken."

"Mary insists that Peter and James put an end to it."

Ezra sighed, "Again, they are called from their duties

to deal with squabbling. I'm sure the deacons will be instructed."

Looking at Mariam, he said, "I fear I had upset some of the priests when I suggested we look to our Lord's teaching on the Law. Some see no need for change. I mentioned the case of the Nazarite. I believe they understand the problem, though none offered another solution."

Mariam smiled. "The year of my vow is nearly complete. I no longer see a need to renew it. I will soon join our brothers and sisters with the cup at the Lord's Supper. But thank you for remembering."

Ezra lightened and said, "More news. God is good and answers prayer! Our persecutor, Saul of Tarsus, is now our brother! He met God on the road to Damascus and now preaches the Good News wherever he goes. The persecutor has become the persecuted, and he was forced to flee. He has returned to Tarsus. Pray for him. He is well trained in the Law. Perhaps the Lord will call upon his gift."

Naomi said, "Ezra, your cup is not full, let me get some more..."

She tried to stand as she spoke but immediately fell to the floor. Ezra and Mariam both raced to help her. As she was lifted back to her seat, she could only say, "Don't either of you make a fuss. I am fine. Just a little tired."

Ezra helped her up, demanding she put her arms around his shoulders, and he walked her to her bed. "Mother, you must sleep. Perhaps, tomorrow, stay here and rest."

Mariam said, "I will sit with you. We can serve the Lord in prayer."

Ezra nodded, "Listen to Mariam. She is both wise and

gracious! You will rest tomorrow. Mariam will stay with you. Yes. Pray. Now tell me you will do as we ask."

Naomi sighed, "I have been a little tired. My legs give me pain. And what woman of my age has no pain? But I will do as you ask. I will spend the time with my daughter, Mariam. We will talk and laugh and pray."

Mariam hugged Naomi tight and said, "Yes, mother. Tomorrow will be ours alone!"

Before the sun rose the next morning, Ezra quietly left the house and made his way to the temple. His thoughts were on his mother Naomi, a very strong woman who never before allowed herself a day off to rest or recuperate. He was thankful that Mariam convinced her to stay home. He worried about her health. Her collapse was more than a sore leg. He prayed his way up the temple steps.

Mariam let Naomi sleep far into the morning. When Naomi woke, she was naturally apologetic for wasting half the day. "How could you let me sleep so late? Did Ezra have his breakfast? You must be starving. Let me make you something to eat."

Mariam smiled and said with all the authority she learned from Naomi, "You are not getting on your feet today. It is my day to serve you. I won't have you under my foot. Now, how is your appetite? Are you hungry? Stay there; I will bring you breakfast."

Naomi smiled and waited obediently for Mariam to return. "Thank you, Mariam. It seems strange to being served in my bed. But as I watch you, I see what a gift you are to me. A precious angel sent from our Father in heaven. Come, sit here beside me, and we shall talk."

Mariam sat beside Naomi, kissed her forehead, and gave her a warm hug, "You have shown me love I have never known before. It brings great joy to serve you."

"And you have filled an empty space in my heart, and Ezra's as well. I called you 'daughter' without your permission. Was I wrong to do so?"

"I called you mother in return. It is from my heart."

Naomi looked silently at Mariam sitting beside her, and after several quiet moments, asked, "This is very forward of me, but you know I am not one to withhold my opinion. I want to ask you..." Naomi paused.

"Ask me what?"

"I am afraid to ask."

"Naomi, you are a woman who knows no fear! You can ask me anything."

"You have been such a blessing to Ezra and me, I wonder..."

"Naomi, please, what is it you wish to ask?"

Naomi looked into Mariam's questioning eyes and said, "Would you marry Ezra if he asked. Would you become my daughter-in-law? Become a true family?"

Naomi sighed, "Ezra has not asked me, he has given no indication..."

"Ezra will do nothing that may cause you to leave us. He treasures you as I do. He fears that if you will not have him, you will leave us."

Mariam closed her eyes and wiped away a small tear. "Ezra is a good man. He is loving and honest with a heart for the Lord. What woman would not be honored to marry him? But..."

Mariam looked into Naomi's eyes, "But I cannot marry him. I would gladly marry him if I could. Nothing would make me happier. But it is not possible. Can't we stay as we are?"

Naomi replied, "You will always have a place in our

house. We will never ask you to leave." Naomi looked down and spoke directly, "I should never have asked you. I'm sorry."

"No! I am honored, truly. With all of my heart. I have never felt so loved and wanted! Look at me, Naomi. Please. It is time I tell you. I will tell you everything."

Mariam began her story, "As I have said, I am the daughter of a Levite. My father is a wealthy man, and he arranged my marriage to another wealthy Levite with whom he does much business. This man is very old and insists on only the best. He will have nothing but the best, and it must be new and untouched by anyone else. I was fifteen when my father arranged the wedding. The bridegroom had only one condition that I proved to be a virgin. My father agreed to permit a midwife to examine me. She announced that I was no virgin. Furious, my father insisted on a second examination by a different midwife. She, too, announced I was not a virgin."

Marian paused, and Naomi allowed her to regain composure. Looking up again, she continued, "My father looked at me and said, 'I will have no harlot under my roof. I will never look at you again,' and he turned his back on me. I stood up, walked out of the door, and have had no dealings with my family since."

Naomi hugged Mariam, "Who could be so cruel? Your mother allowed this"

Mariam replied, "My mother died while I was very young. I have no memory of her."

"Raised only by your father, and him so cruel."

"I hardly know my father. He was away much and never found time to speak with me. Only my uncle. He would sit with me. He made me feel special, but he said nothing when I was accused."

"My dear child. And you have been on your own since then?"

Mariam replied, "That was over two years ago. I felt so guilty and unworthy. That is why I sought out the prophet John. That is why I made the Nazarite vow."

"Know this, my daughter, you are loved here. Never will you be unwelcome here."

Mariam wept, "Ezra is a priest. Under the Law, he must marry only a virgin Levite."

Facing Naomi once more, "Mother, I do not understand...I never...Please believe me. I never slept with a man. Surely, I would remember...How did this happen to me?"

Mariam hugged Naomi, holding her tight as she spoke, "You dear girl, Dear girl. You are safe now. You are loved. Somehow God will bring you justice just as he brings grace and comfort."

Naomi winced in pain. "My arm. That's strange. I can't feel my hand. I can't move my arm."

Chapter Eight

The day of fulfillment of Mariam's Nazarite vow, Ezra arranged with his fellow priests to accept her sacrifices and offerings at the court of the Nazarites. When the sacrifices and offerings were made, her long and uncombed hair was cut and thrown into the fire of the ram cookpot. Naomi had come to the temple with her and warmly hugged her afterward. Even Ezra stepped outside his role and hugged both women. He hugged Naomi as a son hugs the mother he loves and worries as she grows frail. Mariam, he hugged knowing in his heart that he never wanted to let her go.

Mariam lifted a scarf over her head, smiled brightly and said, "We now go to take the Lord's Supper, both the cup and the bread."

"Ezra nodded and said, "You had no trouble with the

steps, mother?"

"Ezra, I am fine. And Mariam does not let me out of her sight. Enough of your worrying!"

Turning to Mariam, he said, "Now remember... "

"I shall watch her carefully. She had no trouble today. Don't you have duties? Good-bye Ezra."

Ezra called out, "I shall bring the ram shoulder for our dinner tonight."

He could not help himself and gave one last plea to Naomi, "Try to get some rest. Don't stay too long with the widows. We shall remember you in prayer!"

Ezra was finishing his duties at the court of the Nazarites when he heard that Peter and a group of six men had come to the temple with the other apostles seeking James. Word passed quickly, and soon, James was surrounded by curious priests and Levites.

Finishing his prayers, James looked at the crowd of believers around him and said, "Our brothers are anxious for the news as well. Is there any reason they should not hear it with me?"

"As you wish brother, this is Good News for all."

Then motioning for all to come near Peter began, "Brothers, the Word of God has been received by Gentiles! I have come from Caesarea, where the Centurion Cornelius, a righteous and God-fearing man, with all his household, has believed the Good News and with many signs and wonders received the Holy Spirit! Seeing that it was divinely directed, I baptized them in the name of the Father, Son, and Holy Spirit."

A voice called out, "Brother, you went into the house of a Gentile? You went to uncircumcised men and ate with them?"

Peter nodded yes, "I was in the city of Joppa praying, and in a trance, I saw a vision of a great sheet coming down, lowered by the four corners from the sky. It came right down to me, and when I looked at it, I saw four-footed animals of the earth, wild beasts, crawling animals, and birds of the air. I heard a voice saying, 'Peter, kill and eat.'

"But I said, 'By no means, Lord, for nothing unholy or unclean has ever entered my mouth.' The voice came a second time, 'What God has cleansed, no longer consider unholy.' This happened three times, and everything was drawn back up into the sky. Now at that moment, three men came to the house. They said they were sent from Caesarea to bring me back with them. The Spirit told me to go with them, and these six men here with me are witnesses. They were told to go with me."

Peter pointed to the witnesses who all nodded agreement. The priests and Levites stood listening carefully.

"In Caesarea, Cornelius told us he had seen an angel standing in his house, saying, 'Send to Joppa, and have Simon who is also called Peter, brought here; and shall speak words to you, by which you will be saved, you and your household.' And as I began to speak the Holy Spirit fell upon them, just as he did upon us in the beginning. And I remembered the word of the Lord, how he used to say, 'John baptized with water, but you shall be baptized with the Holy Spirit.'"

Peter moved his eyes across the crowd and said, "If God gave them the same gift as he gave us also after believing in the Lord Jesus Christ, who was I that I could stand in God's way?"

Peter stood with his hands and arms open before them and waited. All were silent. Turning to James, who had listened prayerfully, James nodded and said, "Well then, God has granted to the Gentiles also the repentance that leads to life."

Ezra turned to Baruch, "Are these Gentile believers under the Law? They did not..."

Baruch interrupted, "It is written, 'I will make you a light unto the Gentiles, that my salvation may reach to the ends of the earth."

Ezra replied, "But the Law?"

"Are you not the one who reminds us we must study the Law as Jesus taught it?"

Ezra tried again, "Under the Law, the Gentiles should have been circumcised first, then baptized."

"You say then, that salvation is just for the Jews. Does God wish to make all men Jewish? Like Caiaphas and the man Saul of Tarsus once was, or does he seek to make all men his?" Did our Lord heal only Jews? Did he not recognize the faith of Gentiles who believed? What were his words to both Jew and Gentile? 'Your faith has saved you. Your sins are forgiven.' The law does not forgive sins; it identifies them. Only God can forgive sin, and he does not need the Law to do so."

Ezra continued to observe the Law, the festivals and all the temple observances as he always had. He was not alone. James, the brother of Jesus, the apostles, the believing priests and Levites and the Jewish Jesus followers from Judea, Galilee and the Greek and Roman cities continued in every way to be righteous Jews, who followed Jesus.

The occasional Gentile in Jerusalem upon whom the

Spirit of God descended and was baptized in the name of Jesus was instructed to become circumcised as a sure witness that the God of Abraham, Isaac, and Jacob was their God. Gentile believers were encouraged to join in worship and the Lord's Supper and the teaching which was held in synagogues around Jerusalem and in the temple Court of the Gentiles.

Naomi's health worried Ezra. He continued to copy the Torah, and with Mariam's Nazarite vow completed, his zeal to question if Jesus' teachings on the Law was indeed like pouring new wine into old wineskins waned. Jesus was a Jewish Messiah who came in fulfillment of the Law and Prophets. His message was to all people, but his father was the God of Abraham, Isaac, and Jacob, and the Jews were his chosen people.

He did not need to know more. He was secure in his faith.

As Naomi's episodes of pain, weakness, dizziness, or blurred vision came more frequently, she became the focus of both Mariam and Ezra. The bond between women became stronger. Mariam never left Naomi's side.

"Mariam, I have rested well this last night. I am anxious to serve today the widows and orphans. The Lord has given me this day. A good day! Come and share my joy in serving!"

"It is a good day! And I rejoice in seeing you strong and fit this morning. But first, let me see you dress and have breakfast. If your strength continues, perhaps we can visit the widows."

After considering her words, she continued, "Ezra is at the temple today, perhaps we should send word to him.

You know his instructions; we are not to venture out without him."

Naomi shook her head, "He is a good son. I love him. But he worries too much, as you do too, my dear. You know I have good days and bad days. This is a good day. Let me make the most of it. You will be with me."

Mariam sighed, "I know there will be no reasoning with you. We will go. But you must agree to stop and rest when I say. Do you agree, Naomi? No fussing. If you love me as you say, you will not make me any more anxious for your well-being."

Naomi replied, "Of course! I will be a good girl. Just for you."

As they walked the crowded streets of Jerusalem, Naomi clutched tightly the arm that Mariam provided her for support. "Mariam, I rejoice in the day that the Lord brought you to us. What a blessing to be given a loving daughter late in my life! I have watched you grow in grace and love. You have made my life brighter, even in the darkest day."

Mariam blushed, "Naomi, your words are far too generous. It is the Lord who has blessed us all. And have you forgotten Ezra? Could any son be more loving and attentive?"

"Ezra is a faithful, loving son. And I never doubt his love and care. But I worry about you, dear. What will become of you? Are you not deserving of joy and security? Should you not have a loving son to care for you when you become old? God forbid you become weak as I, but a husband who will give you a son for your old age is a blessing of the Lord."

Mariam reached with her other hand and gently

squeezed Naomi's arm. "Naomi, we talked before... I... I am thankful for your love for me. I have faith, Naomi. Faith that God will provide for me. Here, we arrive. Remember, you are to rest when I say."

An hour into their service, Mary, the mother of Jesus, arrived, accompanied by the Apostle John. Naomi was serving tables with Mariam. Mariam would carry the tray and Naomi distribute the food and drink with a cheerful word, a squeeze of a shoulder or a kiss upon the head of each widow she served.

When Naomi finally sat for a few moments upon the insistence of Mariam, Mary approached her and said, "Sister Naomi, it is a joy to see you again! I rejoice in the love you show our sisters in need! Tell me, has your strength been fully restored?"

Mary looked to Mariam and saw the concern in her eyes.

Naomi cheerfully said, "It is true there are difficult days, but I rejoice in good days like today. My heart yearns to serve. God has called me to love Him and to love others."

Mary motioned towards the widows being served, "Has not our Lord called all of these to serve as well? Do you think they do not serve? You hear their words. You know they pray powerfully. They love and encourage our brothers and sisters. Sister, I will not take from you the joy of serving. I ask only that your heart be open to being served and one day serving as they do."

Naomi considered Mary's words. "It is true I am a stubborn woman. One who is accustomed to having her way even from those she loves."

Naomi smiled at Mariam. She sighed, and her face

grew sober, "I have peace from the Lord growing old. I have peace that my body sometimes fails me. But I cannot help but worry for those I love. Should I not worry? Does my faith fail me? I look to you, mother of our Savior. You are so full of grace. Did you worry? I am sure you worried. No woman has suffered more than you. Where does the strength come from?"

Naomi's eyes became moist with tears.

Mary answered, "Sister, we must learn to separate worry from faith. We cannot love others without being concerned for them. Never give up your concern but prepare for the darkness that will surely come."

Mary pointed to the Apostle John in earnest conversation with the deaconess. "When John led me away from the cross at Golgotha, our hearts were broken. We believed the pain unbearable. My son chose John, the youngest of the twelve, to care for me. John was beloved by Jesus for his open and loving heart. I am sure of it. He knew our hearts were broken. He knew we needed to be loved in return, and so we were matched, mother and son. Now I know John has faith. I know he loves our Lord. But do you know what John spoke of that night and all the time Jesus was in that tomb?"

Mary caught John's eye and waved for him to join her.

John smiled and came to her side. "John, this is sister Naomi and sister Mariam. They often serve here. I was telling them to prepare for the darkness that will come. Please tell them your words on the sabbath day as our Lord lay in the tomb."

John nodded. Closed his eyes and spoke softly, "The psalm. I could not stop reciting the psalm of tribulation. You have heard it:

O LORD, God of my salvation,
I cry out day and night before you.
Let my prayer come before you;
incline your ear to my cry!
For my soul is full of troubles,
and my life draws near to Sheol.
I am counted among those
who go down to the pit;
I am a man who has no strength,
like one set loose among the dead,
Like the slain that lie in the grave,
like those who you remember no more,
For they are cut off from your hand.
You have put me in the depths of the pit,
in the regions dark and deep.
Your wrath lies heavy upon me,
and you overwhelm me with all your waves.
You have caused my companions to shun me;
you have made me a horror to them.
I am shut in so that I cannot escape;
my eye grows dim through sorrow.
Every day I call upon you O LORD;
I spread out my hands to you.
Do you work wonders for the dead?
Do the departed rise up to praise you?
Is your steadfast love declared to the grave?
Or your faithfulness to Abaddon?
Are your wonders known in the darkness?
Or your righteousness
in the land of forgetfulness?
But I O LORD, cry to you;
in the morning my prayer comes before you.

O LORD, why do you cast my soul away?
Why do you hide your face from me?
Afflicted and close to death from my youth up,
I suffer your terrors;
I am helpless; your wrath has swept over me;
your dreadful assaults destroy me.
They surround me like a flood all day long;
they close in on me together.
You have caused my beloved
and my friend to shun me;
My companions have become darkness."

Mary nodded, "John repeated that psalm over and over. It is all lament. It is a cry to God from one in the darkness. There is not a glimmer of light. I am sure John was not alone. Ask Peter, or Philip, Andrew, James or Thomas. They would agree. They lived through the darkness before Jesus arose."

John nodded and said, "Mary's faith saw past the darkness. She believed. She remembered what Jesus said and believed he would rise again. So, I stand beside her and love her, for she is our Savior's first disciple. And she shows us how to see beyond the darkness. Jesus leads us in the resurrection. He has overcome death for us and brings us out of the darkness and into the light."

Naomi studied Mary's serenity as John spoke and said, "Yes, faith can look beyond the darkness."

Mariam asked John, "The one who betrayed him. Judas. Do you think of him? Was he lost to the darkness?"

John bowed his head and closed his eyes. Nodding, he said, "Yes, I think of him. He was a brother, one of us. He saw what we saw. He broke bread with us. He heard the words, witnessed the miracles. He wanted the kingdom of God to come. But he thought he knew the way things should be done. He chose his own will over the Father's will. Jesus loved Judas. Was he lost to the darkness? Oh yes. The darkness of Jesus laid in the tomb was greater than his faith."

John looked up and smiled at Mariam, "Jesus prayed, 'Father, not my will, but your will be done.' It is a good prayer for all of us."

Ezra returned that evening to find Naomi already in bed. Mariam was by her side. As he entered, Naomi said to Mariam, "Dear daughter, would you bring me a small cup of wine."

When she had gone, Naomi said to Ezra, "The attacks are coming more frequently, and they are stronger than ever. I am not afraid. I look forward to our heavenly home. Promise me, son, promise me you will care for Mariam as you have cared for me."

"Mother, I love Mariam as you do. I pray she will have me."

When Naomi fell asleep, Ezra said to Mariam, "Has not the LORD brought us together? You have come into our lives and brought joy and comfort. Marry me, Mariam. Marry me because we have been brought together. It is not because of my mother's desires that we marry, but because we love God, and we love each other. Is it not better that we wed before my mother passes? Let her eyes see what we both desire and what we know in our hearts to be God's will."

Mariam bowed her head. "Because I love you, and I will not cause you to violate your vows, I cannot marry you."

"Naomi told me of your past. But did not you insist on denying having any man? I do not require a midwife's examination. I know you are a righteous woman. Your word is enough."

Mariam looked into Ezra's eyes and said, "What if it is true? What if the memory was just too painful? You hold to the Law. You teach that it is perfect and will endure for all time. No, Ezra, I will not have your guilt upon my head. You are a good and righteous priest. I will stay with Naomi until her final breath. Only God knows what lies beyond."

Chapter Nine

Baruch's absence from the wine court in the temple alarmed Ezra. When Ezra was told that Baruch had become ill weeks ago, he was overcome with guilt. How long had it been since they debated? How long since Ezra had closed his mind to Baruch's teaching on the Law? The priest in charge of the wine and oil said, "He's gone. He's not coming back. Is there something you need? I have work to do."

Ezra saw a priest whom he knew to be a brother standing nearby and said, "Baruch?"

The priest annoyed, shook his head, "Everyone knows. Where have you been? I thought you were his friend?" And he turned and walked away.

The street to Baruch's house was even more quiet

than usual. All he heard was the echoing of his sandals upon the cobblestones. As he listened, his mind began to put words to the sound, words of condemnation, '*You wanted it easy. Easy for you. Be the good priest. Salvation came to your house. Easy for you. A good life being a priest, Good food, and wine. Only the best bulls and sheep are sacrificed and given to your table. Yes, easy for you. No need for you to walk away from your family. No new commitments for you to be circumcised. You dine on the consecrated bread, not the crumbs that fall from the table and are left for the Gentile who believes. Easy for you. Oh, you did it for your mother! Yes, you had to keep her comfortable. So comfortable that you kept her from the service she loved. Easy for you! You went along to get along. Let Baruch and Paul endure the slings and arrows. Let them find the new wineskins to be filled for those bought by the blood of Jesus. Easy for you, don't let the new wine in your old wineskin. Yes, easy for you!*' Somewhere a door slammed and the voice in Ezra's mind screamed *guilty!*

Ezra knocked lightly on Baruch's door. A priest he recognized from the temple let him in. He was led to an inner room where his old friend was propped up in his bed. Two other priests and a man in rich Egyptian clothes were seated on either side. As Ezra entered, Baruch smiled and called out, "Ezra! Good of you to come, my young friend! I was just telling my new friend, your name? Oh yes, I recall, Apollos. I was explaining to Apollos that Jesus' teaching on the Law is like pouring new wine into old wineskins. It will cause the skins to burst, and the wine will be spilled. No, as our Lord says, we must pour new wine into new wineskins. We must look afresh on the Law and Covenant just as we searched the Prophets to see what they say about Jesus."

Ezra smiled and was relieved to see his old friend in such high spirits. "Please, my friend, do not stop on my account! I am certain that Apollos from?"

"I am from Alexandria, a priest at the temple invited me to hear the teacher, Baruch."

Baruch smiled, "So this is what I must do to get your attention once more Ezra? No matter, I am glad you have come at last."

"Baruch, I…"

"I know, my friend, I know. Now, as I was saying, when Jesus said he came to fulfill the Law, is it not true that his fulfillment was in the atonement for sin, which the Law identified? Do not his words, 'It is finished,' cry out that God's plan of salvation is complete. The purpose of the Law was to show our need for salvation, to show that we are sinners separated from God; that sin required atonement, the shed blood of the innocent for the guilty. Atonement was made, one time and forever. Just as Isaac was bound to the tree, and he before the Law of Moses, intended as a sacrifice to the God of Abraham, our Lord was hung on the tree, and it is written, 'Cursed is anyone who hangs from a tree,' so Jesus accomplished what was shown before the Law, the way of salvation. The work of the Law is complete. We know we are sinners. We know he atoned for our sin. We have forgiveness and new life. But even more, we have the testimony of the Spirit of God who descended upon us and now assures of new life in his anointed one! The curtain to the Holy of Holies is torn! God is no longer separated from his people. He dwells in our very hearts! As Peter preached and as the prophet Joel wrote, 'He shall write his law on the tablets of our hearts.'"

Apollos asked, "What law does he write on our hearts?"

Baruch smiled, "The Law from the beginning. Given to Adam and given to father Abraham, the law that says, 'I am your God, and you are my people.' This is the law that has been fulfilled and lives on. It is the law for all who believe, the Jew and the Gentile."

Baruch reached for Ezra's arm. Grasping him tight, he said, "Scribe and I say a teacher of the Law; you, a priest of the One True God, look to the laws of the priest. Look to the temple worship. Look to the festivals and sacrifices. Look to the Law of Moses and know that in every way it points to Jesus. I pass this calling to you."

Baruch held tight to Ezra's arm. He laid back on his pillow with his eyes open wide towards the ceiling above, and he began to sing. Ezra struggled to identify the psalm. He did not recognize it. It was a new psalm, the song of Baruch:

> O my soul, rejoice!
> My eyes have seen my salvation!
> The salvation of Israel.
> The salvation of all nations!
> Redemption has come to all people!
> The road has been made straight to our God.
> A pathway for all nations.
> The hen has gathered her chicks
> beneath her wing.
> They are gathered as sheep in a fold,
> safe from all alarm.
> They will sit under the shade of his love
> and be refreshed from his well.
> New hearts inscribed with the Law of the LORD

to instruct our way.
New hearts to worship our God.
My heart sings, 'It is fulfilled.'
Your promises are true.
Your love has cured us. Your will is before us.
The redeemed of the LORD come before him
in thanksgiving, singing praises!

When Baruch finished his song, he fell back into his bed and died.

Everyone in the room was silent. No one had words. Slowly the priests got up and left. The Jew in Egyptian dress rose and walked over to Ezra. "I am Apollos of Alexandria. I have many questions."

Naomi's visits to the widows became less frequent and were less about serving tables than fellowship, encouragement, and prayer. Even so, she was warmly welcomed and loved by the dependent widows. Despite hobbling with small unsure steps, and hanging tightly to Mariam's arms, she always wore a genuine smile. Her face shined, and her eyes sparkled as she made her way to each table. She knew everyone's name and had heard all their stories but was patient to listen to them again and again. New residents were quickly introduced to her and loved into the fellowship. Mariam was always by her side, smiling just as brightly. She would see that Naomi was seated and rested a while, and she would ensure that all had been served. Mariam knew the signs of Naomi's weakness and would lovingly assert that it was time to go home promising that they would come back as soon as Naomi was able. Naomi insisted on praying with each sister before they left.

Ezra continued to perform his priestly duties and diligently copied the Torah praising God for each sign of Jesus as he went through the Scriptures. He spent time every day with believing priests discussing the Law as Jesus taught it. But he was torn by the two most compelling duties, his duty to care for Naomi and his calling to continue Baruch's work interpreting the Law as Jesus taught. He was pleased that Mariam was committed to Naomi, but that did not relieve him of his duty. And he felt guilty that Naomi's needs were keeping the woman he loved in his life. In dark moments he would ask himself, *'Is it Naomi's loss that I fear or is it that Mariam would then be free to leave me?'*

The Roman Procurator Pilate was recalled to Rome, and he was replaced by another Roman, Marcellus, who named Caiaphas' brother-in-law Jonathan, High Priest on the recommendation of Annas, Caiaphas' father-in-law. Annas was the real power in the temple, a friend of Rome, and always a confidant of the Roman ruler. When Jonathan lost the support of the people in Jerusalem, on the advice of Annas, Marcellus named his younger brother Theophilus High Priest. Theophilus obeyed his Roman procurator and maintained order in the temple.

Annas and most of the Sanhedrin rejoiced when Caligula crowned the Emperor's close friend Herod Agrippa, King of Judea. Agrippa was now king over all of historic Israel like his grandfather Herod the Great before him. King Agrippa was raised in Judea and Rome, and though he was Greek by birth and Roman to the core, he was drawn to the God of the Jews and temple worship. He chose as his High Priest, the fiery Jonathan, the son of Annas, as High Priest.

After the first day of the Festival of Tabernacles, Ezra stood silently among the priests gathered in the Temple Court of the Gentiles. When the Levites blew their trumpets, and the musicians sang their psalms of praise, King Agrippa walked from the Royal Porch into the Temple Court of the Gentiles with his wife, Cyprus and his court. King Agrippa was radiant, his cloak of spun silver shining and glittering as he moved. All his years in Rome had prepared him for this show of majesty. The trumpets and singers fell silent as Herod Agrippa took his place next to the High Priest. The sparkling multicolored gems of the High Priest's ephod danced in the sun as they magically reflected off Agrippa's silver tunic. A priest came forward carrying the Sefer Scroll of the Law. He stopped in front of the High Priest, removed the gilded embroidered mantle and gave it to the High Priest. High Priest Jonathan unrolled the scroll open to Deuteronomy and read, "And Moses commanded them, 'At the end of seven years, at the set time of the year of release, at the feast of the tabernacles, when all Israel comes before the LORD your God at the place he will choose, you shall read this law before all Israel before their hearing. Assemble the people, men, women, and little ones, that they may hear and learn to fear the LORD your God and be careful to do all the words of this law.'"

Looking up at the people gathered in worship and turning to the King, Jonathan proclaimed, "King Agrippa. It is an ancient custom of our nation, that on the second day of the Feast of Tabernacles that the King of Israel read the Law to the people. This is a holy reminder that the God of our fathers, the God of Abraham, Isaac, and Jacob is our God, and we are his people. It has been many years since we have had a king to remind his people to hear the word of God. King Herod Agrippa read to us our God's commands and law."

The high priest presented the Torah scroll to Agrippa. The King accepted the scroll, his golden laurel crown now glowing as he bowed slightly to read. "These are the words that Moses spoke to all Israel beyond the Jordan, in the wilderness, in the Arabah opposite Suph..."

Agrippa's voice carried across the temple courts. He read gracefully and reverently. His fluent Hebrew and apparent conviction captured the hearts of many who listened. He read on, all of Deuteronomy pausing only once when he read, "You may indeed set a king over you whom the LORD your God shall choose. One from among your brothers, you shall set as king over you." But when he came to the words, "You may not put a foreigner over you, who is not your brother," Agrippa paused and began to weep.

Annas shouted first. "Don't fear Agrippa. You are a brother. You are our brother!"

Immediately Jonathan the High Priest led the people in a chant, "You are our brother, you are our brother!"

King Agrippa looked up, wiped the tears from his eyes and smiling, lifted his arms in a request for silence, and he continued to read the law through the conclusion of Deuteronomy. When he finished, he rolled the scroll tight and returned it to the High Priest who shouted, "Hear O Israel, the LORD our God, the LORD is One!" King Herod Agrippa retreated through the Royal gate followed by Cyprus and the court.

As Jonathan was departing, he stopped in front of Ezra. Resplendent in his robes and ephod and triumphant over the celebration he coldly stared into Ezra's face and said, "This new religion you preach, it must stop. You will come to me tomorrow."

The next morning the High Priest resumed his lecture, "The temple is the one place in Israel, no in the world, where all Jews are one. Yet you preach a new law of a dead and false messiah. I will not permit any preaching which disturbs the peace and divides Israel."

Ezra replied, "Is it the Sadducees like you or the Pharisees that find division taught in the temple courtyards? Is it those who argue for the resurrection or those who deny it? Is it the Zealots who look for a warrior messiah to free us from our Roman overlords or the Hellenists like you who remind us that Rome brings us peace and prosperity? I wish to know which of our brothers can no longer tolerate debate between God-fearing Jews faithful to the Law."

Jonathan was surprised and angered by the insubordinate priest before him, "You are not faithful to the Law!"

Ezra calmly replied, "I have served the temple as a priest for nearly eighteen years. Bring before me any priest who will say I do not serve faithfully in all that the Law requires, just as my father before me and my father's fathers before him."

"It is your teaching that must stop. I have heard you debating the scribes in the portico of Solomon. You speak of a new covenant in the blood of Jesus. You speak of drinking his blood. The Law of Moses is clear; we shall drink no blood of any animal!"

"I spoke of the words of Jesus who took the cup of wine during the Passover feast, the Passover cup when he proclaimed that the wine was his blood shed for our sin. We drink it in remembrance of him. We drink it in accordance with the Law which only Jesus always obeyed and in so doing, he fulfilled."

Jonathan, annoyed, replied, "So you teach a new covenant, a new law!"

Ezra stared back at the High Priest, "Bring before the Sanhedrin anyone who can name a Law that Jesus of Nazareth did not obey! But I see I am not before the Sanhedrin. I only stand before King Agrippa's High Priest who abuses his authority with accusations against a righteous priest. I will not answer to a Roman's priest who would stop lawful teaching and debate in the temple of the God of Abraham, Isaac, and Jacob!"

Jonathan screamed, "Guards! Take him to the jail and let him sit until he learns to respect the High Priest of Israel!"

Ezra was soon joined in prison by other priests and Levites who attended teaching by the Jesus followers. Such a thing had never been done in Israel! The council prison was filled with priests and Levites! These priests and Levites were without charge in fulfilling their duties in the temple worship. The people judged their crime as a failure to satisfy a despised, Roman puppet from a Sadducee family that had grown wealthy and powerful collaborating with the Romans.

When the demands for their freedom by families and friends were ignored, the people took their case to the Sanhedrin. Soon afterward, the followers of Jesus were released, but Ezra knew that Jonathan and his father Annas would look for new opportunities to purge the temple of the Jesus followers.

Soon the Pharisees came to the High Priest with new complaints against 'The Way.' Careful not to repeat his mistakes. He would not underestimate the devotion and lack of fear by these Jesus followers. Jonathan decided to receive them as his father, Annas, would. "You must realize that the people and many Sadducees do not share the concerns you Pharisees have with the Jesus followers in the temple. So long as these Jesus followers follow the temple rules and observe the Law, they will be permitted to teach and meet just as the teachers of the Law and all observant Jews are."

Jonathan paused. He held up his hands, motioning for them to wait as he gathered his thoughts. Jonathan had no use for the self-righteous Pharisees always telling others they did not follow the Law as they so clearly understood it themselves. And their argument of heaven! No, he thought, the Pharisees were alarmed that the people are drawn to this new teaching, this Jesus and his teaching of a law of Love and compassion rather than judgment and punishment.

Once silence was restored, Jonathan took a breath, smiled, and said, "But if the Pharisees could convince the people, well then..."

Ezra and his brother priests were preaching Jesus openly on the porch of Solomon when a wealthy Sadducee, a Levite, waited at the fringe of the crowd. Ezra noticed the man in the costly embroidered robe. He stood silently, without emotion, listening. Ezra thought, '*A spy from the High Priest? Certainly not a Pharisee. Joseph and Nicodemus wore the robes of the wealthy, yet they proved faithful. Who is he? Why is he here?*"

As Ezra finished his teaching for the day and sent off his listeners with the benediction of Leviticus, the stranger walked forward and said, "My name is Nathan. Nathan ben Joseph. I am told you can lead me to my daughter, Miriam."

Chapter Ten

Friend, it is an hour before sunset, I have little time to make my way home for Sabbath. You say you seek a girl named Mariam. There must be hundreds of young girls by that name in Jerusalem. I am a priest and a scribe. Why do you come to me?"

"My daughter Mariam is not a young girl. She is a woman. She serves in your house as a nurse to your mother, Naomi. It is important you take me to her."

Ezra was stunned. He could not hide, nor could he find the words to reply.

"I know about you, Ezra ben Haggai. I know you follow in place of the priest Baruch as a teacher of the Messianic Jews who follow Jesus. I know my daughter lives with you and serves in the Jesus followers' house of widows. I must speak to my daughter; she is in danger, as are you, Ezra."

Ezra replied, "If the Mariam in my house is your daughter, why have you not gone to her yourself?"

Now Nathan was struck defensive, even though he expected the question. "She would not see me if I came alone." He paused and continued softly, "I have hurt her sorely. I treated her most badly and unjustly. I closed my door to her and left her to wander and beg. No. She would surely close her door to me."

Ezra's voice became compassionate, "You seek her forgiveness?"

"Forgiveness is too much to ask for. I desire to confess my sin against her. But it is most urgent I warn her of the danger that is to come."

"She has told us her story. She denied the accusation made against her. She is a most remarkable woman. Strong. Compassionate. She is yet determined not to allow her past and what has been said about her to fall upon others. I will take your request to her. I will allow her to decide."

Nathan sighed in relief, "It is a good thing. But you must tell her also, that she is in danger. You and Naomi and many others are in danger. I will speak only to her."

"If you love her, you would do well not to force her to put others above herself. Do not withhold. Give first and permit her to accept, and thank you."

Nathan shook his head. "No, I cannot risk her rejection. Though she hates me, I must see her and confess to her. Now go and tell her. I will come again to hear her response."

Ezra, Naomi, and Mariam observed the Sabbath according to the Law. They did no work and spent the day in prayer, meditation, and sharing. They restored relationships, first with God and then each other. Ezra taught how the Sabbath was fulfilled in Jesus. From the very beginning, from creation, God, the Creator rested on the seventh day when all his creation was completed. God made man in his image, the image of a creator and worker. God gave the Sabbath to man as a gift. Jesus reminded us that the Sabbath was created for man. So, Ezra praised God for his gift of rest. And he praised God that when Jesus fulfilled the Law, the Law of the Sabbath found fulfillment in the eternal rest that we have in our Lord and Savior.

After the Sabbath evening meal, Ezra mentioned, "Mariam, I must tell you something we have never discussed. Perhaps it is good that you have time for prayer before you make your decision."

Naomi looked at Ezra, "You make this sound serious, husband!"

Mariam's face also showed her concern, "Tell me, Ezra, for I can think of nothing we have not discussed. What is it that requires such prayerful deliberation?"

Ezra took a deep breath, "A man came to see me today after the lessons, just as I was preparing to come home. His name was Nathan ben Joseph. He claimed to be your father and asked me to bring him to you."

Mariam's eyes widened, and her voice rang with urgency, "What did you tell him?"

"I questioned him carefully. He knows you are here. He knows how you care for Naomi and serve the widows. He believes you will not see him unless I convince you. He seeks to confess his sin against you, the injustice and cruelty of his actions."

"Now he comes to me? Now that he is old and seeks to

go to his fathers with a clear conscience? He is right. I have long ago decided never to speak to him again!"

Naomi took Mariam's hand, "Daughter, that is only pain I hear from your lips. I know your heart is one of love and forgiveness. As Ezra says, you have the Sabbath to seek the Lords leading."

Ezra took another deep breath and said, "There is more. He tells me you are in danger. He claims Naomi and I are also in danger. He will tell only you. I insisted if he loved you, he would say what this danger was. I tried to reason with him not to risk harm by withholding what he knew. But he insisted. To him, his confession to your face was more important."

Mariam sat quietly, stunned by the thought of facing her father after more than half her lifetime. She was no longer a vulnerable teenager but a strong and committed follower of Jesus. Slowly she spoke, "Ezra, you met him... I have learned to trust your word... After all these years, he seeks me out? He knows where I am, what I do... I should not fear him... I never considered... Ezra, help me. What should I do?"

Ezra answered, "You must seek the Lord's will. Pray and listen. Consider the love of our Lord and Savior. His grace will carry you. He will lead you in what you do and what you say."

Naomi said, "Let the love in your heart lead you, my dear."

Ezra sighed, "In the morning I return to the temple for the Sabbath sacrifices, and you see to the invalid widows. You have the day for prayer and contemplation. I will not see Nathan ben Joseph before the first day."

Mariam nodded, "Yes, I will pray and seek the Lord. Naomi, please permit me to retire. I am tired, and my head spins. I wish to go to bed."

Mariam was home when Ezra returned from the temple after the sun had set and the end of the Sabbath. The confidence and joy, so natural to her personality, had returned. "Welcome, Ezra, the meal is prepared, wash, and then sit."

"Thank you, Mariam. And you look well today, mother. A good day! Resting in the Lord truly brings blessings upon our house!"

As Mariam went to bring the food to the table, Ezra asked, "Did your prayers bring answers? I see the joyful and confidant Mariam with us tonight."

Mariam did not turn around, "First wash. We eat soon. Then we can talk. All in good order!"

Naomi scolded Ezra, "Must you always be impatient! You know better than to be childish! Now, do as she says!"

Ezra washed and took his seat at the table. He kissed Naomi, picked her up, and carried her to the table, "She hasn't told you either, has she?"

"Hush! She will hear you. Now, help me sit up straight."

When all was prepared, Mariam sat down, and Ezra blessed the food. Both Naomi and Ezra ate silently, waiting for Mariam to speak. Looking at her adopted family, Mariam smiled and finally spoke. "How can I who have been forgiven all by our Lord Jesus withhold the confession of one stricken by guilt?"

"What shall I tell him then?"

"Tell him I will listen to him here. That is if you agree. I want him to see that God has blessed me. That I am loved. That I have a family where I am loved and cared for."

Ezra looked at Naomi, "If that is what you desire... We are honored to call you family. When—"

"When he seeks you, send word to Naomi. I will see him as soon as he desires."

The next day, a nervous Nathan ben Joseph followed Ezra home. "Does she ever speak of me? No, of course, she wouldn't. Is she healthy? Happy? I pray that she has found happiness and... "

"Mariam knows she is blessed. Yes, she is happy. She finds the most joy in serving others, just as our Lord Jesus taught us."

"I have heard that she follows this Jesus. He has been dead all these many years yet still they follow. Still, they follow. And Mariam finds joy following this Jesus?"

"You shall see. Mariam is a woman accustomed to speaking for herself. Ah, here we are. Come in. I will introduce— I will say that you are here."

"Mariam, Nathan ben Joseph has asked... "

Mariam came to the door and interrupted, "You have something to say to me. I will listen."

Naomi alarmed, said, "Perhaps we should sit and offer refreshment to our guest."

Mariam shook her head. "I will hear what he says now."

Nathan began, "Daughter... "

"My name is Mariam, not daughter. What will you say to me, that is, say to my family? You say Ezra and Naomi are in danger. Tell us."

Nathan wiped away a tear and spoke up, "Mariam, I have sinned against you and treated you unjustly. When I learned what truly happened to you, I was cut to the quick. Poor child. I should never have doubted you. You never took a lover. It was. It was... "

Nathan began to cry. "Your uncle. You may not recall. Your uncle did things, unimaginable things when you were just a little child. He confessed to me just before he died. All those years, I let you feel the shame. I let you bear the guilt and suffer. My little girl. You are all I had left. Your mother died so young, and what did I do? I buried myself in business. I made money. I pursued power, but they brought me no happiness. Even the arranged marriage. He was no match for a daughter I loved."

Mariam could no longer remain hardened and aloof. "I have found love here. Naomi is my mother. Ezra, a dear brother. I love them, and I love the widows I serve, and they love me. It is you, you, Nathan, for I cannot yet call you father, you who still carries the pain of sin."

Naomi paused, momentarily closed her eyes before she asked, "You said Naomi and Ezra are in danger. Tell me. How are they in danger?"

Nathan replied, without pride, "I am a member of the Sanhedrin. The Pharisees have convinced the leading Sadducees that the high priest has not dealt with the Jesus followers who they insist pollute the temple with their heresy. They have convinced Herod Agrippa to act against the Jesus followers in the temple. The High Priest, Jonathan son of Annas, seeks Roman guards to arrest their leaders as they enter or leave the temple. He knows the Roman reputation for brutality. He knows what happens to prisoners in the Fortress of Antonia. Let them strike down the leaders. Their blood shall be on the hands of the Romans! Annas and Jonathan have convinced King Agrippa that this is his service to the temple and will be pleasing to the people. They are determined to crush those they call 'The Way.' I know you are one of them. I drove you to them. I cannot see you suffer anymore."

Surprised, Ezra replied, "We have friends in the Sanhedrin. We have heard no such reports."

Nathan answered, "No doubt you speak of your fellow priest, Simon ben Nathanael, son-in-law to Rabban Gamaliel. We know of him. We know that the Rabban has been convinced by his sons and daughter of the claims of Jesus. He has told us that so many new believers all these years after Jesus death testify that his coming must be of God. Anas had Jonathan wait until Gamaliel could not be present. And the other Jesus followers, Joseph of Arimathea is off on a journey and Nicodemus is home in frail health. He was not called. No, I tell you the truth; the Romans will act soon."

Turning to Mariam, Nathan begged, "Please, Mariam. I do this for you. I can bear no more guilt on my head."

Mariam looked into Nathan's eyes and said, "If God is for us, who can stand against us? You have given your warning—"

"Please, daughter... Mariam, let me stay. Let me hear of all that has happened to you. Indeed, I see your strength and courage. Where did you go? How is it you are strong and confident? Please, tell me your story. Perhaps I... I want to understand. I want to have the peace you have."

Mariam looked to Ezra and Naomi and said, "If my family offers hospitality, who am I to deny it?"

Ezra motioned to Nathan, "Come, friend, enjoy the hospitality of our house."

Nathan's face shown throughout the meal, giving nods of approval as Mariam explained how God had blessed her. He could not help himself from shouting, "Blessed is the God of Abraham, Isaac, and Jacob, who redeems his people Israel! Who preserved my daughter, Mariam! Where I failed her, he saved her!"

Mariam saw the tears forming in Nathan's eyes. These were not tears shed from the release from guilt; they were tears of joy of a father finding his daughter safe. She stared at him and saw him vulnerable and open. "The LORD did more than shield me from harm; he led me here to Jerusalem on the day the Holy Spirit came upon Peter and the disciples of Jesus. His Spirit was poured out, and He called to me. I believed the word and was baptized into a new life in Jesus, the Son of God. He has taken all fear. I may not know what will become of me, but I fully trust in his will. You should come. You should hear the teaching. The joy you find tonight in my company is but a small taste of the joy that awaits you in the Savior."

Nathan's lips tightened, and his eyes narrowed. He said firmly, "I will hear what these men have to say."

The morning lesson had just begun when Ezra heard his name being shouted. Nathan, gasping for breath had run up the temple stairs and out to the porch of Solomon. "Where is Mariam? It has begun. The High Priest has sent his temple guard to the Fortress of Antonia to arrange for the Romans to arrest your leaders of 'The Way.'"

"Mariam is serving at the common house."

"The Temple guards know of this house. They will take the Romans there."

Ezra turned to the priest, Nathaniel, "Go warn the others. I will go to the widows and the common house."

They quickly made their way to the common house in the upper city by the Essene Gate. They rushed in to find the widows calmly being served their morning meal.

Mariam could be heard laughing as she placed a large plate on a table of smiling widows. Ezra came over and asked, "Is all well this morning, Mariam?"

Surprised, she looked up at Ezra and Nathan and replied, "All is well," and turning to the widows, "Is not all well this morning, sisters?"

Nathan flushed red with embarrassment, "I was worried, I..."

Ezra interrupted, "Are the apostles upstairs?"

Mariam replied hesitantly, "I believe some are upstairs; they do not check with me."

Ezra said to Nathan, "Come, I will take you to them."

Mariam asked, "Is all well?"

Ezra smiled, "Mothers and sisters, we are all well in God's grace. Do not worry. Do not let our sister Mariam worry, either."

In the upper room, Ezra politely introduced Nathan to Peter who thanked Nathan for the news and told him that all were here this morning except James who was praying at the temple.

Nathan replied, "It is well you are warned. I return to the temple and will share the news with him. But first, I will speak with the High Priest to learn more fully his intentions."

Nathan led Ezra to the house of the High Priest in the upper city. A servant greeted Nathan cordially and said, "Master Nathan, Jonathan ben Annas is not here. I understand he was called to the city gate below the temple in the Kidron valley."

"Who called him there?"

"A temple guard came for him not an hour ago."

Ezra and Nathan hurried to the bridge to the Royal Porch of the Temple, made their way around to the

Horse Gate and down into the Kidron valley the area set aside for the temple ashes and waste. As they made their way down, they met the high priest and a temple guard speaking as a cohort of Roman guards marched off towards the prison gate on their way to the Antonia Fortress. "What have you done?" Nathan shouted.

"The Jesus follower, the one they call James the apostle, they found him in the temple. We gave him to the Romans as a nuisance to the temple worship. We took him publicly to make a message. He is dead. And soon all the others shall be as he is. This scourge will be cut out and destroyed from Israel."

"James dead?" Ezra cried out. "How?"

Jonathan, the high priest, looked at Ezra and turned to Nathan, "This James was beheaded on by King Agrippa's order."

"Without a trial? You delivered a brother, a son of Israel to the Romans for execution? By your authority?" Nathan shouted. "Only the Council can determine if stoning is justified."

The High Priest smiled, "I have only asked our king to preserve peace in the temple. When the temple is defiled or polluted, our guards will arrest the offenders, but once they are outside of the temple, their disorder will now be dealt with as a civil matter by the authority of the king. I certainly, do not instruct King Agrippa in Roman enforcement of civil law."

"You went to Agrippa to seek brutality against our brothers without consulting the Council? You go too far, Jonathan. You are reckless and go too far! The Council shall hear of this!"

Jonathan smiled, "The Council has no use for these Jesus followers. I just made it easy for all of you. Yes, I went to Agrippa. He has more stomach than the Council. It was he who appointed me High Priest and he who granted me the authority to employ Roman soldiers to ensure the security of the temple. Now out of my way! I go to purify myself from this place."

"Agrippa shall hear too! You put yourself above the Council. You go too far!"

Ezra was overcome with the smell of burnt hide as he walked down to the valley of smoldering ash and sacrifice burnings and saw the blood-soaked body and severed head of the Apostle James, the son of Zebedee, tossed onto the pile. He dragged the body out and set the head beside it. He knelt down and wept.

Nathan tasted the acid rising into his throat from his stomach as he stood behind Ezra and placed an arm on Ezra's shoulder. Ezra remained bowed and softly asked, "Nathan, find the priest Nathaniel son-in-law to Gamaliel. Ask him to gather the brothers still on Solomon's Porch. Send them to help me with the body."

Nathan replied, "I will do as you ask. Then I must call the council. Jonathan must not do the same with Peter and the others."

Chapter Eleven

You must come with me, Mariam. It is not safe here," Nathan pleaded as Mariam continued her rounds serving the widows at the common house."

"Please leave sir. You disturb my friends and sisters. I will not speak of it here."

"Then I shall wait for you outside. You must listen to me. I am your father, and I fear for your life."

Mariam's back stiffened, and her eyes narrowed as she turned to Nathan and with steel in her voice said, "That's quite enough, Nathan ben Joseph. My father is in heaven. He loves me, and his son Jesus teaches me: 'Do not fear those who can kill the body but cannot kill the soul. Rather fear him who can destroy both soul and body in hell.'"

Nathan felt his strength fail him, his shoulders slumped, and all his voice could manage was a gasping cough. He closed his eyes and nodded then said softly, "I know I have failed you as a father. But hear my words for the sake of these you serve if not for yourself. I will wait."

Mariam could feel the tension leaving her body. She looked at the bewildered faces of the widows at the table she served. She smiled at them and said, "Please forgive me, sisters."

Mariam glanced over to Nathan as he went out the door and shook her head softly, confirming her regret for the hardness of her words.

"Go after him Mariam," a white-haired widow said. "I do not know how he has wounded you, but you must not hold on to the pain. Who is beyond the grace of our Savior? Who is beyond his love and his calling? Daughter Mariam, it is your nature to love others."

Mariam bowed her head, "It has been so long. I do not know what to say. I don't... "

"Go, my dear. Listen to his words and then listen to your heart. Go."

Mariam forced a small smile and turned and went out the door. Nathan was walking slowly, his head down, and his eyes peering at the dusty street. She walked up beside him and forced the words, "I will hear what you would say to me."

Nathan immediately straightened up and hope lifted his spirits, "Mariam, I cannot change the past. I know that. I know you find it hard to believe that I could love you after all the years we lost. But is it too hard to believe I can show concern for your safety? I could not bear to see you harmed again. What I said about the danger, is true. It is not my reputation, or my honor, or my wealth that concern me. If you remain in the common house of the Jesus followers, you will be arrested. It is only a matter of time. You know the high priest had James the son of Zebedee put to the sword on King Herod Agrippa's word. I have called for a meeting of the Sanhedrin, but I fear too many others, both Pharisees and Sadducees, are pleased with this attack. You have few friends left on the council. Joseph of Arimathea is on a journey and Nicodemus near death. Gamaliel will call for caution, but they will not listen."

Mariam nodded, "All that you say, I have heard from Ezra and others. We have no fear. We will continue to do the will of our Lord."

"I am not asking you to be anyone different than you are. You have found peace and purpose following Jesus. I can see that. But did I not hear that your Jesus once said, 'to be wise as serpents?' Where is the wisdom in waiting for temple guards to come for widows and orphans?"

"Will you speak for us at the council, father?"

Hearing Mariam call him father, brought tears to Nathan's eyes. He could hardly speak and managed only a soft, "Daughter, you know I will. I will speak because I love you, yes, but also because I begin to see...I see courage, and I see the love in those who follow 'The Way.' But promise you will be careful. You must live and teach me. Tell me how I can find what you have."

"I will consider your words. There is so much I want to tell you. Tonight. Come to the house tonight. I will tell Ezra you are coming and Naomi...Naomi likes you. I trust Naomi. Now I must go back."

"Tonight. I will come directly from the council

meeting!" Nathan walked off in the gait of a man filled with determination.

The council room began to fill. The seventy members of the Sanhedrin along with the high priest, were the nearest thing to nobility in the Jewish nation. They were accustomed to power and jealously guarded their authority. Although the high priest presided over the Sanhedrin, Annas, father of Jonathan, Theophilus and Matthias, and father-in-law of Caiaphas, all having served as high priest, was the real leader of the Sanhedrin. Annas spoke for the Jews with the Roman procurators, governors and now the appointed King Herod Agrippa. He rarely spoke in the council, choosing to let his chosen High Priest speak for him.

The High Priest Jonathan pounded the base of his staff on the cold stone floor several times and then called out, "Nathan ben Joseph, you called for this meeting. We all have better things to do than debate your new-found love of the Jesus followers. We are here, speak and let us return to more useful work."

Nathan walked to the front of the council room, "Elders of Israel, our High Priest sees no benefit to our wisdom. He would have us all keep busy away from our sacred duty to Israel. He would make our decisions for us! Is it not true that only the Sanhedrin can determine a man is deserving to be stoned? And then only after a trial before this very council? When have we become redundant? When have we forfeited our authority? It is not enough to say good riddance to any man, especially a blasphemer; 'Let the High Priest do what he thinks best.' Speak. Who has given his authority to High Priest Jonathan? Who has said Annas could order Jonathan to do whatever pleases him? Did you Benjamin? Or you, Joseph? Tell me, Raban Gamaliel, would such a thing even be lawful? No. We all know this should never be! Yet Jonathan has gone to Herod Agrippa, our Roman King and put to the sword a fellow Jew, the Jesus follower, James ben Zebedee! Is it the duty of the temple guards to arrest our brothers for the benefit of a Roman execution? No trial? No decision by this council?"

Jonathan was about to answer when Annas shouted out, "Elders of Israel, hear me!" The room became silent as the muttering between members stopped, and every eye turned to Annas. The old man slowly walked to the front of the assembly. "Our authority? Is that what this is about, Nathan ben Joseph? Protecting our authority? And what authority is that? To do the will of our Roman Emperor and his appointed King? To put a Jewish face on our foreign ruler? Brothers, we must cling to what we have. Hold fast to who we are! If Herod Agrippa serves our temple and our purposes is this, not the Lord's doing? Would we make an enemy of the one who protects us and preserves our temple from the desecration sought by Emperor Claudius?"

A voice called out, "The LORD our God is our protector and shield!"

"Yes," Annas replied, "He sends us Agrippa to defend our worship!"

"What you say is true, Annas. Speak on."

Annas called for silence. "King Agrippa knows the threat these Jesus followers are to the true worship of the LORD our God. He called for the execution of this man James ben Zebedee. When the temple guards came upon him, it was convenient to arrest him. What need was there to trouble the Sanhedrin? He was not stoned under our law but put to the sword under Roman law. A simple matter of convenience to help our King help us."

Another voice called, "The people will not tolerate temple guards arresting a brother for execution under Roman law!"

Annas shouted back, "The people? The people honor King Agrippa! You heard him read the law at the festival of the tabernacles. The people are pleased to see this James, this disrupter of peace in the temple dead!"

The murmuring and talking among the elders grew. Annas shouted, "Hear me, brothers. If you are jealous of your authority, use it! Call the Romans to do what they will not authorize us to do. Put an end to this Jesus sect. Strike hard at their leaders. Arrest them! Give them over to severe Roman justice. Let King Agrippa judge then! Who is with me?"

The chant went up, "Let Agrippa judge them. Let Agrippa judge them!"

Gamaliel shouted, "Are we a mob?"

Jonathan stepped forward and banged his staff on the floor. Staring at Gamaliel, he shouted, "The time for caution is over. We will crush their leaders. What snake survives when its head is cut off? The decision is made."

Annas, again lifted his arms, "You have heard your High Priest, he has acted on the will of this council!" And he walked out of the council house with Jonathan.

Nathan turned to Gamaliel and asked, "Rabban Gamaliel, what has just happened?"

Gamaliel turned to Nathan and said, "Annas has just placed the Council of Israel against the LORD our God. We have joined with our ancestors, who killed the prophets and turned away from the LORD. I fear it will require more than a friendly Roman king to save us from the impending judgment of God. Excuse me, my friend, I must go and pray for God's mercy on our people."

Nathan's posture abandoned him again, and his chin fell into his chest. He gasped weakly but found no words to express his pain. He left the council house and wandered the streets of Jerusalem.

He was nearly at the home of Ezra when he remembered that today was the day of preparation for the Passover. His determination to ensure the safety of Mariam had put every other thought out of his mind. This was a holy night when families gathered to relive Israel's salvation from Egypt and slavery. It was not the day to welcome a stranger. He had pushed Mariam too hard, perhaps dishonoring her before the widows. *Was her invitation sincere? Should he leave her to the warmth of Naomi, the woman she called mother?* He knocked on the door and waited.

Ezra opened the door and recognizing Nathan smiled broadly, "Welcome Nathan ben Joseph! Naomi and I were so pleased to hear Mariam invited you to share this most holy time with us. Come in, come in and wash. It is nearly sunset."

Peace began to replace the fear and anger in Nathan's soul, and a small smile crossed his lips as he said, "Your hospitality is most gracious."

"Naomi, Nathan is here! Truly the Lord is good!"

Mariam was sitting with Naomi. She stood when Nathan entered and with an uncertain smile said, "Welcome father. May God's blessing be upon you today and always."

Again, Nathan's eyes teared, "There is no place I would rather be than in the home of my daughter's family."

Naomi called out, "Come. All is prepared. It is time to

sit at the table. Tonight, we have a new father to tell the Passover story, and Ezra must ask the questions!"

"I would not take the role of the head of the house from Ezra..."

"Nonsense!" Naomi replied, "It is done. Now sit. Everyone sit."

Ezra laughed, "There you have it, Nathan. Even the Sanhedrin must bow to Naomi in this house!"

The Passover was celebrated in the house of Ezra as it was in every Jewish home for generations. It was first a bond that holds a family together, then a bond that tied all Jews together and finally, a covenant that bound the Jewish people to God. It was older and stronger than any problem of the day, and in the celebration, the broken relationship of a long-separated father and daughter began to heal.

It was not until Ezra was preparing a bed for Nathan that Nathan quietly told Ezra, "The council met today. The council agreed to the High Priest's demands to arrest the leaders and turn them over to the Romans for punishment. He is most anxious to please King Agrippa. Herod believes the murder of James and the arrest of the others will please the people. These are dangerous times, Ezra. I have warned them..."

Ezra nodded, "You have done your best. Others too have seen this time of trial coming. A test of faith. Yes, like father Abraham's test when he raised his knife to slay Isaac upon the altar. A hard test. We must remember the faith of father Abraham. Try to sleep, friend. Was it not good to be called father by Mariam? Sleep in that joy."

The next morning, Ezra and Nathan insisted on accompanying Mariam as she walked to the common house. When they arrived, Temple guards were posted at the door. Ezra and Nathan approached the door to enter, but the guard stopped them, "No one enters or leaves by order of the High Priest."

"I am a member of the Sanhedrin. I do not know of this order," Nathan challenged.

"The Romans came to arrest the leader of the Jesus followers. We are to detain all others inside until further notice."

"Has anyone been arrested, or are all still inside? I demand to be allowed entry!" Nathan shouted.

"The one called Peter was arrested yesterday, just before the Passover feast."

"Where have they taken him?" Nathan demanded.

The guard stiffened at Nathan's rebuke. "I have my orders. You can take your questions to the High Priest."

Ezra tried a softer request. "We worry for the widows, mothers of Israel. Let us in, just for a moment to give us peace that they are well."

The guard replied without malice, "My orders are to tell any who seek to enter to move on or be arrested."

Nathan nodded, "Yes, we know your orders. But what happens to the guard who arrests a member of the Sanhedrin?"

The guard nervously looked at Nathan and said, "Yes, Now I recognize you. The prisoner was taken to the Antonia Fortress."

Nathan nodded, "Thank you. Now let me go in. I seek assurance that the mothers of Israel inside are safe."

The guard stood silent for a moment and then said, "Temple guards do not molest old women. Be assured they are well."

Mariam came forward, "They must be fed and nursed. Would you have their deaths upon your head? Now let me enter, or is a sister to great a threat to a temple guard?"

The guard looked in both directions and then opened the door, "You may enter, but you must remain inside."

Nathan let Mariam go in. As she walked by him, he said softly, "Daughter, I go to the council and seek a pardon for the mothers of Israel. I pray that I see the Lord place his shield before you."

Mariam stopped long enough to reply, "His angels surround us. Have faith, father." And the door closed behind her.

Chapter Twelve

Every member of the way and the crowds of Jerusalem were talking. The story was recounted everywhere to the shame of the Sanhedrin and anger of Herod Agrippa. Four squads of seasoned Roman soldiers could not hold Peter in prison! Mariam and the mothers of Israel within the common house of The Way spent the day of his imprisonment in fervent prayer. The brothers at the temple and followers of Jesus met in homes and prayed. All that day, the prayers of believers rose up from Jerusalem, thousands of voices but one heart and one spirit.

The story was retold: On that night, when King Agrippa was about to summon Peter before him, Peter was sleeping between two soldiers bound to him with chains. Guards were standing in front of the prison cell. Peter vividly recounted how an angel of the Lord appeared, and a light filled the prison cell. The angel nudged Peter awake and said, "Get up quickly!" As Peter sat up, the chains fell from his wrists. "Take your cloak and put on your sandals," and when Peter did so, the angel commanded, "Follow me."

In Peter's retelling, he said, "I went out of the prison cell, past the two guards outside and followed the angel. I did not know if the angel was real or if I was dreaming. I thought, perhaps, it was all a vision. I followed the angel past many soldiers, and when we approached the iron gate of the fortress, it opened before us of its own accord. When walked through the gate into the city, the angel disappeared. Only then was I certain that the Lord sent his angel to rescue me from King Herod Agrippa and all that the Jewish people were expecting."

Peter chuckled as he told how the serving girl, Rhoda, left him standing outside the common house door when he first returned, "It is just as he says," Mariam insisted. "I was there. We were inside praying when we heard someone knocking on the door. Some said, 'Don't open it. It is surely a Roman soldier, or the temple guard has returned.' I assured them the temple guard was withdrawn on the orders of the Council. Rhoda cracked the door open and looked outside, then slammed and bolted the door closed and cried out, 'Peter! Peter has returned,' and she ran to the stairs to pass the news. John, who was in the upper room with Mary, heard the commotion and came down. Rhoda again shouted, 'Peter stands outside the door!' John told her, 'Sister, open the door and let him in! Never have I seen such rejoicing! Our God saves!'"

King Herod Agrippa responded to the embarrassing news of Peter's escape by executing the guards that had been chained to him. Unwilling to face his subjects rejoicing in Peter's freedom, Agrippa took his court and moved to Caesarea, but not until deposing High Priest Jonathan once again and appointing Josephus ben Camydus High Priest, ending the line of Annas, his sons, and son-in-law. The new High Priest was careful not to embarrass the King, and the persecution of The Way in Jerusalem abated to cold stares and harsh words by Pharisees and Sadducees in the temple courts.

It was not until the third pilgrimage festival of that year, the festival of tabernacles, that a new time of testing began. A drought had come to Judea. In the autumn of the year, Jerusalem again swelled with pilgrims who lived in tabernacles, that is, tents or booths, and daily attended rituals at the temple. Merchants could not supply all the fruit and grain demanded. Even with higher prices, the supply could not meet the demand. Pilgrims at the Festival of Tabernacles were no different than any market; the wealthy paid the higher price while the poor bought less or went without.

Mariam brought the urgency to Ezra, "Fear is growing among the widows. Even those who showed courage in the face of the arrests and persecutions now fear they may starve. The deacons do their best to find food, but all know the pool of common funds is draining quickly. What can the priests do? All of the food at the temple, there must be some way..."

Ezra was quiet. His closed eyes told Mariam a debate was being argued in his mind. Finally, he took his debate to Mariam and Naomi. "The Law is clear. The offerings made at the temple are set aside for the Levites.

Certainly, any Levite widow or orphan is entitled to bread, meat, grain, and oil. But then Jesus taught that David was justified when he gave the showbread to his hungry men. Would that justify the Levites in sharing with widows and orphans? Does not the Law command us not to despise the widow? Again, Jesus sent his disciples into the wheat field on the Sabbath to gather grain, and to him, it was not sin. Surely our brother priests would share..."

Mariam replied, "The High Priest must approve it. He must find it within the Law."

Ezra was surprised, "Go to the High Priest?"

Mariam nodded, "It must be so. If you break the Law regarding the temple offerings, you will be barred from the temple. I will not, none of the widows would take such guilt upon their heads. Only if the High Priest agrees. Josephus is not like the sons of Annas; perhaps he will show mercy."

"Perhaps if both Levites and the Sanhedrin advise him. I will try. I know those among us who are blessed with wealth can be urged to give. Pray. Pray for the Spirit to lead. Speak to your father, Nathan. He has wealth and influence in the Sanhedrin."

Ezra was surprised to learn his request to meet with the High Priest Josephus to discuss helping widows and orphans suffering the impact of food shortage, was quickly granted. At the appointed hour, Ezra was welcomed to the High Priest's court. Josephus welcomed Ezra and promptly said, "Please sit, brother. I am pleased you have come to me. My heart is burdened for the mothers of Israel. Now, tell me what you have seen and what we can do."

Ezra found a leather strap chair of carved acacia and

sat down. The very high ceiling and tall columns made the room feel much larger than it was. Josephus wore a clean white robe of fine linen but uncharacteristically plain, lacking any embroidery. His short black hair and beard were dusted at the edges with the first strands of gray. Josephus was still a young man, only a few years older than Ezra. He struck Ezra as earnest and unassuming. "The prices in the market continue to rise. On most days, there is still food to be had for all, if poor quality is accepted. But during the festivals, the festival of tabernacles most recently, everything was sold, and some went hungry."

"Yes, I heard complaints from the pilgrims; some could not find what they needed for the offerings."

"There is a house near the temple, home to widows and orphans with no one to care for them. Some have sold all and put the proceeds in common. Others give generously to support them. But now their funds are nearly depleted. I have been asked to come to the temple for help. Perhaps some of the grain offering or bread set aside for the Levites..."

Josephus interrupted, "You speak of the Jesus followers. Their common house. The Law is very clear. Only the Levites can eat the showbread, and of the offerings. Surely, Ezra, you know this? Now if there are Levites among them, and only Levites, then of course..."

"I know the Law and have followed it my whole life. I ask you to consider an exception."

"There is no exception to the Law."

Ezra moved forward in his chair, "Master Josephus, I remember King David taking the showbread for his men and being justified by God. The same Law commands us not to forsake the orphan and the widow."

"Was David indeed justified by God? The account you recall is perhaps historical or perhaps mythical. There is no exception in the Torah, the five books of Law given to us by our father, Moses. I cannot make an exception to the Law on history, psalms or the prophets for they are not of the Torah."

Ezra nodded. He knew Josephus was a Sadducee to whom only the five books of Moses were Scripture. "In Deuteronomy, the LORD our God established an office, His voice to us through His prophet. Can you agree that God's voice through His prophets is in accordance with His Law?"

"God does speak to us through His prophets, and their word is to 'love the LORD our God and obey His Law.'"

"It is as you say, Master Josephus, the prophets were sent to show us our disobedience and to instruct us on how to obey. They can also help us when we must decide between two righteous acts."

Josephus immediately replied, "Is the food offered in sacrifice the only solution to caring for our widows and orphans? Is there a decision between two righteous acts? Or is this a decision for two righteous acts?"

Josephus smiled at Ezra, "Tell me, Ezra. These widows you choose to serve, must they be followers of Jesus, or any mother of Israel?"

"Truly, Master Josephus, we will turn away none. Even the foreigner will be cared for."

"I have heard of your good works among the widows and orphans. My mother speaks of it often. She has friends among them. She insists she would be better off in the common house of The Way than living under my roof with my wife. Can you imagine living with an unhappy mother and an angry wife?"

Ezra could not suppress a chuckle, "Master, my authority ends at the door to my home. My mother lives under my roof. She is happy, and we are blessed that a faithful sister has come into our lives, and they are of one mind. But it is also true they have a heart to serve the widows and share in their lives as well."

Josephus sat back and smiled, "You are a blessed man, Ezra to have a happy home. I was surprised you sought me out. It seems to me, you Jesus followers have more in common with the Pharisees. You both look to the chronicles, the prophets the psalms and the wisdom to build on the Law and find your evidence of the resurrection of the dead. Yet, it seems the Pharisees are your strongest critics in the Council."

"Indeed, the Pharisees can be both enemy and friend. Many have joined us, those who believe that salvation cannot be attained by the Law but only by the atoning sacrifice of our Lord Jesus. You, a High Priest, know that there is no end to temple sacrifice. The sinning and the need for atonement continues. Jesus has come to make atonement one time forever. Where the Law shows we are sinners, Jesus came to bring us salvation—sent by God to show us the Father—baptized into him, and His Spirit puts his Law in our hearts."

"And yet you still come to the temple to worship. You still offer sacrifices of atonement and offerings of thanksgiving. You participate in a Law you say is insufficient, one that has been replaced by a new law written in your heart. Why do you wish to have both the old and new?"

Ezra's face went blank. He softly asked, "Would you bar us from temple worship?"

Josephus shook his head, "I, a High Priest of all Israel

would not hinder any Jew from observing the Law. I observe the Law in obedience to God's command, and in return, I know I have lived a righteous life, and that is all my reward. But, you, you seek a higher reward. You must come again, Ezra. I would hear more from you. You remind me of your father, Haggai, a good and faultless priest."

"You knew my father?"

"Haggai trained me when I entered the temple service. He showed me kindness and respect."

As Ezra stood to leave, Josephus said, "Would you take me to the common house, that I might see your service to the widows?"

"Yes, of course…"

"Tomorrow. Yes, tomorrow after the morning worship."

Nathan sat with Mariam in a corner of the common house. "I fear I have little support in the Sanhedrin. They will not petition the High Priest to care for any of the poor, and they are most opposed to aiding any who follows Jesus. But I can help. All that I have stored in my barns save the seed for next year, I will give to the widows. I still have my share as a Levite. I will give grain, oil, and wine. It will feed many. Would Peter accept my gift?"

"Peter accepts gifts given with a thankful heart. I know of no gifts but those of followers of Jesus. But you must tell me, father, is the gift for the widows, or is it to please me?"

"Is it wrong to please you, daughter? I give knowing it buys food for the mothers of Israel. You have taught me to see what I ignored in the Law. You have taught me not to forget the widow, the orphan, or the foreigner among us. It is better to give here where it can be used than for me to wander Israel judging who is in need."

Nathan paused, the eyes of a father on his only daughter, "Let God judge my heart. I want to give."

"Come, you shall make your offer known."

Mariam led Nathan up the stairs to the upper room. She stopped at the top and knocked on the door. The one called Matthias opened the door and said, "What is it you seek, sister?"

"I seek Peter; here is a man who offers food for the mothers of Israel."

Matthias led Mariam and Nathan into the upper room. The very place Jesus ate his last supper before he was betrayed and handed over to the Romans as a sacrifice for the sins of the world. It was a very plain room with high windows and a narrow ladder to the roof. There were tables, chairs, and cushions about the walls and men sitting in small groups, talking and praying. Peter was at the far end, looking over the shoulder of a seated young man writing a letter. "John Mark, please inform our brother Paul of our dire need for food. Not just the widows but all our brothers and sisters in Judea. The drought shows no sign of ending. Entreat our brother to pray, yes he and all our friends and new brothers and sisters in Asia should pray fervently…"

"Peter, one has come forward offering food for the widows, can you speak with him?" Matthias called out.

Peter looked up and waved for them to come over. He nodded to Mariam and said, "Sister Mariam! You bring more than a sweet smile this day!"

Mariam's cheeks turned red as she smiled, "My father, Nathan, has heard of our plight and offers the grain, oil, and wine of his barns to the care of the widows."

"I do not recall meeting you, Nathan, but your daughter has served faithfully for many years."

"I have found my daughter here but recently. It is a hard thing to say, but I wronged her, and we parted bitterly. But I find her a woman of strength, full of love for the LORD our God and the mothers of Israel. I have seen the good work she does, that is done here for those in need. I have the means and a heart to help. If you will accept food from a foolish old sinner."

"Old or young, foolish or wise, we are all sinners here. We will accept the food you offer, and I pray you will accept the offer of salvation that our Savior makes to you."

"I fear it is too late for me... I am unworthy."

Peter put an arm on Nathan's shoulder, "The Spirit is calling you, Nathan. Sit here with me. There is good news for you to hear... "

When Ezra introduced the High Priest, Josephus to Peter, he replied, "I know your coming is of the Lord! Please, come and see how we serve the widows, orphans and brothers and sisters that choose to live, sharing all that they have."

"I have heard of your good works, and now I hear of your need. Will you continue as you have been?" Josephus asked.

"Come. Sit and speak with the mothers. Speak with those who serve. God has provided. You ask if we can continue — a fair question to ask in this time of drought. Just as the LORD, our God saved his people in Egypt, he still provides for his children here. To be sure, our savings are gone, they have been for some time, but God provides as we need. New brothers and sister come and bring what they have. Friends give to the work. Just this morning, an elder in Israel has promised the grain, wine, and oil in his barns to the widows."

"Are all welcome?"

"Surely no one in need is turned away. The door will always be open to any who desires and gives what he has. Is this not what the Law has commanded us? And Jesus, too, has reminded us not to forget the widow, the orphan and foreigner among us."

Josephus nodded, "A Law too often forgotten by our people. I come because my mother will no longer live under my roof with my wife. Some find this selfish and sinful. She has friends among the widows here and longs for their fellowship. I will never declare my responsibility for her as Corban. I love my mother and desire for her long life and happiness. I will give of my wealth more than her share, to see she is welcomed and cared for. And I will praise your works of mercy in the council."

Peter nodded. "Let your mother come and see. If she desires to live among us, she will be welcomed and cared for."

Chapter Thirteen

Ezra was wakening when he heard the cry of Mariam, "Naomi! Naomi! Please, Lord, no!"

Before Ezra's feet hit the floor, Mariam ran into the room, "Ezra, come quick! Naomi lies in her bed, trembling and shaking. She does not answer me. Her eyes stare, but she does not see."

"Does she breathe?"

"Yes, I think so—I don't know."

Moments later, Ezra was bent over his mother. He lifted her frail body and held her close. The trembling did not stop. He held her head against his chest, brushed her hair from her face and rocked back and forth, aware only of her labored breath on his arm. "O Lord do not take my mother from me. Preserve her, Lord. Do not fear, mother. You are surrounded by love. Please find comfort in those who love you."

Ezra began to weep. Mariam sat beside Naomi gently stroking her and sobbing, "Please Lord. Not yet."

Ezra continued to rock her back and forth in his arms. The trembling stopped. He could no longer feel her warm breath on his arm. All he heard was the quiet sobbing of Mariam. He stopped rocking but clung tight to Naomi. He did not hear any sound or feel any movement from Naomi, limp, and silent in his arms. Mariam's head fell back, and she began to wail. Crying and sobbing in anguish, she cried out, "No. No Lord. Mother Naomi, O Naomi."

Ezra stopped rocking, clinging even tighter to the mother he loved. He tasted her hair, wet with his tears. He inhaled her scent fearing he would never remember its calming familiarity. He began to sob uncontrollably.

Ezra and Naomi were both startled when Naomi's small body forcefully began to straighten. She gave out a loud gasp for air, her head rose and her eyes blinked before she smiled and said, "Ezra! Mariam! I just had the strangest dream!"

Ezra kissed her forehead, sniffling as he wiped away his tears, "God is good. God is merciful! Mother, you gave us such a fright!"

Mariam was giggling through sobs of joy, "O thank you, Lord. Thank you, Lord!" Smiling brightly, she reached for Naomi, "Let me hold you. I never want to let go!"

"What is this?" Naomi asked. "I was sleeping, only sleeping. I remember praying for Jesus to come. Yes, I prayed over and over 'come Lord Jesus.' Then I was floating. I floated in front of a great door. More beautiful than the golden doors of the Temple. I saw the door open, just a crack and light spilled out. Such light! I had to turn my head and close my eyes. Then I heard a voice speak from the light. It was His voice. I'm certain. He said, 'My beloved Naomi, it is not yet your time. Soon. Very soon, but first teach them to love each other. They are a gift, one to the other.' Who, Lord? Who must I teach? And He said, 'Those whom you love. I have given you wisdom and years. Teach them, and soon you shall return to me.'"

Ezra and Mariam bowed their heads and closed their eyes. Each embracing Naomi. Ezra whispered, "Thank you, Lord, for returning Naomi. Thank you for loving her,"

The noise of the market outside the Temple took Nathan away from his thoughts. Noise belonged in the market. Merchants and buyers haggling over prices followed a ritual as ancient as the Temple itself. But this noise, harsh, angry arguing, was not the perfunctory haggling that was almost comforting in its normalcy. The shoppers, few compared to a festival day, were enraged. Voices were sharp. Hands which should be gesturing along with the asking and offering were instead shoving and pushing.

As Nathan neared one merchant, fists were thrown, and a merchant pulled across his table spilling his meager offerings. As the merchant lay on the ground, eyes bulging at the sight of a foot being lifted to kick, he pointed a finger from his trembling outstretched arm, "It's his fault! He is the real thief!"

The assailant turned to look at Nathan, dumfounded by what was happening. "Look at him," the merchant continued to point as he got up on his knees. "Look at him rich on our misery! Look at how he can dress. Can you or I afford such robes! Yes, his name is Nathan ben Joseph. Greedy! Rich and greedy! I know how he became wealthy, but it wasn't enough! It never is for the rich. I have bought from him. For years I have sold his grain, oil, and wine. I have made him rich. Now, when Jerusalem starves, he stops selling! Yes. I have been to his barns. They are filled with grain, wine, and oil. And this man waits for the prices to go higher!"

"Is this true, Nathan ben Joseph? While my children go hungry, you hoard in your barns what all of Jerusalem needs?"

Nathan shook his head, "No! My barns are empty! I have nothing to sell."

The merchant stood up, "Ask any of the merchants if they have bought from Nathan ben Joseph this year! They will tell you he has not sold. Greedy and full of himself! A member of the council, so much better than the rest of us! And a Levite! He will always eat. The best portion of the sacrifice goes to the priests and the Levites. Does he look like he has missed a meal?"

The angry man grabbed Nathan's robe at the collar and pulled him close. In slow, angry words coming with the hot breath on his face, "Is this true, Levite?"

Turning to the crowd that was beginning to circle them, the enraged man shouted, "Brothers and sisters! Who is with me! We shall have what he has been holding back!"

Anger came from behind clenched teeth as he said to Nathan, "Take us to your barns, and we shall take what we need from your hoard, and perhaps, perhaps we will not kill you!"

Nathan's voice trembled as tried to reason, "Friends,

my barns are empty! I have given what I had to the mothers and orphans of Jerusalem. I gave because I saw the need..."

A voice cried out, "We don't need him. I know where he lives. Stone him, and we shall take all that is his!"

A new sound began to grow. The sound of iron studs in wooden Roman sandals striking the paving stones rang in the unmistakable cadence of Roman soldiers. Paving stones were dropped, and men began to run.

"I gave all to the widows and orphans at the common house near the Temple," Nathan tried to explain unaware of the approaching soldiers.

A stone thrown from a fleeing rioter found its mark and hit Nathan in the back of the head just below his ear. His eyes went sightless as they widened, and his knees crumbled. Nathan fell in a heap in the street.

The merchant quickly gathered up his trade goods and straightened his table. "He gives to the Jesus followers? Worse than a thief!"

The Centurion stopped his men in front of Nathan, drew his sword, and walked to the merchant, "Who is this man?"

The merchant stood up and said, "His name is Nathan ben Joseph. He is a member of the Sanhedrin."

"Is this how you Jews treat your leaders? Pick him up."

The merchant hesitated, and the Roman stepped forward and put his blade against the man's robe just below his ribcage. "Pick him up, or your blood will run in the street."

The merchant nodded, stepped over, and lifted Nathan over his shoulder.

"You will carry him to the council house."

Nathan opened his eyes in the darkness and silence of

solitude. His back told him it was an unfamiliar bed. His head throbbed, and somehow, he knew better than to try and move it. He stared straight above into the blackness but could discern nothing other than his own thoughts. *'So, this is sheol. I did not expect the pain. Am I to lie here and relive my sins in my mind forever?'*

Nathan let out a long sigh of despair. And then, a sound. He heard the light rustling of clothing, a robe brushing against something, followed by the creak of a chair. He felt a hand on his forehead and then heard the sweet words, "Father! You're awake! I, we have been so worried. But God has answered our prayers, and you are returned to us!"

Nathan could feel Mariam's breath on his face, then her hair brush against his cheek and finally her soft kiss on his forehead. "Mariam, how my heart is refreshed! Can you open the curtain or light a candle that I may see your face?"

Mariam kissed him again and with a soft sob said, "The curtain is open, papa. The noon sun brightens the room."

"Nathan slowly lifted his arm and softly put his hand on the back of Mariam's head, "Daughter, how I have longed to embrace you. If I were to descend to sheol now, I would remember this moment forever."

"Jesus promises us joy forever with Him in heaven. That is the gift He brings to all who believe. But you see nothing, father? Let me light a lamp over your eyes."

Mariam lifted her head but took Nathan's hand as she reached for the lamp beside the bed. Kissing his hand, she gently placed it on his chest as she went to light the oil lamp. Nathan could hear her soft steps coming and going. "I shall be careful not to burn you with the flame. I am going to bring the lamp close. Tell me if you see anything."

Nathan smelled the burning oil and felt the heat of the flame, "Nothing. I hear, I smell, I feel the heat, but I see nothing."

"I know of a physician. A Greek, a very learned man. We shall send for him. And rest; you must rest."

Nathan tried to move his head and stretch his back, "My head. So much pain."

Mariam lightly touched the large swollen knob on the back of Nathan's head, "Here is where the stone hit you, papa. Perhaps a cool, wet cloth. I will bring one at once. Please try to rest."

When Mariam returned, Nathan was asleep.

The physician first looked into Nathan's eyes. He moved his hand back and forth. He then turned his attention to the swollen wound at the back of his head. "When was he injured?"

"Little more than two days ago,"

"It appears he lost little blood."

"The cut was not deep. I cleaned what little blood there was."

The physician put his hand on Nathan's shoulder, "My name is Luke. I am a physician. Tell me about your pain. Does it come and go?"

Nathan answered, "It never ends. It throbs."

"I am going to help you sit up. Mariam, please help me. Gently. Now bring him forward."

The physician supported Nathan's head as they lifted him forward. As Nathan groaned, Luke asked, "Are you dizzy? Lightheaded? Your stomach, do fear you will vomit?"

Nathan mumbled, "Yes, light-headed, and a bit dizzy. But it seems to lessen as I sit. My stomach turns. Vomit, no, I don't think so."

"I will let you sit for a short time, and then I want you to rest. Once you feel better, sit up again. Again, and again. Once you feel strong sitting, you can try standing. But only if someone is with you to steady you. Do you understand? Mariam, I will leave you some herbs. Boil them in water and when it is cool enough, let him drink."

"We will do as you say."

"My eyes? Will I ever see again?"

"We shall cover your eyes by day and uncover them by night. Your vision may return. The blow you received was severe. There is still much swelling. Perhaps..."

"How long shall I wait?

"I have no answer. There is one, the Great Physician who can heal you. If it pleases you, I will pray to him."

Nathan replied, "You speak of Jesus. My daughter prays. It pleases me greatly."

Nathan's breathing slowed, and his body relaxed as he listened to the prayers made for him. "I am at peace. I am at peace."

"I shall come again tomorrow."

Nathan asked, "How is it a Greek comes to Jerusalem and speaks of Jesus?"

"The brothers and sisters in Antioch of Syria. They call themselves 'Christians,' they shared with me the good news. I come to Jerusalem seeking one Paul of Tarsus. I heard he comes here to speak with Peter and the apostles."

"Christians?"

"Yes, Christians, we follow the Christ, the anointed one. Now you must rest, Nathan. Until tomorrow then."

Mariam helped Nathan lay down and said. "Ezra, Naomi and all of the widows pray for you, papa. God is good. You should trust him. He can heal you. He can heal your heart."

"I am blind, Mariam. Blind. What will become of me?"

"I shall care for you, papa."

"How can you, daughter, you have Naomi to look after? How is Naomi? Is she well? I have grown quite fond of her. A very wise woman."

"Naomi grows weak, papa. She sleeps most of the day. She speaks of a vision. She believes she will soon be called to our Lord in heaven."

"I am sorry to hear of it."

"Naomi is not unhappy. She tells me she waits to see me love whom I hide from. You, papa, I see I have withheld my love for you for far too many years. She will be happy to know we share the love of father and daughter."

"And Ezra? How is Ezra? A good man and faultless priest. Why don't you marry him? I see that you love him, and he loves you. Let me speak to him. I can convince him to ask for you."

"Papa, Ezra has asked me to marry him several times. You know that I cannot marry him. He is a priest and I..."

"And you have slept with no man! An evil man hurt you! Do not remind me of the pain! You are no adultress. Marry Ezra! He is a faultless priest, and he knows the Law. Does he not say the Law serves man? The Law instructs us in justice? Where is the justice in denying consecration to a daughter violated in her youth and mercifully has no memory of the evil done to her? Have I not heard it said of Jesus, 'Your sins are forgiven?'"

"Father, I am not forbidden marriage, only marriage to a priest. And our Lord also said, 'If you love Me, obey My commands.'"

151

Taking Nathan's hands, she continued, "Papa, it is not just the Law that stops me, but there is you. I must care for you. Ezra and I understand. We know what we must do. We know how we must serve and sacrifice. Now, enough! Try and sleep, papa."

Mariam kissed Nathan and left.

James, the brother of Jesus, now an apostle and called James the Just, entered the Temple in the early morning for prayer as was his habit. Ezra met him at the porch of Solomon. "Good morning brother! And what should I pray for today?"

James answered, "Good morning, Ezra. Why do you ask me the same question every day? You know there are not enough hours in the day for all that needs prayer. But as you ask, there is something new. Paul of Tarsus has returned and requested a council with the apostles and the leaders. I must forego precious time with the Father to hear his charges."

"Charges?"

"Brother Paul complains we Jews make too many demands upon the Greeks who follow Jesus! Too many demands? Our God sacrificed His only Son that we might have eternal life, and circumcision is too great a demand? A few days pain to demonstrate the covenant made by God with His people to declare He is their God and we are His people?"

"Brother James, the Gentiles have received the same Spirit we received, and they make the same declaration in public baptism. Do they not confirm their old life in sin has been buried, and they rise in new life with Christ? We have determined not to require them to follow the old law because it did not bring salvation. If they are not under the law, why hold them to parts of it? Why put new wine into old wineskins? The Law is a stumbling block to the Jews, do not make it a stumbling block for the Greeks."

"Ezra, again you remind me of wineskins! I find beauty in the Law. For in It, I see our Savior's atoning sacrifice portrayed. It reminds me of all that He has done for me."

Ezra nodded, "There is beauty in the Law. We see it because it is familiar to us. Perhaps the Greeks will see the beauty as well. But circumcision will not help them see it and provides no atoning value."

James put his hand on Ezra's shoulder, "I will hear what brother Paul has to say. Now, my heart yearns to pray."

Ezra replied, "I shall pray for discernment—that our Father makes His will known to the council."

As Ezra walked off, he stopped and turned to James once more. "I would like to hear what brother Paul has to say—As a priest and a scribe. I knew him—before.— When he persecuted our brothers. I knew him as Saul, the disciple of Gamaliel. How mysterious are the ways of our LORD!"

"You may listen. Tomorrow in the upper room."

Chapter Fourteen

The upper room was full. The apostles were there seated at a table at the far end of the room. Many believers from the Pharisees were standing near the table passionately making their position known. The deacons were graciously urging everyone to be seated. The room was still alive with loud conversation. Everyone was talking such that no conversation was heard mere feet away from the speaker. Then the loud banging of a shepherd's staff on the worn wood floor rang above the cacophony of voices. Again, the deacon drove his staff against the floor three times, and the voices silenced. Paul and Barnabas had entered the room and were walking forward.

Peter rose from his seat and said, "Welcome brother Paul and brother Barnabas. We are eager to hear from your own testimony of your work among the Greeks."

Peter motioned to two seats reserved for them at the table of the apostles.

The room was silent except for the sound of wooden sandals on the creaking oak floor. Every eye watched Paul and Barnabas walk in and greet Peter and James with a kiss. Paul turned and dropped a large leather pouch which sang with the voices of many coins as it landed on the table. "The brothers from Asia, Gentiles mostly, have heard of your hardship and send this offering."

Peter nodded, "Their gift is most gracious. May God bless the gift and the giver. Please, brothers, sit with us and tell us of these new brothers."

Paul spent several hours recounting the places he went and the reception he received. "It was our habit to go first to the synagogue and the Jews and then to the Gentiles where we were better received. Greeks of all ages; men, and women, young and old, wealthy and poor, heard the Good News and believing, received the Holy Spirit just as you did here in Jerusalem. We instructed them as Peter instructed our brothers here. We baptized them into the same faith. Their heart is to fellowship with all believers, and most assuredly, with their brother Jews here in Jerusalem."

When Paul came to the recent events upon his return to the Christians of Antioch, his voice hardened, and anger flashed in his eyes. "But in Antioch... "

Peter, alarmed by Paul's passion, interrupted, "Brother, we heard stories, but what you tell us today is of great encouragement. God be praised! Our new brothers, tell me, they have forsaken their idols and follow only our Savior? And their hearts are filled with worship and love for God and neighbor? You have found them in no way lacking in the faith?"

Paul exhaled, and his body relaxed. He nodded and with a small smile, answered, "It is just as you say. They believe, they love, they serve. I train and appoint leaders in each city before I move on, and I instruct by messenger or letter."

James smiled and nodded, "Brother Paul, the brothers who went down from Judea to Antioch, what was their message."

Now wholly composed, Paul explained, "Certain brothers, once Pharisees, as I, myself was once, came to Antioch and commanded our Gentile brothers: 'Unless you are circumcised according to the custom of Moses you cannot be saved.' Barnabas and I debated them. I would agree there was great dissension between us, so we determined to come here—to the apostles, to this council, for resolution of this issue."

Paul had not finished his sentence when a Pharisee shouted, "It is necessary! They must be circumcised! You must direct them to observe the Law of Moses!"

Ezra listened as the debate began again, certain priests and Pharisees insisting that the Gentile believers be circumcised, that is become Jews according to the Law. Only then to be counted as believers and find salvation in the atoning death of Jesus. First, Paul spoke, then Barnabas, who encouraged understanding and acceptance of those unfamiliar with Jewish Law. Men began shouting. No one listening, only shouting. Peter's face flushed, he bit his lip and finally jumped to his feet and shouted, "Brothers! Brothers! Hear me!"

Peter pounded on the table and waited for silence before speaking, "Brothers, you know that in the early days God made a choice among you. That by my mouth, the Gentile Cornelius and his household, should hear the Word of the Gospel and believe. And God, who knows the heart, bore witness to them, giving them the Holy Spirit, just as He did to us. He made no distinction between us and them cleansing their hearts by faith. Now, why do you put God to the test by placing upon the necks of these disciples a yoke which neither we nor our fathers were able to bear?"

The room was silent. Paul was listening with his head down and eyes closed. Barnabas fixed his eyes on Peter, who looked at James and the others before continuing, "But we believe we are saved through the grace of the Lord Jesus, in the same way they are."

Peter sat down. No one spoke. James the Just, president of the Council, slowly stood up, "Brothers, listen to me. Simon Peter has related how God first acted to take from the Gentiles a people for His name. The words of the Prophets agree. Just as it is written: 'After this I will return and I will rebuild the tent of David that has fallen; that the remnant of mankind may seek the Lord, and all the Gentiles who are called by My name, says the Lord, who makes these things known from old.'"

James turned to Paul and spoke directly to him, "Therefore my judgment is that we should not trouble those of the Gentiles who turn to God but should write to them to abstain from things polluted by idols, and from sexual immorality, and from what has been strangled, and from blood. For from ancient generations Moses has had in every city those who proclaim him, for he is read every Sabbath in the synagogues."

Paul watched and listened closely. He turned to Barnabas; both men smiled and nodded when James finished.

As Ezra walked home, the debate replayed in his mind. He wondered: if the Law was, in fact, a yoke which could not be born and if it was unnecessary for the Gentiles who were now deemed saved by grace and the same as the Jewish believer, was there any remaining value to the law? Did he hold to it merely for the beauty he found in its foreshadowing of Christ? Or the privileges of the priesthood? Had the Law become a stumbling stone to knowing the grace of Jesus Christ?

When Ezra opened the door to his house, Mariam immediately ran to him. Hugging him tightly, she wept, "I am so worried. Naomi would not eat. Nothing. All day she wanted only to sleep. A little wine, Just a few sips. That was all. What shall we do? We are losing her Ezra. What shall we do?"

A deep sigh was all Ezra could muster. "I know. She is going. We can love her. That is all. Let me see her."

Ezra quietly sat on the bed next to his mother. He bowed down close to her face and still barely heard her faint breath. He held her hand close to his heart and whispered, "Lord, I know you love her and call her to joy in your presence, but she is so dear to me, so very dear. I don't want to lose her. Please."

Naomi opened her eyes and smiled, "Ezra, my son, my joy. Ezra, promise me..."

"Yes, mother..."

"Promise me you will care for Mariam. She is strong, I know. But she too has needs. Do not let her grow old with no one."

"I promise, mother, I could never abandon her. I love Mariam, as you do."

Naomi gazed lovingly at Ezra, smiling warmly, "I feel

very tired. I think I will sleep."

"Yes, mother. Sleep. Sleep well."

Ezra kissed Naomi. She closed her eyes and fell asleep.

Ezra sat up straight and wiped the tears from his eyes. Standing, he saw Mariam behind him, wiping tears from her eyes. He stepped over to her, hugged her tight while gently stroking his hand over her back shoulder. "I promised her. You heard me."

Mariam sobbed.

Ezra took a breath and said, "Tell me, Mariam, how is Nathan?" He let go of his hug, and they quietly stepped out of Naomi's room.

"Mariam nodded slightly, smiled and said, "He is encouraged. Today he saw the light as I passed the lamp across his eyes. He has hope. Hope, and with it joy. Come, he will want to speak with you."

The morning found Ezra walking up the steps to the Temple and out on the Court towards Solomon's porch where brothers in Christ awaited him. The tall man in the robes of a Pharisee took his mind back to an earlier time. "Brother Paul! Surely you shall give the lesson this morning!"

Paul smiled wryly, "Should I call you Rabban? Is this not the very portico where you sat with me at the feet of Gamaliel?"

Paul's face became serious, "I saw you at the council meeting yesterday. It is you? The one who insisted on challenging the trial of Jesus?"

Ezra nodded, "Yes, and now I teach with our brother, Simeon ben Gamaliel, those who seek to know how the Law tells of Jesus. He is with the Rabban Gamaliel, who is very frail. Simeon would regret not seeing you."

"I called on Gamaliel last night. Simeon was there. My teacher and my friend did not wake for my visit. There is much I wanted to share with him."

Ezra nodded, and then asked, "Yesterday, at the council, Peter said the Law is a yoke that cannot be born. You claim you are not under the Law. It is the truth I find in our Lord, but I struggle to apply. Yet, here you are at the Temple. You come to worship following the Law?"

Paul pointed his arm to the pilgrims, and worshippers crossing the court of the Gentiles and then to the great Temple doors. "To the Jews, I become like a Jew to win Jews. You heard my accusers among our brothers. To those under the Law, I become like one under the Law—though I myself am not under the Law, so as to win those under the Law."

Turning back to the disciples gathered for their lesson, Paul smiled, pointed to the fortress Antonia and continued, "To those not having the Law I became like one not having the Law—though I am not free from God's Law but am under Christ's Law, to win those not having the Law. To the weak, I became weak, to win the weak. I have become all things to all people so that by all possible means I might save some."

Ezra looked to the Temple and then back to the young disciples, "I have been teaching that pouring the truth of Jesus into the traditions of the Law is like pouring new wine into old wineskins…"

"And such it is," Paul commented.

"But I come to the Temple every day. I am a priest. I eat from the sacrifices. I tell myself—and others—that there is beauty in the Law. The Law points to Jesus, who in all ways fulfilled the Law."

"All that you say is true, but there is more…"

"Yes. I stop short of living in faith, not trusting in the grace of Jesus alone. And—And not considering our brothers and sisters caught in a struggle to find righteousness in a Law they can never fully keep."

"That is the unbearable yoke."

Paul looked at each of the young Jewish disciples of Jesus, smiled, and said, "I must take my leave. I go to offer a sacrifice of thanksgiving."

Turning to Ezra, he grasped his forearm and said, "This truth must be made known. You must help them understand."

A rare rain fell over Jerusalem as two funeral processions made their way out of the city to hillside cave tombs in the wall of the Kidron valley. Two Levites were laid to rest in their family tombs. Two lines of mourners following the families bearing the wrapped bodies occasionally stopped and sang lamentations for the dead.

Rabban Gamaliel ben Simeon would be remembered as one of the great teachers of the Law in all the days of Israel. He dedicated his life to the Law of Moses. His son Simeon sang this psalm as a tribute to his father:

"Teach me, O LORD the way of your statutes;
And I will keep it to the end.
Give me understanding, that I might keep your Law
And observe it with my whole heart.
Lead me in the path of your commandments,
For I delight in it.
Incline my heart to your testimonies,
And not for selfish gain!
Turn my eyes from looking at worthless things;

And give me life in your ways.
Confirm to your servant your promise,
That you may be feared.
Turn away the reproach that I dread,
For your rules are good.
Behold I long for your precepts;
In your righteousness give me life!"

Simeon ben Gamaliel spoke as his father was laid in the tomb. "My father loved the Law. He saw in it, perfection. He saw justice and mercy and trusted in the atoning sacrifices for sin and offerings of thanksgiving. He loved the Great Giver of the Law."

Naomi would be remembered only by those who loved her. Her name would not be recorded in the history of Israel. But how she loved, touched many lives. Ezra and Mariam chose a different psalm to sing in her memory:

"Bless the LORD, O my soul,
and all that is within me,
Bless his holy name
Bless the LORD, O my soul,
And forget not all his benefits,
Who forgives all my iniquity,
Who heals all your diseases,
Who redeems your life from the pit.
Who crowns you with steadfast love and mercy,
Who satisfies you with good,
So that your youth is renewed like the eagle's.
The LORD works righteousness
and justice for all who are oppressed.
The steadfast love of the LORD is from everlasting."

At the tomb of Ezra's fathers going back generations

to the building of the second Temple, Ezra wept bitterly and began, "Jesus on the night before he was betrayed said, 'This is my commandment, that you love one another...'" Ezra's voice broke into cries, his head fell to his chest, and his shoulders slumped.

Mariam placed her arm around him and finished, "...that you love one another as I have loved you.' Mother Naomi always knew the heart of the Law, for it is written: 'Defend the weak and the fatherless, uphold the cause of the poor and the oppressed."

Ezra sniffled, wiped his eyes and added, "Yes, even as the LORD spoke through the prophet Isaiah, 'Is this not the fast I choose? Is it not to share your bread with the hungry and bring the homeless poor into your house; when you see the naked, to cover him?'"

Ezra gently straightened the grave clothes of Naomi. When he finished with the linen cloth over her face, he bent over and kissed her forehead. Fighting back tears and sobs, he said, "Jesus said, 'In my Father's house are many rooms—I go to prepare a place for you.'"

When they had finished laying her in the tomb, and they were about to seal it again, Ezra turned and said softly, "Oh, how she loved."

And the rain grew heavier.

Chapter Fifteen

Simeon ben Gamaliel joined Ezra at their favorite portico on Solomon's porch of the Temple. "I have heard of your great loss, brother. I share in your grief."

"And you, as well, brother Simeon."

"Ezra, I come with news and with an opportunity, perhaps your calling with the passing of your dear mother, Naomi..."

Simeon stopped. He frowned and said, "I am sorry, brother, forgive me for saying that the grief you suffer is anyway an opportunity—I meant—I, I am sorry, truly sorry."

"Please, brother, I know your heart, I take no offense. What is the news you bring?"

"Paul and Barnabas have departed for Antioch. They carry the decision of the Council to the Gentile disciples. From there, they will visit the disciples in the cities of Asia and Greece."

"Yes, all of this, I know."

"James the Just is sending a letter to the Christians at Antioch confirming all that has been decided. He has determined that this letter should also be carried to Mark the Evangelist and the believers in Alexandria. I suggested my friend Apollos deliver it."

"Apollos? Apollos?"

"You met him. Remember, he was there the night Baruch died."

"Yes, now I remember him. He was a disciple of John the Baptizer."

"He follows Jesus. He stays at my house now. He often comes to Jerusalem for the festivals. James asks that one of us, from the Jerusalem fellowship, carry the letter—that is, I go with Apollos. I thought, well, with Naomi gone and your father buried, nothing is keeping you here—I mean you no longer see the need for sacrifices and..."

Ezra adjusted his head scarf, the top of his head hot in the midday sun. He closed his eyes and sighed, "There is Mariam and her father, Nathan, who recovers in my house. Why don't you make the journey with your old friend?"

"When the Rabban died, I promised my mother... "

"Say no more, brother. I know the duty a son owes his widowed mother. I will give you my answer tomorrow."

The sun had set before Ezra began his walk home. Yesterday's rain had washed the dust from the streets of the upper city, but the occasional puddle was a painful reminder of the tears that fell from the sky as Naomi was laid to rest. Several of the merchants who regularly watched Ezra go by nodded and warmly greeted him with the blessing, 'Shalom,' as he passed. Ezra smiled absently and repeated the blessing, but his mind was elsewhere. He would not remember who he passed or who he greeted on his first return home without Naomi waiting for him.

Nathan was sitting near the door when Ezra came in. "Ezra, perhaps you can talk some sense to her. She has her mind set on leaving."

Mariam stepped away from preparing the evening meal and scowling at Nathan blurted, "Enough, father! No discussion! I have kept my word to Naomi. Now it is time to leave!"

Ezra's jaw dropped, "You're leaving? Why?"

"I stayed for mother Naomi. She is gone. So now I leave. I will take father home and care for him there."

"We never talked of such a thing. And so soon. Your work?"

"There are others who do the work. They will do well without me. Father's dizziness is gone, and he has some vision, blurred though it is. He can safely ride a donkey. He must see to his house and fields."

Nathan snorted, "Hah! I have servants, good and loyal. They tend to my fields and barns. Stubborn daughter! It is you, Ezra, she flees. She refuses your marriage proposal. Foolish girl—loves you! I know she does, even a blind man can see that! I have pleaded with her! Is it not a father's duty to find a husband for his daughter? Sons! She must have a son to care for her in her old age just as you loved and cared for Naomi. Naomi said the same to her."

167

Mariam's lips tightened, her fingers became fists, and through clenched teeth, she snapped, "What do you know of the duty of a father to his daughter? When did you protect me from *him*? And that husband you chose for me? The old man without a heart!"

Ezra's face tightened, his brow creased and eyes widened in surprise, "Mariam, you don't mean that!"

Turning her glare to Ezra, she snapped, "And you. I got along well before I came here. I do not need you or any man. I can take care of myself!"

Nathan and Ezra were frozen speechless. Dumbfounded, mouths open, they stood, waited and stared.

Mariam stopped, covered her face with her hands, and she began to sob. "I am sorry, father, forgive me. I love you, papa."

She sniffled, turned to Ezra and whispered, "I will not bring disgrace upon you, Ezra. I leave tomorrow." She began to cry.

Ezra went to Mariam and hugged her tight. His chest absorbed her sobs, and he buried his face in the top of her head. He whispered, "I would not see you struggle with guilt. I love you too much to see you in pain. No. I cannot do such a thing. Perhaps someday. There is no one else for me. But stay here. Continue the service you love. I will leave. I was asked to carry a letter to the believers in Alexandria. I will go. You and Nathan stay. Remember my promise to Naomi. As long as I live..."

Ezra felt Mariam's body relax, "You're leaving? Alexandria? When will you return? I don't know if I will be here when you return."

Mariam stepped away and wiped her eyes and with one last sniffle said, "It will give me time to think, to consider all that you have said."

Ezra closed his eyes and sighed, "I don't know how long. Perhaps weeks, perhaps months. I can wait to hear from you. Yes, consider what we mean to each other, then write. Simeon ben Gamaliel will know how to reach me. Seek him out."

Mariam stepped back; her eyes flashed her voice strengthened, "Your duties. You cannot leave tomorrow! Your priestly duties have not completed for the year - How..."

"My duty—our duty is to make disciples. Jesus commanded it. Simon Peter sees it. Paul sees it. Mark the Evangelist, Phillip, others—Jesus is a light to the Gentiles. He did not die that all men become Jews failing under the yoke of the Law or for Jews to become freer under the Law. He died to free all men from their sin. I hid behind my priestly duties far too long even as I teach that the Law is fulfilled and the sacrifices for sin and atonement are met forever in His sacrifice on the cross. Just as the Law is fulfilled, the need for atoning sacrifices in the temple is no more. All that remains of the priesthood is to intercede for God's people. God has moved his presence from the Temple to the hearts of his people. Isn't that what we received on the day His Spirit filled our hearts and baptized us in His Holy Spirit? The day you came into my life. I know you remember, just as I do."

Mariam's shoulders narrowed drawn in by her arms as she clutched her elbows, "You abandon your priesthood? A man asks you to carry a letter to Alexandria, and now you say the Temple is meaningless, the priesthood is ended?"

Ezra grasped Mariam's shoulders, his eyes wide in excitement, "I do not abandon my calling. I am determined to fulfill it! In my heart, I have never been more certain that I am called to a new priesthood, other than the Levitical priesthood. A priesthood that always existed. If God can give his Spirit to all who believe, can He not, in so doing, consecrate every believer into a holy priesthood to serve and intercede for His people? I need to find this new priesthood. I won't find it at the Temple. Perhaps I will find it where His Spirit is working among the Gentiles."

Mariam stared.

Ezra continued passionately, "Scripture. Scripture tells us of a Priest of the Most High God, before Moses. Greater than father Abraham, Melchizedek. There is a lesson. I must study this priest in the light Jesus has brought to Scripture."

Mariam's brow wrinkled, but she could only muster one word, "But."

Ezra and Mariam stared at each other in silence. Nathan, listening and almost forgotten, broke the silence, "It seems, daughter, you can no longer be a disgrace to his priesthood. He seeks no more than what you seek, to serve God according to the best of his ability. Marry him. Serve as one and let me fulfill my duty as your father."

Mariam and Ezra turned in unison towards Nathan. Finally, Mariam announced, "Dinner is ready. Papa, it is your favorite."

It was Mariam's practice to serve Ezra and Nathan dinner and then takes hers with Naomi confined to her bed. She placed the plates in front of Nathan and Ezra, took hers and started for Naomi's room. After two steps, she stopped and stood silent. After a moment she lowered her head turned around and sat beside Nathan.

She wiped a tear from her eye, smiled, and said, "I will join you tonight."

They ate in silence. When Nathan had finished, Ezra said, "Let me help you to your room."

Mariam closed her eyes and said, "Wait. Tell me about the letter you are to carry, and why Simeon asked you. Could I meet Simeon before you leave? I will stay here with father and continue to serve the widows—if that is what you want. And—and I will consider your offer of marriage. If you still desire it when you return."

When she finished speaking, she opened her eyes and looked at Ezra. He smiled at her, stood up, and kissed her forehead.

Ezra looked at the shoulder bag on the floor packed with his things. He scanned the room to see if there was anything else he would need. Of course, his Sefer Torah would be safe with Nathan and Mariam. *'Perhaps some memory of Naomi? 'No,'* he thought, *'I will only be gone a short time, and surely I need nothing to help me remember.'*

"Coins! Small change. I need some coins," he grumbled.

"Surely you can make change as you need it with money changers," Nathan offered.

"Yes, yes, but I need coins for the walk."

"For the walk? Nathan asked.

"Something mother taught me. Always take something to give others, even if it is only a smile."

Nathan asked, "Must it be a coin?"

Ezra looked up, "I really don't know how to smile at people. So, I give coins to the beggars."

Mariam nodded and laughed lightly, "I have seen your

smile, Ezra. I find it very pleasing indeed!"

She went to the blushing man she loved, hugged him tight and demanded, "Come home to me safe!"

Chapter Sixteen

Apollos was waiting for Ezra at the house of Simeon ben Gamaliel. Ezra was late. When Ezra knocked at the gate, Apollos met him warmly. "There you are brother! I see you wisely packed light. It is the best part of two days brisk walk to Joppa. I look forward to our fellowship as we travel."

Ezra's face tightened, "Two days? Brisk walk? I never— I have never been more than a few miles from Jerusalem. I have never walked, walked briskly for two days!"

Apollos smiled broadly, "My friend, be glad we sail to Alexandria, the walk or ride would be more than two weeks at a brisk pace!"

Apollos wore a natural smile. The smile of a man happy with his lot in life, delighting in the people he met. He was younger than Ezra by a few years but confident in himself and cheerful. Ezra was surprised to find him a most likable man. His charm instantly put Ezra at ease. His smile was not forged but an ever-present expression of the joy within the man who wore it. His dress was distinctly Alexandrian, not true Egyptian, but not quite Greek. Elegant and exquisite, a man of wealth and high social class, even so, any apprehension Ezra felt was now put at ease.

Handing Ezra a small shoulder purse, Apollos apologized, "Here is the letter of the council to Mark the Evangelist, it is only proper that a believer from Jerusalem should carry and deliver it. And a well-chosen apostle, you are Ezra ben Haggai, a priest, scribe, and teacher of the Law! Our brother Simeon would see us before we depart. He excused himself as his mother called for him."

Ezra smiled and hung the purse opposite his shoulder bag.

Apollos nodded, "Perhaps we should sit. Please put down your bag. Tell me, Ezra, how is your Greek?"

Ezra set down his bag, wondering if he needed everything he now carried and sat at a bench beside the gate. "I can speak Greek in the market to buy what I need. I understand the Hellenized brothers, pilgrims, at the temple. I have never read their philosophies or dramas. Will that be a problem?"

"The market Greek and the Greek of the philosophers are nearly two different languages! But it is the *koine* or market-place Greek that is spoken by everyone. Once we depart, we will speak only koine so you should feel confident in the language once we arrive. Ah, here is Simeon."

Simeon walked forward blushing with a sheepish smile, "Sorry brothers. Mother is still unsettled. She mourns and fears to be alone. Ezra, I am so grateful that you have chosen to make this journey. I will make your excuses to the High Priest. He may grumble, but with so many temple priests, it will be no problem. I am more concerned with the disciples you teach. I shall do my best to carry on as you have led us."

Ezra smiled, "Please consider Melchizedek, priest of the Most High God in the account of father Abraham. What would Jesus teach us of this mysterious priesthood? It is on my mind. I will discuss it with you when I return."

"Certainly, brother. I should not keep you and brother Apollos from your journey. I thought a prayer and blessing before you depart."

Turning to Apollos, Ezra replied, "We would be favored."

The two men made their way out the Gennath Gate and took the road to the left past the pool of Amygdalon, below the three towers and Herod's palace, and out the west road to Joppa.

"I sent my servants ahead with the trade goods. They will arrange for our passage to Alexandria. I thought the walk would give us time to talk—become better acquainted."

Ezra shifted his shoulder bag and nodded.

Apollos apologized, "I fear I presumed too much. We can return to the city for riding donkeys if you prefer."

"No, I will be fine. The walk will do me well. Our Lord rode a donkey but once. I must put my privileged life behind."

"At least let me share your burden, I should have sent

it ahead."

"You say you sent servants and trade goods ahead. You are a merchant then?"

"Yes, grain primarily. From Egypt. Though I buy and sell throughout the Roman world. There is only one market, the Roman market. It is straightforward to understand but requires some skill to navigate. It begins with Rome itself. The city's demand for grain comes first. Did you know, Ezra, that the Emperor gives free bread to the people of Rome? Free bread and games to buy their peace. First, we must feed Rome, and then we must feed Rome's legions. Of course, the legions move from place to place enforcing the Pax Romana. The governors and procurators set their requirements. And then there is everyone else, the markets in every city and village."

"I did not know this. So much of the world I do not know."

Rome demands the best price. Fortunately, the emperor does not buy the best grain for bread that is free and poorly valued by the people. Grain for the legions is the same. Believe me, brother, the Temple priests would not accept such grain for a wave offering. Only the merchants to wealthy households and the temple require the best. And it may come from anywhere. It moves about as drought and plenty move and as needs move. And as it moves, and as it changes hands, the price increases."

Apollos stopped and turned to Ezra, "Let me take your bag, brother. The sun is getting high. Perhaps a drink of water?"

Ezra humbly accepted Apollos' offer and handed him his bag. "Tell me how you came to follow our Lord."

"It was my first visit to Jerusalem, years ago.

Everywhere I went I heard of this prophet in the desert, John, baptizing repentant sinners. I was curious—something new. I found him—I went to the desert, and he was—different—a true prophet. Well, I repented of my sins, and he baptized me. I went home to Alexandria, many there had heard of him. But my father—well, he didn't believe. When I returned to Jerusalem the next year, John was in prison, and many of his disciples followed Jesus. I never saw Jesus, but I heard the stories. Simeon convinced me, and I believe."

Apollos, smiled, "I have been doing all of the talking. What about you, Ezra?"

Ezra soon exchanged worry over the hot sun above for the warmth of friendship and camaraderie of his new friend. It was just past sunset when they arrived at a gritty roadside inn between Emmaus and Lydda for supper and the night. Ezra shook his head in amazement at the dust that covered not only his feet but his legs arms, face, and neck. Not even a pilgrim would enter the Temple as dirty as he found himself. Both men cheerfully shook the dust from their robes and drew from the large water jugs outside the door to wash away the souvenirs of their journey.

The men were not halfway through their evening meal when the door of the inn was violently flung open. A Roman officer in full armor and a soldier marched in. The centurion's eyes were ringed by the mud of dust and sweat. The officer shouted for the innkeeper while the soldier, panting from a hard ride, watched everyone in the room. The officer barked, "We seek two men traveling alone on foot from Jerusalem."

The wide-eyed innkeeper silently pointed to Ezra and Apollos.

"Seize them!"

As the frozen innkeeper held out his arm, finger still pointing, the soldier drew his sword rushed to the table, grabbed Apollos by the collar of his robe, and yanked him to his feet.

"Is this how a Roman citizen is treated in Judea?" Apollos roared, "A Roman of a noble house cousin to your General Tiberius Julius Alexander lately procurator of Judea?"

"Hold!" The officer shouted. "Release him!"

The Officer walked over to Apollos. "You are a Roman citizen?"

"I am Apollos of Alexandria, nephew of the Alabarch and cousin to Tiberius Julius Alexander. I travel with my friend from Jerusalem to Alexandria."

"Pardon my soldier, Apollos of Alexandria. We are in pursuit of two bandits who ambushed and killed a Roman soldier, a messenger of the legion. They were reported traveling this road."

Apollos straightened his collar and brushed his robe smooth, then looking into the centurion's eyes, smiled and said, "Your zeal is understandable. Please, sit for a moment. We will tell you of all we saw on the road today, though I do not recall two men traveling alone on foot, do you, Ezra?"

"Ezra shook his head no, his eyes wide with fear.

"Some wine? Perhaps someone else here has seen them or can tell of places such men may hide — innkeeper wine for the officer. I'll pay and for all his men, ask them in. We must help them keep the road safe."

The Centurion sat down and removed his helmet. "Yes, I shall want to speak with all here. Bandits are no use to anyone. We seek only peace and justice. My messenger was a good man. He leaves a widow and orphan. Bandits indeed! Cowards!"

The room was silent. The door opened, and four more soldiers filed in. They cautiously removed their helmets and sat down; their gaze fixed on their centurion.

Apollos turned to his right and said, "You men. We will start with your table. Come and speak to the centurion."

One by one, every patron stood before the centurion and told what they saw on the road that day. Several volunteered that perhaps the bandits had gone north to Arimathea or south to Gezer or Nicopolis and that the hills to the south afforded many places for bandits to hide. The centurion and his cohort left peaceably with every eye left in the room alternating between the departing Romans and the skillful peacemaker sitting next to Ezra.

Ezra also stared and pondered, 'Who is this man, Apollos? Cousin to a Roman general and procurator? Nephew to the ruler of Jews in Egypt? Yet he chooses to walk with me and stop at a humble roadside inn?'

When the noise of conversation returned to the inn, Ezra asked Apollos, "Is all that you said true?"

Wearing the same pleasant smile, Apollos replied, "It is true. Tiberius Julius Alexander is my cousin, and he would take offense at a family member being humiliated, not that he cares for me, but it would be a sign of disrespect for himself. No, my cousin was born a Jew but honors what serves him, and that is his position as a Roman."

Ezra leaned in, "I have heard of Jews who became Roman citizens, brother Paul of course, but a general and procurator? How does such a thing happen?"

"Any Roman citizen of great wealth can be enrolled as Equestrian class, not as noble as Senatorial class, but suitable for senior positions in the armies of Rome and after ten years of service, suitable for appointment to a senior official to the emperor. There is a long history of the Jews in Egypt serving the armies first of the Ptolemy's and later the Romans. Their service was rewarded with position and rights for Jews in Alexandria, even the right of self-government of the Jews second only to Roman law."

"And you, Apollos, a Roman citizen, you do not seek office, authority?"

"I do not deny my citizenship. It serves me, just as it has today. But, no, I do not pursue office and authority. I am a Jew, and I will not give up my worship of the One True God. My desire is to see the Gentiles follow our God. Jesus reminded us that we had forgotten that we are a light to Gentiles. Mark the Evangelist believes this, and I help him in the work in Alexandria. I am blessed by God, and I also do my share in providing for the brothers and sisters in Jerusalem as well."

After the first day's journey, all downhill from Jerusalem, the road connected with the coastal road along the flat coastal plain. It was a hot, dusty walk just out of reach of the cooling onshore breeze. Joppa was crowded with carts, donkeys, horses, and men. The road through the gate led past warehouse after warehouse straight to the harbor filled with ships. Once through the gate, the sea breeze cooled the city within. Ships were berthed three and four abreast with planks crossing between them and men bearing baskets, casks, and amphora out on one lane of planks and back on another. Crewmen were shouting instructions as cargo came aboard and holds were filled.

Apollos led Ezra directly to the harbor where Apollos's

servants were waiting. A young man in a clean Egyptian linen tunic, unstained by dust or sweat, approached and said, "Greetings Master Apollos! The baskets of raisins are loaded, the wine and olive oil are finishing as we speak. You have time for refreshment before we sail, about two hours. I can put these bags aboard if you like. There will be one stop at Pelusium."

"Thank you, Demetrius, yes, washing the dust of travel and a change of clothes would be most refreshing. We shall join you in an hour. I do not want to keep the pilot waiting. You know where to find me."

The pier-side inn at Joppa provided a cool, shaded place to wash and enjoy a bowl of wine and fresh fruit. Ezra sat down and rubbed his thighs and knees. "An excellent walk, indeed. So, this smell, is it the sea? I have never been to the great sea before."

Apollos laughed, "You smell the low tide and the foul water of the harbor! No, my friend, once we are offshore, you will smell the true sea air. All this noise will be gone. You will hear only the muffled voices of the crew, speaking softly only when needed. It is a wondrous thing to see, Ezra, men working without words, knowing what is needed, and doing without being told. A ship at sea is a special place. Men are only visitors upon the sea and must be courteous to God, who alone rules upon the deep."

"Demetrius, your servant? He spoke of raisins, wine, and oil..."

"Demetrious is my steward and chief servant. A most capable man. Yes, we bring grain suitable for Temple worship to Jerusalem and take back raisins, wine, vinegar, and olive oil to Alexandria. A ship must find cargo for each port of call, so merchants must trade for both directions. Wine and oil must be brought into Egypt, Judea is close. The wine is not the best but satisfactory for soldiers and the market. The oil too is much closer than that of Greece."

Apollos leaned back in his chair and stretched his shoulders. Smiling again broadly, he filled Ezra's cup and said, "Help me finish the wine and let us go to the ship. I am anxious to get underway. I love sailing the sea."

An hour later, the ship had slipped its lines, and the crew rowed out past the breakwater. Ezra could feel the fresh breeze as the crew boated their oars and hoisted the lateen mainsail. Soon the small ship had settled on its left side and a wake formed behind the stern. Apollos smiled when he finally heard the joyful sound of water running against the side of the boat. Taking in a deep breath, he turned to Ezra, "Ah, the sea air!"

Ezra was holding onto the thwart with white knuckles, "Are we going to tip over? Is this safe? How long to port?"

On the second morning, the color returned to Ezra's face. He managed some solid food in addition to his water. Still holding onto the thwart, but with only one hand, he pointed to a tower on the horizon and nudged Apollos.

"Yes, that is Pelusium. We will offload and load some cargo there. Shouldn't take long. Pelusium anchors the eastern approach to the Nile delta. It has been a stronghold and gateway to Egypt for many centuries. Marc Antony ruled the city for a while, and the great Roman General Pompey was murdered there. The city is now some miles from the harbor as the sands have shifted, but still it is an important port for flax linen. Tomorrow we sail around the delta."

Apollos watched as Ezra stared longingly towards the shore. "We can stretch our feet a bit and have some cool fruit and wine while the crew does their work."

Then patting Ezra on the back, he said, "You will gain your sea legs, friend, and all of this will become quite pleasant. Much more pleasing than the road from Judea."

Suddenly, there was an abrupt change in the wind. The small ship went deep on its right side as the captain lunged to undo the main sheet from its cleat. Once loosened, the sail soared out, the boat spun behind the sail and righted itself. The helmsman used his great sweep oar to bring the ship to a new and stable course. The wind began to howl, and the ropes and lines sang in the breeze. The air thickened and the tower on the coast disappeared in a shroud of sand.

Apollos motioned for Ezra to follow him below the deck underneath the cargo tarp. Demetrius was immediately at their side with clean linen face cloths to protect them from the dust that penetrated every crevice and opening. Apollos grinned and shouted above the roar, "It happens. Usually gone in an hour or two."

Ezra's eyes widened. He gripped the thwart he sat on with both hands. He shook his head and said nothing.

Apollos tried once more, "It happens on the road as well. Don't worry. We are safe.

The small vessel lurched again. All three men tumbled to the other side of the boat. Water poured over the gunwale, soaking them and flooding the hold to their shins. Apollos said softly, "Perhaps we should pray?"

Chapter Seventeen

Three days later as the Pleiades was fading into to the dawn and only Venus continued to shine in the brightening sky, Apollos pointed to a light showing on the horizon far ahead of them. "There. Where the water and the sky meet. Ezra, do you see it? That is Pharos, the famous Alexandria Lighthouse. It is a beacon both day and night. It is lit by fire at night, but watch for the sunrise, and you will see the most incredible flashes of light. The great mirror will capture the sunlight and flash it out across the sea."

Ezra craned his neck and squinted at the horizon, finally nodding, "I can see it! The Alexandria Light—It looks so distant, how far?"

"Yes, it is at least six hours sail with a good wind. We should be in Alexandria midday."

"So long as we are not overwhelmed by another sandstorm." Ezra muttered.

"Have faith, brother. God has preserved us for this mission."

Ezra shouted, "Ah! the flash, I saw it!"

Turning around and looking over the stern, Apollos answered, "Yes. The sun just breaks the eastern horizon. Is it not a marvel? Many more await you, my friend. Alexandria is filled with wonders and marvels. It is a joy to share them with you!"

The sun was still high and the heat scorching as they sailed through the narrow harbor entrance. Ezra stood tall, holding onto a mast stay and studied the lighthouse as the crew rowed the small ship into the large, protected harbor. "A true marvel of the world!" Apollos proclaimed. "Only the Great Pyramid is taller. Two hundred and fifty cubits tall! Note the distinctive architecture, the square base holding the main octagonal tower and topped by a cylinder wide enough for two horsemen to ride abreast in the internal spiral ramp!"

"I've not seen anything like it!" Ezra replied, his eyes following the soaring height from base to top. How did they build such a thing? Surely the rounded cylinder is the same great white stone as the foundation and the octagonal tower."

"The lighthouse is nearly three hundred years old and is as sound as the day it was completed! And the road, the heptastadium, seven stradia long, forming both a breakwater and bridge to the great light—Builders—Egyptians and the Ptolomys are great builders!"

Ezra nodded, his mouth agape, as he contemplated the enormity of the effort. Apollos was not finished with his guide work. Pointing to a magnificent palace on an island in the eastern end of the harbor, "That is Antirhodos and the Ptolemaic Palace. The quarter of the city on that shore is the Jewish quarter, perhaps the finest in the city."

"I have never seen such a large and magnificent city! And you say the Jews here govern themselves?"

"Tomorrow, you will deliver your letter to Mark. We look for him at the central synagogue. It is also the seat of the Gerusia, the Jewish ruling council of seventy-one not unlike the Sanhedrin in Jerusalem."

"Yes, the letter. I must not forget our mission. Can I visit the great library before we return? Could you arrange that?"

Apollos smiled broadly and slapped Ezra's back, "Of course! and the theatre and market as well!"

Once the ship moored, Apollos told Ezra, "Demetrius will attend to the cargo. You will come with me to my villa. You have earned the taste of fine wine and a well-prepared meal. I will see that you're refreshed for tomorrow. Now, you must agree that travel by ship is far more refreshing than a long, hot and boring walk."

"You might have convinced me if we were not nearly shipwrecked."

"The little dust-storm? I've survived worse."

"I prefer not to put the Lord to the test. No, I will not be content until my feet are safely on firm ground!"

Apollos' family villa faced the harbor, looking out to the Ptolemy's palace, now the home of the Roman Prefect of Egypt. They dined in the open court which was refreshed by the sea breeze which serenely filtered through alternating rows of finely open filigreed stone-work and intricate iron latticed windows in the wall. The soft sound of small waves washing against the beach did much to soothe any remaining tensions of the day. The lilt of laughter and light conversation mingled with the waves and songs of birds nested in the eaves. The aroma of roasting lamb and spiced dates played with the nostrils as an exquisite wine satisfied the tongue. That night, Ezra's tired frame still felt the rolling of the waves as he slept peacefully in the comfort of his friend's home.

The Central Synagogue was a powerful, towering presence in the Jewish quarter. Its architecture, classic Greek with distinctly Hebrew motifs, assured everyone who visited that this was Alexandria, not Jerusalem. It spoke of a different culture, but a shared faith with the same wheat sheaves, pomegranates, vines, palms, and menorah relief chiseled into the stone walls and massive columns. The large open interior was divided into three large common spaces. Worshippers passing through the massive doors entered an outer courtyard, a busy place of meetings, with many groups of disciples encircling teachers of the Law or philosophy. Inside of the great court was a circle of seventy-one chairs, the seat of the Gerusia, where the Alabarch and seventy Ethnarchs, Jewish elders, met to conduct Jewish affairs, a prized right of self-governance granted by Rome. It was inside the last chamber where the most exceptional craftmanship exalted the God of Abraham, Isaac, and Jacob. In this magnificent vault, several thousand Jews could worship, hear the word of God read from the Sefer Scroll displayed prominently against the back wall and listen as the most learned rabbis teach the lesson standing between two magnificent golden menorahs.

Ezra instinctively clutched the small pouch containing the letter from James and the Council in Jerusalem, his eyes scanning the brightly painted ornate architecture of the great court, glancing down every couple of moments not to lose sight of Apollos circling through the gaggle of teachers and their disciples, searching for Mark the Evangelist. Finally penetrating a large crowd, Apollos stopped, elbowed Ezra for his attention and pointing discreetly whispered, "Mark. We shall wait until he finishes. It would be most rude to disturb him."

Mark argued from Scripture familiar to Ezra, speaking the words of Peter on the day the Holy Spirit brought His vision to Ezra and came in power upon Naomi and Mariam—the day all three were baptized. Mark called for his listeners to believe that the crucified Jesus was the true messiah and reigns today at the right hand of the Father in heaven. He patiently listened and answered every question from an open inquirer and returned to the invitation, "A decision on Jesus should not put-off. God is calling, His Holy Spirit speaking, inviting, calling you unto Himself. Today is the day of salvation!"

Those who believed were asked to stand together. Slowly the group of new believers grew as the large crowd divided into those seeking baptism and those who, though interested, were not ready to commit. When the last of the undecideds wandered off, and only Apollos and Ezra were standing in front of him, Mark asked, "Apollos, will your friend follow the Way this day?"

Apollos bowed slightly and said, "Teacher, Ezra comes from Jerusalem with letters from Peter, James and the Council, we did not want to interfere..."

Mark smiled, "Brothers, give me a moment to address our new brothers and sisters before we take them to be baptized. Then I will gladly see the letter you bring."

When Mark finished instructing the new believers,

after praying and laying hands on each one, he returned to Ezra and Apollos. "I have a few minutes as our new brothers and sisters are led to the river to be baptized. Let me read what has been sent."

Ezra opened the pouch and handed the sealed letter to Mark, "The first is a copy of the instructions given to Paul regarding the Gentiles who follow Jesus. The other is a letter of instructions from James the Just."

Mark sighed, "I pray someday, brother Paul forgives me for abandoning him and cousin Barnabas on their mission journey. I was too young, too homesick. No. There is no excuse. I failed him. I pray the Holy Spirit strengthens me, that never again will I fail in His service."

Mark nodded as he read the letters. When he finished them, he rolled them up and gave them back to Ezra. "I will share Brother James' letter of encouragement with our brothers and sisters.
Please join me this evening — you, brother Apollos, as well. There is much I wish to share with you. My table is much simpler, brothers, than yours, Apollos, but please come. Sunset."

Mark walked off briskly to catch up with his new flock of believers.

"Let us go in and worship. The Lord has brought us here safely, and the council's epistle delivered," Ezra said as he watched many Jews making their way into the sanctuary."

Just then a Shofar sounded, its distinct mellow blare echoing throughout the cavernous synagogue, calling Jews to worship. As they passed through the hall of the Gerusia and into the sanctuary, Ezra's eyes were drawn up to the high ceiling, far above and circled with windows, sending shafts of light down upon the worshippers. Still looking up, he walked through a bright shaft remembering the words of Jesus, "I am the Light of the World. Whoever follows me will not walk in darkness but will have the light of life." Once again, he thought, a fulfillment of the Law and the prophets who spoke of God's desire to be seen and known, His word and his work were not hidden in darkness. Ezra found himself singing from the psalm, "The unfolding of your word, gives light, it gives understanding to the simple..."

Bumping into another worshiper brought Ezra's eyes back to the ground and the crowded sanctuary. He watched as the rabbi took a scroll from the ark and climbed the steps of the bema. The rabbi unrolled the scroll and looked out upon the congregation. He read in Greek from the Genesis account of father Abraham obeying God, leading his beloved son Isaac off to be sacrificed in a distant place where God would lead him. Hearing the Law read in Koine Greek shocked Ezra. He listened carefully and understood, but the words, the rhythm, the familiarity was gone. He heard the story differently, almost like hearing it for the first time.

Apollos whispered in Ezra's ear, "While it is customary for any man to pose questions to the rabbi on the lesson, and there are many synagogues in Alexandria where this is the rule, the etiquette at the Central Synagogue permits only esteemed teachers invited by the Gerusia to speak here."

Ezra nodded, "I will be a listener only."

As the rabbi unwound the passage, challenging the congregation to be open to God's calling. Instructing that God calls us away from home and comfort to follow in obedience as He tests our love for Him. Our love must be above every blessing, He has generously, and lovingly given us even to the point of sacrificing the very promise of our heart—to prove that we love God first, with all our heart, and soul and mind. The rabbi was interrupted by another, "Would you agree, Rabbi, that father Abraham was found righteous in the eyes of our God by his faith. And his righteousness preceded the sacrifice of the ram caught in the thicket when God saved Isaac at the last moment?"

"You ask if atonement is found in faith rather than sacrifice. Certainly, the prophet Hosea has spoken, 'For I desire mercy and not sacrifice, and acknowledgment of God, not burnt sacrifices' Truly this is God's desire for us, yet we are taught sin requires atonement, that is why... "

The debater replied, "That is why the sacrifices at the temple never ceased, for sin never ceases. Sacrifice satisfies neither God nor man. It reminds us of our sinfulness. That is why our Lord sent His son, crucified He shed his blood one time forever to be a final atonement. With this atonement made we, like father Abraham, can delight our God with righteousness borne of faith, a faith found in loving God."

"Many believe as you say, but was not Abraham's faith, or abiding love, demonstrated in his willingness to sacrifice the most blessed gift God had given him?"

"It is as you say. In the atoning blood of Jesus, no longer does God require the blood of bulls and rams. It is written, 'The sacrifices of God are a broken spirit, a broken and contrite heart you will not despise."

When the service was over, Ezra walked silently alongside Apollos. No longer transfixed by the splendor of the Synagogue, he remarked, "It is good to hear the message of our Lord in the synagogue. The Greek, the sanctuary is so different than the temple in Jerusalem, but the message—the message was at once the truth of the apostles, yet fresh and new. It is as if the Spirit is speaking to me again. What does it all mean?"

Mark lodged in a small apartment adjacent to a villa. "He chooses a servant's quarters," Apollos commented. "Be assured he would be welcomed in half the villas in Alexandria."

Inside, they were warmly welcomed with a kiss of friendship. Their host motioned for them to sit at the small table in the center of the room. Against the wall, beneath the single window was a small bed, no more than a cot. Along the opposite wall, a small table supported a single washbasin and a jug of water. Next to the wash basin, a towel and a robe hung from hooks. Ezra and Apollos sat on simple chairs around the table which was set with a generous roast lamb, date and raisin cakes and a bowl of spiced wine.

Mark smiled, "My host indulges me. I do not cook and agreed to accept the food of a servant, but as you see, it is his desire always to give more."

"You honor him to accept his gift, brother," Apollos replied.

"I remember our Lord Jesus accepted the gifts of those who loved him, so who am I to…"

"Forgive me, brother," Ezra interrupted, "Did you know our Lord—that is see Him before…"

"Many times. He stayed in the house of my mother… yes, I first saw Him in Cana, at the wedding. I was hired out as a servant. I was very young, and my mother knew the groom. I helped fill the large water jars, the ones for washing—the very water he turned into wine! I am told it was his first miracle. I said nothing, of course, I was as surprised as everyone else. His mother Mary knew all along. Nothing he did surprised her."

Ezra's eyes lit up, "You said many times, tell us more."

Mark sat down. He cocked his head back slightly and stared off into memory, "He visited when he came to Jerusalem for Passover and the festivals. On the night He was betrayed I followed Him from the upper room to the garden where they went to pray. I wasn't supposed to be there, but I was waiting, I had helped prepare the room. I was there when the temple guards came to arrest Him. I saw Peter take up his sword and cut off the ear of one of the guards, and then—then I ran. I ran in fear, losing my tunic as I ran. It is a hard thing to remember. I ran."

"You were not alone. Peter denied Him that night. All the disciples, the men closest to him abandoned him," Ezra replied softly.

"Yes. But that does not make the memory any easier. And when Jesus was crucified, some of the disciples came to our house. My mother provided shelter — the fear. I shall never forget the fear and the despair."

Mark sighed deeply, "But thanks be to God, he arose! He lives! He has restored my soul!"

Mark lowered his eyes, "But I failed Him again. On the journey when—when I abandoned Paul and Barnabas."

Mark looked up, "Barnabas wanted to give me a second chance. He wanted me to go with them on their next journey, but Paul would not have it. To my great shame and despair, Paul and Barnabas parted over me. I pray daily to be found faithful one day at a time. God is good and has answered my prayer—so far—Eat! Brothers eat! And then I have questions for you!"

Apollos sampled the lamb and the wine, nodding his head affirmed, "Your host does you well indeed! I have never tasted better!"

Ezra took a bite, and his face radiated the pleasure of excellent food. But slowly his face grew reflective and he said, "Brother Mark, you should take up the pen and write what you remember. There are so few who were witnesses to our Lord, who remember his words and can provide a first-hand account. It would be of great value to new believers, both Jew and Gentile."

"There are the disciples they can write."

"They are scattering. They are busy in the work. Perhaps they should write. Perhaps they will. But someone must be the first. You have a story to tell."

"You think so? I will consider the matter. I will seek the Spirit's guidance. But there is a letter I must write — a report to the council and the apostles in Jerusalem of the work here. I want you to take it back to them. Many Jews here believe and now follow. But then—but then the letter speaks of rules for Gentile believers. There, I have not done well."

Apollos swallowed his food and pointing with greasy fingers said, "Brother, you have done very well, this morning, how many did you baptize?"

Mark wiped his mouth and sat back in his chair, "Indeed, many Jews believe. You see Paul and Barnabas always went first to the synagogue, to the Jews and only after they believed or rejected the word, did they go to the Gentiles. When I came here, I went to the synagogue. There are a million Jews in Alexandria. Jews and synagogues all over the city. I have not yet gone to the Gentiles!"

Pausing with his eyes on his food, he continued, "A few Greeks and Romans, God-fearers, have believed and joined our Jewish brothers and sisters who follow Jesus, but so many others. They must hear the word."

Ezra nodded, "With so many followers, surely some will take the Good News to the Greeks and Egyptians?"

"It is as you say, brother Ezra, but it is difficult for the Jews of Alexandria. There is history…"

"What history?"

Mark inhaled deeply, "The riots. Many Greeks despise us Jews. The Romans have taken from the Greeks the right of self-rule and given it to the Jews. The Romans have not forgotten that the Greeks of Egypt revolted. Positions of authority now reside with Jews, and Roman soldiers protect us. And then there are the true Egyptians. To Rome, everyone in Alexandria is Egyptian, but this is a Greek city, by language, culture, and founding. Few Alexandrians even speak Egyptian. They labor among us as little more than slaves, loading and unloading ships, cleaning stalls, and threshing wheat. Even the Jews have forgotten that the Lord sent us into Egypt to save us. It was here that we became a nation. True Egypt, the Egypt of the Nile, must hear the word as well. I will write to the council and invite others to come…"

Ezra closed his eyes and began to think aloud, "You believe, Jews without Hellenic accent and culture may be more acceptable to the Egyptians? And the Greeks of Alexandria? Could you use a temple priest? One who knows that Jesus is the fulfillment of God's Law and a light to the Gentiles?"

Mark looked into Ezra's accepting face and replied, "Such a man could do much good. But better if there were two men and one had been blessed with wealth and influence." Mark turned and smiled at Apollos.

Apollos returned Mark's gaze silently. Mark went back

to his dinner. "Tomorrow, I will have a letter for you. I want you to stop at the Temple of Leontopolis on your return. Perhaps the priests of Onias there will listen to you as well."

Mark swallowed his food and added, "I will consider writing the story of Jesus."

Chapter Eighteen

Apollos and Ezra walked back through the quiet streets of the Jewish quarter, cooled by the evening sea breeze. The occasional muffled sounds of conversation escaped through the artfully carved stone tracery of noble courtyards. The soft flapping of linen canopies and ruffling of palms overhead added to the lullaby.

"Where is Leontopolis? Ezra asked. "On the way back to Judea, I hope. And these priests? I have heard of them. They are forbidden to serve in the Temple in Jerusalem."

"Leontopolis is in the eastern delta. It is an easy connection to the trade route along the Great Sea. The Temple of Onias was built by Priests who fled to Egypt after the desecration of the Temple in Jerusalem by the Syrian Antiochus IV. The tyrant installed a statue of Zeus in the Temple spurring the Maccabean revolt. Many of our people hired themselves as mercenaries to the Pharaoh Ptolemy IV. They have served the Ptolemy Pharaohs since. Unfortunately, they found themselves on the wrong side of Rome, though they would serve any master, even Rome."

"Warriors and Priests," Ezra replied.

"Apollos, nodded, "For two hundred years—Listen, Ezra, I can go as far as Leontopolis, but then I must return to Alexandria. I must—I promised my parents. They have chosen a bride for me."

Apollos stopped, "I do not know if I am ready for marriage. There is so much I need to do. And travel. The work. I agreed to marry, but she must be a follower of Jesus."

Ezra put his hand on Apollos shoulder and smiled, "Marriage is a good thing brother, I long to marry someone. She believes as we do and serves faithfully. She has—she believes she cannot marry a priest under the law. I have promised her I would have no other. I expect her decision on my return to Jerusalem. Brother, consider the strength a wife may bring."

"Your word to Mark? You are returning to Egypt?"

"It is my earnest desire, to return, and I pray she returns with me."

"I pray for your return as well, and may God answer all of your prayers!"

The men resumed their walk, "If I am to marry, Ezra, will you be my groom's friend?"

"I would be most honored!"

Ezra breathed in deeply of the moist and fragrant evening air and added happily, "Along the coastal trade route. Happily, no risk of shipwreck!"

The heat came early that morning in Jerusalem. Nathan insisted on walking with Mariam to the Temple. The street was busier than usual, pilgrims were beginning to arrive for Passover. Squads of Romans soldiers were marching towards the market. The procurator had dispatched a full Roman legion from Caesarea to control the crowds and maintain order during Passover and through the festival of tents fifty days later. The recurring swelling of Jerusalem was routine to Nathan and Mariam, something they no longer noticed.

"Tell me, daughter, is it true, Jesus was able to cure the blind?"

Mariam squeezed his hand. Nathan knew she was smiling, "Yes, papa several times. Even a man born blind."

"How did he do it? Did the blind men have to pray, or wash in the pool of Bethesda? I would like to see again, I mean as before, not just the shadows I see now."

"Faith. Papa. Jesus said to them, 'Your faith has healed you.' And he would also say to them, 'Your sins are forgiven.'"

"Was their blindness because of sin. I know I am a sinner."

"The disciples asked Jesus about the man born blind. They asked who sinned? The blind man or his parents. Jesus said his blindness was not because of sin. Jesus was more concerned with forgiving sin, then healing the body."

Nathan sighed, "But He did heal people."

"Yes. But not everyone. His healing was a sign of His authority. But, yes, He did, that is, He does heal. The healing comes from faith."

They continued to walk towards the temple in silence. Nathan asked again, "And Peter, he healed people, and the apostles as well?"

Yes, papa. Peter healed a lame man, begging at the temple. There are many stories."

"Tell me about faith. I know you have faith in Jesus, Ezra has faith and Naomi, too, had faith. If it heals, how can I have faith?"

Mariam stopped, still holding Nathan's hand turned to him and said, "It is hard for me to explain my faith. I think my faith was a gift. On the day the Holy Spirit was given with power, and Peter preached to the whole city, God's Spirit called to me. He wanted me to trust Him, and I did, with His help, I believed. I think... Papa, I think God sends His Spirit to call us, assuring us we can trust Him, and we can. Not all do, but we can. He doesn't force us. He invites us."

"Mariam, I see your faith. Truly, I see your heart and your love. Does God invite me to have the faith I see in you?"

"Papa, Jesus said many are called but few are chosen. Let me tell you a story as we walk. Jesus told many stories, but before He rose again, we did not understand them. After He gave us His Spirit, then we understood. He said, 'The kingdom of heaven may be compared to a king who gave a wedding feast for his son and sent servants to call those who were invited to the wedding feast, but they would not come. Again, he sent other servants, saying, 'Tell those who are invited, 'See, I have prepared my dinner. My oxen and fat calves have been slaughtered, and everything is ready. Come to the wedding feast.' But they paid no attention and went off, one to his farm, another to his business, while the rest seized his servants, treated them shamefully, and killed them. The king was angry, and he sent his soldiers and destroyed those murderers and burned their city. Then he said to his servants, 'The wedding feast is ready, but those invited were not worthy. Go, therefore, to the main roads and invite to the wedding feast as many as you find.' Those servants went out into the roads and gathered all whom they found, both bad and good. So, the wedding hall was filled with guests.'"

Nathan nodded, "The Pharisees and Sadducees—The Chief priests and all who rejected him are unworthy."

Mariam added, "And those who were too busy to care. But the story isn't over, 'But when the king came in to look at the guests, he saw there a man who had no wedding garment. And he said to him, 'Friend, how did you get in here without a wedding garment? And he was speechless. Then the king said to the attendants, 'Bind him hand and foot and cast him into the outer darkness. In that place there will be weeping and gnashing of teeth. For many are called but few are chosen.'"

Nathan sighed, "I don't understand this part."

"This part is for you, papa. It is for all those who want the blessings of God -the healing—salvation— fellowship—to go to heaven. They are not clothed in faith. They have not been made righteous in Jesus. They are not brides of Christ or His people. Papa, you cannot be accepted on the faith of someone else. Yes, you are invited, but the invitation must be accepted in the Spirit. Do you understand?"

Nathan stopped and pulled Mariam's arms till she stood in front of him. "Mariam, I believe Jesus is the Messiah, the Son of God. I believe, but still, I doubt. I doubt He forgives me. I am unworthy of his love."

Now Mariam pulled Nathan close and hugged him, "Papa, we are all unworthy. Trust Him despite the doubts. Only trust Him. Do you want Him to forgive you? Ask Him!"

Nathan nodded with sad eyes, "I do. I trust He has forgiven me. I do trust Him. I feel His love. I do."

"Father come with me to the common house. Someone there will baptize you. I am so happy!"

Deacon Nicolas, a proselyte Greek, from Antioch, chosen to replace Philip who was sent to lead the church in Caesarea, joyfully agreed to take Nathan to the pool for baptism. Nathan was encouraged by the enthusiasm and joy he saw in Nicolas and listened with interest to his stories of the 'Christians' in Antioch.

Nicolas offered, "Brother, I have not been given the gift of healing, like Simon Peter and some of the others, but most assuredly I will make known your need for healing to Peter or one of the other apostles."

Nathan asked, "The gift of healing?"

"It is just you say. Healing is a gift given by the Holy Spirit. We all may pray for healing, but some are specially gifted to see who God is calling to heal. We all receive a gift or several. My gift is helping and perhaps administering. Our sister Mariam has the gift of mercy, like few others. Brother look for your gift and employ it joyfully where you are called."

As they returned to the upper city, the noise of an angry crowd interrupted their conversation. Someone was shouting in Greek, "Who threw the stone?"

Now the narrow streets echoed with the sound of iron-studded Roman sandals announcing the deliberate march of soldiers. A Roman officer again shouted, "Give us the bandit, and you may continue your business in peace!" First, the pilgrims began to rush off, and then the shopkeepers lowered their shutters and moved their goods inside.

The officer shouted, "Clear the street!"

The soldiers formed a line shoulder to shoulder, raised their shields, and drew their swords. They marched abreast in a line traversing the street wall to wall driving the crowd before them.

"Zealots," Nathan mumbled, "How many will be killed because of a coward's stone thrown in hate?"

Ezra waited in Alexandria for Mark to complete his letter to the elders in Jerusalem. He visited the famous library. He heard Philo debate the logic of the possibility of only one, all-powerful God, a view surprisingly popular among the Greeks and many Egyptians. But mostly, he was anxious to return to Jerusalem. With haste, he believed he could home for Passover. One afternoon a servant of Apollos carried a letter for Ezra from Simeon ben Gamaliel in Jerusalem.

Simeon wrote, 'Mariam visited me. She asked if it is true that Jesus has brought a new law or if the Law of Moses was still binding on priests. I reminded her what Peter has preached from the beginning, that the Law was given by Moses to show our sin, but now the Spirit has written the Law in our hearts. Jesus has overcome our sin and gives us the freedom to love and serve Him. All the requirements of the Law are satisfied in Him, just as all our sins are forgiven one time and forever. To this, she replied, "Please send to Ezra in Alexandria that my answer is yes."

Brother, I must warn you, the zealots have become bolder, attacking Romans even in Jerusalem and stirring up the people. I fear for Jerusalem this Passover. Pray for *us.—Simeon*

When Ezra finished the letter, he looked to the sky and cried out, "Thank you, Lord! Lord, keep her safe!"

Apollos stared at Ezra, "What is it, brother? Good news?"

"I must return to Jerusalem. I am to be married!"

"Brother, good news, indeed! Let us drink to your happiness! Truly, we shall call on Mark tomorrow and not leave until he gives you the letter. How I wish I could go with you and share in your joy. But you will bring her back here with you, certainly, and I will finally meet the woman you never stop praising!"

Ezra took a deep breath closed his eyes and said, "Twenty years. I've waited twenty years for this answer. Thanks be to God!"

Leontopolis, the 'City of Lions,' rose from the flat marshy lands of the central Nile Delta. A high stone wall surrounded the city, but within the walls rose up a sixty-cubit tall stone fortress, long the guardian of the Jewish military colony and the Temple of Onias. Ezra and Apollos entered the city and followed the street to the temple hidden inside the massive fortress wall. The fortress gate was open and once inside the beautiful doors to the temple, brightly painted and gilded in gold, invited Jews to worship. Hidden from the city outside, was a Temple and sanctuary similar in layout to the Temple in Jerusalem, Ezra's eyes were drawn to a large golden lamp which shone in place of the Menorah candelabrum.

Ezra was anxious to meet his commitment to preach in the temple court and then hurry on his way to Jerusalem. He walked to the center of the court and called out, but before he spoke, a Spirit within him said: "Pray."

He lowered his head and closed his eyes and prayed quietly, "Holy Spirit fall upon all those who you are calling. May Jesus be glorified. In this place."

Ezra opened his eyes and nodded to Apollos. Raising his arms, he called out the words of Peter on Pentecost, "Brothers, I come in the name of Jesus of Nazareth, a man attested by God with miracles and signs and wonders which God performed through him, as I am sure you have heard. He was delivered up by the predetermined plan and foreknowledge of God; He was nailed to a Roman cross by the hands of godless men and put to death. But God raised Him up again, putting an end to the agony of death since it was impossible for Him to be held in its power..."

The Spirit spoke through Ezra as he quoted the Scriptures, how they looked ahead and spoke of the resurrection of Christ, "He was neither abandoned to Hades nor did His flesh suffer decay...therefore having been exalted to the right hand of God and having received from the Father the promise of the Holy Spirit which He pours forth upon you...Therefore let all the house of Israel know for certain that God has made Him both Lord and Christ—this Jesus whom they crucified."

Ezra stopped and waited. One voice cried out, "Brother, what shall we do?"

Soon a chorus of voices joined, "What shall we do? What shall we do?"

Ezra raised his arms seeking silence then cried out, "Repent and be baptized in the name of Jesus Christ for the forgiveness of your sins, and you shall receive the Holy Spirit."

Men began to swarm around Apollos and Ezra calling out, "Baptize me in the name of Jesus!"

Apollos diligently gathered the men, encouraging them, "Today you will be baptized. Wait and pray. Ask for His forgiveness."

Over the tumult, the horn of a shofar trumpeted, and a robed priest flanked by two temple guards came forward demanding silence. Those called by the Holy Spirit continued to go forward, crushing in around Ezra. The robed priest shouted, "Who disturbs the worship of our God?"

Ezra walked towards him, stared into his face, and said, "The Spirit of God has come upon these our brothers. Jesus, our Savior, and Messiah is glorified!"

"Jesus? Savior? God is our savior, and without the shedding of blood, there can be no forgiveness of sin. That is the work of the Temple and our priests. That is the work of the Law of Moses, our father!"

"The blood of Jesus atoned for all sin one time and forever! He has redeemed and called us His own. You do not atone for sin in this place! Sacrifice? Is it ever enough? There is always more sin, there is the unknown sin but even the sin we know, do we sacrifice for each one? You speak of the Law of Moses—it is like the great wall you have built around this place. A wall of separation. Sin is the great wall of separation, and Jesus has torn down that wall."

"But God gave Moses the Law..."

"Yes. He gave the Law to a stiff-necked and disobedient people to show them their sin and to remind them that the cost of sin is death. Moses consecrated the sons of Aaron to be his priests, as I myself am, but this priesthood was but for a time. God had a plan for a new priesthood. A priesthood of His people filled with His Spirit and in whose heart the Law of God was written forever. He gave us a sign of this priesthood in Melchizedek, King of Salem and Priest of the Most High God, a priesthood not by blood and birthright, for he was a man with no genealogy, a priesthood which required no consecration and no atonement. A Priest greater than our father Abraham who bore him tithes and offerings and who received the blessing from him—the blessing of the Most High God, the God of Abraham, Isaac, and Jacob!"

Ezra turned and pointed to the crowd calling to baptized, "Look to these our brothers and sisters. The Spirit of God has called them. Join us repent and be baptized in the name of Jesus!"

The robed priest stared at Ezra and the Spirit-filled men and women before him. He said nothing, turned around a walked off.

Ezra closed his eyes and prayed silently, "Thank you, LORD. Preserve all who follow our Savior Jesus, for surely today His name is glorified!"

As Ezra and Apollos led the new believers to be baptized a messenger ran towards Apollos, bending over and gasping for breath he announced, "Master Apollos, your father is taken ill and begs you come at once."

Ezra smiled at his friend, "Go. Go at once. I will stay here, baptize, and teach. I will not arrive in Jerusalem for Passover, but I shall be there for the festival of tents. God has worked His blessing this day. Go rejoicing! I will pray your father is healed and is refreshed by your presence. Go."

Chapter Nineteen

The day of preparation before Passover, Jerusalem had swelled with pilgrims. Jews from the known world had come to celebrate Passover in the City of David and worship in the Temple. Many would stay through the feast of Tents, some seven weeks later. The zealots openly taunted and agitated against the Roman soldiers determined to keep the peace. As the afternoon wore on, a steady line of Jews made their way up the grand steps to the temple court.

Nathan had insisted on walking with Mariam to the market to purchase the required bitter herbs and the traditional items for the Passover feast. Their purchases completed, they started back from the market wiping the sweat from their brows as they walked. Everyone was tense. Everyone was hot, and goodwill was in short supply.

"Papa, I told you, you should have stayed home and rested in the shade," Mariam chided.

"It's not just the heat," Nathan observed, "Everyone is so irritable. The zealots have put everyone on edge. Let us hurry home. I sense something bad is about to happen."

The heat, the crowds, combined with fatigue and monotony, wore on some of the soldiers stationed at the foot of the stairs. Simmering resentment against the taunting of the zealots and the boredom of the duty led one Roman soldier to turn his back on the line of pilgrims, lift his tunic, bare his backside, and loudly fart in their faces.

For a moment, there was a stunned silence. Then came the angry shouts and stones were pelted at the guards. Before the first stone found its mark, swords were drawn, shields lifted and Roman soldiers came together, shoulder to shoulder, and marched towards the pilgrims. Jews began to run in every direction. Most tried to get away from the temple, fearing they would be followed and massacred in the great courtyard. As the phalanx worked its way across the street, the pilgrims found themselves against a wall. They pushed and shoved in panic and fled back into the market and the relative safety of the streets of Jerusalem. Fear gripped the people. Zealots appeared from rooftops and side streets with slings and rocks, raining them upon the armored Romans. Market stalls were overturned, people fell, but no one stopped. Stopping meant being trampled and left behind.

More soldiers arrived at the far end of the market, and the two formations closed in on the frenzied mass of humanity between them. Swords cleared the way in front of them as they marched. The once bored Romans became a disciplined killing machine dispatching without mercy everyone they overtook. The screams of the dying drowned the taunts of the zealots. That day thirty thousand Jews lay dead in the streets of Jerusalem, most of them trampled by fellow Jewish worshippers.

Not an hour after the riot began, the only sounds heard in the market were the moans of the injured. The soldiers had marched off, and the steps to the temple were clear. An overturned cart leaning against baskets of dates creaked as its wooden side scraped against the paving stones. Sticky dates spilled from baskets as a prone body pushed its way from beneath the cart. With the cart off him, Nathan slowly and carefully moved aside, uncovering Mariam who he sheltered beneath him.

"It is safe to get up. Are you hurt? I pray you are well. Please, Mariam, answer me!"

"I am well papa. God has preserved us."

Mariam slowly found her feet and helped Nathan up from against the wall where he sat in shock. "Papa stand up. Stay very close to me. There are many... the street is... O Papa, the street is filled with the dead!"

Mariam hugged Nathan, who held her tight as she cried. "Papa, so many. Why Papa?"

As they stood, slowly, people began to appear, walking through the dead, helping the injured and searching for family and friends.

Nathan held tight to Mariam and said, "I prayed. As we lay there, I prayed. I trusted God. I trusted he would save us and many. He heard my prayer, Mariam. God heard, and he answered. I am certain."

Nathan straightened his back and lifted his eyes.

"Mariam," he said urgently. "Mariam, look at me."

"What is it Papa," Mariam replied, looking into Nathan's face.

"Have we both not prayed again and again that I might see?"

"Yes, Papa."

"I see the face of the daughter I love. A face much lovelier than I recall!"

Looking at the grisly scene around him, Nathan wept, "So many dead, yet I am healed? I don't understand."

Mariam hugged Nathan again, "Your faith has healed you, Papa. Good and evil travel together, papa. God can reward faith even in times of evil. Come, let's go home."

Nathan looked at the carnage all around him. "We must help our brothers and sisters, any that still breathe."

"Yes, father, we will stay and do what we can. But I fear..."

"Daughter, it is time we leave Jerusalem. It is no longer safe. Let us go to the villa, the farm where we will be safe. We will help who we can help, but we must leave!"

Mariam leaned over and kissed Nathan's cheek. She straightened her back and furrowed her brow. "Ezra. I cannot abandon Ezra. I have sent word that I accept his offer of marriage."

"We will leave word for him. He loves you like no other man. How many years has he waited? No, Mariam, do not fear. Ezra will come for you. He will come. Pray. He will come."

"There, the young man. That one. He moves!" Nathan rushed a young man of Cyrene lying beside the wall.

"Your eyes are better than mine, Papa. Yes, I see him

now."

The roads from Jerusalem were crowded with refugees. Jews, both pilgrims, and residents flooded the streets, all fleeing the riots and carnage in Jerusalem. Roman soldiers seemed everywhere, coming and going, only the rhythmic pounding of their marching warning all to stand aside or be trampled. The dust of Roman cavalry and the shaking ground beneath them brought terror to the exodus of Jerusalem. Fires could be seen rising from villages, country farms, and villas in every direction. Nathan clutched onto Mariam as they silently walked the road to the city the Romans called Nicopolis but known to the Jews as little Emmaus. Nathan's villa in the hills outside of the city would afford peace and safety.

Skirting the city, Nathan led Mariam south into the rolling hills along a small stream which fed the Zephathah River as it meandered through fields of wheat, past vineyards, and olive groves. It was a fertile land dotted with houses and barns, crisscrossed with irrigation canals, ponds, and cisterns which collected the precious seasonal rainwater which brought abundant crops to the dry and arid land.

As Nathan and Mariam crested the last hill, they were accosted with the acrid smell of ash and burnt embers and stopped in their tracks. At once, they turned to one another, "Please God, No!" They rushed to the top of the hill and looking down in the gentle valley below they saw the embers that were all that remained of Nathan's villa and barns. A few blackened posts still stood upright. Four men were beating the last of the flames with heavy rugs in a futile attempt to salvage a bit of grain. Beyond the destroyed house and barns were parched fields blackened by fire.

Nathan ran to the once beautiful villa and cried out, "What happened? How did it—everything is gone!"

The men put down their rugs and slowly walked to Nathan. "Master, we did all that we could. The Romans. Bandits. Zealots were found in a barn. We did not know. We know you are a man of peace and seek no trouble with the Romans. The Zealots have been raiding along the road. They go back and forth from the hills and caves to the south. The Romans burn any home or villa that shelters them. We did not know, truly!"

Nathan walked towards the barn, "Does anything remain?"

"No master, we stayed and did our best. What shall we do? Where shall we go?"

"And the crops?"

"The Romans took what they could carry and burned the rest. Master Asa came by. He left word if you returned, we were to say you are welcome in his house. Master, may we go with you? We have not eaten or slept in two days."

Asa owned the fields next to Nathan's estate. He and Mariam played together as children. Nathan suspected perhaps they were more than friends after the midwives pronounced her a fornicator and she ran off in shame. After Nathan learned the truth, he came to trust the earnest young man living in the villa next to his.

Standing in front of Asa's gate, Nathan called out, "Asa, neighbor, it is Nathan and Mariam. We seek your hospitality."

The gate began to swing open. A servant, standing inside, pulled it wide open and Asa could be heard calling, "Good neighbors, please come. For indeed, I know of your hardship. You are welcome in my house!"

A handsome man walked towards them wearing an exquisite white linen robe embroidered in red, green, and gold. His trimmed black hair faded to gray above his ears and the back of his neck. He went first to Nathan and greeted him with a welcoming hug and a kiss on the cheek. He turned to Mariam and said, "What a joy it is to see you after all these years! Happy memories! How much fun we had together as children! And to see you now, even tired and distressed as you must be, an elegant and gracious lady. Permit me to give you a welcoming kiss."

Mariam smiled at her childhood friend, and he politely kissed her cheek. Mariam, still smiling, looked into his eyes and said, "It is indeed a joy to see you again, Asa. I see God has blessed you. How are your parents? They were always most gracious towards me."

"Passed. Over a year now. I am afraid it is only me to enjoy the fruits of their labor. But when the resurrection comes, well then. But come in, Nathan and Mariam let there be life in my house! I have room to share."

Turning to his servant Asa commanded, "Prepare something for our guests to eat. Something warm and filling. And wine. The good wine. They have had a hard journey and suffered great misfortune. Then prepare rooms."

The servant bowed and hastened off.

Nathan bowed slightly to Asa before engaging his eyes, "My servants, they..."

"Of course, they can stay. There is room."

Asa clapped his hands, and another servant quickly appeared. "The servants of Nathan will stay. Find them a place in the workers quarters. See that they are fed and rested for now."

As Nathan's servants were led away, Asa said, "Now you must come to my table. Some wine while the meal is prepared."

Asa continued, "It was most alarming. The smell of the fire woke me. The smoke and flames—you know what fire can do in this land. It is a good thing you were away, my friend. The Romans show no mercy. Your servants are good men. They did their best. These are hard times. The zealots. What do they accomplish with their hate? For every Roman they kill, what? A hundred innocent Jews may die! Fools! Devils, they are to me! Perhaps you should have stayed in Jerusalem where it is safe."

Nathan bowed his head and sighed, "Jerusalem is no longer safe. Worse. Indeed, thousands upon thousands of our people were killed in a riot. Mariam and I only survived by the grace of God and the protection of our Lord Jesus. There too, the zealots provoke the Romans. We fled the city in haste. Hard times. Yes, hard times they are."

"You follow Jesus, the Way?"

"Mariam has followed Jesus since the beginning. She served the widows and orphans of Jerusalem alongside Mary, the mother of Jesus. I have seen her faith, and now I believe. I know Jesus is Lord. He has healed my soul and removed my blindness."

"Blindness?"

"Blind in the eyes and blind to faith. A long story. But you, Asa, you follow Jesus?"

"Yes. There are many of us in Nicopolis. Seekers of wisdom and truth. Truth hidden until now. Your stay in Jerusalem, Nathan, so long. And no word."

Nathan, Mariam, and Asa found pillows and reclined

around the table. Nathan filled a cup with wine before answering, "It was a routine business trip, but then I heard someone say they had seen a woman, named Mariam, one who reminded him of my Mariam, so I sought her out. And found her, my greatest blessing!"

Asa smiled and turned to Mariam, "You found a husband and good home in Jerusalem? And children? A son to care for you?"

Mariam shook her head, "I found Jesus and I found a family. A mother to serve and her son, a priest and righteous man. And of late, I have accepted his long-tendered offer of marriage. Ezra. Ezra ben Haggai, we will marry when he returns from Alexandria."

"You waited so long! Forgive me, but you hope for sons?"

Mariam's eyes shone, "I hope in the return of our Lord and Savior Jesus. If God gives me sons, I will rejoice. If I have no sons, yet will I praise Him!"

Nathan smiled, "Mariam is a strong woman. Strong in faith and strong in heart. No son could please me more."

Asa nodded, "Your betrothed, Ezra? Will he find you here?"

Nathan replied, "We left word for him in Jerusalem to follow us here. He is a most determined man. A good man who loves Mariam with all his heart. He will find her."

Asa smiled and nodded. After tasting his wine, his face grew serious, "Tell me, my friend, what are your plans? Will you rebuild your barns and villa? Do you have seed to replant?"

"Tomorrow, I will walk my fields and examine what remains. I will go to Nicopolis and speak with the money lenders."

Asa nodded, "Mariam will be safe here. Let her rest. I would enjoy hearing her stories. Stories of the apostles and the preaching—accounts of the Holy Spirit. But you both are tired. Please, sleep well, we can speak of it in the morning."

Nathan and his servants left after breakfast the next morning. Asa was waiting for Mariam when she came out. "Mariam, I pray you slept well and are refreshed this day. There is fresh fruit and sweet cakes. Come, the morning breeze is fresh, and the sun not yet hot. The songbirds are sweetly singing. You deserve a day of peace in the garden. I wish to hear all of the secrets of the way."

Mariam stretched her neck and back, then pushed her shoulders back and yawned sending the stiffness of the morning away. She inhaled deeply of the fresh morning air, smiled, and said, "Truly a good night's sleep is a gift from our Lord. Yes, Asa, I will sit with you and taste the fruit and sweet cakes."

Sitting by the table, she said, "Has papa gone?"

"He and the servants were off early. He wished you a long rest. So, tell me, you have seen the power of the Spirit. I have heard that Peter and Phillip, and Paul of Tarsus work miracles in the name of Jesus. Tell me, do you have this power?"

"It was Pentecost. The first Pentecost after they crucified Him. I was there in the market. Simon Peter, filled with the Spirit, preached. The Spirit moved with power through the city. Jerusalem was filled with pilgrims. Pilgrims from everywhere. They heard—They heard Peter in their own tongue. And visions. Many had visions. Ezra was lifted in the Spirit and saw Jesus on the cross of crucifixion and heard Him speak. He was transported to the Temple. He saw, just as he did on that day, the curtain in the Holy of Holies torn by the hand of God. And this time he heard Jesus speak as it happened. I heard the rushing of the wind and the Spirit calling me, 'Come. Believe and be baptized.' I went forward, and it was there that I met Naomi, the mother I needed, with Ezra. We were baptized, and we follow Jesus."

Asa nodded, "I was baptized, along with many others in Nicopolis. There are some among us who speak of the hidden wisdom. Hidden in the past but given by the Spirit. The Spirit is everything and the body nothing. Have you heard this?"

Mariam looked puzzled, "Ezra speaks of Jesus as the fulfillment of the Law and the Prophets. He claims that the eyes of the chief priests, Pharisees and Sadducees are blind. They do not see that the Messiah has come."

Asa nodded urgently, "Yes, yes, that is true, but there is more. Jesus releases us from the Law for the Law is only for the flesh. But we received the Spirit of God and live in the spirit, not the flesh. The flesh is of no significance. The sins of the flesh are forgiven. Forgiven and forgotten forever. We live only in the spirit and for the spirit."

Mariam sat back and studied the man across from her. "I have heard our sins are forgiven. I know we have received the gift of the Holy Spirit who lives within us. But the flesh is of no matter? This I have not heard. Our Lord has said, 'Be Holy as I am Holy.' He lived without sin. He promises a resurrection. He rose in body and in Spirit. I will think on your words."

Mariam sampled a raisin cake and asked, "Tell me, Asa, you never married."

Now Asa sat back at took a cluster of fresh grapes.

Popping one in his mouth, he smiled, "When we were young, I desired only you. I dreamt of you and was heart-broken when I learned your father arranged your marriage. But when you ran off, I rejoiced. I wanted to follow after, find you and make you mine."

Mariam laughed, "You would not have enjoyed my life before Ezra and Naomi. Your servants fare better than I did. I cannot imagine you following the Nazarite oath. But you did not run-off, and you are still unmarried."

"Nazarite? You were a Nazarite? Indeed not. No. My father prevailed on me to stay and learn. There would be time for marriage after I was established. And then he died, and there was my mother. And after she passed, well, there is much to keep me busy. I am sought by many wealthy men as a husband for young girls. I will choose one—someday."

Mariam smiled at Asa. "You are a handsome and desirable man; you will make a woman happy to be your husband."

Asa stood up and slid around the table next to her. He put his arm around her shoulder, bent over and whispered in her ear. "We are free. Free to enjoy all that God has created. Is this not a beautiful day? Fresh with fragrance and joy. Mariam, I know how to bring pleasure to a woman. Let us find pleasure now."

Asa held her tight and tried to kiss her lips. "Stop. Asa. No! I am betrothed to Ezra. You would not have me sin against him and against God?"

Asa held her tight, his mouth close against her ear. "No sin. It is but the flesh. Your spirit still belongs to God. There are many of us in Nicopolis, men, and women. We share the joy of our freedom. We do not sin. We find the pleasure set apart for us here and now. I know your story, Mariam. You were not fit to marry a Levite, but now you claim the freedom to marry a priest! It is a good thing! Marry him! But enjoy our freedom. Come to my bed. We have loved one another for years. Come. You are a beautiful woman. Many are the pleasures I will give you. My body has longed to find release in yours. Years I have waited. I will wait no longer."

Mariam jammed her elbow into Asa's side, pushed the table away, not saying a word, eyes straight ahead, she walked through the gate towards Nicopolis.

Chapter Twenty

Ezra remained in Leontopolis teaching daily in the temple and in the evenings in the home of a priest named Joseph. Joseph was a fervent disciple with a strong knowledge of the Scriptures. Ezra often found Joseph ahead of the lesson points Ezra intended to make. A passionate man, Joseph found himself urging Ezra along, pointing out the consequences and applications faster than the deliberate and careful Ezra could make them. "Brother Ezra," he would say, "You teach like a scribe, counting jots and strokes, ever careful not to overlook a single point. Can you not see the urgency of the message? You hold the good news of Jesus in a saltshaker, serving a few crystals at a time. I would have it all poured out at once!"

Ezra laughed, "Indeed, you see where my argument goes. It is the Spirit that has come upon you, which speaks the truth to your heart. But not all are so gifted as you in the Scriptures and receptive to the Spirit's leading. To many, the Law has become a stumbling block, and we must carefully walk with them around a lifetime of beliefs and habits. Change can come hard for the best of men. I speak here of my own walk. Since the day of Pentecost, I believed Jesus to be the Messiah, the Son of God. I searched the Law and the Prophets for how they spoke of Him. Yet I clung to my duties as a priest, the Law, and Temple sacrifice. But when brother Paul resisted requiring the new Gentile believers to be circumcised, that is to become Jewish. It was to me a stumbling block. I am certain many others still believe as I did. You will cross paths with such brothers who fervently cling to the traditions of men. I want your preparation to be as strong as your passion, Joseph, to show these brothers the way around the stumbling blocks. I will soon leave Leontopolis, but you will stay. And you will lead the brothers and sisters here."

Joseph was stunned, "Me? Lead the brothers and sisters in the Lord?"

Ezra smiled at Joseph, "Do you fear your responsibilities, Joseph? God has prepared you. He has shown me your heart. He has assured me of your strength."

Joseph looked down, but his eyes were looking inward, "If I have faith in God, I, therefore, must trust Him to—I would hear every crystal, every grain expounded! Brother Ezra, leave nothing out!"

When Ezra's time to leave had come, he was surprised to see Apollos waiting for him in the courtyard. "Brother

Ezra! I return only to find you intent on leaving!"

Ezra greeted his friend with a hug, "Your father? He is well?"

Apollos shrugged his shoulders, "He is ill, but not to death. He insists he sees me married and with sons of my own before he goes the way of all men. He arranged for me to meet a young woman, suitable to him as my wife. I will tell you all about it. But I am happy to have found you before you departed. I feared the unrest in Jerusalem..."

"Unrest in Jerusalem?" Ezra asked in surprise.

"You have not heard? It pains me, brother, to tell you. Riots. A most terrible loss. On the Passover day of preparation. Thirty thousand, some say more, killed near the steps of the temple and in the market. Pilgrims and citizens of Jerusalem alike are fleeing the city. The Romans are determined to crush the Zealots and any who support them."

Ezra was stunned, backed himself into a chair, and collapsed into it. "The temple stairs? Then the market as well? Fleeing? I must get back. I must get back to Mariam!"

Apollos instantly read the pain in Ezra's face and voice, "Brother, let me go with you. There is great danger. I can help. You saw my skills with the Romans that day in the inn on the Joppa road."

His eyes not seeing, and his mind faraway, Ezra replied softly, "No. But I must go."

Turning first to Joseph and smiling weakly before focusing on Apollos, he was emphatic, "No. Apollos, you must stay here with Joseph and help him with our new brothers and sisters in Jesus."

Ezra patted the pouch hanging from his shoulder with Mark's letters to apostles in Jerusalem. "Letters. I carry

Mark's letters to Jerusalem. Just as Mark will share the Council's letter to Paul and the letter of James, I am certain Paul will share Mark's letter and the Jerusalem letters with all the churches in Asia. We must keep the believers here informed by letters. Mark can instruct Joseph and all believers in Egypt by letters. Just as Paul writes to the churches, he leaves behind. We must share the teachings and the work of the Spirit in His church."

Apollos nodded, "It is as you say, brother. I will carry a letter to Mark telling him of the church here and see that Paul's letters are carried to the new churches in Egypt, the churches of the Nile."

Ezra stood and hugged first Joseph, "Trust in the Lord, Joseph. Trust His Spirit to lead you." Then wrapping his arms around Apollos, he said, "I will send word to you in Alexandria. Pray for me, brother. Pray for Mariam and the brothers and sisters in Jerusalem!"

"I will brother, God speed," Apollos replied, his hand clasped to Ezra's shoulder.

Ezra picked up his bag and started for the gate. He stopped and turned to Apollos and with a warm smile, asked, "Will there be a wedding, my friend? Am I still to be the groom's friend?"

"Wedding or no, you are the groom's friend. Write. And when you find her, return to us."

Ezra was persuaded to take a Nile riverboat north to the great Coastal Road. He gave no thought to the weight of his pouch, the hot sun overhead, or the dust in the air. He walked briskly, with purpose, east towards Judea. All along the way, he encountered Jews fleeing Jerusalem. Most were going to Alexandria, where relations with the large Jewish community were common. Many witnessed the riot and spoke of God's grace in saving them. None were acquainted with Mariam or Nathan. No one could offer information on their fate.

Ezra stopped at an inn in Gaza. He met a brother he recognized from his teaching in the Temple. The brother confirmed all that Ezra heard along the road. He added that many of the apostles had left the city as well. To his knowledge, Peter and James were determined to stay. The brothers among the priests also remained. Many of the faithful followed John to Ephesus. Still others were bound for Antioch, as the believers there were known to be generous to their Jewish brothers and sisters in Jerusalem.

North of Gaza, the road forked. Ezra chose the route to the right, the way into the Judean desert to Marisa and Jerusalem. It was a long, hot climb away from the sea, but the shortest road home. Stopping only at the Jewish town Beth-Gabra, near the Idumean city of Marisa, Ezra soon found himself in the Mountains of Judea with Jerusalem on the horizon. His worst fears were realized when he made his way onto the city. He could not shake the feeling that he had entered an occupied city. The Romans offered no respect for any citizen, no concern for the daily life of its inhabitants. The market was open, but no one lingered to talk. He did not hear the customary "shalom" as he passed by a merchant. Eyes were down, robes were held tight, and women were all chaperoned by husbands, brothers or fathers.

The streets in the upper city were empty. Ezra was alone on the street of his house. He called out as he approached the gate, "Mariam! Nathan! Come open the gate!"

There was no response. Ezra shook on the gate handle. Silence. He went next door to his neighbor's house and called out. More silence. Ezra returned to his home, trying with all his might to hold back the fear generated bile rising from the pit of his stomach. His arms felt heavy and weak as he forced the gate open and entered his house. The silence crushed him. He was overwhelmed by emptiness. Nothing was out of place. Dust had preserved the house as it appeared the day long past when Mariam and Nathan left.

"Simeon ben Gamliel! Mariam's letter. He sent it on to me at the home of Apollos. They have spoken. He will know where they went!"

The Temple was closer than Simeon's house. He would try there first. Entering the great court of the Gentiles, Ezra was surprised by how empty it appeared. No pilgrims were to be seen, just a few faithful Jews praying. There! In his customary place, on his knees, 'Old Camel Knees,' James the Just! Praying as he always does. Next to him a group of priests, brothers! Among them, Simeon!

Ezra rushed to Simeon who caught his approach from the corner of his eye, "Brother Ezra, you have returned! God be praised!"

"Mariam! I cannot find Mariam! Have you seen her?"

Simeon stood up and hugged Ezra, "She is safe, brother, and has left word she returns with her father to his villa and fields near Nicopolis. She was determined to stay here and wait for you. But her father and others insisted she would be safer away from Jerusalem, away from the unrest and riots."

Stepping away from the praying James, Simeon, with an arm around Ezra's shoulder motioned, "Come. I have your Sefer scroll. Mariam asked me to hold it for you. And what of your journey? Peter will want to hear of your meeting with Mark in Alexandria."

Simeon stopped and looked into Ezra's eyes, "Most of the brothers have left Jerusalem. They visit family among the Hellenized or our friends among the Gentiles. Everywhere there are new believers! All hungry for the Word and the Spirit. They hunger for teachers and to hear the accounts of the apostles. Brother, the church in Jerusalem has become the church everywhere! Come. First, we go to Peter; then you can refresh at my house."

Ezra sighed deeply; the tension built over many long days drained from his weary body. A smile came to his lips, "There are many believers in Alexandria. Apollos, our brother, is most gifted in sharing the Good News. And Leontopolis—I stopped at the Temple of Onais, many of the priests and Jews of the city believe."

"You bring words of encouragement! They will be welcome."

Ezra nodded, "I carry letters from Mark the Evangelist." I believe he has written an account of the life and sayings of Jesus."

In the upper room of the common house, Peter welcomed Ezra warmly. He nodded with a broad smile as he heard of the growing church in Alexandria, the Spirit-filled leadership of Mark and the work of Ezra in Leontopolis. Peter warmly reminisced of his journey with Mark visiting churches in Pontus, Galatia, Cappadocia and Bithynia after the harsh words against the young man by Paul. Mark was remembered as both an excellent travel companion and interpreter. They shared memories of Jesus life and teachings. It was clear Peter had high regard and strong confidence in Mark.

Peter opened the pouch containing Mark's letters. As he began to read, Ezra spoke, "Letters should be read in the churches…"

Peter continued to read. Ezra continued softly, "…For the building up of faith, and the instruction of the churches by the apostles and the council. Just as the council instructed the church of Antioch, such instruction must be shared. Mark's gospel must be shared. Shared everywhere, even as the faith moves where the Spirit blows."

Peter looked up from the letter and smiling, warmly replied, "Scribes. Our apostles, those sent into the world. They need scribes to record. To report and to share with others. Yes, the Good News must be preached, and the preaching and acts of our apostles must be recorded and shared."

Leaning close to Ezra, Peter said softly, "You must read Mark's account. Have I not been told you are a scribe? Take this letter and copy it. Give it to your fellow scribes and let them copy it. We must share our brother's gospel account, for surely the Spirit of God fell upon him just as it fell on the Prophets in the past."

Ezra nodded enthusiastically, "And the letter of James the Just as well."

Ezra and Simeon set about the task of copying Mark's gospel account. Their plan was simple: get copies in the hands of others in Jerusalem to copy and send a copy to every known church.

"We must recruit scribes for this work, brother," Ezra told Simeon as they began copying.

"We have good men. Men who are fluent in Greek. We shall instruct them to make the most accurate copies."

Ezra muttered, "The text must not be corrupted. The

letters will most certainly be copied again and again by those who receive them. I worry.…"

Simeon reassured his friend, "God's word will be neither lost nor forgotten. Neither the Romans, the Jews, or the schemes of the enemy from the gates of hell shall stop it from planting God's seed of revelation into the hearts of men."

Ezra replied, "We must instruct the leaders in the local churches. Surely, they will direct more copies be made for the small house churches and for those who would carry the Good News to other cities and villages. I am fearful that others may not be as careful as we scribes are. We are accustomed to counting every stroke. I worry some enthusiastic men may add their comments to the letter they copied. Even if well-intended, in years to come, the Church Fathers will be called upon to compare and edit conflicting copies to determine the original text."

Ezra and Simeon worked together in Simeon's home. Simeon was an open and congenial man. His habit was to chat happily as he worked, and it in no way compromised his excellent work. Ezra enjoyed working in silence, concentrating, counting, and finding satisfaction in perfection and focusing on the task at hand. Ezra more than once, cleared his throat with loud 'ahem' hoping Simeon would take the hint, but to no avail.

As they worked, Simeon's cheerful banter took a more serious tone as he asked, "Brother, do you not see how Mark's account in all ways shows the superiority of Jesus? He is superior to other men, to kings and rulers. He is superior to the angels. He is superior to the prophets. He is superior to Moses. He is certainly superior to the High Priests."

Ezra kept copying and counting. His eyes on the text, he mumbled, "Yes. Jesus is superior to all."

Simeon's eyes were no longer on the text. He was looking with the penetrating gaze of concentration, "Remember, before you left, you asked that I consider the priest Melchizedek?"

Ezra looked up, "Yes. Melchizedek, King of Salem and Priest of the Most High God."

Simeon rubbed his beard and answered, "Though little is written about Melchizedek, we know nothing of his genealogy, where he came from or what became of him—there is prominence to him. A superiority, if you will."

Simeon took a breath and coughed lightly, clearing his throat, "Does it not seem strange that Father Abraham brought a tithe to him? Was not, therefore, the priest, Melchizedek superior to Abraham? And as Abraham was the father of Levi and this before Moses was declared righteous, was not Melchizedek therefore superior to Moses? Superior to all the Levitical priests before and after him? And superior to the priesthood of Moses? Melchizedek does not offer sacrifices to cleanse himself before his priestly duties…"

Ezra closed his eyes and let his head roll back in concentration, "His was a priesthood that had no beginning and no end. A priest forever?"

Ezra opened his eyes and stared into the eyes of Simeon, "We know Jesus to be a prophet and a king. But is he not also a priest? Not a Levitical priest, one by blood. One marred by sin. But a priest He is. A priest forever seated at the right hand of the Father on High! Interceding! Pleading for us! Superior to every other priest! Like Melchizedek, a priest of the Most High God and a king of peace, and as the name Melchizedek means, a king and priest of righteousness!"

Both men became silent as they pondered this truth. Ezra concluded, "We must think, my friend and pray that the Holy Spirit guide us in this truth."

Chapter Twenty-One

Nathan called on his friends in Nicopolis, inquiring into the cost of seed and the current rate for borrowing against the next year's crop. While he was greeted warmly in each house, the conversations took the same course, "A Terrible thing, brother, to lose you villa, your barns, and your fields. Where will you live? The crop is one thing, a very risky investment. Are your cisterns dry as well? Will they yet hold water? And the irrigation channels? Were they damaged? What money have you to rebuild? Perhaps it is better to sell than to risk a poor crop and a loan you cannot repay. My good friend, my brother, Nathan, I would not offer a loan that put you at such great risk! But buy? Yes, I would pay a fair price for your fields."

The land had been Nathan's inheritance going back

many generations. He longed to gift it to Mariam. The thought of selling was beyond painful. Dejected, Nathan made his way out of Nicopolis walking back towards the house of Asa. He had just passed through the gate when he saw Mariam walking towards him. Nathan hurried towards here and said, "Mariam, why do you walk alone? Is all well?"

Mariam gave her father a hug, "Papa, I cannot stay in that house. Asa. Asa has changed papa. He is a man with no shame and no honor. He says he follows Jesus, but his only desire is for pleasures of the flesh! He lusts, papa, he asked me to his bed!"

Ezra hugged Mariam even tighter. "My dear child, I am sorry. I should not have left you alone. I never thought..."

Mariam took comfort in her father's embrace, "How could you know, Papa? No. Do not blame yourself. The Lord is my shield and defender. Has He not saved us in Jerusalem? Has he not restored your sight? He will not abandon us."

Nathan kissed her forehead, "Come. We shall find room in an inn."

As they walked back to Nicopolis, Ezra sighed, "We must pray, Mariam. Pray in faith. I found no one to loan me money. They see me weakened and seek only to buy my fields. I have sent my servants to examine the cisterns and the irrigation channels. I don't know how I can pay them. If I sell, there is nothing to give to you and Ezra."

Mariam squeezed Nathan's hand, "Yes, Papa, we will pray. And let us seek out our brothers and sisters in Christ. But we must be careful, Asa claims others in Nicopolis believe as he does that the flesh is of no account, and there can be no sin for the lusts of the flesh for those who have a special knowledge of the Spirit."

Nathan stopped and turned to face Mariam, "Have you heard such talk before?"

"No, father. We must be careful."

Nathan inquired at the synagogue after the leader of the Jesus followers. Joel, the president of the synagogue, looked at Nathan with surprise, "Nathan, you, a Levite, who only came here on the High Holy Days? You cared more for your profits than for worship. And now you ask about the Jesus followers? Is it because the Romans have ruined you? You seek the handouts of the Jesus sect?"

"Rabbi, all that you say is true. But I am changed, thanks be to God! I have found the daughter I have lost and the God I ignored. Now tell me where I can find those who follow Jesus."

"Which sect? There are those called the Gnostics who follow in the Greek way. They speak of a secret wisdom. And there are those who remember the Law and the prophets."

Nathan looked confused. "Jesus came to fulfill the Law and the prophets. He taught openly. He spoke of no secret knowledge. God hates sin; that is why Jesus came to us. He suffered and died for our sin. He called sinners to repentance and forgiveness, not to license and depravity!"

Rabbi Joel smiled, "Come, Nathan, I will take you to our brothers and sisters."

The Christians of Nicopolis met in a house in the old city, once a small village called Little Emmaus, before the Greeks ruled Judea and built a large garrison and trading center and named their city Nicopolis. Nathan recognized several men with whom he had conducted business. Few remembered Mariam, but her scandalous story was well known among the people. Joel and many Jews in the city were committed followers of Jesus. They worshipped both in the synagogue and in their house churches. They prayed with and for their non-believing Jewish community, determined that their love for them be known, a living invitation to follow Christ.

Nathan and Mariam were each asked to speak a word of encouragement or request prayer. Their testimonies, the story of their reconciliation and the plight of Jerusalem, touched the hearts of many. When Nathan described the destruction of his home and fields, sighs of dismay rose from the listeners. And when Mariam told how she fled from the house of Asa, one claiming to follow Jesus, loud shouts of 'no,' and 'shame' spread through the gathering.

Nathan concluded by asking, "Can a brother provide me a tent, that I might shelter my daughter and inhabit the land of my fathers, while I wait upon the Lord to restore my fields?"

The rabbi stepped forward, "Surely our brother and sister must have shelter. We cannot leave them to wither under the hot sun and be blown away by the dry winds! No! We must offer hospitality and support! Not a tent, a home!"

Turning to Nathan, Joel said, "Brother, you and Mariam shall live in my house and eat at my table until all is restored."

Turning to the gathered believers, he said, "Let us pray. Let us pray that God has mercy and provides justice to our brother and sister..."

As he began to pray, the sky turned quickly dark. A wind came from the sea. A loud clap of thunder shook the heavens above. Immediately the sky was lit by bolts of lightning and heavy rain began to fall. Those in the center of the courtyard moved under the protective eaves and sun- shades. The rain-soaked souls murmured, "Rain? In the dry season? What can it mean?"

The rabbi shouted out, "God sends His rain upon a dry and thirsty land! Go in peace, knowing the LORD has heard our prayers!"

That evening Mariam and Nathan were seated at the table when a servant announced to their host that four men were at the gate asking for Nathan. "My servants!" Nathan shouted. "I sent them to my fields this morning! Please. May they be given food and shelter?"

Rabbi Joel nodded, and the four wet servants were brought into the room. "Forgive me," Nathan begged, "So much has happened today. I should have sent word that we could no longer stay in Asa's house."

"Yes, master Nathan, we were told that you and mistress Mariam were unlikely to return and to seek you in the city—Master, we have news! We have come from the fields. We found nothing this morning and were about to leave when the rains came. We sought shelter in the remains of the barn. We found a tarp and crawled under it to escape the rain. Master—there was seed grain under the tarp! I swear we never saw it before! We thought the soldiers took everything. But there is seed!"

"Praise God!" Nathan said with his eyes closed and head facing heaven.

"There is more. The cisterns are now full. The irrigation canals are intact. The fields are watered. And—And, the burned grain—the burned grain show green stalks again growing from the root."

Nathan began to cry, "I have seen the salvation of the

LORD! Who is like Him? He has forgiven my sins, and He has saved my soul. He brought my daughter back to me, and we are reconciled in love. He has restored my vision and saved me from death in Jerusalem. He has healed my land and brought new life! My soul rejoices. All that I have is His and I will serve Him joyfully all the days of my life."

Mariam began to weep and hugged her father, sobbing as tears of joy flowed from her eyes.

Joel smiled broadly, "Amen brother Nathan. Amen."

Ezra entered the gates of Nicopolis and found his way to the market. "I seek Nathan ben Joseph. He has a villa and fields..."

"I know Nathan ben Joseph. Yes, he is here and his daughter, Mariam."

"Please, tell me the way to his villa."

"Oh, you will not find him there. The Romans destroyed it. He and Mariam lodge with the Rabbi Joel, president of the synagogue. Are you a brother? A follower of Jesus?"

"I am Ezra ben Haggai, a brother from Jerusalem."

"Welcome, Ezra ben Haggai, I have heard of you. Mariam will be most happy to see you. Come. I will take you there."

Mariam was seated in the cool shade of the courtyard next to a small fountain. The gate was opened for Ezra. Seeing him standing there, her eyes opened wide and she squealed, "Ezra! Ezra!"

She ran to him and threw her arms around his neck, "Ezra you came! Please say you received my message! Please say it is not too late for us! I have made you wait too long. Please say you have come for me. Say that I am to be your bride!"

Ezra hugged her tight and buried his face in her dark hair. His eyes teared up, and he whispered, "Mariam. Mariam. There is no other for me. I never want to leave you. Yes, I come for you. And I will ask your father..."

"I am a grown woman. I make my own decisions..."

Mariam stopped, then laughed and said, "Of course. You must ask Papa. It is good that you ask him, and I honor him as well."

Mariam stepped back but held both of Ezra's hands, smiling broadly she said, "Let me look at you again. I see a fine and handsome man! Oh, Ezra so much to tell you! I am so happy! God is good. Come. Let me tell you all."

Mariam excused herself and waited in her room when Nathan returned from the fields. His eyes lit when he saw Ezra waiting in the courtyard. "Praise God you found us—found Mariam who waits for you! And, God, His name be praised, has restored my sight that I might behold you, my son, may I call you my son, Ezra? For that is how dear you are to me!"

Ezra greeted Nathan with a hug. "May it be as you say! Nathan ben Joseph, I..."

"Nathan ben Joseph is it? Sounds very formal..."

Ezra nodded and began again, "Nathan ben Joseph, I have come to ask for your daughter, Mariam to be my wife."

Nathan again hugged Ezra, then put his arm around his shoulder, "Please sit. Hear the advice of an old man. Please sit."

Ezra's face became serious. He sat and waited for Nathan to speak. Nathan smiled and said, "You have my blessing. It was never my decision. I knew the day I found my Mariam in your house that God had brought you together. How many times did I counsel her to marry you? I know my daughter is a strong woman. A woman of faith and determination. And I know that you love her like none other. But hear the word of a father and a husband. Love her. In your love, let her follow her path of service. Not just allow—encourage. Encourage and support her. She was a gift. Surely, Ezra, you know this."

Ezra smiled. "She is, indeed, a strong woman. Such strength is rare among women!"

Nathan smiled and shook his head no. "Not so rare! It is the foolishness of husbands to require submission first and then seek to please their wives with trinkets and gifts. No. Encourage Mariam as your wife. Support her as she ministers in love. This is the true love you must show her. If she is encouraged in her walk, she shall submit to the love you share with her in the LORD."

Nathan smiled, "She is to me a force not to be stopped! I love her and can only do my best to be one with her."

"Shall we call for my daughter, your betrothed wife? Truly this is a joyful day!"

The Christians warmly received Ezra in Nicopolis. He took the opportunity when he was offered to speak a word of encouragement and to read Mark's gospel account of the life and sayings of Jesus. Joel praised God, and the brothers immediately set about copying the letter for the benefit of the local churches. Ezra also shared the Council's decision regarding Gentile believers and James' letter on righteous living. As Necapolis was a Hellenized city, there were many God-fearing Greeks, and Romans encouraged by the word.

Mariam was already much loved in the fellowship. The news of her betrothal to Ezra was cause for a grand celebration. The brothers and sisters insisted that the wedding celebration be provided by the fellowship so that Nathan's hardships would not cause a delay in such a joyous event. Of course, Nathan protested, arguing it was his duty as the father of the bride, but the will of his brothers and sisters in Christ could not be denied.

Nathan did his best to hold back his tears as he thanked them, "Good friends, I thank you for your love towards Mariam and me. Is not God good? Does He not shower us with His love and His blessings? Has He not loved us before we loved Him? In times of troubles, riots, insurrection, fire, even blindness, He has rescued me, saved me from harm, brought me close to the daughter I had lost. He is bringing new life to my fields and has given me back my sight that I may see the marriage of my daughter to a good and righteous man. And He has established me here in this fellowship to be loved and accepted. Friends, there is no end to the love of God and His blessings to those He gathers under His wings."

The marriage of Ezra and Mariam followed every custom and ritual observed by the Jews for a thousand years. A jubilant procession escorted the finely robed and crowned Ezra to the house of Mariam where the maids and maidens called in song for Mariam to come out and follow her bridegroom. The robed and veiled Mariam joined the procession as they walked around the well and on to the bridegroom's house. The Rabbi asked Mariam if she agreed to the marriage covenant. He then turned to Ezra and asked if he accepted the dowry gifts and would take Mariam as his wife. Both smiling and happily agreeing, he commanded Ezra to take his wife home. When Ezra took Mariam into his room, the weeklong party began.

While every guest played his or her part, they knew this marriage was different. Certainly, Ezra appeared in every way to be the man ready for a bride and wife: settled, established and of an age to start a family. And Nathan was in every way, the proud father giving away his daughter to the security of a husband who would provide for her. But this had not been by his plan. This marriage was different. Mariam was no young, innocent girl untested by hardships, disappointment, and pain. She was a woman, not a girl. She knew who she was. She knew the man she was marrying. She knew how deeply she loved him and was secure in the knowledge that he loved her. She knew the costs of love and the price of commitment. She knew this marriage was planned not by her earthly father, loving as he now was, but the wonderful gift of her heavenly Father. Mariam knew this sweet gift was one of justice for a young girl wrongly condemned, a fulfillment of a long expectation granted after a season of testing, preparation and wisdom, all of which made it sweeter in satisfaction.

Ezra and Mariam were surrounded by love, encircled by brothers and sisters determined to help them, love them, and pray that their union never be divided. They were one; from then on, Ezra and Mariam. Never again one without the other.

Chapter Twenty-Two

With the help of the Christian brothers of Nicopolis who reminded Nathan that the essence of love is giving, and with the faithful service of his servants, Nathan set about the task of rebuilding his house and restoring his fields, vineyard, and groves. He was happy. Ezra thanked God in all things. He considered how God did not spare him from adversity but shielded him, and even sent blessings during hard times—the good to carry him through the bad—and a reminder that he was not forgotten.

One Lord's day when the Christians of Nicopolis were gathered for worship and the Lord's Supper, a brother, returning from Ephesus, reported on a new teacher he met there. He told how the visitor to that city, one Apollos of Alexandria, convincingly expounded how the

Scriptures all pointed to Jesus. He reported that Apollos made many converts among the Jews of Ephesus and was asked to stay by Aquila and his wife Priscilla, leaders of the church in Ephesus.

Ezra sought out the man and asked; "I know an Apollos, a brother from Alexandria. A man about my age. Wealthy. A trader in grain, oil, and wine."

"Apollos is such a man. Wealthy, yes, but most pleasant and congenial. No airs of privilege. Truly gifted and persuasive in speech. A friend to be valued."

"Did he say how long he would remain in Ephesus? Is he to return to Alexandria? Did he mention a marriage?"

"He mentioned a desire to go on to Achaia, but Priscilla was most persuasive that he remain a season in Ephesus and continue his preaching among the Jews. I expect he is still there. I know nothing of his marriage; certainly, no wife accompanied him. If you desire to find him, go to Ephesus and ask for the house of Aquilla, the tent maker."

Ezra turned to Mariam who was holding his arm and smiling broadly, "Mariam..."

"Husband, go. I know you wish to find your dear friend. Husband, what a wonderful word to me! Ezra, go to Ephesus. I know it is what you ask."

"Come with me. Nathan is busy. He is among friends, better, he is among brothers. Come with me to Ephesus. You must meet Apollos. I was to return to Alexandria. I am to be his bridegroom's friend. Mark the Evangelist asked us to go to the Egyptians, not the Hellenized, but the Copts, people of the land. Those up the Nile. We are called to make disciples!"

Mariam thought out loud. "I am a wife. No longer under a father's roof. A wife under the authority of my husband. Yet he asks, not demands. Yes, Ezra. I will go with you. We shall tell Papa, but we will go to Ephesus!"

Ezra hugged Mariam and kissed her. "We walk a new road, Mariam. God is calling us to walk a new road!"

When Simeon found tenants for Ezra's house in Jerusalem and sent the money and the price of Ezra's Sefer Scroll, Mariam and Ezra set off to Joppa in search of a ship bound for Ephesus. Nathan and many brothers and sisters from Nicopolis went to Joppa with them and prayed for a safe journey. Ezra did his best to appear confident about their journey and reminded Mariam how Apollos had learned to love the sea, and worshipped God for such a wondrous creation. Mariam saw through his bluff and said simply, "The Lord is our shield."

The summer winds were light and their voyage, though slow, was pleasant, with time for meditation, prayer, and intimate conversation. The evenings found them sitting together on the deck watching the sunset, Mariam wrapped in Ezra's arms. Knowing each other for so many years, they were surprised how they longed to hold on to one another, to feel the warmth, the comfort and security that came by touch.

Ephesus reminded Ezra of Alexandria, but on a smaller scale. The busy port was congested and much like Joppa. The harbor was safely within the mouth of the river, but it was narrow and shallow, which required ships to moor alongside each other three and four deep. Two Agora's served the people, one a large commercial market and the second a square where Roman officials conducted business as Ephesus was the capital city of the Roman Province of Asia. The Temple of Artemis dominated the central square. It was known as a great wonder of the world. Ezra and Mariam explored the city, discovering its vast library was a center of learning and philosophy. They passed the amphitheater, amazed at its size and curious as to the entertainment it provided. The city rose in prominence under Rome, and the Roman influence was apparent.

They returned to the busy market and asked after the tentmaker Aquilla. They were directed to a stall among cloth merchants, drape makers, and tentmakers. A small man with kind eyes greeted them with a distinctly Roman accent. "I am Aquilla, what is it you are looking for."

Ezra replied, "I am Ezra, a brother from Jerusalem, and this is my wife, Mariam. We seek Apollos of Alexandria. We were told he was here."

Aquilla smiled brightly, "Welcome brother, sister! Indeed, Apollos is here. Well, not now. He is at the synagogue teaching. He teaches the Jews about Jesus. Priscilla, my wife, and I lead our fellowship. She is more persuasive than I and gifted in preaching. They shall be most pleased to see you. You must stay with us. Jerusalem, you say?"

Ezra felt a comfortable smile grace his face, "We left Jerusalem several months ago, after the riots. We saw many thousands killed — a terrible sight. We fled to Nicopolis where we now live. A brother returned there from Ephesus and brought word of Apollos. He is a friend and co-worker in Christ. Apollos and I carried a letter from the council in Jerusalem to Mark the Evangelist in Alexandria, and in return, I carried the Apostle Mark's account of the life and sayings of Jesus to Jerusalem. Apollos went with me as far as Leontopolis, where we preached the good news and made many believers among the priests of the Temple of Onais."

"Apollos spoke of his work in Leontopolis. He mentioned a brother, a priest of the Temple in Jerusalem."

Smiling at Mariam, he offered, "Mariam, you must be tired from the journey and the heat of the day. Please come with me to our home."

Aquilla removed the poles holding the shade over his booth and let it fall to the crude wooden counter, the universal sign that his shop was now closed. He led them down a quiet street, and said, "I know the pain of leaving your home in times of trouble. Priscilla and I came here from Rome when Claudius exiled we Jews. Rome was my home since childhood, though I was born in Pontus on the Black Sea. As we traveled, we sought out Christians—brothers, and sisters who assisted us. We sought work as tentmakers, and that is how we met brother Paul. He spent much time teaching. He affirmed my dear Priscilla's gift and sent us here to shepherd the brothers and sisters."

Aquilla brought them into a villa with a large courtyard and small apartment. "It is well suited for teaching and observing the Lord's Supper," he commented.

No servants came to help. Aquilla pointed to a small room, "It offers little in the way of luxury, but I hope you will find it comfortable."

Mariam smiled, "Hospitality is the true measure of comfort. We are most grateful."

Aquilla bowed and smiled, "Indeed, you are kind. We are blessed that you have come to us."

Aquilla looked about and said, "Priscilla will be home soon to prepare our meal. I must return to the market for our dinner. Please rest. There will be many brothers and sisters joining us this evening."

Ezra and Mariam did not hear Aquilla return. He quietly slipped into the kitchen to begin preparing the meal. When Priscilla came in, she called out, "Husband, did you remember to shop?"

Aquilla replied, "Yes, of course. Please, we must be quiet. We have guests resting after a long journey. A brother and sister from Jerusalem. Friends of Apollos."

"You brought them here? Where are they to stay? We have no room."

"They are in our room, resting. We will sort it out. We are tentmakers, are we not. Perhaps Apollos will agree to…"

Priscilla shook her head, "What can I do with you, husband?"

Priscilla hugged Aquilla and kissed him warmly, "It was your big heart that made me love you and ask my father to arrange our marriage. He warned me there would be times like this! But I would have it no other way. I leave it for you to arrange. Did you buy enough food?"

Ezra and Mariam heard Priscilla's call and meekly came out to greet their hosts. A fashionably robed, middle-aged woman with finely coiffed black hair in the Roman style stood before them. Her intelligent blue eyes watched them approach. A smile came to Priscilla's lips, and she walked over to greet them. "Welcome. I am Priscilla. You are from Jerusalem? Friends of Apollos?"

Ezra bowed his head and said, "Mistress Priscilla, I am Ezra, and this is my wife, Mariam. God bless this house. We are most grateful for your hospitality."

Priscilla smiled, "Brother Ezra, sister Mariam, you are most welcome. Please do not take my surprise for anything but that. You are most welcome. Sister Mariam, can I ask you to help me with the cooking. We could talk as women. I dare not let Aquilla cook."

Mariam nodded, "It has been some time since I enjoyed the company of a woman in the kitchen. My fondest memories are such moments with Ezra's dear mother, Naomi. Yes, send Ezra and Aquilla to the shade in the courtyard."

"You would send our husbands off?" Priscilla said with raised eyebrows and a smile.

Mariam laughed, "Ezra is the dearest man. Though I have known him for twenty years, we are only recently married. Perhaps I spent too much time with his mother. She became a mother to me as well. She was not afraid to step in. There are things a man, even a loving husband does not understand and places he should not go. The kitchen being one."

Priscilla turned to Ezra and Aquilla and opened her mouth to speak. Ezra lifted his hand to show the message was received, "You see now the strength of Mariam. Be assured her strength is equaled only by her works of mercy. Come, Aquilla we have been exiled to the courtyard!"

An hour later, Apollos came in. "Ezra!" He called, "It is a blessing to see you, my brother! I was worried. I heard of the riots and the massacre. I sent word to Simeon asking after you. But here you are safe! And your betrothed, Mariam, is she well?"

Ezra hugged Apollos, "My wife helps Priscilla prepare the meal."

"Wife! I knew you loved her and were anxious to marry, brother, but you could not send for me to be your groom's friend?"

Ezra shouted, "Mariam! Come meet Apollos!"

Turning back to Apollos, Ezra continued, "So much has

253

happened, brother. I could not find her in Jerusalem. She fled to Nicopolis. Mariam's father, Nathan, a good man and an elder in Israel—his villa and fields were burned by the Romans. Bandits—bandits were found hiding his barn. And then Mariam was—well she and Nathan found refuge among the brothers and sisters in Nicopolis. When I found her, I could wait no longer—we married. But then I heard you were here, so we came!"

Mariam and Priscilla came out of the kitchen. Apollos smiled warmly at Mariam, "Brother Ezra has spoken of you so often I feel I know you, though you do not appear the lioness for I see a woman of warmth and beauty."

Priscilla laughed, "Brother Apollos, you have my word; she has the strength and courage of a lioness. But as you say, a kind and warm heart."

Ezra put an arm around Apollos' shoulder, "Brother, what of your marriage? I was to return to Alexandria."

Apollos sighed, "It was not to be. I could not marry her. She said she followed Jesus. But her's is not the Jesus we follow. She spoke of hidden wisdom, knowledge for the few. She spoke of ancient Jewish myths and strange Greek philosophies. She saw no honor in the marriage bed. She tried to—well, I do not believe the Spirit dwells within her. We could not be of one mind and one spirit. Do not fret for me, brother, I am called into service to our Lord. And God has directed me here. Priscilla and Aquilla have been most helpful and instructed me more fully on the baptism of Jesus. Truly they are one and brother Aquilla has the true heart of the shepherd. Such hospitality!"

Priscilla motioned, "The meal is prepared. Come wash and we shall eat. There is time to talk."

As they made their way towards the basin, Aquilla

mumbled, "Brother Apollos, speaking of hospitality. I have given Mariam and Ezra the bedroom. As our people once dwelt in tents, I ask would you..."

Apollos laughed, "I shall be happy to employ one of your tents!"

During supper, Ezra put down his wine cup next to his plate and turned to his host, "Forgive me, I have something for you, for the church here in Ephesus."

Glancing at his friend, he continued, "Apollos, you will recall I carried letters from Mark to the brothers in Jerusalem."

Apollos nodded, "Truly, it is so."

Turning back to Aquilla, he said, "The Apostle Mark wrote an account of the life and sayings of Jesus, a Gospel, the good news of His coming. It was decided to make copies and give them to all the churches. Mark walked with Jesus. It is his first-hand account, so there be no confusion. I bring a copy for you and a copy of the letter of James the Just. And please, I encourage you, brother, to find trustworthy scribes to copy them just as they are—word for word with no change or corruption."

Aquilla put down his food and with a warm smile, said, "You must first read them. Read to all the brothers and sisters! Yes! We shall arrange it."

Turning to Priscilla, he asked, "I think the next Lords day. Before the Lord's Supper, dear. We will announce it tonight. I want as many as we are to hear it."

Ezra nodded, "I will gladly read them."

Pausing and bringing his hands together beneath his lips, Ezra said, "Perhaps it is my past work, but I must insist that the copies be without error. Let me oversee the task while I am here."

Mariam smiled, "My husband is a scribe. He would

treat the story of Jesus as the Scripture, the Very Word of God."

Apollos nodded, "Was not the Apostle Mark filled with the Holy Spirit? Did not the Spirit bring all to his remembrance? Is not Jesus greater than the prophets? Brother Ezra is right. Mark's Gospel is Scripture!"

Priscilla smiled, "It is just as you say!"

After dinner, brother and sisters began to arrive for an evening of prayer, fellowship, and teaching. Aquilla warmly greeted each one asking prayer needs. He smiled with the happy and comforted the hurting. When all prayer requests were made known, he earnestly prayed. The love he bore for the brothers and sisters, his encouragement, his tears, and his petitions lifted hearts and renewed strength. When it came time for the teaching, Priscilla spoke. She spoke as a teacher of the law, with authority, and with the rhetorical skill of Roman orator.

As Ezra listened to her soaring exhortations, Apollos whispered in his ear, "Aquilla speaks in the synagogue, where no woman is permitted to teach—but here, among the brothers and sisters—well listen."

After a few minutes Ezra whispered to Apollos. "Truly a gift from the LORD. Aquilla is the heart and Priscilla his voice."

On the next Lord's Day, Ezra first read the Epistle of James and then the Gospel of Mark. The church of Ephesus, Jews, and Gentiles were astonished by what they heard. "Is it true?" One Greek brother cried out, "Some I have heard, but there is so much more, so much new!"

Apollos came forward and said, "Brothers and sisters in our Lord, you have heard the Apostle Mark's account.

Now allow me to show how the Scripture you have just heard, for that is what I now believe it to be, how the prophets foretell Mark's Gospel of Jesus."

He began with the Scriptures quoted by Peter on Pentecost and going through the Talmud and all the prophets, Apollos confirmed by the Scriptures what the Spirit told them in their hearts, that Jesus was the promised and long-awaited Messiah.

A Jewish brother standing for the reading raised his arms and said, "Truly it confirms all that Priscilla and you, Apollos, teach us about Jesus and the Prophets! We have His very words! Yes, it is as the Prophets are speaking. A great gift, indeed!"

Ezra came forward and lifted his arms, asking for quiet before speaking, "Brothers and sisters of Ephesus, you have heard the Good News of Jesus recorded by the Apostle Mark. And brother Apollos has proven how the Prophets spoke of Jesus as our Messiah. Consider how He is superior in every way. He is superior to all the prophets, for He was before them, and there is no end to His prophecy as He sends His Spirit to live within us. He is superior to every king, superior to David, whose throne He inherited. His Kingdom is forever. He said His Kingdom is not of this world; it is now a heavenly Kingdom until He comes again. He is the Son of God who sits on the throne, first promised to David. But He is more. Consider how He has fulfilled the Law. He alone has obeyed the Law. Christ is the end of the Law; its role is now complete. He has fulfilled the Law, and He has satisfied the Law. He is the lamb of God. His blood was shed for us. He has atoned for our sins. No longer will God accept the blood of lambs and bulls sacrificed on the great temple altar in Jerusalem. There is no need. Christ

257

has atoned for all our sins by His willing sacrifice. He was cursed and hung from a tree for us. And now He sits at the right hand of the Father. Christ intercedes for us with the Father in heaven. No High Priest can make the sacrifice Jesus made. No temple priest can intercede as does our Lord. Jesus is our High Priest. Do you say a priest must be a Levite? Before Moses was born. Before Aaron, there was another High Priest, Melchizedek, King of Salem and Priest of the God Most High. A man with no genealogy, a man greater than Father Abraham who brought his tithe to him and sought his blessing. A pries of God of High—not a priest by the descent of Blood. Jesus is such a High Priest. His sacrifice was perfect, and his blessings fall upon us. He intercedes for us. Brothers, Jesus is our perfect Prophet, Priest, and King!"

Ezra paused and read the faces of the believers, listening carefully. He lifted his arms and said, "Brothers and sisters, what does this mean? Have the priests stopped sacrificing at the altar? No. Has sin and evil been removed from our world? No. The Romans still occupy Jerusalem and enforce their Pax Romana throughout the known world. What does it matter that Jesus is our Messiah, Prophet, and Priest? Brothers and sisters, it means freedom. It means we are free from the condemnation of the Law. He has freed us from seeking salvation under the Law. He has granted us His salvation. A blessed salvation! But more. Yes, He gives us still more! He has called us His brothers, heirs with Him as children of God. And if we are brothers to the Great High Priest, then we too are a priesthood. We who bear His Law written on our hearts. We who have received His Spirit are joined with Christ as priests also, called to serve and intercede with our Heavenly Father. Such a gift, such a calling should not be taken lightly. Such great a salvation demands our all!"

A chorus of 'amens' rang through the assembly. Ezra nodded humbly and then said, "Now who among you will help us make careful copies that we share this Gospel with brothers and sisters everywhere?"

Chapter Twenty-Three

Mariam was happy. She treasured the time she spent with Ezra. She was proud of him. She saw him mature as all his many questions regarding the Law and the temple worship were answered. It was as if a veil was lifted, or a familiar face far in the distance was brought close and clearly recognized. The search he began with his mentor Baruch was complete. He understood his priesthood, and he was eager to share it with her and everyone who believes. She found the fellowship of Aquilla, Priscilla, and Apollos refreshing, full of hope and dedication. And Mariam found comfort in the night in the arms of the one man she loved. *Never,* she thought, *never again will we be separated.*

Ezra was surprised to learn how much he enjoyed overseeing eager brothers who carefully copied the

Gospel. He insisted on counting the words on each page and proofreading each text. Deep down he knew these copies would be copied again and again and before too long the text would be corrupted by errors, additions, and deletions. Admitting this to his friends, he declared, "Surely, even with the best of intentions, corrupted copies are certain to be made. I hope that the many faithful and true copies maintain the true word is carried to all people."

It was Priscilla who opined, "Brother Ezra, may the Lord reward your diligence! I look for His return before any error may occur."

Aquilla gave Apollos more and more time to preach and teach in the fellowship and in homes of Gentiles, still allowing Priscilla the opportunity for summation and admonition for commitment and application in life. Evenings were a warm time of sharing around the supper table. Mariam and Ezra cherished the quiet time with their new friends. Apollos sought advice from Priscilla on his efforts. During one such critique, Aquilla turned to Ezra and Mariam and said, "I think she has found a disciple. My wife spent many happy hours first listening and then joining the teachers and debaters of rhetoric. Oh, rhetoric is highly regarded in Rome. To many Romans, the rhetoric is more valued than the truth of the argument. It is all about persuasion."

Ezra nodded, "Truly, Priscilla is most persuasive to the truth. Jesus is truth!"

Aquilla smiled, "Happily, it is just as you say."

Mariam cleared her throat, interrupting the side conversation between Priscilla and Apollos. "Priscilla, please explain to Ezra and me your use of rhetoric in preaching."

Apollos stopped speaking and smiled, "Please, Priscilla share your secrets!"

Priscilla laughed, "Shall I give away all of my secrets to Apollos? Where would I be?"

She smiled and nodded, "Good rhetoric persuades the listener. I have found I am most persuasive when I remember my words must be pleasant and memorable to the ear. Perhaps poetic or like waves of the sea both ascending and descending. They must engage the mind offering new insight—a new perspective to the mind's eye. And most importantly, they must touch the heart, for in the end it is the heart that persuades us."

"A contest!" Mariam smiled brightly. "A contest between you and Apollos! Do you agree, Apollos?"

Apollos smiled his eyes bright with excitement, "Yes! Let me use Priscilla's advice. What shall we discuss?"

Priscilla replied, "In the end it is not the speaker of the beauty of the words, but the Holy Spirit that calls the hearer unto Himself."

Mariam nodded and said, "Sister Priscilla, is not your gift from God? All wisdom is His. Let us see what Apollos has learned."

Aquilla raised his arms and looked at each friend around his table. "I should like you both to expound, first Priscilla one statement followed by the Apollos' statement, persuade us of the love of Christ!"

Priscilla leaned over and kissed Aquilla's cheek. "I know how dear the love of Christ is to you, husband. And I must confess, Apollos, that I may have an advantage over you as I have heard brother Paul the Apostle preach on the love of Christ but let us each do our best!"

As Priscilla began, Mariam moved close against Ezra, laid her head against his shoulder, and squeezed his arm.

One morning as Ezra was supervising his cadre of newly trained scribes, Aquilla returned to the house with a visitor. Aquilla called out, "Ezra, a messenger for Mariam and you from Nicopolis."

Mariam, hearing from the kitchen dropped what she was doing and ran out to the courtyard, wiping her hands as she hurried. "News for me? From Nicopolis? Is it Papa? Is all well?"

The downcast face of the messenger told her it was bad news, "It is Papa! She screamed, "Please tell me!"

Now Ezra was beside her, an arm about her waist, "Speak up, friend. What news?"

The man looked up, his face sober, "Your father, Nathan, has been arrested by the Romans and carried off to prison. He is accused... He is accused of..."

Ezra shouted, "Out with it! Accused of what?"

"He is accused as a bandit. Zealots. Zealots attacked a Roman messenger on the road to Joppa. It was a trap. The Romans were watching and waiting in the hills. They followed and captured them in Nathan's tent at his fields."

Mariam screamed, "No! No! Lord please, this cannot be!"

Ezra pressed the messenger further, "Nathan is no Zealot. Certainly, no bandit. He lives in the city. His villa is not yet rebuilt. Why arrest him?"

"Brother, it was his servants. His servants were among the Zealots. They used his tents and fields as a refuge for Zealots — a place to hide their weapons. The Romans searched quite thoroughly and confirmed this. They insisted Nathan permitted this. They say he is a Zealot himself. He was taken away in chains."

Ezra shook. He closed his eyes and snorted. Composing himself, he asked, "Where did they take him?"

The frightened messenger replied, "They did not say. But they took the road towards Joppa."

Mariam was crying, shaking, and sobbing. Ezra squeezed her tight and said, "There is no prison in Joppa. They took him to the prison at Caesarea. That is where we will find him."

Ezra nodded to the young man, "Thank you, brother, for coming. Please forgive us — the shock. Now take refreshment and rest. Mariam and I will prepare to leave at once. Our God is sovereign. His will be done!"

Aquilla sent for Priscilla and Apollos, and they arrived before Mariam and Ezra had finished gathering their things. "I am going with you," Apollos announced. "As a Roman citizen and one familiar with Roman law, I insist on going with you."

"God will go with us," Ezra replied. You have your work here."

"God has brought us together, brother, perhaps for a time such as this. My cousin's name still carries weight among the Romans. No. I will have it no other way. Mariam can wait here or perhaps Nicopolis…"

"I am going to find my Papa. I will not wait in suffering and doubt. I am going."

Ezra turned and stared at Apollos.

Apollos insisted, "It is decided then, we all go. Let me find a fast ship to Caesarea. I will send for you at once." Apollos immediately ran out the gate towards the harbor.

When Ezra and Mariam had bundled their things together, they found Aquilla patiently sitting with the young messenger from Nicopolis. "Stephen and I were about to pray. You and Mariam are most welcome to join us."

Mariam sat down and smiled, "You are Stephen, son of Joel, president of the synagogue. Thank you for coming, Stephen. Was the voyage difficult? Do wish to return with us by way of Caesarea or stay and rest here. Brother Aquilla and his wife Priscilla are very gracious. You would find time spent with them most rewarding."

Aquilla smiled, "You are most welcome, Stephen. Rest a few days and return to Joppa. It would save you from a dangerous walk from Caesarea."

Stephen smiled bravely, "I am not afraid. But perhaps a ship to Joppa would be easier."

Ezra nodded, "Give our blessings to your father and all the brothers and sisters in Nicopolis. Ask them to remember us in their prayers. And forgive me for my anger..."

Stephen shook his head, "O no master Ezra. I know your anger is not with me. I am honored to have been sent to you."

The late summer winds, although they were light were westerly, and the ship sailed on a comfortable reach directly to Caesarea. The ship entered the large man-made Sebastos harbor between two jetties built out into the Great Sea. Safely inside the breakwater, hundreds of ships could securely anchor while waiting for cargo or passengers to load or unload on the wharves and jetty. Built by Herod the Great, the city of Caesarea was named in honor of Augustus Caesar. It was in every way, a Roman city. The palace of the Procurator of Judea, formerly the palace of Herod the Great, was built on a promontory jutting into the sea, reminiscent of the island Ptolemy Palace in Alexandria. Caesarea was both the Roman capital and a major military stronghold. The city was known for its gladiatorial games that were held every four years.

Apollos led Ezra and Mariam directly to the house of Philip the Evangelist, once a deacon in Jerusalem, now leader of the church in Caesarea. Philip immediately recognized Mariam from their days serving the widows, and he greeted her warmly, "Sister Mariam! God be praised! You are well?"

Philip kissed both cheeks of Mariam as she introduced Ezra and Apollos. "Brother Philip, we come here on urgent business. My father, a good man, and believer, stands accused as a bandit, a Zealot and we believe he is now in the prison of the fortress."

Philip sighed, "That is hard news, sister. Hard news, indeed! If only Centurion Cornelius were still with us. The soldiers and the guards honored him as a Roman and man of great honor. Still, there are other brothers among the legions."

Apollos interrupted, "Brother Philip, first we must confirm that Nathan, for that is his name, that Nathan is indeed here. We need to know his well-being and the status of his case. Then I would ask the name of the Commander of the prison and the Garrison. My cousin is the Roman, Tiberius, once procurator of Judea now the military commander for Quadratus, Legate of Syria. Quadratus is overseer to Ventidius Cumanus, Procurator of Judea. I hope to enlist my cousin's help in this cause."

Philip stared at Apollos, but his thoughts were elsewhere; finally, he motioned, "Please, sister and brothers, sit. Where are my manners?"

Philip sighed and continued, "It is a hard time in Judea. So many killed in the riot at the temple..."

Mariam answered, "I was there. Both my father and me. Only by the grace of God did we live. So many dead."

Philip nodded, "The people will not forget what happened that day. But then there was the murder of pilgrims to the temple by a Samaritan mob. Justice was demanded, but Cumanus did nothing. More discontent. More riots. The Romans carry many off to prison. Already he has crucified James and Simon the sons of Judas the Zealot. The Chief Priest, Ananias, received no assurances from Cumanus, he has petitioned Quadratus and the emperor for justice,"

Apollos replied, "Cumanus will be dangerous. Rome will not countenance too much unrest."

Philip folded his hands under his chin. "I know a brother, a Roman in the garrison. I will send for him tomorrow. In the meantime, we shall pray."

The Roman brother arranged for Apollos, an important Roman citizen, to meet with the Officer of the prison guards. The prison commander was wise enough to recognize the careful treatment of prisoners with friends in high places, but also aware of the danger of releasing political prisoners. He agreed to receive Apollos of Alexandria.

Mariam was not permitted to enter the prison compound. She was told it was not an appropriate place for a woman, but she would be allowed to wait in the shaded courtyard just outside the iron strapped gate. A soldier escorted Apollos and Ezra through a courtyard surrounded by stone walls, three stories high, with barred gates leading to the darkness inside. In the middle of the courtyard was a large post rising from a small platform. Chains hung from an iron collar at the top of the post. The cobblestone floor beneath and around the whipping post was wet with puddles in the low spots and near a floor drain.

The prison commander was seated in a room opposite the gate, open to the courtyard. Everything that happened in the yard was within his view. The commander, Flavius, stood when Apollos was introduced. His everyday leather armor and short sword told Apollos that this was no place to stand on ceremony.

Flavius greeted him, "Apollos of Alexandria? Is it true you are a cousin to Tiberius Julius?"

"You are well informed. It is as you say."

"Flavius. I am Flavius. Please, sit and perhaps a cup of wine? And this is?"

"My name is Ezra ben Haggai of Jerusalem, son-in-law to Nathan ben Joseph from Nicopolis. We believe he was brought here by mistake."

"Everyone brought here believes it to be a mistake. I can assure you, Ezra of Jerusalem, we don't often make mistakes."

Flavius poured a cup of wine and handed it to Apollos, "Tell me, Apollos, what is your interest in this man?"

"I am acquainted with his family. An honorable and prosperous family, not given to politics and certainly not a bandit or Jewish Zealot. I seek to know his well-being and plead for his release. Can you tell me if he is indeed here?"

"I do not release prisoners without authority. Ventidus Cumanus is Procurator of Judea. He has authority over Nicopolis and Jerusalem. Do you believe you can persuade the Procurator?"

"Perhaps I can persuade those who can persuade the

Procurator."

"You speak of your cousin, Tiberius no doubt. Tiberius is no longer procurator of Judea. He is in service to Quadratus the Legate of Syria."

"Indeed. And Quadratus has authority over Cumanus. So, tell me Flavius, is Nathan prisoner here? I wish to know his health."

Flavius put down his wine cup and stood up. "Come back tomorrow. I will make inquiries and tell you then. The guard will show you out."

The next day Apollos, Ezra, and Mariam returned to the fortress prison. Again. Mariam was told to wait outside. Apollos and Ezra were escorted across the courtyard to the Commander's room. There seated on a crude wooden stool, sat Nathan, slumped over and his head down. He was dressed in a clean robe, washed and his gray hair combed. He did not look up as Apollos and Ezra were introduced.

"Is this the man you seek?" Flavius asked.

Ezra knelt beside Nathan and tenderly lifted his head. The bruised face with the black, closed and swollen eyes was that of Nathan. Ezra fought back tears as he nodded, "Yes, this is Nathan."

Nathan did not respond. He sat motionless, barely breathing.

"As you see, he is alive and well. Out of respect for Tiberius, a good Roman officer, I will see that he is well cared for…"

Ezra stood up, his eyes on fire, "Well cared for? He has been beaten to the edge of death!"

Flavius let him finish, with no emotion in his voice he continued, "I will see that the prisoner is well cared for, and I will delay his trial until you, Apollos, return. I know

270

Tiberius. He is a hard man and well respected by his soldiers. He is not one to grant favors. But I will wait."

Then turning to Ezra, Flavius said, "He is well treated here. Bandits know their fate if they are captured. This is what happens when they resist."

Apollos smiled weakly, "Thank you, Flavius. I shall not be long in returning. I have one small request of you. Nathan's daughter, his only child, waits outside. I ask she be permitted a short visit with her father."

Flavius nodded, "Guard, escort the woman... what is her name?"

"Mariam"

"Escort Mariam here."

When Mariam saw Nathan, she cried out, "Papa," ran to him and threw her arms around him. "Papa. Papa, It's me, Mariam. All will be well Papa. All will be well."

Nathan slowly raised his head, and tears could be seen flowing from beneath his puffy purple unopened eyes.

Chapter Twenty-Four

The three day sail up the coast from Caesarea to Antioch, capital of the Roman Province of Syria was helped by a favorable beam wind. The pilot was careful to stay well offshore aware of the dangers of being driven onto the lee shore at night. Only when the tall cone of Mount Cassius came into sight did the pilot steer the stout cargo ship around the mountain into a river which flowed behind the base to the south. Antioch was a long day's sail up the river even with the crew pulling on oars. The land along the river at the foot the tall mountain range was green, fertile, and well-watered. The narrow plateau along the shore was patchwork green with garden vegetables of every variety. Further up the slopes of the mountains, olives, figs, and vineyards spoke of a luxuriant verdant land.

The harbor of Seluceia served Antioch. It was a busy port which connected with caravan routes east to Persia. The city was built by the Greeks four hundred years earlier and improved first by King Agrippa then Herod the Great who paved four miles of the main colonnaded street along the river with marble. The Romans added to its beauty great public buildings, a hippodrome near the palace on an island in the river. The amphitheater and massive library faced them from across the channel. A temple to Apollos retained a prominent place in the center of the city. Antioch's pleasant climate, the abundance of fresh vegetables, food, and strategic location made it an ideal capital and military base protecting the empire from invasion from the east.

The citizens of Antioch disparagingly referred to the followers of Jesus as 'Christians.' The believers soon gladly accepted the title, and it carried from Antioch to believers throughout the Roman world. Apollos knew Antioch. He had been here before. He knew the Christians had long since severed any relationship with the synagogue and met separately in houses of its leaders. Apollos led Ezra to the home of a Gentile believer, a man named Jason, with whom he had stayed before.

Jason greeted him warmly, "Brother Apollos! Welcome! And your friend?"

"This Ezra from Jerusalem. It is good to see you again, my friend! Is all well with the fellowship?"

"We grow in numbers daily! God continues to bless us! Come in! Come in and be refreshed. Wine and some fruit? How long will you be in Antioch? You will stay here, of course!"

Apollos and Ezra followed Jason into the quiet

courtyard of his house. "We come on urgent business. We seek an audience with Tiberius Julius Alexander, military commander under Quadratus. He is my relative, and we seek his help in righting an injustice. Tell me, does he quarter at the island palace or in the citadel on the mountain?"

Jason was surprised, "Tiberius is a hard man. Not a friend to Christian or Jew. He is your relative?"

"A cousin. I know he is a hard man and one not known to grant favors, but perhaps out of respect for our fathers in Alexandria, he will hear me."

Jason sighed, "A subordinate commands the citadel. Though Tiberius visits there often, it is said he sometimes seeks distance from the Legate Quadratus. But he is quartered in the palace. A Roman brother, a centurion at the citadel, may be able to help you."

Two days later, Tiberius responded to the letter the centurion carried from Apollos. He and Ezra made their way to the citadel in the western wall on the side of Mount Silpius. Apollos presented the pass given him and followed the guard to a room inside the thick stone walls of the tower which dominated the massive fortress. Inside the well-lighted space, a Roman general in a linen tunic and scarlet cloak and wearing white armor trimmed in gold sat in a leather strapped oak chair. A small table beside him held a bowl of wine, drinking cup, dates, and grapes.

"I've been expecting you cousin," the general said as Apollos was led into the room.

"Flavius wrote to me of your visit. You should know, cousin, that your visit is a waste of your time and mine. I see you only out of respect for our fathers."

Apollos bowed and looking up smiled, "But I have

come, and you have received me, so allow me to have my say."

Apollos looked around and said, "You would not allow your cousin to sit? You do not welcome him and his friend?"

Tiberius laughed and commanded a guard, "Two chairs for my visitors!"

Once seated Apollos began, "Cousin I do not come here for my benefit, or even for the justice deserving my friend Ezra's father-in-law. I know you are not one to grant favors. Cousin, I come because you know Judea and the troubles there. You have heard of the petition that the High Priest makes to Legate Quadratus. You see the benefit of keeping peace in Judea. The Emperor is likely to remember those who keep small troubles from growing."

"You say these cases are related, cousin?"

Apollos smiled as said, "Listen and judge for yourself. The man Nathan was arrested because he owned a villa used by bandits. I need not tell you these so-called 'bandits' were Zealots. The Zealots have been fighting the rulers of Judea since the days of the Greeks. Their desire—and it is madness—they desire to rid all of Judea of foreign rulers and restore the Kingdom of Israel."

Tiberius nodded, "Of course, You tell me nothing new."

Apollos continued, "The Zealots seek a messiah. A Jewish King to rule. The accused man, Nathan ben Joseph, or Nathan of Nicopolis, could never be such a man. He is a wealthy man. He is a Levite—his family is Sadducee. Such men—such families—do not find their interests served by riot and rebellion."

Tiberius replied tersely, "He had a motive! Zealots used

276

his villa and fields in the past. They were burned to the ground! Revenge is a strong passion! He joined the Zealot cause."

Apollos nodded and smiled, "Nathan was away. He was living in Jerusalem. His villa in the hands of servants—servants who betrayed him. There is more you must know of Nathan. He is a Christian, a most devout follower of Jesus..."

"As you are my cousin. So that is your interest in this man!"

Apollos continued to smile, "You know of the Christians. You know they do not seek a messiah to rule over Israel. They have found the Messiah, and He rules in Heaven. Christians have no dealings with Zealots but to convince them to follow Jesus as well, submitting to authority as they do."

Tiberius sat back and stretched his neck. He sighed and then said, "Flavius writes that a neighbor accused this Nathan of Nicopolis. He reports Nathan knew of the Zealots and was in league with them."

Ezra shouted, "Which neighbor?"

Tiberius stared at Ezra for several seconds, looked at the letter beside him, and said, "Asa. Neighbor to Nathan in Nicopolis."

Ezra snorted, "Asa. I have heard of this man. He tried to force his way on the daughter of Nathan. He had offered them his hospitality when they returned to find their home destroyed. When he would have his way with her, she fled his house and they never returned. The man is... what man violates our law of hospitality on a woman under his roof!"

Tiberius continued to stare at Ezra as he thought. Apollos interrupted. "Ezra is husband to Mariam, the daughter of Nathan. Surely you understand his response. But cousin, there is more you do not know. More that Flavius did not report. Nathan ben Joseph is a member of the Sanhedrin. Would such a man conspire with Zealots? Should an elder of Israel be dragged off in chains, and beaten near to the point of death, with no notice to the Chief Priest? Procurator Cumanus ignores the chief priests and the Sanhedrin. He fills his prisons with Jews while Samaritans murder Jewish pilgrims on their way to the Temple. You are the military commander. Are you ready to petition Caesar for more legions to put down a revolt in Judea? What would Quadratus say if he knew you withheld your counsel?"

Tiberius looked up, his mind racing. "I know where to find you, cousin."

Ezra and Apollos returned to the home of Demetrius. That night, Ezra read the Gospel of Mark to the Christians gathered. Apollos listened attentively and then preached persuasively on the topic: 'Christ, the Servant.' Remembering the lessons of Priscilla, he argued how Mark's Gospel demonstrated the service of Christ the servant, the sanctification of Christ the servant and the success of Christ, the servant. He finished with a challenge, "Brothers, sisters if you have not yet believed that Jesus is the Christ, the Messiah sent from the Father, you have heard the evidence. Now is the time to listen to the Spirit speaking to your spirit. Believe. Ask Jesus to forgive your sins, and He will hear your prayer in heaven, forgive your sins, and send His Spirit. If any here hears this word, come. Be baptized in the name Jesus. And to my brothers and sisters, Christians of Antioch, the message of Mark's Gospel to you is one of obedience. If we love God, we must obey His commands. Jesus said,

'Be Holy as I am Holy.' Jesus took the form of a servant. How can we be greater than Him? Christians of Antioch, I am called—we are called to be servants like Him. Serving sacrificially knowing that He brings the success."

The following morning, Quadratus, Roman Legate of Syria summoned Apollos and Ezra to the palace.

The house meeting in Caesarea was crowded with refugees from Jerusalem. Many others had come, curious to see if the four prophets, daughters, of Philip the Evangelist, would prophesy. Philip always allowed any brother or sister to speak a word. He lifted his arms to call the fellowship to order. He prayed, "Father God, bless these Your children. Bless this time of worship. Send Your Holy Spirit to lead us into your truth. May Jesus Christ be praised to the Glory of God our Father. We pray in the name of Jesus, Son of God, Amen. Lifting his head, Philip asked, "Brothers and sisters is there a Word from the Lord this evening? Now is the time to share."

At once, his four daughters, prophets of God, stood. Irais spoke first, "The Lord sends His word to our sister Mariam."

Eutychus closed her eyes and said, "God has heard your prayers and the prayers of your father, Nathan. Nathan's wounds are healed, and his pain forgotten."

Chariline looked straight out and said, "Brother Nathan shall be released and live out his days in peace."

Hermione lifted her head, eyes closed and said softly, "The Lord will bless Nathan with the desire of his heart."

Mariam wept.

Apollos and Ezra were instructed by Tiberius Julius to

wait in the house of Philip in Caesarea. The day they arrived back in Caesarea, they heard a soldier had come for them earlier that same day, commanding them to appear before Flavius at the fortress prison. Dropping their bags, Apollos said, "Pray for us brothers. We shall not delay but go at once."

Ezra hugged Mariam tightly. He smiled at her warmly. Saying nothing, he followed Apollos out the gate.

As they approached the gate to the fortress, Apollos and Ezra passed four men hanging from Roman crosses. Apollos bowed his head as they passed. Glancing up, Ezra recognized the servants of Nathan, bodies slumped and hanging limp. Their eyes were closed, their heads hanging in pain, chins against their chests. One, groaning in agony pushed with his feet to gasp for air before collapsing once more. "God be merciful. Have mercy on their souls," Ezra prayed as he walked past.

The guard at the prison gate was expecting Apollos. He led Apollos and Ezra across the courtyard to Flavius, seated alone in his customary place, his wine, and fruit set beside him.

Flavius spoke as they approached, "Apollos. Ezra. Word from the Legate Quadratus. He has chosen to intervene. Events in Judea concern him. There is too much unrest in Judea. He fears Tiberius Julius may require another Legion at a minimum if the order is not restored soon. Quadratus has heard the Procurator and Ananias your High Priest. He orders them to the Emperor himself. Claudius will hear the petitions of the Jews."

Apollos asked, "You have summoned me to hear of the petitions of the High Priest?"

Flavius studied Apollos' face carefully and said, "No. There is more. He tells me the Zealots, for that is his word for them, the Zealots guilty of rebellion and crime against Rome should be crucified."

Flavius paused. He took a deep breath, still contemplating the two men before him. He turned to a guard and called out, "Bring the man."

A few moments later, the guard returned with Nathan. He was dressed in a clean white toga. His face clean. His hair combed, and his eyes open. Flavius looked at Nathan and said, "Nathan of Nicopolis, you are free to go. Be more careful in the selection of your servants."

That night there was great rejoicing in the house of Philip. Nathan repeated over and over, "I never lost faith! The pain passes soon, but God's love is forever!"

Chapter Twenty-Five

Philip chose the quiet of the morning to spend time alone in prayer and meditation. Apollos did not disturb Philip but found another quiet place in the courtyard. When Philip completed his prayers and walked over to his breakfast table, Apollos spoke softly. "Brother, I have something for the church. Ezra and I carry back copies of letters from brother Paul. Letters to the churches in Galatia and Thessalonica. They are helpful to all Christians as we are called in Antioch."

Philip took the letters and began to read. After a few moments, he set them down, and replied, "I shall indeed study them. I—we shall teach what our brother Paul teaches for truly, brother Paul is an apostle called by God."

Apollos smiled, "It is as you say, brother. Ezra was

most excited by Paul's strong teaching on faith in his letter to the Galatians. Paul explains that our justification by faith alone goes back through all time to father Abraham. He does not contradict what James the Just commands regarding righteous living rather, Paul explains it is faith alone that brings God's salvation to us, and faith that takes root in our very soul yielding good work through a renewed spirit."

Philip smiled nodding, then turned as asked, "And the letters to the Thessalonians?"

"He addresses some concerns peculiar to beliefs among some of them concerning the 'Day of the Lord.' But there is much else to commend his instruction."

Philip smiled, "We shall add brother Paul's letters to Mark's Gospel and James' letter."

"Ezra is most insistent on copying the letters, most carefully. He is, by training, a scribe. Ezra's heart is to share the Gospel and letters of the Apostles with all who believe. He regards them as coming from God just as the words of the prophets were recorded. He would regard them as Scripture."

As Apollos and Philip were talking, Ezra and Mariam entered. Ezra greeted them joyfully, "Brothers! Is this not the Lord's day? Has he not been gracious and loving? His mercy endures forever!"

Philip smiled, "Brother Ezra, sister Mariam. Indeed, the Lord is good! Apollos has just given me Paul's letters that you carried from Antioch. Be assured, brother, that we will copy them carefully, share them widely, and teach them confidently!"

Mariam put her arm around Ezra's waist, "Brother Philip, you bring great joy to my husband. But I ask that you do not keep him long here in Caesarea, for I long to return to Nicopolis with my father and share the good news of my father's release with our brothers and sisters still praying for us."

Apollos nodded and said, "And I must return to Alexandria. Mark the Evangelist still awaits my mission to the Copts, the Egyptians of the upper Nile. Ezra was to journey with me."

Ezra sat down. "The mission. I gave my word to Mark—I was to return. And Peter has affirmed the mission as well. I have delayed too long—So much has happened. Mark desired a brother without the speech and dress of Greek Alexandria go to the Copts. Greeks and the Alexandrians have badly treated them. I have been most selfish."

Ezra burried his face buried in his hands. Mariam knelt beside him, "Husband, the delay is not your fault. You have not forsaken your word, and I shall never require it of you. You must go with Apollos. Go and do as Mark has asked."

Ezra looked up, "Will you come with me? I cannot part from you. I have waited so long, and I find such comfort in your presence."

Mariam replied softly, "And I praise God for each day I share with you. But we are now one. We have been joined in body and spirit. Though we are apart, we are still one. Husband, you must go. I will see father home and wait in Nicopolis for your return."

Ezra sat silently. Mariam continued, "But Nathan is well. He is strong again. Surely, he loves you and would see you happy with your husband. Has he not said so many times?"

Mariam kissed Ezra and added, "Indeed God has saved him. Allow me to bless him, as well. I fear his years grow short. Go with Apollos but do not tarry too long and return to me."

The church in Nicopolis rejoiced to see Nathan return safely with Mariam. The fellowship reported all that happened in the weeks they were gone. Nathan's fields were tended, his groves and vineyard pruned and the reconstruction of his barns and house continued. Hugging each brother and sister, Nathan could not hold back the tears of joy he shed for the friends he dearly loved.

Mariam, too, was greeted with warm hugs and kisses, "But where is Ezra?" They asked her.

"My husband returns to Egypt with Apollos of Alexandria. He has given his word to Mark the Evangelist to make a mission to the upper Nile and bring the Good News to the Copts, the ancient people of Egypt."

Nathan spoke up, "My son-in-law has not forgotten you, friends. He has sent along copies of letters from brother Paul to churches in Galatia and Thessalonica. We add these to Mark's Gospel and James the Just's letter. I give them to you, Joel, leader of our church. Perhaps this Lord's Day, you will read them and comment on Paul's lesson."

Joel accepted the letters and smiled, "A blessing indeed! Let me read them and consider the lesson. Then, of course, we shall endeavor to make accurate copies, just as Ezra has instructed us. But come, we wish to show you the progress on your house and fields. We shall make it a celebration of God's great gift to you and us, brother. He has heard our prayers, the prayers of many, blessed be His name!"

Nathan and Mariam were surprised by joy to see

Nathan's house nearly complete. Nathan stopped at the gate and turned to Joel, "Brother, how? So much has been done! How can I repay you? I see so many workers!" Joel smiled, "Brother, you repay us with your love and fellowship. Repay us by doing as we do in obedience to our Lord, who commands us to love one another. Your fields and vineyards are healthy, your cisterns full. You should have a good crop. You will be able to find new servants, faithful—perhaps from among the brothers. Now let me show you the barns."

Mariam's heart was warmed yet she longed for Ezra. She missed having him beside her at night. But she found joy in knowing that he was obedient to God's call in his life. Though they were apart, she knew they remained one in spirit.

Mariam and Nathan were only in Nicopolis a few days when Mariam woke up feeling ill.

Mark warmly received Apollos and Ezra. Ezra delivered the letters of to the churches Paul had established and eagerly told Mark of the growing effort to spread Mark's account, his gospel, to all the churches. Mark's Gospel and the letters of James and Paul were being read, discussed, and taught throughout the Roman world.

Apollos shared the fervency of Christians in Antioch and Caesarea, while Ezra reported on Jerusalem and Nicopolis. Both were eager to take the Good News. They carried many copies of the Gospel and letters bound for Egyptians in the upper Nile.

"I shall not delay you, brothers," Mark declared. We shall set about copying the letters. It warms my heart to see you returned. The church in Alexandria grows by the day. We have become many! I spend my days training leaders who host the faithful and offer the Lord's Supper. Our numbers are far too great for all to meet in one place. And I have been delaying my return to Pentopolis, my home in Cyrene. The brothers there plead for my return. They desire that I preach and instruct."

"Truly, many of our people are answering the voice of the Holy Spirit and putting their faith in Jesus! Apollos replied.

Mark nodded, smiling, and replied, "More and more are Greeks, Apollos. No longer Jews, but Greek! And it is all the more urgent you go to the Copts!"

Apollos and Ezra were soon aboard a Nile riverboat slowly making its way up the current. Their first stop was Heliopolis, at the fork to the eastern branch of the Nile into the vast Nile delta. The city, once a great center of learning and the royal depository of records of the pharaohs was now little more than a village, bypassed by the times and traders. The once great and influential Temple to Ra-Atum, the god of the sun, still dominated the city. The market was small and shabby. The town now populated with priests trying hard to hold onto their tradition, and Arabs, shepherds, and merchants carrying good from the Red Sea. The newcomers had moved into the long-abandoned houses on the outskirts of the city. The Romans maintained a small outpost collecting taxes on the goods coming from the Red Sea that may have by-passed Memphis. They monitored the boat traffic recording the destination of cargoes and boats that could disappear in the many channels of the Nile delta.

Ezra was surprised to see the foundations of once-great structures still standing in the vacant city center. "Bases for Obelisks and columns," Apollos explained. "They have been taken to Alexandria and Rome itself.

Only the foundations remain. And look at the Temple of Ra-Atum. Never a favorite after the Ptolemies conquered Egypt. Oh, the priests try to preserve the old worship, but the peeling paint and leaking roof tell you all you need to know. The temple has more feral cats than priest and worshippers. The Egyptians and even the Greeks have long ago deserted. A few still find work when the priests find the money or the Romans seek servants. The Arabs, a few bring trade goods and the others, well the others have nothing but sheep."

Ezra nodded and took a deep breath, "Well, our Lord has commanded us to make disciples of all nations. It is not for us to overlook any, whether rich or poor, weak or powerful. Let us find a gathering and preach!"

The two spent a month in Heliopolis. The son of a priest of Ra-Atum, and two Egyptians, servants in Roman households, heard the Good News and led by the Spirit believed and were baptized. Apollos and Ezra taught them daily from the Scriptures and left them a copy of Mark's Gospel, the letter from James' and each of Paul's letters, Apollos promised to visit them again on their return.

Not far south of Heliopolis was the city of Memphis, the first large trading city above the many branches into the delta, where the river became one large channel. Apollos swept his outstretched arm across the cityscape, "It was here in Memphis that Alexander the Great was crowned Pharaoh of Egypt. The Romans still maintain a large garrison. The citizens are diverse, with many Greeks, Jews, Arabs, and Copts. My uncle, Alexander the Alabarch of Alexandria's second son, Marcus Julius, brother of General Tiberius Julius, maintains a palace here. Memphis is second in Egypt only to Alexandria in importance and in the collection of taxes which cousin Marcus, chief tax collector, oversees."

Ezra stood scanning the ancient city, more than three thousand years old when the Romans first marched in. He listened as Apollos continued, "It was the first capital of Egypt and never lost its prominence. Even when middle kingdom Pharaohs moved their capital to Thebes, Memphis remained the center of Egyptian commerce and art. It remained the first city of Egypt until the Greek conquerors established Alexandria."

Memphis was a city of temples, statues, sculptures, and overwhelming Egyptian architecture. The massive buildings were brightly painted with distinctive Egyptian writing, murals of victorious pharaohs mounted in chariots leading massive armies, protected by the gods they worshipped. It was nothing like Alexandria. It was thirty-one centuries of Egyptian glory and history. The great pyramids outside the city matched the sights of the cityscape. Stepping off the boat, Ezra could only exclaim, "Now we are in Egypt!"

Apollos nodded, "This was once Egypt, and certainly some Copts remain, but the Greeks and the Romans have become comfortable here. Most true Egyptians, the Copts, live further south. There is a small synagogue. Perhaps we should start there. My cousin, Marcus Julius, rarely uses his villa here. He stays in Alexandria where the sea breeze fends off the great heat. Perhaps the servants will remember me."

Ezra looked at Apollos, shook his head, and laughed, "You are not a man one forgets!"

Apollos was immediately recognized and welcomed into the home of his cousin. "Master Apollos, your cousin, Master Marcus, will regret missing you. But as he has often said you are always welcome here."

"Stepping out of the gate and looking into the street, the servant asked, "Just the two of you, master Apollos? Your steward and servants? Are they yet at the boat with trade goods? How many shall I expect?"

Apollos smiled, "Just me and my friend Ezra this time Quintus. Different business this trip. If you will see to our things, we will wash and immediately go to the synagogue."

"Certainly, master Apollos. Can I expect you at the table this evening? Sunset?"

"You are most attentive, Quintus. Yes, we shall come to the table at sunset."

The synagogue appeared Egyptian on the outside, except the brightly painted murals were distinctly Jewish. Inside was a smaller, more welcoming copy of the Great Synagogue in Alexandria. The entrance of two Jewish strangers to the outer court caught the attention of the men there. "News brothers? Do you bring us news or perhaps a word?"

Apollos, began, "I bring news of the salvation of our God. I bring good news of the long-awaited Messiah, Jesus Christ, Son of God..."

The small group around Apollos began to grow as he preached. A voice spoke, "Amen brother, we have heard this news!"

The man said, "Are you a disciple of Joseph of Leontopolis? For he preaches this man Jesus."

Ezra smiled, "Joseph of Leontopolis? Once a priest of the Temple Onias?"

"He is the man."

"Indeed, a good man and brother in the Lord! Tell me, who leads the Jesus followers in Memphis?"

Another man stepped forward, "I am Michael, the fellowship meets in my house. Welcome brothers. There are not many here who believe as we do and none so skilled in the Law and the Prophets as Joseph."

Apollos nodded, "Michael, I am Apollos of Alexandria, and the is Ezra of Jerusalem, a priest, a scribe and a teacher of the Law. My friend Ezra brought the truth of Jesus to Joseph in Leontopolis. We would be honored to share in your fellowship."

The fellowship meeting in the house of Michael included Jews and God-fearing Greeks and Romans. The God-fearers were attracted to the monotheism and the ancient religion of the Hebrews. Apollos became deeply involved in teaching, arguing from Scripture and the new writings of Mark and the Apostles. Ezra recruited several Roman and Greek brothers to preach in the agora and the library among citizens debating the philosophies of the day. Philo of Alexandria was much respected throughout Egypt, and Ezra often used his argument for one God to begin his preaching.

New believers were added to the church in Memphis. Many Greek and Romans joined, and soon, a second and third house church was needed. Ezra turned over the ministry to the Greeks and Romans to Michael and determined he would preach to the Copts. Apollos circulated among the churches, teaching and building up the body. Apollos often joined in the preaching among the philosophers, distinguishing himself in Memphis for persuasive rhetoric and fervent faith.

Ezra visited the gate to the market. It was the place laborers would wait to be hired. He spoke with a young man waiting, "Tell me, friend, what is your skill?"

The young man smiled, "What skill do you require

master?"

"A guide to help me during my visit. One fluent in the language of the Copts and perhaps the Arabs."

"Certainly, I am your man! Tell me, master, why do you wish to speak with Copts? Greek is the language of the market. Even the Romans speak Greek here. The Copts have nothing to trade."

Ezra smiled, "What is your name?"

"I am Abanoud."

"Abanoud, my name is Ezra. Tell me, do all Copts speak Greek as you do? Be truthful Abanoud, for I still need a servant."

"Indeed, Master Ezra, most speak Greek, or they can find no work other than in the fields or building for the Romans."

"Show me where the Copts live. Tell me the wage they require."

"Come, master Ezra, I will show my house. You will see other Copts as well. Wage? We have learned to live without. There is always some grain and vegetables or fish that we find. But coins are good. We buy when we have them."

"You find grain, vegetables, and fish?"

"Well, not me, but others. I am clever with language. I work for coins."

Ezra was led down a narrow street of low, small, mud brick houses. Abanoud stopped in front of one and opened a curtain across the doorway. A woman nursed an infant while two small, skinny children sat beside her. "My mother. You may tell her I am now your servant. Tell her you will pay Abanoud with coins."

Ezra tried to smile, but his eyes betrayed his pity. "I have hired, Abanoud as my servant. He will be well treated and permitted to come home to you. Do the children eat raisin cakes?"

The woman looked up at Ezra and said nothing. She bowed her head and continued to nurse.

Ezra turned to Abanoud. Tomorrow morning you start. Meet me in the same place as this morning."

Ezra reached into his purse and took out a small coin and gave it to Abanoud's mother. "He is to start work tomorrow. Take this."

That evening Ezra told Apollos of his new servant. "Brother, you do not need a servant."

"The Copts, their men to need to work. We must find work for them. Tomorrow I would like to bring fresh raisin cakes. But work. Will our brothers in the church not find work for them? Mariam's whole life was one of service to the widows and orphans in Jerusalem. These people need our help, and they need the joy of God's salvation. Can we not find a way to serve them?"

Apollos sighed, "The peasants of Egypt have never been permitted to own land or livestock. All property belonged to the Pharaoh who provided work, food, and shelter. This did not change under the Greeks or the Romans. What did change was that now nearly all Egyptians are either priests to the fading gods, laborers or peasants. The priests are little better off than their brothers in the fields and servant's quarters of their new masters. Mercy and charity are unknown. That God could love a peasant and that a Copt is welcomed as a brother to a Greek or Roman is unthinkable."

Ezra looked at Apollos, "Unthinkable brother?"

Apollos smiled, "Until now. Until now, brother. With God's help, we shall make it happen!"

Soon the Christians of Memphis were providing food

and clothes to the needy Coptic Egyptians of Memphis while sharing the simple message of God's love for them and His hope of eternal salvation.

Ezra's mission to the Copts required patience and persistence, but soon Abanoud believed, and then others, often family members of believers. Ezra prayed with them, worshipped with them, cried with them and laughed with them. The Copts in the church of Memphis soon outnumbered the Romans and the Greeks.

Chapter Twenty-Six

Mariam finished her morning prayers and quiet meditation. She sat in the shaded courtyard of Nathan's villa beneath a grape arbor. The sun was still low in the morning sky. There was a light breeze. Birds sang cheerful songs. She looked down, smiling as her hands gently ran over the growing bulge of her stomach. *'Ezra would be so pleased,'* she thought. *'The Lord is so good! At my age? I never believed this blessing would come to me. And Papa is so happy! Thank you, Lord! O how I love you, Lord! A baby, I never thought...'*

"Do I hear you laughing, dear daughter?" Nathan asked as he approached.

"O Papa, I am so happy. Are you happy, Papa?"

Nathan sat beside Mariam and said, "My whole life has changed. I spent years chasing the wind. I lost you, and I lost God. A lifetime of pain and misery, but if it was all necessary—if it was God's plan, to find you again and the love of God our Father, it was all worth it. O yes, Mariam, I am most blessed. This is the blessing I long for. I long to see you love your child. And me a grandfather! My prayer is for Ezra to return soon and complete your happiness, dear child."

Three months became six then nine in Memphis as Apollos and Ezra trained Michael to lead the new church, fellowshipping and sharing with Greeks, Romans, and Copts. Soon even some Arabs were welcomed into the church. Deacons were appointed to oversee the ministry to the widows, orphans, prisoners and poor. Messengers were sent to Mark in Alexandria. They reported the outpouring of the Holy Spirit upon the citizens of Memphis. Ezra urged that money be sent to help care for the new brothers and sisters, mothers and fathers in great need, just as believers in Asia and Galatia supported the church in Jerusalem.

A year after returning to Egypt, Apollos, Ezra, and Abanoud continued up the Nile to Oxyrhynchus, or 'Sharp snouted Fish,' named for the fish plentiful in the shallow Lake Fayum, where they established a small fellowship. Then on to Abydos with its temple to the Egyptian god, Seti, and many ancient tombs, finally reaching Thebes, the great city of Upper Egypt.

Thebes, like Heliopolis, was no longer the great city of kings and Pharaohs. It was now a small but active trading city. It was Rome's southernmost citadel, the home of two full legions kept busy with a rebellious and troublesome diverse population and incursions from the Kingdom of Kush to the south. Everywhere the monuments to the glory of Egypt remained, but most were in disrepair and decline. Many centuries had passed since Thebes ruled Egypt. Before Rome, Thebes was ruled by the Greeks. Before the Greeks, it was part of the Kingdom of Kush, a people from further up the Nile who adopted Egyptian culture and gods but were never content to be ruled by the Pharaohs. The Egypt of the Kush Pharaohs was then reduced to a Satrap of Assyria. Mighty Egypt may have lasted thousands of years, but it was no stranger to foreign conquerors.

Thebes was now two small cities in one. The Romans, Greeks and a few Jews lived in new spacious villas with garden courtyards and quiet streets off a well-provisioned Agora in the new city, while the Copts, Kushites, and Arabs remained in the old city, centered around the Pylon of Lexor and ancient temples. Apollos made his way to the new market while Ezra and Abanoud went to the Copts, Arabs, and Kushites in the old city. Ezra had no intention of remaining long in Thebes. He found himself staring south at the Nile, his heart yearning to continue up the river to Meroe, capital of the Kingdom of Kush, home of the Candace, their queen mother.

Ezra preached in Greek and Abanoud repeated his words in Copt. Long after Ezra finished speaking, Abanoud continued, "Brothers I testify to this truth! Join me as I follow the one true God who writes His law in your heart. Jesus, His Son, has come. He sends His Holy Spirit, and He finds a home in your heart. He is the only God whose temple is always alive, growing, and speaking truth in the hearts of believers everywhere. He does not hide, blind and deaf in a crumbling temple of fading glories past. Friends, how can a god be only a god of Copts or Greeks or even Romans? There can only be one creator, God. One God over all people. His Son Jesus said all who believe are my brothers and sisters. The true God is God to all, and all who believe call Him Father. He calls to Copts, Arabs, Kushites, Greeks, Romans, and Jews. Brother Egyptians, Listen! His Spirit calls to you!"

With the Spirit-led work of Ezra and Abanoud, the church in Thebes grew daily. Apollos urged the Jews, Greeks, and Romans to welcome their Coptic, Arab and African brothers into fellowship. Deacons were appointed to oversee the ministry to the widows, orphans and poor among their destitute brothers.

One hot day as Ezra and Abanoud finished preaching, a young man nervously came forward for baptism. The man, not yet bearded, barefoot, clutching a cloak and headscarf tightly against his thin body, lowered his eyes and softly whispered, "My name is Asim, and I come to Jesus. I come for salvation. I had a dream, and a man said, 'Go to the Pylon and hear the words of the man preaching. I have sent him.' I heard the words, and my heart was warmed. A voice kept whispering 'My word is truth.' So, I have come."

Ezra smiled, "Welcome Asim, the Spirit spoke to me as well before I came to believe. God has called and invited you. Your spirit has accepted His gracious invitation. Come, we will take you to be baptized."

At the river, Ezra walked in up to his knees and asked Asim to follow. Asim removed his threadbare cloak and scarf and waded into the water in a stained and tattered linen tunic. His head, once shaved, was now covered in black stubble except for a lock of braided black hair, clasped at his scalp with a gold ring. The braid fell as a tassel over his right ear.

Several Copts whispered as they watched Asim be

baptized, Abanoud's eyes widened as he watched.

Ezra smiled, "Kneel Asim."

Asim kneeled and bowed his head. Ezra filled a bowl of water from the river and poured it over his head, "Asim, I baptize you in the name of the Father and the Son and the Holy Spirit. Amen. Brother Asim rise up in new life!"

Ezra reached down and helped him stand, "Welcome brother, can I see about some shoes and new clothes for you? Let me take you to your new brothers and sisters who will help you."

Asim wiped his wet dreadlock out of his face trying not to show the tears he wiped from his eyes. He quickly covered his head with his dirty scarf, looked up at Ezra, and smiled.

Ezra asked softly, "Tell me, Asim, where are you from? Your Greek is quite good. Who are your people?"

Asim smiled sheepishly, looked up, but up and hesitated. "I have been taught Greek and Arabic and also Hebrew. Though my family speaks only the language of the Copts and the Kushites."

Asim stopped speaking. He closed his eyes and gritted his teeth. He had said too much.

Ezra smiled, "God hears you, Asim, in whatever language you speak to Him. I do not know your story, but you are safe. You have brothers and sisters to love and protect you. I take you to the brothers now."

As they walked, Ezra spoke, "I have a desire to visit the Kingdom of Kush. I once had dealings with an official of the Candace. I have always wondered..."

Asim kept his eyes down and said nothing.

Ezra honored Asim's silence.

Asim was warmly received by a brother who said, "Come, brother. Perhaps new clothes and a clean robe.

You must have shoes! Have you eaten today? Perhaps some cakes until the meal? The LORD would have us hungry for His Word but satisfied in the body."

The young man smiled, "Cakes would be most generous. And clean clothes. Where may I bathe?"

Now smiling broadly, Asim followed the brother, his face shining with hope.

Out of Asim's hearing, Abanoud said to Ezra, "Young Asim's head is groomed for the royal court of Kush."

Ezra nodded, "God has called him. He was sent to us. I wonder why he has run away? Do not push him. He will tell his story when he is ready."

One evening, Ezra was teaching from Isaiah, "The Spirit of the LORD is upon me, for the LORD has anointed me to bring good news to the poor. He has sent me to comfort the brokenhearted and to proclaim liberty to the captives, and the opening of the prison to those who are bound."

Asim asked, "Master Ezra, does the prophet Isaiah speak of himself or another?"

Ezra smiled, "Truly, the prophet Isiah, and all of the prophets speak to us even today, of the Messiah, the Righteous One, promised of God. He speaks of Jesus who has come. He has died, and He has risen."

Asim nodded, "I have heard this before. If the prophet speaks of Jesus, are the captives now free?"

Ezra looked at the young man and said, "We, all men, were once captive to sin and death. But now we are free to live in Christ. We are free from the price of sin, which is death. And we have a greater freedom. We are at liberty to stand before God in righteousness, fearing no condemnation from Him or any man. God's heart is for the widow, the orphan, the prisoner, and the poor. The poor in spirit know their need for His love and salvation. It is the proud who stand afar off and refuse His salvation. God's heart is to heal the wounded, comfort the mourning, and to lift up the humble."

Asim lowered his eyes and then quoted Isaiah in Hebrew, "But you shall be called priests of the LORD; they shall speak of you as ministers of our God you shall eat the wealth of nations, and in their glory, you shall boast. Instead of your shame, there shall be a double portion; instead of dishonor they shall rejoice in their lot; therefore, in their land, they shall possess a double portion; they shall have everlasting joy. For I, the LORD love justice; I hate robbery and wrong; I will faithfully give them their recompense, and I will make an everlasting covenant with them."

Ezra nodded, "And so we are in Jesus, as Isaiah says, 'I will greatly rejoice in the LORD; my soul shall exult in my God, for He has clothed me in garments of salvation; He has covered me with the robe of righteousness as a bridegroom decks himself like a priest with a beautiful headdress, as a bride adorns herself with her jewels.'"

Ezra walked over to Asim and sat beside him. "Brother, it is time you told me your story."

The small boat struggled to make headway through the strong currents in the rocky shallows of the cataract. Ezra gripped the thwart tightly and cringed as he heard rocks scraping against the bottom and side of the boat. He stared into the swirling waters around him and silently prayed. After minutes of terror, the waves were gone. The surface of the Nile once again smooth as the river widened. The oarsman continued to pull in unison, and the pilot loosened the sheet and let the sail glide outboard.

Asim smiled, "The next cataract is even shallower. We shall be required to get out and push the boat through. But that will not be for several days. The next cataract is the border. We will be in Kush."

Abanoud asked, "No more Romans?"

Asim nodded, "There is a treaty. There is peace, but it came at a great price. Years ago, before I was born, when the Romans first came, the Candace traded with the Romans, but she became greedy and sacked Thebes. That is when Rome sent a legion and burned our ancient capital Napata. The city lies in ruin, and the capital was moved to Meroe. It is a sad thing. You shall see for yourself."

They slowly made their way up the Nile in a broad valley between mountains to the left and right. The flood plain was green with wheat and vegetables up to the sharp red walls of the mountains on either side. After crossing the third cataract, the river made a great arching sweep into the Nubian desert. Passing Napata, only a single column was left to mark where the city once stretched out on the plain. In the distance stood the ancient tombs of the Kings and Candaces of Kush. Large pyramids stood atop square bases, eroded by centuries and millennium of wind and sand.

Asim stared at the ruins as they slowly made their way past. He sighed and turned to Ezra, "Only one more cataract, and we shall come to Meroe." He lowered his eyes and mumbled, "I shall learn my fate."

Chapter Twenty-Seven

Meroe captivated Ezra. He saw no Romans or Greeks. The buildings and the market were Egyptian in all the ways Alexandria was not. The citizens did not dress in the manner of Egyptians, like the Greeks down the Nile. They dressed Egyptian. The Kushites were for millennia connected to Egypt. They were sometimes subject to the Egyptians, sometimes master of the Egyptians and always envious of the Egyptians. They bowed before the Egyptian gods and built pyramids and obelisks. Their sons drove chariots for the Pharaohs and were known as the best bow makers in the world. They adopted the Egyptian culture yet maintained their Kushite identity with fierce pride. Meroe was a smaller mixing pot of cultures. Its villas and huts housed Kushites, Copts and Ethiopians, their neighbors and trading partners to the south.

Ezra made his way to a service gate in the palace and asked the guard for Melech. The guard eyed the foreigner before him, not a Copt, not a Greek. Certainly not a Roman. "What business do you have with the Eunuch to the Candace?"

"I bring news of a runaway who wishes to return."

The guard said, "Let the scoundrel show himself and accept his fate."

Ezra smiled, "Melech knows of the young man. He agrees to comes only because I will speak for him."

"Very well. I shall inform the Candace's Eunuch. What is his name?"

"His name is Asim." Ezra reached opened his hand and held up the gold braid ring from Asim's lock. "You may give this to Melech as proof I speak for Asim."

Ezra sat in the shade outside the gate and waited. He did not wait long before the guard returned, accompanied by a tall Ethiopian man in flowing white linen robes. Graying hair showed under his white, feather dressed turban with a large sapphire in the center. He hurried in the manner of a high-ranking official who could not be seen to hurry. He walked in long, elegant strides which forced the guard to trot alongside.

"You have news of Asim? Where is he? Is he safe?"

Ezra bowed and replied, "I am Ezra of Jerusalem. I travel here with Asim. He asked me to speak for him. He repents of his sin and seeks forgiveness. But he fears. The ring is from his braided lock. I could not read the inscription, but surely you have. Please, allow me to share what has happened in his life."

The tall Ethiopian nodded, "Yes, come with me, Ezra of Jerusalem? I recall an Ezra I met in Jerusalem, briefly, many years ago. Forgive me my name Melech. I am Chief Eunuch to the Candace."

Ezra stared at Melech, "God sent a Eunuch of the Candace to my house in Jerusalem. He paid me handsomely for a Sefer Torah. He asked me to show him the writings of the prophet Isaiah."

Melech stopped and studied Ezra, "God has brought us together once again, Ezra. Tell me, friend, do you follow Jesus the Messiah?"

"I was baptized in the Spirit and in water on the day of Pentecost, fifty days after the crucifixion of our LORD."

Melech raised his head, closed his eyes, and asked, "There was a man of God—Philip. Do you know of him?"

"You speak of Philip the Evangelist. Yes, he was a deacon in Jerusalem, and now he leads our brothers and sisters in Caesarea in Judea. He spoke of being transported in the Spirit and coming upon an Ethiopian standing in a chariot reading Isaiah. The man believed and was baptized by Philip. You are that man brother Melech?"

Melech smiled, "'Who has measured the Spirit of the LORD, or what man shows Him His counsel?' God has brought us together again, brother, now come, tell me all."

Inside the cool palace room of the Candace's Chief Counselor, Ezra began, "I met Asim when he came forward to baptized while I preached in Thebes. He told me a voice sent him to the Pylon of Lexor to listen. He is now a brother and a most capable young man, gifted in many ways!"

"Has he told you his story? Melech asked.

"He told of his life here—the training, the preparation for service. It was the... the... "

Ezra held out his right hand and made a scissor motion with his index and middle finger. "He was not prepared to become a Eunuch."

Melech sighed and looking into Ezra's eyes, asked, "And now?"

Ezra nodded, "And now he returns. He still does not want to become a eunuch, but—Asim has many questions about liberty. When I taught from Isaiah of our Messiah giving liberty to the prisoner, it touched his very soul. I told him that the freedom Jesus brings is the freedom from the grip of sin and the sentence of death. It is freedom to live righteous in the eyes of God and before all men. Asim seeks to be free from his sin. He has confessed to God and desires to confess to you. He will put his life in your hands."

Melech smiled and stood up, "You have taught him, well, brother. I will hear his confession. Bring Asim to me. Come with him, for I shall like to hear more of our brothers and sisters in Jesus. Come tomorrow."

Ezra stood up and bowed, "I shall bring him tomorrow. And letters. I have letters from the Apostles and an account of the life and sayings of Jesus. They are most profitable for instruction."

"Yes, bring them, and young Asim. Tomorrow."

The following morning, Asim crept into Melech's chamber behind Ezra, head down and silent. Melech spoke firmly, "Asim, do you have something to say to me?"

His eyes still on the floor, Asim whispered, "I have sinned against you and against God. I come to confess my sin and place myself in your hands."

Melech's deep voice boomed, "You know it is a grievous thing for a slave to run away."

"Yes, Master Melech. Very grievous."

Melech's voice softened, "But you have returned on your own accord. This weighs in your favor. Why have you returned and confessed to me?"

"My LORD Jesus commands obedience. He teaches us to confess our sins to Him and our neighbor and repent. So, I have come."

"And now you follow Jesus?"

"Yes. I have been baptized in the Spirit and in water. Now I follow Him."

Melech clapped his hands. A man entered with a stool, a bowl and a razor. Another man carried a clean white linen tunic and headdress.

Melech said, "Shave his head properly and see he is dressed. Here is his braid ring," and he handed the gold ring to the barber."

Turning his focus on Asim, he said, "We shall speak again when you are presentable."

Melech sat down and motioned for Ezra to sit. "Brother Ezra, the gospel and letters you mentioned, would you read them before our fellowship this evening and give an account to the brothers and sisters? News from followers on the outside is always welcomed. You may leave Asim with us. You shall see him this evening. Come to the gate before sunset. Someone will meet you there."

Ezra bowed to Melech and smiled at Asim as he left.

When Asim was shaved and dressed as a servant to the Candace, he presented himself to Melech. "Stand up straight, Asim. Brother Ezra, a priest, a scribe and a teacher of the Law spoke highly of you. He tells me you are reluctant to become a eunuch. Your selection is a great honor but can be withdrawn for the disloyalty of running away. Only a Eunuch may be trained as a counselor and wise man to the Candace. If this honor is withdrawn, you will become a household slave for the remainder of your days but you will never be allowed in the presence of the Candace."

Melech paused and watched Asim stare ahead. He continued, "Brother Ezra only confirms my judgment that you are skilled and capable. There are costs to accept such a life. The desires of the flesh will depart, and you will view men and women the same. The pain comes when you see a father holding up his son, his face and heart soaring with pride. I have learned to view special young men, men that I groom, to give me a similar pride of fatherhood. You have been such a son to me. There is also the forfeit of your life and your time to serving another as they demand."

The color returned to Asim's face which softened and opened into a smile as he listened. Melech continued, "But with this honor comes great reward. Not in wealth, though the Candace can be most generous. The reward is a position of trust, knowing that your counsel may benefit our people. Do you remember the stories of the Hebrew Daniel? A man who served the rulers of three successive empires. His people were slaves. His faith was tested, yet he persevered and served his conqueror and captors to his fullest ability remaining faithful to God. No wife or children of Daniel are recorded; only fellow Jews faithful to God. And of Queen Esther and her uncle Mordecai? Consider her sacrifice. They answered God's calling."

Melech waited for Asim to answer, "I remember the teaching, Master Melech." Asim paused and then stammered, "You believe that becoming a Eunuch to the

Candace is a calling?"

Melech smiled, "Meditate on my words. Pray to our Father in heaven and wait for the leading of His Holy Spirit. Eunuch to the Candace is a path open before you. You know where it can lead. There is another path, but its destination is, well, it is for you to ponder. I shall give you some time to consider."

Asim smiled, "Thank you, Master Melech. I will pray and seek an answer."

"Now concerning your punishment. You will spend your nights in prison for one month. You shall be released for your duties. And, you are to attend the fellowship. I shall not separate you from the fellowship of brothers in Christ. Now go to the hall of instruction. I must not keep the Candace waiting."

Ezra met with the fellowship of believers in Meroe for several evenings, reading and teaching from the Gospel of Mark, the letters James and Paul, and the Council's instruction regarding Gentile believers. Ezra's teaching was greeted with enthusiasm and thanksgiving. He offered to carry letters north to Mark and Jerusalem to encourage others in the Spirit's work in Africa. Ezra and Melech determined to establish regular reports to Mark. Melech agreed he should recognize the apostleship of Mark as his overseer. Asim affirmed the calling of the Holy Spirit to follow Melech into service as a Eunuch to the Candace. Before Ezra and Abanoud departed, Melech had already shared the Gospel of Mark with the Candace, and he asked for prayers that she would find the faith they shared.

Ezra and Abanoud found the trip downriver much faster and more pleasant than the slow voyage upstream. Even running cataracts downriver proved an exhilarating adventure. They stopped in Thebes and sought out Apollos. They carried letters back to Mark from the leaders of each church. Abanoud was introduced to each elder as a messenger to Mark the Evangelist. As they worked their way downriver, Ezra found himself drawn to the unique wildlife of the Nile. Magnificent birds and herons like he had never seen and crocodiles lurking among the reeds and sunning on the mudflats. The boat's pilot gave a wide berth to what the Greeks and Romans called hippopotamus, the gentle appearing river horses who fiercely attacked anything that ventured too close.

He witnessed the floods which deposited thick black mud on the riverbank which was spread across the fields where wheat, cotton, flax, and vegetables were grown. Below Thebes, the Egyptians called the Nile the black river for the nutrient-rich flow that made this land the breadbasket of the Roman Empire.

Ezra, Apollos and Abanoud called on the churches at Abados which boasted three times the followers. In Oxyrhynchus, the port city on the great inland lake, he learned three new churches had been planted in the fertile farmland around the shore of Lake Fayum. Memphis too had seen considerable growth and church planting in several neighborhoods with a council of elders overseeing the teaching. But downtrodden Heliopolis was special. The small fellowship was visited regularly by Joseph of Leontopolis and led by the former priest to Ra-Amun. They established a ministry to the Arab traders who carried the Good News to ports on the Red Sea and the into the heart of Arabia connecting with churches founded there by the Apostle Paul.

In Alexandria, Mark the Evangelist received Apollos

and Ezra joyfully. He insisted on sharing each letter and learning the names of the leaders. Mark enjoyed hearing again and again of the work of the Spirit in each city. When Ezra shared his experience with Melech and Asim, he shouted. "Praise God! Even the Candace of Kush hears the Good News of Jesus Christ!" Mark ordained young Abanoud his messenger to the churches of the Nile. Mark called for a celebration of thanksgiving for his new churches and for a special blessing of his two, now three apostles from Alexandria.

After all the festivities Ezra stood and thanked Mark, "Brother Mark, Apostle of the Lord Jesus Christ, I thank you for sending me with Apollos to the Egyptians, Copts and Kushites, Arabs and Greeks up the Nile River. It is a wondrous thing to see God's Spirit calling all men unto him. Men have seen visions. Miracles were common, and God's truth will not be stopped. I urge you to send brothers from your new churches even deeper into the land, for God is with us. But now I beg you, allow me to go home to my wife for I have been absent from her longer than we have been married. Let brother Apollos continue to serve you, for surely he carries the voice of the Lord."

Mark stood, walked over to Ezra, and hugged him. "Well done good and faithful servant! Go to your wife and find comfort in her love. But brother, know this, your labors in the Lord are not complete. New ministry awaits and a greater reward will come!"

Chapter Twenty-Eight

Ezra approached the gate of Nathan's villa set down his bag and was about to call out when he heard the laughter of a child. He straightened up and listened, his head cocked, and his ear bent to the gate. *Do I hear giggling?* "It is Ezra, come open the gate." He called.

The calm voice of Mariam could be heard, "Jonathan, it's your Papa, are you ready to meet your Papa?"

The gate swung open, and a beaming Mariam stood inside cradling a rambunctious baby boy. Ezra stood and stared. Slowly his surprise turned into a great smile. He reached for his son and lifted him high above his face. He studied the big brown eyes shining from beneath a mop of thick, black hair. The boy stared back at this strange man that held him high. Ezra began to laugh, "You're a bright-eyed little fellow, Jonathan! And a good name it is, Jonathan..."

"Our son needed a name, Ezra. I hope you like it," Mariam said with a smile.

"Just look at him!"

Ezra lowered the boy to eye level. Jonathan smiled, slowly straightened his pudgy arm and with a single finger, touched the smiling lip of his father. "You are a curious one, my son, and brave!" Tears streamed from Ezra's eyes as he brought him close to his chest. Putting the boy's face over his shoulder and patting his back, Ezra closed his eyes and wept. "Can a man know any more joy?"

Ezra stepped towards Mariam and pulled her into his hug. "No word? I would have come home. I would not have left you alone,"

Mariam leaned up and kissed Ezra, "I know, husband. I sent no word so you would not be troubled. You have a calling, Ezra. You must be true to your calling. But God has answered my prayers, and you are here. Safe."

Ezra could not let go of his wife and son as he stood in the gate, tears flowing into Mariam's hair, his cheek alongside Jonathan's. When his sobs ceased, Ezra lifted his head, "And Nathan? Is Nathan well?"

Mariam let go her hug. "Come inside. You can hold our son, though he crawls and soon will be walking. Nathan is in his fields. He is well. He is happy."

"Jonathan, yes, a good name. His grandfather Nathan must be pleased. So much better than Haggai or the old names from my family. Will you look at him, Mariam! He is so big!"

"He is well past his first birthday! You're such a big boy, aren't you, my precious son? You must show your

Papa how well you play. And talk—Ezra, sometimes he just talks—babbles on and on. O he is a happy baby, no trouble this one!"

Mariam sat close to Ezra and leaned against him. She sighed. "It seems we spent our whole lives waiting. Is it our time now, Ezra? Tell me you have returned for good."

Ezra wrapped his arm around Mariam, "I have returned. I need only deliver letters to Jerusalem. I should see Simeon and the brothers. But, yes, it is our time. We shall watch our Jonathan grow and his brothers and sisters as well!"

Mariam laughed, "Brothers and sisters? Do you not think one son is gift enough at my age?"

Ezra rubbed his hand in Mariam's hair, "Have you forgotten Sarah?"

Mariam pushed Ezra lightly and sighed, "I am so happy..."

Jerusalem appeared the same busy place Ezra left nearly three years earlier. The pilgrims filled the streets. The market was crowded, and the Roman soldiers were ever-present. As he walked the streets, he looked about for familiar faces, trying to reconnect with the past. He laughed to himself when it occurred to him that Jerusalem was never a city of familiar faces. It was always crowded with strangers. Even so, a melancholy flooded over him as the city of the magnificent Temple now seemed foreign. He went first to the common house in the upper city, determined to deliver the letters of Mark to James and the council, not knowing if any of the apostles even remained in the city.

Ezra was greeted at the door by a deacon he did not recognize and was told to wait in the serving hall. The room was filled with widows, orphans and poor, being served as they had been for over a quarter-century. The deacon returned and announced that James the Just would see him in the upper room. James was rising from his bony calloused *camel* knees as Ezra come in. "Welcome brother," James said as he came forward and gave Ezra a kiss of fellowship on the cheek.

"You carry letters from Mark in Alexandria? Please, sit with me while I read. I should like to hear all the news from Egypt."

James motioned to the deacon, "Brother, some wine for Brother Ezra, while he waits."

James opened the pouch and scanned the headings of each letter before going back and reading one in detail. "You and Apollos, up the Nile.?—Philip's Ethiopian Eunuch!—The Candace of Kush?"

James lowered the letter and looked at Ezra. "Truly, it is as our Lord commanded. Disciples of all men! Soon the whole world will hear the Good News! Tell me, brother, what is it like? What is it like to preach to a foreigner, to strangers? What is it like to see the Spirit call men unto him? I see none of it. I stay here in Jerusalem in my familiar room or at the Temple courts. I do not see the world changing."

Ezra, taken aback, thought for a moment, "James, it is your prayers. You are here on your knees before God! You send us. You encourage us and instruct us! You know the power of the Spirit of God!"

James nodded, "Yes, but to slip away as Peter and the others do... and see."

"You have strength and discipline. That is why you lead us. Tell me brother James, is the Temple yet safe for worship? The riots? The Zealots?"

James sighed, "The unrest is the same. The Temple is as it was. But there is something troubling. Some of the brothers—our Jewish brothers of the Pharisees mostly—they will not fellowship with our Gentile brothers. Unless the Gentiles are circumcised and submit fully to the law, they will have no dealings with them."

"But the letter. Your letter from the Council to the Gentiles in Antioch? It is shared around the world."

"Many of our Jewish brothers have withdrawn. They meet inside the temple, in the court of the women, the Nazarites, or lepers. They fellowship where Gentiles are excluded. It is a hard thing, indeed. Their numbers do not grow, but their opposition is well known. Tell me, Ezra, is it such in Alexandria? In Egypt?"

"Alexandria has many Jews. I do not know—there may be some who believe as the Pharisees, but I saw brothers, Jews, and Greeks in warm fellowship. But better still, I saw the wealthy Jews and Greeks welcome the Copts of Egypt and the Arabs and the Kushites, even Ethiopians. This has never been seen in Egypt since before the days of the Ptolemies."

James smiled. "And where do you go now, my friend?"

"I shall call on Simeon ben Gamaliel and then return to my wife and son born in my absence. I will live in Nicopolis and fellowship with the brothers there."

James smiled warmly, his eyes locked onto Ezra's, and said, "Simeon remains steadfast and teaches the law rightly. Take my blessings to your family. Let me give you a kiss of fellowship as you depart."

Both men stood. James leaned in and kissed Ezra once again on each cheek. "Brother Ezra, the Lord has more for you to do. Go in peace!"

Joel, still leading the fellowship in Nicopolis took Ezra aside. "Surely, Ezra ben Haggai, you are filled with the Holy Spirit. You teach the Law with knowledge and authority. You preach to Jew and Gentile baptizing many that hear. I know it is your heart to remain with us in Nicopolis and watch your son Jonathan grow into a man of God. With so many gifts, do not deny me this request. Lead our brothers and sisters here. I am old and tired. It is time for me to give my place to a younger man. You, Ezra, are that man."

Ezra did not know what to say. "Brother Joel, you are loved. You are a man of wisdom..."

Joel did not let Ezra finish. He shook his head no as he smiled, "It is true. I have been blessed by the love the fellowship pours upon me. But love is not limited to one man. God pours it out for all His people to share. Wisdom, you say?—Old age and experience. But you have learned God's lessons and truth. Do you not discern His Law? Have you not preached His Word and counseled His people? No, it is your time to lead, and I will remain. I will listen, and I will pray, but you will lead."

"But the others..."

"The others have decided. You will lead!"

After Mariam gave birth to a daughter, Ruth, word came that Paul had returned to Jerusalem with a generous offering from the churches of Greece. Before leaving Corinth, Paul wrote a letter to the church in Rome, declaring his strong desire to visit them. A copy of the epistle and two others to the church in Corinth made their way to Ezra in Nicopolis.

Ezra poured himself into Paul's letter to the Romans. His eyes bright, a smile tight on his face, he found himself nodding and repeating: "Amen! Amen brother Paul! Here is the true telling of the Law! Brother you expound on the truth you wrote to the brothers in Galatia! Yes! You go to the beginning, God's very revelation of Himself from creation. It is just as you say. He has always shown us the truth. It is evident. We are indeed without excuse, exchanging the Truth revealed for a lie, worshipping images of creatures rather than our Creator. From the very beginning, we are lost!"

Mariam heard Ezra as he reasoned out loud the words of Paul, "Husband, Paul's letter, it excites you?"

Ezra looked up, "It is so clear, Mariam, consider: 'The lusts that fell upon men, the depraved mind, all wickedness, and greed, that all who practice such things are deserving of death. Not the Gentiles only, but the Jews as well. For though we were given the Law we did not obey and rather than being a light to the Gentiles, we came to blaspheme the name of God to them. So, all people are condemned. That is the message of the prophets, but the message of Jesus is that all men may be saved. They may be justified and stand righteous before God through faith in Jesus—a gift of His grace through the redemption, which is Christ Jesus!' Mariam, we must share this. The argument is made and cannot be assailed; it is faith alone!"

Mariam smiled at her husband as he absorbed each word he read, "Husband is that not what your work is about, calling all to faith in Jesus?"

"Ezra nodded, "Yes, of course, but the question remained, 'What shall I make of the Law?'"

Mariam kissed Ezra's forehead and went back to the children, leaving Ezra to continue. Trying to be silent, he thought, 'Abraham, yes. Our father of the faith—apart from works—apart from circumcision—apart from the Law! His righteousness was imparted—His sanctification—separation from sin—no longer under the law. Our brother says the Law is not evil! It does not bring death but understanding! O look at the power of living in Christ Jesus! Look at the freedom we now have! Look at the brotherhood in Jesus, the very adoption by God to be his sons, daughters, and heirs!

Ezra 's fingers pierced his beard and massaged his chin, Yes, what of Israel? What about Israel's rejection of Jesus? He says it is temporary—there is hope! They shall recover their sight. What a blessed day that will be. And our responsibility? What should we be doing? Yes, present our bodies as a living sacrifice—a spiritual worship. Be transformed. Unity in the body, yes, of course! And be steadfast doers of His will—enduring—giving -loving. Obedient citizens, even to Rome? Ah, not judging others. Here it is—of course!—be imitators of Christ!"

Paul's letter to the Romans made an impact everywhere it was read. To Gentile believers and many Jewish Christians, it thoughtfully and powerfully defended the ancient teachings of the prophets that God's desire was not for sacrifice, but 'a broken and contrite heart.' It affirmed Israel's role as a light to the Gentiles and God's desire to call all people unto Himself. Paul proved that faith was always God's genuine desire for man. The Law is a means not an end. But Jews holding onto the traditions of the Law and Temple worship read this teaching as a threat to Judaism. They determined that these Jesus followers were no longer Jews. Synagogues would no longer allow Jesus followers to speak. Jews and Christians separated. The Jewish Christians holding to the Law would not permit Gentile brothers to enter their homes, and fellowship was broken. These same Christian Jews of the Law were excluded from the synagogues and were cut off, their witness lost, and their message silenced.

Ezra found Paul's two letters to the church in Corinth filled with practical instruction on dealing with sexual sin and marriage and the growing dissension in the church. Paul urged unity and spiritual growth.

"Mariam, come hear what Paul writes to the church in Corinth," Ezra called out.

Mariam came into the room holding baby Ruth against her shoulder. "Corinth?" She asked.

"Corinth. Famous for its canal cut through the Isthmus of Greece. It is a major trading city, very wealthy and accustomed to ostentatious wealth and worldly lifestyle. It is a place where sin is not hidden in society or, as Paul condemns, within the church."

"It sounds like a city I would not want to visit!" Mariam replied, gently patting Ruth's back.

"First, Paul teaches it was right that we married, for we had been promised. Though Paul thinks it best believers stay unmarried in service to Christ until He comes again."

"Well, I'm pleased to hear brother Paul would not leave our children outside of marriage."

Ezra ignored her remark and continued to read, "Paul calls the Corinthian Christians to account for sexual sins tolerated within the church, most sternly but with love. He urges spiritual maturity and the proper exercising of spiritual gifts within the church."

Ezra looked up at Mariam and continued, "Even in a broken church like Corinth, where spiritual gifts became a source of pride, Paul teaches that God grants all spiritual gifts for the ministry of the Good News. Here, in this stern letter to Corinth, Paul reminds all Christians that love is our first calling and greatest gift; love for God, and love one another. He extolls that love is greater than faith and hope for it is the very foundation on which our salvation rests."

Mariam smiled and replied, "Husband, did you not read from the letter to the Romans, Paul's command to be imitators of Christ? What greater way to imitate our LORD and Savior than to love? Love Him as he has loved us and love others unsparingly, for surely He loved them before us."

Ezra stood up hugged Mariam and Ruth and kissed her on the cheek. "I praise God for giving me a wife who teaches me how to love."

Ezra expounded on Paul's teaching, and the church in Nicopolis continued to grow, but fewer Jews were listening, and they would not enter a home welcoming Gentiles. Jews observant to the Law permitted relations with Gentiles only in public areas, markets and courts set aside for them. The Pharisees were especially vocal in demanding this separation. Ezra was accustomed to the harassment he received, but he was surprised when he learned that Paul was arrested at the Temple in Jerusalem. Paul was accused of bringing the uncircumcised, a Gentile, into the temple when he visited the court of the Nazarites to fulfill a vow. The story varied considerably by the teller, but it was clear that Paul had demanded his right as a Roman citizen to be tried before Caesar!

Ezra traveled to Jerusalem to see Simeon and learn the truth. He found his old friend at the Temple and returned to his home. "Tell me, Simeon, Paul is arrested? Is it the Jews or the Romans who imprison him? I have heard he is accused of profaning the Temple."

His old friend sighed, "He was first taken by the Romans outside the Temple to protect him from the Jews seeking to murder him."

"Murder him? Why?"

Simeon waved his hands, "Listen to me brother, I will explain. When Paul returned to Jerusalem with his gift for our poor, some brothers came with him. Both Jew and Gentile. When Paul met with James and the elders, he was told of complaints, lies mostly, that Paul was teaching Jews not to circumcise their children or follow any of the traditions of the Law. It was decided that Paul should go to the Temple and observe the right of purification to assure the Jewish brothers the accusations were false. But some Jews, Jews of Asia it is said, identified Paul as a blasphemer and profaner. They accused Paul of bringing Gentiles into the inner courts. They drove him from the Temple and sought to murder him as he left."

"Surely, they did not..."

"The Romans, they are everywhere now with so much unrest, the Romans would not permit a riot on the Temple steps and sought to take Paul away. But our brother entreated them, insisting he reason with his accusers. The Jews accusing him would not hear and became more determined to stone him. The Romans took Paul to the Antonia fortress seeking to find the truth by scourging him with the whip. There Paul told the commander he was a Roman citizen. Well, the officer was rightly concerned and instead took Paul to the Sanhedrin as this was a Jewish matter. Ananias, the High

Priest, joined with the accusers. He sought to stone Paul. Paul shrewdly put the Pharisees and Sadducees to arguing their old disputes and such dissension ensued that the Centurion feared another riot! So, fearing a conspiracy, Paul was taken to Caesarea, where he is to this day."

Ezra sighed, "It is just as brother Paul wrote in his letter, 'But Israel, pursuing a law of righteousness did not arrive at that law. Why? Because they did not pursue by faith, but as though it were by works. They stumbled over the stumbling stone, just as it is written, Behold I am laying in Zion a stone of stumbling, and a rock of offense; and whoever believes in him will not be put to shame.'"

Simeon agreed, "Yes, the Law has become the stumbling stone to our Jewish brothers."

Ezra looked up, "Who is seeing to the needs of brother Paul in Caesarea? Perhaps I should go."

"The brothers in Caesarea care for Paul. He is served. He is held in house arrest, not in prison. The Procurator Antonius Felix is a careful man. But he remembers that Cumanus was exiled for denying justice to the Jews when he appeared with the Chief Priest before Caesar."

Ezra closed his eyes and thought before speaking. "Simeon, how long I have struggled with the Law, the Levitical priesthood, and Temple worship? A priest, I held onto the traditions for more than twenty years. It is a hard thing for our people to understand. Brother Apollos teaches the words of Isaiah 'But you will be called priests of the LORD, you will be spoken of as ministers of our God.' This is a promise of a priesthood by faith. A priesthood to all who believe."

Simeon nodded, "Yes! It is the priesthood for those who do not stumble over the Law. It is not a priesthood of works but one of faith. And Jesus is such a priest! Indeed, He is the High Priest like your old friend Melchizedek. Yes, I have considered him as well. Like father Abraham, before the Law, before the Levitical priesthood. And consider this, Ezra, greater than Abraham who brought his tithe to him. Jesus is such a High Priest! Melchizedek foretells His coming and His everlasting priesthood!"

Chapter Twenty-Nine

Ezra was surprised and delighted to see his friend Apollos standing outside his gate. He hugged his friend and stepped back to look at him. "Your hair goes gray, my brother, but your smile is as honest as ever! Come in! Mariam, Apollos is here! Come, greet our brother! A feast, we must feed him! This is a day of celebration!"

Apollos followed Ezra into the courtyard, "Yes, call for Mariam, brother. I have urgent business with Mariam!"

Mariam came out carrying young Daniel with Jonathan and Ruth by her side. Apollos, smiling as brightly as ever went to her and hugged her, "Sister Mariam! But now there are three? Ezra, three children?"

Stooping down Apollos lightly patted the heads of Jonathan and Ruth, "Master Jonathan of course and I know Ruth as well, though she grows so quickly!"

Standing up, he peered at the baby in Mariam's arms, "And who is this precious gift from the Lord?"

Mariam smiled, "This is Daniel. Brave and stout like his brother and sister. As you say, dear Apollos, a gift from the Lord. Now, what is this urgent business that you bring to me rather than my husband?"

Apollos gave Mariam a kiss of fellowship on the cheek as he began, "Sister, I have need of your husband, that is brother Paul has need of us, and I know Ezra will not leave you unless you send him."

Mariam's face grew serious, "Come in, brother, and tell us all."

Apollos spoke as they walked, "Brother Paul is to have another trial in Rome. He is no longer under house arrest but in a dungeon cell. Peter, too, is under arrest. Emperor Nero rails against the Christians in Rome. He accuses them falsely, even as the people grow weary of his debauchery and evil. John Mark has been called from Alexandria. Luke and Silas remain with Paul."

Ezra sat down, "Another trial? Both Paul and Peter in prison? This is very hard news. Only a year ago we learned that James the Just was stoned to death on the orders of Ananus ben Ananus, the High Priest, with the approval of the Sanhedrin—and now Paul and Peter?"

Ezra's face drained of color, "But why send for us? You, Apollos—you serve with him the churches in Greece and Asia, but me? What can I offer brother Paul?"

Apollos nodded, "The Spirit has come upon brother Paul. He writes. He writes to the churches, to Ephesus, Colossae, and Philippi. More letters. He instructs. He writes to his elders, to Timothy and to Titus instructions on leading the churches. He puts his house in order. He prepares for his homecoming with our LORD."

"It is good that he writes. His letters are clear and powerful, full of the Spirit. But, again, my dear Apollos, why send for me?"

"I have spoken to him of our work and of your teaching on the High Priesthood of Jesus. I spoke of Melchizedek, and of Isaiah's prophecy of the church—a church of new priests of the LORD. He remembers his favorite priest—that is how he remembers you, Ezra— his favorite temple priest and debater of the old Saul."

Ezra's face could not hide his confusion, "Brother Paul knows the Law like no other. He sat under Gamaliel. Just read his letter to the Romans. I am no one to instruct him."

Mariam sat beside her husband and slid her arm around his waist, "Brother Paul is gathering his children, those who will carry on the work. He gathers them that they might see what he sees, that they witness the power of the Holy Spirit in this work. And Peter, as well. Peter who opened the way of salvation to the Gentiles!"

Mariam took a deep breath, kissed Ezra, and said, "You must go. I have always known, Ezra that you belong to God. We will celebrate with Apollos tonight, but tomorrow you travel to Rome."

Ezra studied Mariam's eyes and saw the determination. He knew her mind was made up. She sighed and smiled, Ezra, you know Papa's sight is gone, and he sleeps most of the day. He lives only to sit with the children. I will stay here. The brothers and sisters are nearby. They know that God has called you."

Apollos' impatiently asked, "James dead?"

Ezra nodded, "And several of the deacons. There was a great outcry among the people for they knew James to be a righteous man steadfast in the law, always at prayer for the people. The new Procurator, Albinus, has removed Ananus ben Ananus but the common house is abandoned. The brothers and sisters have departed Jerusalem. Only the separated Jewish Christians remain." Mariam gripped Ezra's arm. "Enough of this talk! Our Savior lives and reigns! Now we will show Apollos the hospitality of our house."

The journey from Joppa to Rome was long. The winds came mostly from the west but varied one hundred eighty degrees from south to north. Sailing north above Cyprus offered more shelter but also more variation in the wind. Apollos and his pilot, experienced in sailing grain ships to Rome, believed the west wind would hold and chose the southern route which left either Crete or North Africa as potential stopover ports for fresh food and water. The ship was filled with grain to be sold in Rome, and the proceeds used to support Paul and Peter.

Ezra never became truly comfortable at sea but was happy to listen silently as his friend Apollos effortlessly maintained the conversation. *'How does the man never want for something to say?* Ezra thought. But he found his dear friend's chattering comforting. They spent much time praying for the diminishing number of apostles and the church. They prayed for a speedy voyage, and they debated their deepening understanding of the 'new priesthood' of all believers under our Great High Priest, Jesus Christ.

Only once was Apollos lost for words. Ezra asked, "Brother, no wife? Do you not see the benefits of marriage? The special joy that it brings?"

Apollos sighed and looked at his friend, "I... it did

not..."

Apollos sighed again, "Perhaps I shall tell you... sometime. Now, let me get us some wine."

After stops in Crete and Rhegium in southern Italy, the ship made its way up the west coast of Italy. Apollos insisted, "We will not go to Pontus! I know the road to Rome is shorter, but the place should instead be called, 'Pompous,' for that is what it is. A large man-made harbor built by Claudius into the sea. But it failed to stop a storm, and many grain ships at anchor were sunk not two years ago. No, we shall go to the old port, small and inefficient and farther from Rome, but safely in the mouth of the Tiber. We shall go to Ostia Antica and walk a bit longer."

While Imperial ships were ordered to Pontus, many merchants preferred the safety and long developed partnerships with buyers in Ostia Antica. The city was crowded, but clean and organized and within a day of arriving, Apollos had sold his cargo. He led Ezra out the gate of the city on the via Ostiensis, a broad, stone-paved road to Rome. Ezra marveled at the chariot and wagon grooves cut into the stone by centuries of commerce. The wide road was lined with pine trees unlike any he had ever seen. Massive tall pines topped like giant green umbrellas shaded the road all the way to Rome.

"Magnificent! Are they not, brother? They tell every Roman returning from every corner of the empire that this is home. This is Rome!" Apollos slapped Ezra's back, "It is a pleasant walk. There are many fine inns along the way." The road followed along the east side of the Tiber as it wound its way northeast, a long day's walk or a pleasant two-day stroll with an overnight stop at an inn.

Nothing Ezra had seen prepared him for Rome. Never

had he seen such grandeur surrounded by poverty. It was a city of magnificent buildings, the forum, temples, palaces, villas, a great circus surrounded by dilapidated tenements overflowing with dirty, desperate people, trapped in hopelessness. Ezra shook his head as they passed the poor of Rome, vacant stares on the faces of little children, "Now you see why the emperor gives free bread for their bellies and games to occupy their time. They come from everywhere hoping to find a better life in the capital of the empire, of the world!"

"Is there no work for them? No hope?" Ezra asked

"The legions send fresh supplies of slaves. Every revolt, every resistance to the Pax Romana sends thousands upon thousands of slaves. Many educated, many skilled. Many beautiful young women. Why pay a poor servant when a strong slave can be had for the taking?"

Apollos put an arm around Ezra's shoulder, "Come. I know of an inn for merchants and the Equestrian class near the forum. It is close to where brother Paul is imprisoned. We will stay there until we meet with the brothers."

As they walked by a charcoal brazier next to a pile of filthy straw, Ezra remarked, "The whole city looks like a great fire waiting to happen. But it will be the poor trapped and burned!"

"The tenements occasionally burn, but they are soon replaced with more rooms and less space. Here, across from the Temple of Vesta. We shall stay here and inquire tomorrow."

Ezra was surprised, "You are comfortable living across from a pagan temple and the house of the Vestals?"

"I fear no idol or pagan god! But there is no safer place

in all of Rome. The people greatly honor the Vestal Virgins—Honored above all others in Rome. Vesta is their goddess of the hearth. The six virgins maintain the sacred fire. But they are honored for their chastity and integrity. They remind the people of a better time. Theirs is a belief in sacred marriage, of the legacy of children and the strength of family. Thirty years they serve, they train the one who will replace them. After their service, they may marry. They are sought out even by the senators as wives."

Apollos paused a moment and stared. "They remind all Rome of what has been lost in the decadence of Nero and the emperors. It is said Nero lost the last of his support among the people when he raped the Vestal named Rubria. No, brother, any hand lifted against the Vestals would bring an uprising in Rome no legion could put down."

Ezra mumbled, "God's truth is not hidden, even among the pagans."

The next day, Apollos led Ezra past the Roman forum, up the side of the Capitoline Hill to a building across from the Curia, or Roman court. The front of the building overlooked the forums, or markets of Nerva, Vespasian, and Augustus. The Tulianum prison inside housed prisoners awaiting execution or enemies of the state too dangerous for house arrest pending the formality of a trial before execution. The floor of the prison was covered with a grate which could be opened, allowing prisoners to be lowered into the dungeon below. Visitors offering a few coins to the guards could stand above and shout to the prisoners below.

Apollos recognized Luke standing above the iron grate. "Brother Luke! We have come. How fare our brothers Paul and Peter?"

Luke shouted, "Brothers! Apollos and?"

"Ezra, the priest from Jerusalem."

"Brothers Apollos and Ezra have come," Luke shouted down the grate.

Paul could be heard calling back, "Yes, good that you could come, Ezra. I desired to debate with you once more, our priesthood."

Ezra stood over the grate and peered into the darkness below, "Debate, bother Paul? It has been many years since we sat under the feet of the Rabban Gamaliel at Solomon's porch."

"Indeed, brother, many years. I remember you saw the truth before me. Tell me, brother Ezra, are you still a priest?"

"Indeed, brother, as the prophet Isaiah wrote, just as you, I am a priest of our LORD and a minister of our God. And Jesus Christ is our Great High Priest in the order of Melchizedek!"

Paul laughed, "My friend, it just as you say!"

Another voice spoke from the darkness, "We are a royal priesthood! All who believe in Jesus. For our Jesus, our brother, is forever prophet, priest and king!"

Paul replied, "Peter agrees! Friends, I have long desired to write a letter, but it is better we write this letter—A letter to our brother Jews, who still do not see. I have heard of your struggles, Ezra as a Christian and as a priest. I have heard of your climbing over the stumbling block of the Law and the Temple worship. How long was it, brother? Twenty years as a Christian before you stopped pouring new wine into old wineskins?"

Ezra spoke to the blackness, "Brother, your letter to the Romans, did it not set forth the truth of our justification, bought by the blood of Christ?"

Paul replied, "The Gentiles received the message, but everywhere I went, the Jews rejected the good news. I would try again, a letter to the Hebrews but I fear that we—that my name most assuredly—has become a stumbling block to the Jews as well. Perhaps I have been too hard, or too long away from our brothers, so I ask you, Ezra, and Apollos join me and our brother Simon Peter, for the plight of our people weighs greatly on our hearts."

The prison fell silent. Drops of water could be heard falling into a puddle. Apollos spoke up, "Where should we begin?"

Paul called out, "We begin with the superiority of Christ—superior to the prophets—superior to the angels -his divine person -superior to Moses..."

Peter shouted, "Scripture! They know the Scriptures— 'For to which of the angels did He ever say, 'You are My Son. Today I have begotten You?' Or again, 'I will be to Him a Father and He shall be to Me a Son?'"

Apollos replied, "Yes! And do not forget His delivering purpose, the founder of our salvation. Now in putting everything in subjection to Him, He left nothing outside His control. At present, we do not see everything in subjection to Him who was for a little while made lower than the angels, namely Jesus, crowned with glory and honor because of the suffering of death, so that by the grace of God he might taste death for everyone... For he who sacrifices and those who are sacrificed all have one source. That is why He is not ashamed to call them brothers, saying, 'I will tell of your name to my brothers; in the midst of the congregation I will sing Your praise. And again, 'I will put my trust in Him.' And again, 'Behold,

I and the children God has given me.' Since therefore the children share in flesh and blood, He Himself likewise partook of the same things, that through death he might destroy the one who has the power of death, that is the devil, and deliver those who through fear of death were subject to lifelong slavery."

Ezra finished the thought, "For surely it is not the angels that He helps, but He helps the offspring of Abraham. Therefore, He had to be made like His brothers in every respect, so that He might become a merciful and faithful high priest in the service of God, to make propitiation for the sins of the people. For because he Himself has suffered when tempted, He is able to help those who are being tempted. Therefore, holy brothers, you who share a heavenly calling, consider Jesus, the apostle and high priest of our confession, who was faithful to Him who appointed Him, just as Moses also was faithful in all God's house..."

Peter added, "Christ is better than Moses because Christ is the builder of God's house while Moses was but a servant in God's house. It is just as the Holy Spirit says, 'Today if you hear His voice, do not harden your hearts as in the rebellion, on the day of testing in the wilderness, where your fathers put me to the test and saw my works for forty years. Therefore, I was provoked with that generation and said, 'They always go astray in their heart; they have not known my ways.' As I swore in my wrath, 'They shall not enter my rest.'"

Paul picked up the argument, "Since then we have a great high priest who has passed through the heavens, let us hold fast to our confession. For we do not have a high priest who is unable to sympathize with our weaknesses, but one who in every respect has been tempted as we are, yet without sin. Let us then with confidence draw near to the throne of grace, that we may receive mercy and find grace to help in time of need."

"Amen brother Paul," Ezra shouted, "For every high priest chosen from among men is appointed to act on behalf of men in relation to God, to offer gifts and sacrifices for sins. He can deal gently with the ignorant and the wayward since he himself is beset with weakness. Because of this, he is obligated to sacrifice for his own sins. Christ did not exalt Himself, but was appointed by Him who said to Him, 'You are My Son, today I have begotten You.' And in another place, 'You are a priest forever after the order of Melchizedek.' While in the flesh, Jesus offered up prayers with loud cries and tears to Him who was able to save Him from death...Although He was a Son, He learned obedience through what He suffered. And being made perfect, he became the source of eternal salvation to all who obey Him, being designated by God a high priest after the order of Melchizedek."

The guard interrupted, "It is time. You must leave. Tomorrow. You may return tomorrow."

Apollos and Ezra left the prison with Luke in high spirits. Still excited by their time with Paul and Peter, Ezra remarked, "I find it most strange to feel such joy while our brothers lie in a dungeon."

Luke smiled, "Our brothers know the peace and joy of our Savior. They have no fear. They look forward to seeing Jesus. Indeed, spending time with them refreshes my soul. The others feel the same. Come, they will welcome you."

"Others?" Ezra asked.

"You shall see. Someone attends Peter and Paul every day. Aristarchus sees to their food and ours. Tychicus carries letters to and from the churches in Greece and Asia. Onesimus has just returned to Philemon, his master, but his service to Paul was done in love. Brother Epaphras of Colossae was sent to Timothy with a letter. Epaphroditus recovers in the house, he was near death in his service, but God heard our prayers and he recovers. He brought gifts, money from the church in Philippi. We wait for John Mark and pray for his safe travel here."

Apollos nodded, "Brother Luke, your faithfulness is a gift from above. I saw you writing as we debated."

Luke smiled, "I am a careful listener. Something I learned as a physician. Someone needed to record today. The Holy Spirit was speaking to all men."

The next morning, Ezra and Apollos walked with Luke to the prison. As they approached, they heard singing, the voices of men echoing from a chamber. Luke gave the guard a few coins and went to the grate. Luke called down, "Brothers, should we join in song or shall we continue yesterday's discussion?"

Paul's voice echoed, "Are the brothers here?"

Peter asked, "You do record, brother Luke? And my letters from before?"

Luke laughed, "Brother Peter, your letters have been sent. I maintain a copy if you wish that I reread them and refresh your memory."

Peter replied softly, "Perhaps another time. We should continue where we left off. Where Paul, Apollos, and Ezra left off. I have had little to contribute."

Paul called out, "Not so, brother! You have proclaimed the Scriptures accurately since the Spirit came upon you on Pentecost. You have run the race brother. Surly, a crown awaits."

"Amen!" Luke shouted

Paul's voice swelled and rose from the dungeon below, "Now let us leave behind the elementary teaching about Christ and let us press on to maturity. There is no need for further talk of washings and laying on of hands and the resurrection of the dead and eternal judgment. But we are convinced of better things... we desire that each one show the same diligence so to realize the full assurance of hope until the end, that all become imitators of those who through faith and patience inherit the promises. We have God's oath, He swore by Himself, for there is no one greater. We have strong encouragement, laying hold of the hope set before us. This hope we have as an anchor of the soul, both sure and steadfast, and one which enters within the veil, where Jesus has entered as a forerunner for us, having become a high priest forever in the order of Melchizedek. For this Melchizedek, King of Salem, Priest of the Most High God, who met Abraham as he was returning from the slaughter of the kings, and blessed him, to whom Abraham gave a tenth of all the spoils was first of all, by translation of his name, king of righteousness and then also King of Salem, which is king of peace."

Paul paused for a moment, and Apollos continued, "Without father, without mother, without genealogy, having neither beginning of days or end of life, but made like the Son of God, he continues as a priest forever."

Ezra added, "Now consider how great this man was to whom Abraham, the patriarch, gave a tenth of the choicest spoils. And those, the sons of Levi who receive the priest's office have indeed, been commanded in the Law to collect a tenth from the people, from their brothers, although they are descended from Abraham. But the one whose generation is not traced from them collected a tenth from Abraham and blessed the one who had the promises! Without any dispute, the lesser is blessed by the greater!"

Paul spoke again, "If perfection was attainable through the Levitical priesthood (for under it the people received the Law), what further need would there have been for another priest to arise under the order of Melchizedek? For when there is a change in the priesthood, there is necessarily a change in the law as well. This becomes even more evident when another priest arises, who has become a priest, not on the basis of a legal requirement concerning descent by blood but by the power of an indestructible life!"

Peter interrupted, "It is written of Him: 'The LORD has sworn and will not change His mind. You are a priest forever in the order of Melchizedek.'"

Apollos added, "The Law made nothing perfect. On the other hand, a better hope is introduced through which we draw near to God."

Ezra interrupted, "Jesus has become the guarantee of a better covenant... He is able to save forever those who draw near to God through Him since He always lives to make intercession for them. He does not need to daily offer up sacrifices, first for His own sins, and then for the sins of the people because He did once for all when He offered up Himself. For the Law appoints men as high priests who are weak, but the word of the oath, which came after the Law appoints a Son, made perfect forever."

Apollos nodded to Ezra, "The first covenant had regulations of divine worship and sanctuary..."

Ezra interrupted, "The tabernacle, the lampstand, the sacred bread. This was the holy place. Behind it, the Holy of Holies, having the golden altar of incense and the ark. And above it the cherubim of glory overshadowing the mercy seat. The priests ministered daily in the holy place. But only once a year did the high priest enter the Holy of Holies and not without taking blood which he offers for himself and for the sins of the people committed in ignorance."

Apollos continued, "By this, the Holy Spirit indicates that the way into the holy places is not yet opened as long as the first section is still standing, which is a symbol for the present time. Accordingly, both gifts and sacrifices are offered, which cannot perfect the conscience of the worshipper... until the time of reformation."

Paul had been listening patiently. Now his loud voice rose, "But when Christ appeared as a high priest of the good things that have come, then through the greater and more perfect tent (not made with hands, that is not of this creation) He entered once for all into the holy places not by means of blood of goats and calves but by means of His own blood, thus securing an eternal redemption... How much more will the blood of Christ, who though the eternal Spirit offered Himself without blemish to God, purify our conscience from dead works to serve the living God? Therefore, He is the mediator of a new covenant, so that those who are called may receive the promised eternal inheritance since a death has occurred that redeems them from the transgressions committed under the first covenant... Indeed, under the Law, everything is purified with blood, and without the shedding of blood there is no forgiveness of sins... And just as it is appointed for man to die once, and after that comes judgment, so Christ having been offered once to bear the sins of many, will appear a second time, not to deal with sin but to save those who are eagerly waiting for him."

The prison fell silent. The dripping water the only sound as they pondered their words, not recognizing them as their own but rising from within them as they spoke.

The sound of a deep breath and shuffling of feet on damp stone awoke them and Paul's voice again echoed up, "For since the Law is but a shadow of the good things to come instead of the true form of these realities, it can never, by the same sacrifices that are continually offered every year, make perfect those who draw near. Otherwise, would they not have ceased to be offered? They are but a reminder of sins every year."

Peter's voice rose, "When Christ came into the world, He said, 'Sacrifices and offerings You have not desired, but a body You have prepared for Me; in burnt offerings and sins offerings You have taken no pleasure.' Then I said, 'Behold, I have come to do Your will, O God, as it is written of me in the scroll of the book.' And the Holy Spirit also bears witness to us for after saying; 'This is the covenant I will make with them, after those days, says the LORD: I will put My Laws upon their heart and upon their mind, I will write them.' Then He says, 'And their sins and their lawless deeds I will remember no more.'"

Ezra added softly, "Now where there is forgiveness of these things; there is no longer any offering for sin."

Apollos finished the thought, "Therefore brothers, since we have the confidence to enter the holy places by the blood of Jesus, by the new and living way that He opened for us through the curtain, that is, through His flesh, and since we have a great high priest over the house of God, let us draw near with a true heart in full assurance of faith, with our hearts sprinkled clean from evil conscience and our bodies washed with pure water. Let us hold fast the confession of our hope without wavering, for He who promised is faithful. And let us consider how to stir up one another to love and good works, not neglecting to meet together, as is the habit of some, but encouraging one another, and all the more as you see the day drawing near. For if we go on sinning deliberately after receiving the knowledge of the truth there no longer remains a sacrifice for sins, but a fearful expectation of judgment and a fury of fire that will consume the adversaries...'The LORD will judge His people'...It is a fearful thing to fall into the hands of the Living God."

Paul added, "For you have need of endurance, so that when you have done the will of God, you may receive what is promised. For, 'Yet a little while and the coming one will come and will not delay; but My righteous one will live by faith, and if he shrinks back my soul has no pleasure in him.' But we are not of those who shrink back and are destroyed, but of those who have faith and preserve their souls."

Again, the prison fell silent. Those above in the light bowed their heads and closed their eyes. Peter and Paul could not be seen or heard in the darkness below. Luke spoke softly. The Spirit has spoken. Brothers rest. Let us think upon these words. Tomorrow. Yes, we will return tomorrow and consider what it means to live by faith."

Paul sighed, "Yes. Brothers let us meditate on that faith."

Luke asked, "The food. Do they give you the food? There is meat and vegetables in addition to the bread."

Peter shouted back, "Be at peace brother, we receive all that you provide."

Paul added, "Brother Epaphroditus, he is well?"

"Yes, he recovers and longs to see you. Soon. He shall share his joy with you soon. We receive no news on Mark. Tychicus has not yet returned. There is no other news today," Luke replied.

Paul shouted, "Brothers Apollos and Ezra, it is good that you have come!"

"Amen, brother, amen," Peter echoed.

Chapter Thirty

Walking down the Capitoline Hill, Luke mentioned, "Tonight I go to a gathering of brothers and sisters. The fellowship is one of the oldest in Rome, once led by Priscilla and Aquilla. You will be welcomed."

Luke paused, "You have no objections to eating in the house of a Gentile?"

Ezra nodded, "It will be a joy to gather with them and pray for our brothers Peter and Paul. As for Gentiles, we have accepted the hospitality you and all the brothers serving Peter and Paul have offered. You say one of the oldest, are there others?"

Luke smiled, "Oh yes, there are many small groups of believers, all through the city. Though many of the Jewish brothers never returned after being expelled by

Claudius. And some who have returned choose to remain separate from uncircumcised Gentiles."

Ezra sighed, "Even here?"

"I fear it so. But Jews and Gentiles alike will gather tonight."

Apollos nodded, "Aquilla and Priscilla would be pleased. Of course, brothers Peter and Paul as well."

Apollos and Ezra were led to a pleasant villa on the Esquiline Hill. More than thirty Christians were gathered for fellowship. Ezra was surprised to see wealthy Romans among the brothers and sisters mixing with others whose dress appeared working class. When a slave came out with a tray of bread and wine, an immaculately dressed Roman said, "Thank you, brother Secondus, now you must join us. We are all capable of serving ourselves."

Luke reported on Peter and Paul and assured the fellowship their prayers for Epaphroditus were answered. Apollos and Ezra were warmly received and welcomed. Apollos shared greetings from Aquilla and Priscilla in Corinth calling out many they had asked to be remembered. Ezra was invited to read Scripture and preach.

Ezra came forward and said, "I am a Levite, a priest and by training a scribe and teacher of the Law. But I will not unroll the Sefer scroll copied in Hebrew for millennia nor will I read from the Septuagint, a Greek translation. No, I will read in the Gospel as written by our brother Luke, who has undertaken a careful account of the life and sayings of our Lord. Our brother's account is most welcome as he records many of the parables our Lord spoke not recorded by Mark the Evangelist. The parable of the wineskins has been on my mind these days as I join brother Apollos in a debate with brothers Paul and Peter."

Ezra accepted Luke's gospel and read. When he finished, he said, "Brothers and sisters we have been called to Rome by brother Paul. We spend our days debating the Law. But you ask, 'Has not Paul taught us in his letter that we are no longer under the Law but under grace?' And this is true. And as Gentiles, you rejoice in this gift of God. But for many Jews, this has become a stumbling block. You must not judge your brothers on this account but understand their struggle. Jesus brings a New Covenant to all people, a covenant of salvation by grace. He pours it forth abundantly, but the old wineskin of the law cannot withstand this new wine. Why should you care? You, who have been freely blessed."

Ezra looked into the faces of the brothers listening, took a breath, and continued, "You must know the Law, for it was given by God with a purpose in His great plan of salvation. You must know the Law to know the full gift of grace. You must know the sin that it reveals. You must know the price of that sin. But most dearly, you must know the full cost paid by Jesus to redeem you from that sin."

"Brothers and sisters, you must know the heart of Paul and your many fellow Jewish believers. Their heart is for their people, chosen by God to reveal His will—Chosen by God to be a light to the Gentiles. You who have gained so much must have open hearts, filled with prayer for our brother Paul in this holy work and love his people as he does, even when they reject your love for surely our Father in Heaven loves them no less than He loves you. Show your love with prayer, true hospitality, and fellowship."

Apollos stood up and said, "Amen and Amen!"

Ezra nodded, and lifted his hands, "One other admonition brothers and sisters. There are those who say our grace brings the license to sin. May it never be said! We are called out of sin and made new to live free from sin's entrapment. Our God has made this promise known. He has not hidden His will from us. His revelation is not hidden to some. There are no secrets of the Spirit to the few. Be alert those who teach such things do not have the Spirit of God. These two teachings, the holding of the Law and the secret knowledge of the Spirit, are snares to entrap you. Continue to fellowship with your brothers and sisters appointed by the elders and hold steadfast to our faith in Jesus Christ. God bless you, brothers and sisters!"

The leader led the fellowship in the Lord's prayer and the Lord's supper. After they sang a hymn of praise, they returned to their homes filled with peace and joy.

The morning found Luke, Apollos and Ezra back in the prison, standing on the grate above the dark dungeon. The sound of chains dragging across the stone told of stirrings below. "Brother Peter, are you awake, the brothers are here," Paul said.

Peter stirred, "Yes, brother, not asleep, just in prayer. Good morning brothers! Who visits us this morning?"

Luke called down, "Brothers Luke, Apollos and Ezra. We come to continue the argument of faith. But first, brother Paul, still no word from Mark. Tychicus has not returned from Timothy. Be assured they will be brought directly as soon as they arrive."

Paul could be heard saying, "Yes, yes, we will wait. We have nowhere else to go. Now brothers, on faith—Faith is the assurance of things hoped for, the conviction of things not seen, for by it the people of old received their commendation. By faith, we understand that the universe was created by the Word of God so that what is seen was not made out of things that are visible. By faith Abel offered to God a more acceptable sacrifice than Cain, through which he was commended as righteous, God commending him by accepting his gifts—And through his faith, though he died he still speaks."

Apollos replied, "And by faith…"

Paul did not let him interrupt. He continued, "By faith, Enoch was taken up, so that he should not see death, and he was not found because God had taken him. Now before he was taken, he was commended as having pleased God. And without faith it is impossible to please God, for whoever would draw near to God must believe that He exists and that He rewards those who seek Him."

Apollos joined in again, "By faith Noah, being warned by God concerning events as yet unseen, in reverent fear constructed an ark to save his household. By this, he condemned the world and became an heir of righteousness that comes by faith."

Before Apollos could take a breath and continue, Paul was speaking, "By faith, Abraham obeyed when he was called to go out to a place to receive as an inheritance. And he went out not knowing where he was going. By faith, he went to live in the land of promise, as in a foreign land, living in tents with Isaac and Jacob, heirs with him of the same promise. For he was looking forward to the city that has foundations, whose designer and builder is God. By faith, Sarah herself received power to conceive, even when she was past the age since she considered Him faithful who had promised. Therefore, from one man, and him as good as dead, were born descendants as many as the stars of heaven and as many as the innumerable grains of sand by the seashore."

Ezra and Apollos listened as Paul expounded out of the darkness, "These all died in faith, not having received the things promised, but having seen them from afar, and having acknowledged that they were strangers and exiles on the earth. For people who speak thus make it clear that they are seeking a homeland. They desire a better country, that is a heavenly one. Therefore, God is not ashamed to be called their God, for He has prepared for them a city."

Paul paused, and Apollos considered his words. Ezra spoke, "By faith Abraham when he was tested offered up Isaac, and he who had received the promise was in the act of offering up his only son, of whom it was said, 'Through Isaac shall your offspring be named.' He considered that God was able even to raise him from the dead, from which figuratively speaking, he did receive him back. By faith, Isaac invoked future blessings on Jacob and Esau. By faith Jacob, when dying, blessed each of the sons of Joseph, bowing in worship over the head of his staff. By faith Joseph, at the end of is life, made mention of the exodus of the Israelites and gave directions concerning his bones."

Paul and Apollos continued with examples from the history of God's revelation through the Israelites, "By faith, Moses, when he was born, was hidden... By faith, Moses, when he was grown up, refused to be called the son of Pharaoh's daughter—He considered the reproach of Christ greater wealth than the treasures of Egypt. By faith, he kept the Passover—By faith, the people crossed the Red Sea—By faith the walls of Jericho fell down—By faith Rahab, the prostitute did not perish with those who were disobedient. And what more shall I say" For time would fail me to tell of Barak, Samson, Jephthah, of David and Samuel and the prophets who through faith conquered kingdoms, enforced justice, obtained promises, stopped the mouths of lions, quenched the power of fire, escaped the edge of the sword, were made strong out of weakness, became mighty in war, put foreign armies to flight. Women received back their dead by resurrection. Some were tortured, refusing to accept release so that they might rise again to a better life. Others suffered mocking and flogging, and even chains and imprisonment. They were stoned, they were sawn in two, they were killed with the sword. They went about in skins of sheep and goats, destitute, afflicted, mistreated—of whom the world was not worthy—wandering about in deserts and mountains, and in dens and caves of the earth."

Apollos' voice rose in crescendo, "And these, though commended through their faith, did not receive what was promised, since God had provided something better for us, that apart from us they should not be made perfect."

Chains scraped the stone floor as Paul moved to edge of his cell, clasped the bars, looked up into the light and cried out, "Therefore, since we are surrounded by so great a cloud of witnesses, let us also lay aside every weight, and sin which clings so closely, and let us run with endurance the race that is set before us, looking to Jesus, the founder and perfecter of our faith, who for the joy that was set before Him endured the cross, despising the shame, and is seated at the right hand of the throne of God."

Paul shuffled his feet and softened his voice, "Consider

Him who endured for sinners such hostility against Himself, so that you may not grow weary or fainthearted... Have you forgotten the exhortation that addresses you as sons? 'My son, do not regard lightly the discipline of the Lord... for the Lord disciplines the one he loves.' Therefore, lift your drooping hands and strengthen your weak knees, and make straight paths for your feet, so that what is lame may not be put out of joint but rather be healed. Strive for peace with everyone, and for holiness without which no one will see the Lord. For you have not come to what may be touched, a blazing fire and darkness and gloom and a tempest and the sound of a trumpet and a voice whose words made the hearers beg that no further message be spoken to them. But you have come to Mount Zion and to the city of the living God, the heavenly Jerusalem, and to innumerable angels in festal gathering, and to the assembly of the firstborn who are enrolled in heaven, and to God, the judge of all and to the Spirits of the righteous made perfect, and to Jesus, the mediator of a new covenant, and to the sprinkled blood that speaks a better word than the blood of Abel."

Chains rattled their complaint as Paul stretched his arms. His voice began to grow. "See that you do not refuse Him who is speaking... let us be grateful for receiving a kingdom that cannot be shaken, and thus let us offer to God acceptable worship, with reverence and awe, for God is a consuming fire."

These words echoed through the dank prison air. Then a moment of silence before Ezra spoke, "Let brotherly love continue. Do not neglect to show hospitality to strangers, for thereby some have entertained angels. Remember those in prison. Let marriage be held in honor. Keep your life free from the love of money. Remember your leaders who spoke to you the Word of God. Consider the outcome of their way of life. Jesus Christ is the same yesterday, today, and forever. Obey your leaders and submit to them, for they are keeping watch over your souls, as those who will have to give an account..."

Peter, who had been silent, called out, "Pray for us, for we are sure that we have a clear conscience, desiring to act honorably in all things. I urge you the more earnestly to do this in order that I may be restored to you the sooner."

Paul followed his brother in a blessing, "Now may the God of peace who brought again from the dead our Lord Jesus, the great shepherd of the sheep by the blood of the eternal covenant, equip you with everything good that you may do His will, working in us that which is pleasing in his sight, through Jesus Christ, to whom be glory forever and ever. Amen"

When he finished, Luke spoke softly, "Brothers, truly the Spirit has spoken. I am humbled to record these words. Brother Paul, do wish to add a salutation to affirm your authorship?"

Paul could be heard sighing, "No salutation is necessary. These words come from the Holy Spirit, the brothers and I just mouthpieces. But perhaps add a final greeting. Tell them that brother Timothy has been released from prison, with whom I shall see them if he comes soon. Write also that those who come from Italy send their greetings. Tell them, 'Grace be with all of you.'"

As Ezra and Apollos made their way into fading daylight outside, a guard followed Luke outside, looked in both directions and said softly, "Master Luke, here is the money you have paid me to visit the prisoners. It is yours. You need never pay me."

Luke graciously accepted a pouch of coins and looked into the man's eyes, "Thank you. Janus, is it not?"

Janus again looked left and right, sighed and asked, "Master Luke, I have been listening as you speak and I... well I believe these men are sent from God—the God they confess is unlike the Roman gods—can I... can you take me... I wish to know this God."

Apollos and Ezra stood off a few steps, waiting and praying silently as Luke spoke with the guard.

Luke smiled, "Janus, you are most welcome to join us. I shall take you to brothers, many are Roman, like you, who follow Jesus. They will hear your confession. You will be baptized for I believe it is the Holy Spirit who calls you. When shall I call for you?"

"Janus smiled, "Tomorrow at sunset, I and my wife and children shall be waiting. I have shared this truth with them, and we shall all come."

"Tomorrow at sunset then, brother Janus. May God's blessing be upon your house."

That evening Mark and Timothy arrived together and were taken immediately to visit Paul and Peter. The brothers were cheered by their coming, and they stayed late into the night rejoicing and praising God.

Ezra and Apollos set about copying the epistle addressed to the Hebrews. Tychicus the messenger, and Aristarchus joined them in the work. The ever happy and verbal Apollos asked Aristarchus, "Brother, we are gone all day, and you stay behind and labor here. It now occurs to me as selfish. Please, brother, do not let us keep you from visiting our brothers in prison."

Aristarchus smiled, "Brother Apollos, I thank you for your kindness. I love the brothers, and I know of their love for me, but the Spirit has given me a gift as well. I see what must be done when others are about the work of Peter and Paul. I step in to help, often unasked, with a clear mind to see everything is in order. I see there is food. I see there is a place for everyone who comes and goes. I see their clothes are clean, the water jugs are filled, and the household is in order. I find joy in this. Indeed, I find joy in copying the letters for it brings me into their presence, into their very minds and work in the Spirit. No, but thank you, brother, I do the work of my calling."

Ezra asked Luke for the recent letters of Peter to be copied as well. "I shall like to carry the letters to Jerusalem and the brothers there, though I do not know who now leads. But I trust that God is good, and our people in Jerusalem yet worship him."

Luke nodded, "You shall have them. They have not yet been sent to Jerusalem. Yes, they should be read together for our brother Peter wrote, 'But you are a chosen people, a royal priesthood, a holy nation, a people for His own possession, that you may proclaim the excellencies of Him who called you out of darkness into this marvelous light.'"

Ezra smiled, "The Spirit has proclaimed it, Jesus our prophet, Jesus our King and Jesus, our true High Priest! And we, well, we are called His royal priesthood, His holy nation, and His own possession! His kingdom come! His will be done!"

Ezra breathed deeply before continuing, "Brother Luke, coming here with Apollos, my good friend, has been a blessing. What hope is there for Paul or Peter with the Romans?"

Luke lowered his eyes for a moment then looked up and smiled thinly, "Few are ever released from the Tulianum prison. Waiting is part of the punishment for the day of execution is never announced. Of all men, only Nero knows."

"Only Timothy and Mark were called... "

Luke nodded, "Yes. Titus is in Crete. He is a man, mature in wisdom and strong in faith, instructed closely by Paul. There has always been an understanding between them. Brother Silas as well. He remains in Macedonia, leading the church. But Mark and Timothy. Timothy is a young man... "

Ezra smiled, "There is hardly a hair on his face! He has the face of a child, and he defers to his elders politely. But when he speaks! His wisdom! There is maturity far beyond his years! He is the most amazing young man!"

Luke laughed, "Indeed! Young Timothy is filled with the Spirit! But he is more to brother Paul. Paul never took a wife. He sacrificed his comfort for service to our God. Timothy was to Paul his son, the son he gave up in order to serve. Paul loves him most dearly, and indeed, Timothy loves Paul. Paul knows he is still young and untested by the death of those he loves. So, he called for him."

Luke paused and then added, "Should not each of us equip such a man to follow us in service?"

Ezra closed his eyes and said, "And John Mark, a reconciliation... "

Luke nodded, "Yes. Paul has long desired to see Mark again. To affirm Mark's ministry for the Lord in Alexandria, in all Egypt and North Africa. And Peter has always loved him as well. It has been reported that Mark yet grieves over his early failings. The brothers seek to lift his spirit and bless his faithfulness."

Ezra mumbled, "It is just as Mariam said."

Ezra was disappointed to hear that Apollos had decided to remain in Rome while he returned to Jerusalem alone. "It is a long journey, brother, I shall miss your company."

"Is it my company you shall miss? Or is it the sea journey itself you dread? I will accompany you to Ostia Antica and arrange a comfortable ship for your passage. Brother, the prevailing winds will be with you and the return voyage much faster than the voyage here. But I must stay, there is talk of a mission to Gaul. I would carry the letters to our brothers and sister there. It is well known that brother Paul has long desired to visit them. We shall meet again, brother, God willing not too long."

The walk down the via Ostiensis was pleasant, the towering pines of Rome now familiar to Ezra as he savored the friendly chattering of Apollos as they strolled towards their farewell. Ezra wore a melancholy smile, but his heart was warm. Apollos snorted a "humph," as he brushed several ashes off his clean tunic. Stopping, he looked up to see the sky filled with ash. Both men turned around to see a red, orange light filling the horizon. "Fire?" Apollos asked.

Ezra stared, "Surely a great fire, indeed!"

They stepped up their pace and hurried towards Ostia Antica and the port. Soon many Romans, running, passed by screaming, "Rome burns!"

Chapter Thirty-One

Inside the villa which Ezra shared with Mariam and their children was an Eden untouched by the violence and cruelty outside its brightly washed walls. Beneath the shade of the arbor and date palms, Ezra felt blessed watching his family grow. Mariam and Ezra kept the world outside their walls. Nathan had passed away quietly while Ezra was in Rome. Young Jonathan, now in his teenage years, had become an accomplished vinedresser and winemaker. His young brother Daniel followed his older brother like his shadow. Ruth went everywhere with Mariam, serving the widows, orphans and poor of Nicopolis. Ezra led the faithful of Nicopolis teaching them the Scripture, leading them in the Lord's Supper and encouraging them in the exercise of the gifts the Holy Spirit poured upon the church.

In the years since Ezra returned from Rome and he delivered the epistle to the Hebrews and the two epistles of Peter to his friend, Simeon ben Gamaliel, in Jerusalem, the unrest in Judea increased. Taxes had always been an issue in Judea, but the rioting and attacks against the occupying Romans escalated in Caesarea when Roman pagans sacrificed pigeons in front of a Jewish synagogue. In retribution, a Roman legion marched to Jerusalem and removed treasures from the temple as a tax on enforcing the peace. After the raid on the temple, old rivalries between Jewish factions dissolved and a widespread resistance by nearly all Jews emerged. Many Romans and King Agrippa II fled Jerusalem. Jewish rebels quickly overthrew the Roman garrison and Ananus ben Ananus, Joseph ben Gurion and Eleazar ben Hanania were elected leaders of a provisional Jewish government in Jerusalem.

Ezra urged restraint to his flock in Nicopolis. "A revolt against Rome will bring only death and destruction upon us," he advised, "And to what end? More legions, more death! No, our Savior, Jesus, the very Son of God, with all the power of the Father and all the angels of heaven, chose not to destroy them. Are there not Romans among us—our brothers in the Lord? We are called to make disciples of them! This is our task. Anything else is not of God but of man."

Cestius Gallus, the Roman Legate of Syria, sought to put an end to the growing rebellion and sent the Twelfth Legion to put down the new provisional government in Jerusalem. The Romans were forced to fight their way into the city but could not take the Temple Mount and Gallus ordered a retreat. On the Gibeon–Aijalon road, in a narrow canyon near the town of Beth-Horon, the retreating legion was attacked from above and all sides.

Unable to form a cohesive defense in the tight canyon, six thousand Romans were massacred, stripped of their weapons and armor and left as carrion for scavenging birds and dogs. Gallus himself fled, abandoning his command and escaped to Antioch only to die shortly after.

Word of the defeat of a Roman legion spread false hope through Judea, Samaria, Galilee, and Idumea. Jews listened to the calls of the Zealots in Galilee and Idumea, The Jews of Judea and Jerusalem followed the Pharisees and Sadducees, united in support of the provisional government. Ezra found his words questioned by brothers determined to join the rebellion. All the while, more Romans were sent into the rebellious province. Garrisons were established in cities along the major highways from the coastal road, the ports of Joppa, and Caesarea and all the way north to Antioch. Nicopolis was now garrisoned as well.

On the hot afternoon that Apollos called at Ezra's gate, Mariam was alone with Ruth. "Brother Apollos! God be praised you are safe! Come in and be refreshed. Ezra will be so pleased. Good news and pleasant company are hard to come by these days."

Apollos kissed Mariam on the cheek and then turned and kissed Ruth as well. "Truly, you are now taller than your mother! Ezra, your father must be proud!"

Standing and entering the courtyard, Apollos remarked, "Romans everywhere and not smile on one. I hear only of rebellion. God be praised you are safe."

Mariam closed and barred the gate, "Ezra and Simeon shall be back soon. They urge the brothers to have patience. Patience and prayer. Some have gone to Jerusalem to defend the city."

"Surely, not Jonathan or Daniel?"

"Jonathan and Daniel tend the vineyard and the fields. The servants go with them and keep a sharp eye. I pray you go and refresh yourself, brother. Rest. I shall call for you when Ezra returns."

Ezra and Simeon had washed and refreshed before Jonathan was sent to call Apollos. Surprised that he had fallen asleep, Apollos quickly got up and greeted his friends, "Brothers, God has saved me from sorrow upon sorrow! Dear friends, I had feared..."

Ezra hugged Apollos, "We have had too much fear! But you have brought joy! Is this not true Simeon?"

Apollos hugged Simeon, "What could have caused you to leave Jerusalem? It is your habit never to travel, brother."

"It is hard news. Hard news friend, those leading our city, make it a fortress and every man a soldier. I was able to leave. I decided early. For others, it is now, agree to fight or be stoned. There has been division among the defenders, fighting within the city between the Zealot militia and the Sadducees. The Sicarii have been expelled, their leader executed. The Roman Legate of Syria, Vespasian has routed the Zealots in Galilee and lays siege to Jerusalem. It is rumored he has been recalled to Rome and his son Titus now commands six legions in Judea."

Apollos nodded quickly, "Recalled to Rome? Yes, a strong commander, and now that Emperor Nero is dead by his own hand..."

Apollos stopped sighed deeply, bowed and slowly shook his head no, "Then my news only brings more pain. Brothers Paul and Peter are dead. Paul beheaded. Peter crucified—Crucified upside down. Peter told his executioners he was unworthy to be crucified in the manner of our Lord. There is more. Sadly, there is more. Mark is dead. He was taken in a riot in Alexandria and a rope placed around his neck. He was dragged from a chariot through the streets until dead."

Ezra, Simeon, and Mariam all fell to their knees in grief and cried. Apollos could no longer contain his grief and wailed with his friends.

Apollos mumbled, "I fear brothers, these are the end times. Did not our Lord warn us? Does not Mark's gospel warn us of this disaster? Did He not say, 'Then let those in Judea flee to the mountains. Let no one on the roof of his house go down or enter the house or take anything out. Let no one in the field go back to get his cloak?' Brothers, it is not safe. You must leave while you can, for Rome will not leave Jerusalem standing. Countless numbers will die, and those who survive the sword and the fire will be taken as slaves. Perhaps then, after the destruction, our Lord will return, and we will return with Him."

Ezra shook his head no, "I lead the church here. I cannot abandon them."

"Brother, I do not ask you to abandon them. I beg you to lead them to safety. You live on the road from Joppa to Jerusalem. Rome will leave no threat remaining along this road. You must not wait. You must leave!"

Simeon was nodding his agreement, "Brother, I was fortunate to leave Jerusalem before it was too late. Apollos is right. Consider Mariam and your children. You have a father's duty to them."

Ezra buried his face in his hands, "Yes, I shall urge our people to go. Simeon, I ask you to lead the first group. Mariam, Jonathan, Ruth, and Daniel shall be among them. I shall stay until the last to agree leaves."

Lifting his face, Ezra asked, "Apollos, where shall we go?"

Apollos closed his eyes and thought. He began to reason aloud, "It must be outside Judea, Idumea, and Galilee. Away from the revolt. A city where brothers will receive you, but where Jews are not a threat. I go to Alexandria, but it is not safe. My cousin, Tiberius Julius Alexander is now Prefect of Egypt. He has suspended self-rule from the Jews and his soldiers rule the city. Antioch in Syria. There are many brothers there, and no rebellion. I believe many Jews will go there."

Simeon interrupted, "Many brothers from Jerusalem fled to Persia, beyond the Euphrates and out of the Roman empire."

Apollos replied, "A dangerous journey through the battle and war. No, it is better to go to Antioch—or there is Ephesus. There are many brothers and sisters in Ephesus, and they have a heart for our people."

Mariam looked up and said, "I hear John the Apostle is in Ephesus."

Apollos nodded, "The last I heard, he still leads the church there."

"It is agreed then. I will counsel our people to seek shelter with the church in Ephesus."

The church in Ephesus warmly welcomed Mariam and her children. Some remembered her from the visit she and Ezra made two decades earlier. She asked for prayer that Ezra would soon follow with more brothers and sisters from Nicopolis. She asked prayers too, for the Greek and Roman brothers who remained behind determined to protect the property and interests of those who sought refuge elsewhere. Mariam was delighted to hear that

John the Apostle, now called John the Evangelist, was leading the church. Mariam was disappointed that they missed him on their first visit to Ephesus, but John was prone to travel about Asia, encouraging the leaders and widows alike. The leaders soon found they would have his ear more if they followed him into the homes of the widows and sick.

Mariam waited nervously for her audience with John, rehearsing an appropriate greeting. When she called, John opened the gate to his house and immediately stepped forward and kissed her cheek. "Sister Mariam! At last, you come to join me in ministering to the widows and orphans! At last, a woman with a true servant's heart! And who do you bring with you? She is tall and straight with the determined eyes of her mother. Tell me, Mariam; she has not taken the Nazarite oath?"

Both Mariam and Ruth blushed. Mariam wept a tear as she smiled, "Brother John, do you truly remember one so small in service as me? I praise God that I am permitted to see you again!"

John smiled, "Please, come in. Truly it is safe. There are other sisters and brothers inside. They, too, will welcome one honored by out Lord's mother. There are not many whose ministry was affirmed by Mary."

John turned to Ruth, "And do you have the heart of serving like your mother, sister... dear child, what is your name?"

"Ruth. She is daughter to Ezra ben Haggai the priest and scribe."

"Yes, I recall brother Ezra, a good man. A teacher of the Law."

Ruth spoke, "My father leads the church in Nicopolis. He has preached in Egypt and Rome."

John smiled, "She is not afraid to speak up. Indeed, she is your daughter. How proud you and Ezra must be. Well, we shall put you both to work. Yes, we shall teach her the joy of serving. Now come in, meet the others."

During the two happy years Ezra and Mariam lived in Ephesus, they agreed that Ezra should accept the proposal of the marriage of Ruth to James ben Joel, the son of their dear friend and first leader of the church in Nicopolis. James was ten years senior to Ruth, a shy and quiet man skilled as a goldsmith. They were surprised that the outgoing Ruth found this quiet, serious, and unassuming young man so attractive. But each shared a love for the Lord and a commitment to service. When questioned Ruth would always say, "I don't know why you say James is quiet or shy, he is never quiet when we are together. Papa, Mama, if you only knew his heart as I do..."

When Mariam told Ezra to expect Joel's proposal to Ruth, his response was immediate. "Ruth is too young for marriage!"

Mariam replied, "She is older than I was when I was first betrothed and ran off. No, husband. It is a good match."

Ezra fumed for a few moments but saw the determination in Mariam's eyes. "I shall consent, but they shall wait a full year," he replied firmly as a good father concerned for his daughter's future. "Perhaps when go back to Nicopolis."

The dreaded news finally reached Ephesus. The Jewish revolt had been crushed. Vespasian, now Emperor, had ordered the Temple razed and the city of Jerusalem burned. More than a hundred thousand Jewish soldiers and one million other Jews were dead. Another one hundred thousand surviving Jews were enslaved, exiled from the land to serve their conquerors throughout the Roman world. Most were sent to Rome, rebuilding itself bigger and grander than the city burned by Nero and adding a new Coliseum to host its games of death for its bloodthirsty population.

Few of the Jewish Christians of Nicopolis decided to return. They chose to stay with their Gentile brothers in Ephesus or moved on to find relatives in Antioch, or Alexandria, Corinth or even Rome. Apollos made one more visit to Ezra. He was off again to another mission, this time the end of the Roman world. He was headed back, first to Gaul and then on to a small church in a remote Roman island province called Britain. It was reported that Joseph of Arimathea founded a church in a village called Glastonbury Tor. Apollos was determined to take the gospels of Mark and Luke, The Acts of the Apostles, and the letters of James, Paul, and Peter to this remote outpost of Christianity.

Mariam listened to Apollos' bold plan, squeezed Ezra's arm and said, husband, we are told 'Go and make disciples of all men.'"

Ezra kissed Mariam and then turned to Simeon, "Apollos tells of a great opportunity, but first, I must go back to Jerusalem. I have a message that must be delivered."

Simeon replied, "Jerusalem is no more. I will go to Persia and preach among the Jews there."

Ezra, spoke louder, "The work in Jerusalem is unfinished, come with me, Simeon, you too, Apollos. Our mission shall not take long. From there we can go our ways and follow our calling."

Simeon nodded, "I go that way."

Apollos shook his head and then said, "If it means you will come with me to Britain, then I will go with you on this mission to Jerusalem."

Ruth and James were married in Nicopolis in the warmth of the church who loved them. The few brothers and sisters remaining in Nicopolis, all Gentiles, were disappointed when Ezra and Mariam sold their villa. They begged them to stay and teach them as he had before. The price was set much less than the Roman brother who had cared for the villa in their absence offered to pay, but Mariam insisted he must be rewarded for his faithfulness. Jonathan and Daniel asked to inspect the vineyard before departing and commended the brother for the excellent pruning and fine wine.

Mariam said her goodbyes to Simeon in Nicopolis where she waited with Ruth, her son-in-law James, and sons Johnathan and Daniel. Ezra, Apollos, and Simeon trudged off to the ruins of Jerusalem. The day's walk was painful. The scars of war and destruction were everywhere. When the city came into view, their hearts were torn. The walls were gone. Behind piles of rubble were charred timber and ashes. Neighborhoods were indistinguishable. They judged the upper city by elevation and the temple mount as a focal point.

The city was unguarded. There was nothing left for looters. But they were surprised to see wagons traveling in out of the city. The wagons coming out carried stone. As they made their way to the temple mount, they saw gangs of half-naked men chained together at the waist, prying about the piles of rubble, pulling out blocks unbroken by the fire. The limestone facade of the temple had crumbled, but many blocks of the stone floor and the foundation were suitable for military construction projects in Caesarea or the garrisons throughout Judea.

Apollos, Ezra, and Simeon walked across the stone floor of the temple. They avoided the rubble pile in the center and made their way across the court of the Gentiles, stopping where Solomon's portico once stood. Looking back, there was no sign of golden doors. No evidence of the giant bronze seas, or cooking pots. No golden menorahs or candle holders. Nothing but rubble and burnt wood. Where Simeon and Ezra once sat in the shade of Solomon's portico at the feet of Gamaliel with Saul of Tarsus, the three bewildered men kneeled and prayed. They prayed for Jerusalem and Judea, and they prayed for all those who mourned.

Simeon cried as Ezra spoke softly, "Forty years ago, Lord, I stood here while Jesus was suffering on the cross. I wondered, 'Why do the hands of the Lord tear the curtain to the Holy of Holies? I asked, Why did God shake the very foundation of His own Temple? I did not know that the temple had fallen that very day. I did not know that You, O God had made new temples in the hearts of Your people. O Father, I pray that now Your people Israel will understand this message. I pray that they will cry out to Jesus praising Him and saying, 'Hear O Israel, the LORD our God, the LORD is one!"

Simeon and Apollos listened to Ezra's prayer, and humbly affirmed, "Amen."

Ezra stood up and brushed the grit and ashes from his knees. "Come, brothers, I have one last task."

They followed Ezra off the temple mount, down below the western wall. There beneath the solid foundation of the Temple, he stopped. Ezra took a neatly folded letter, kissed it, and carefully worked it into a crevice between two great stones.

Simeon asked, "Brother? What is it you do?"

"I deliver the Epistle to the Hebrews that they remember for all time that Jesus is our great high priest. He takes no delight in sacrifices and the burnt offering, but a broken and contrite heart He will not despise. Christ died once to make atonement for all the sins of all people for all time. I remind them that all who believe are a royal priesthood. And I remind them that salvation is a gift of God through faith—that we are accounted righteous before our God by our faith."

Ezra stared at the temple ruins and said, "For a time this Temple showed we are sinners in need of redemption. The time of the temple has passed, only its lesson remains."

Made in the USA
Middletown, DE
03 March 2020